UNDER THE TRILLIUM SEA

A NOVEL

LINDA MCGEARY

THE TRILLIUM TRILOGY

BOOK THREE

UNDER THE TRILLIUM SEA

For friends and family,
especially my husband, Duncan,
who adventures with me in the stories we share.

ACKNOWLEDGEMENTS
Editor: Lara Milton
Computer wizard: Aaron Leis
Cover image © 2007,2009 Roy Tabora of Tabora Studio,
LLC
The author thanks artist Roy Tabora
For graciously providing his painting,
"Black Sand Magic," for the cover of this book
http://www.tabora.com and www.taboragallery.com
Map and cover design by Andy Zeigert
Thank you all

HADRIANNA ISLAND

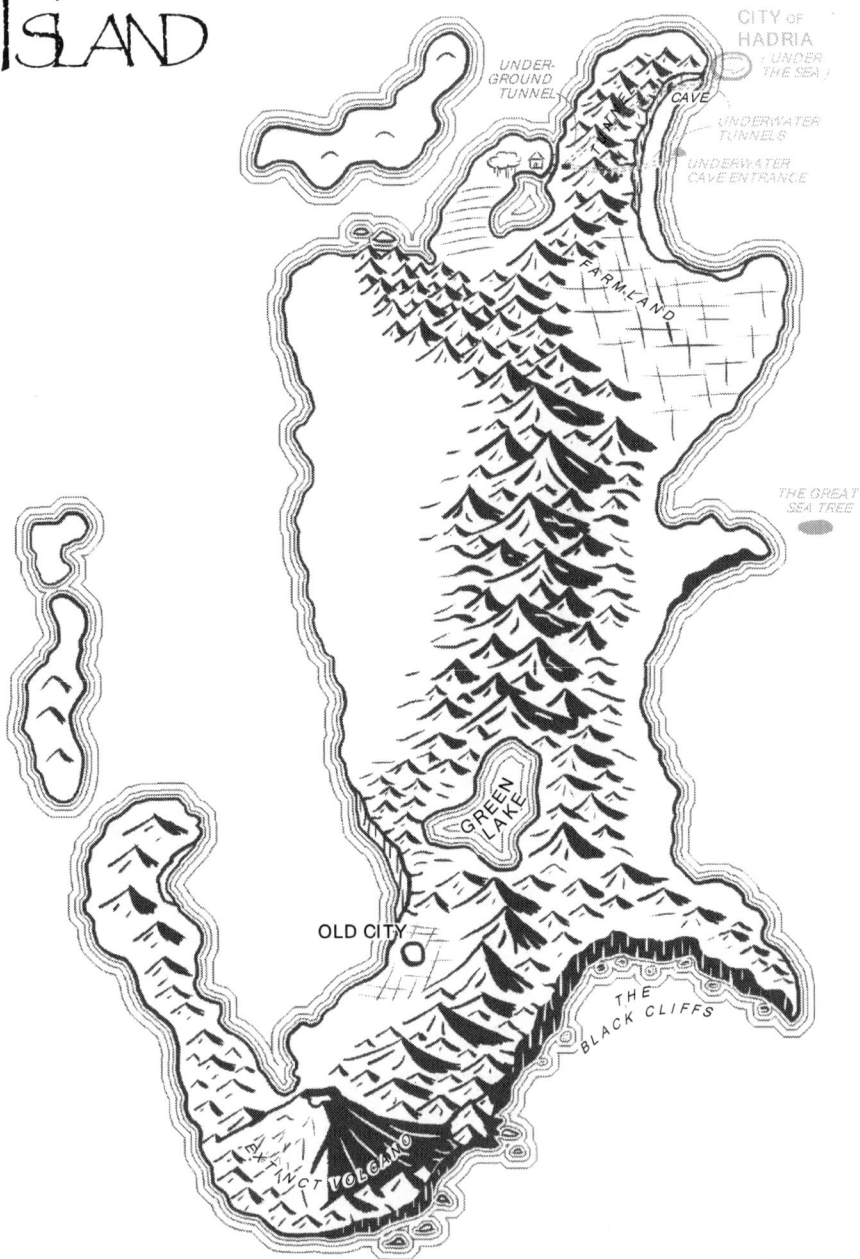

CITY OF HADRIA
(UNDER THE SEA)

UNDER-GROUND TUNNEL

CAVE

UNDERWATER TUNNELS

UNDERWATER CAVE ENTRANCE

FARMLAND

THE GREAT SEA TREE

GREEN LAKE

OLD CITY

THE BLACK CLIFFS

EXTINCT VOLCANO

CHAPTER ONE

My friends and I really had no choice. It was go with Verity and the Stella Mara people or go to war with a more technologically advanced enemy. I hoped we could become allies, if not friends. But to be forced into a year of citizen exchange on the brink of a possible civil war among my own people did not bode well for friendship.

It had taken three hours to fly over the land and sea, which had taken days to travel just weeks ago by ship, before we dipped into the ocean and kept going under the dark water. Another couple of hours and I began to see the glimmer of lights.

"Hadria," I breathed.

Verity turned and smiled at me. "Home!" she said. "Mea cara Hadria."

This I knew. It meant "My dear Hadria."

We drew closer to the glowing domes of the underwater city. The spiraling shapes within the domes looked like giant seashells that quickly resolved into elegant, magnificent buildings. The domes looked like glowing glass. The buildings within were clear in some places and opaque in others. Each building seemed to have the barest hint of a different color from its neighbor, and with most of them, you could see through their walls. We were traveling to the left of the city now, where the dome hugged the side of an underwater mountain. To the right, the ocean floor flattened out and stretched away, going deeper into the dark Trillium Sea.

We glided into an open, glasslike tube, and, turning as much as I could while still strapped into my chair, I watched as the other nine ships came in after us. Ibera climbed up on the seat next to me and looked around. The opening behind us closed, and the water began to recede. When the water was gone, Verity continued to lead the ships, now moving through the air like cyna-cycles do, through another doorway and down a tunnel to a large bay area, and each ship pulled into an empty dock. Other ships, larger and smaller, were also docked there, all in neat rows.

Once out of the ships we all gathered around Verity with our things.

"Venire," Verity said, indicating the direction she wanted us to go. "Superus Domas," She pointed up the underwater cliff face to another, higher dome. Verity nodded and pointed again.

"She says we must go to ... High Dome," LaBo translated.

We gathered our things and followed Verity: Lucus Tallman, Rifkin Steel, Jorame Oath, Dray, Kid, Willobee, Reia, LaBo, myself and Ibera, my hound. Ibera didn't seem at all bothered to be under the ocean. Though she seemed alert and watchful, she didn't react in any negative way. Our ears popped when we swallowed; the higher pressure in this place took a bit of adjusting to, but it wasn't uncomfortable. How far down we were was impossible to tell, being as it was night when we arrived and the sea was inky black just a few yards past the lights of Hadria.

We loaded all our gear onto an air platform, and Verity set the platform to keep pace with us. We were all quiet amid this new underwater strangeness, looking at everything as we followed Verity.

We walked through the long bay, past fifty or sixty different-sized ships in their docks. There were more than a hundred docks, and I wondered where the other ships were, or if this was all they had. LaBo spoke to Verity in Sabostienie, and at the end of their short, choppy conversation, she turned to us and said, "We will go to our apartment for the night. Tomorrow we will meet the First Woman, when we are all fresh. I also asked her how far below the surface we are. She said it's two fathoms from the top of High Dome, three fathoms from the surface to Mid Dome and four to the Low Dome. I'm not sure what they consider a fathom, but where I come from, it is six feet. If we are in Mid Dome, then we are eighteen feet below the surface."

"Oooh," Lucus moaned, "eighteen feet! This will be the death of me." His slight frame shuddered a bit in protest.

Through the lighted dome wall, we could see many kinds of fish of many shapes, sizes and colors close beyond it. Visibility faded the farther into the dark we tried to see. There was a brilliant red, many-limbed thing with sucker feet all along its long limbs inching its way up the outside wall. Then it suddenly turned bright blue, which made us gasp. We were all fascinated with the teeming life outside the dome, except for Lucus, who was trying not to look. And at that point, Verity named in her language some of the things we were seeing, going slowly, and LaBo told us those names in English—or as close as she could come to them.

"Uh ... Tiger Nar-fish," she said, and pointed to a square-faced fish that had a short, spiky horn between its eyes and fangs that hung over its bottom jaw. When it opened its mouth, we saw that there was a second and third row of jagged teeth inside.

"That thing with the many legs ..." LaBo pointed, "that one, with the shifting colors, is a Neon Octo Ped."

Willobee piped up. "We have them on the Blue Moon don't we?" She looked up at LaBo.

Before LaBo could answer, our attention was grabbed by a school of small blue, crimson and yellow fish that hugged the wall, gliding along together, darting left, then right suddenly, all in perfect synchronization.

"Those ..." LaBo pointed after the school, "are Neon Zippers. And yes, we do have the Octos on the moon, Bee."

We did our best to repeat the names Verity said when she pointed out some new aquatic creature. Then we stopped, stunned to see two of the Fish Children who had come with Verity to escort us here appear outside the dome. They waved and gave her a hand signal, and she answered back in kind. Their naked, shimmery selves hung in the water as small sliver-green fish circled around them. Tiny bubbles rose up from what I now realized were gills on their necks. Verity spoke again with her hands, and they sped away faster than any of us might run on land. A new and clearer meaning to the name Obaskillian, Fish Children, came into my understanding as I remembered the faces I'd seen in the Trillium Sea when I had cast the Life Stealers into those ocean waters only a few weeks before.

"But how?" several of my friends whispered. Their faces shone like children on Winter Festival Day, pressed close to the dome wall.

"Now that is the strangest thing I have ever seen in all my years of roaming," Jorame said. "Strange, but *beautiful.*"

Verity led us to a bank of large elevators, and we all crowded into one, along with the air platform. We rose up a large vertical tube that separated the smaller dome on the side of the mountain from the main dome—the middle dome that was three fathoms deep, however deep that was.

After following the outer rim walkway, we arrived at a large apartment, big enough to house all of us comfortably, with communal living space to share and a bedchamber and private sitting room for each of us for when we needed time alone. We carried our belongings into our apartment. Verity waited outside as we dropped off our things in the middle of the communal room and returned to her as instructed.

The area outside the apartment had a clear glass balcony with a long bench where we could watch the wildlife of the sea just outside the dome wall. From this balcony, there was a spiral hallway that led up a gentle slope, wrapping around other apartments like ours, spacious and with many visible luxuries. These people didn't seem much for privacy, as most of the front living spaces were visible to the world.

Only a few apartments away from ours, we came to a bright orange door. Verity said, "Doma mea cara."

"I think that means 'my dear home,'" I said, and Jorame agreed. Wydra and Jorame had never learned Sabostienie in depth, but knew enough to get by, if they had to, in the old language. English had taken over in the Wells and on the Blue Moon hundreds of years earlier, the people there believing it is better to speak the language of a possible enemy in order to pursue peaceful resolutions if you are discovered by them. Wydra knew somewhat more than Jorame. *More's the pity she isn't here, but on second thought, if Wydra had been taken, that would have killed John.* I wondered about Julka and Jorame, how would they deal with this separation? Then my mind leapt to LaBo, the historian-librarian. She spoke Sabostienie fluently, and though there were slight differences between the two languages, she would continue to do a fine job of being our interpreter until we learned more ourselves, if we needed to.

I could certainly understand the concept of wanting to know the language of an opposing force and wished I had spent more time under the neurocap learning Sabostienie when I was on the Blue Moon. Instead, my curiosity had sidetracked me into history, culture and philosophy, which meant I had learned a little bit about each one, but none of them in depth, thinking I would have more time later to learn anything I set my mind to.

LaBo spoke with Verity for a while. What I could follow was if we needed anything, Verity was here. LaBo confirmed this by saying

"This is Verity's home. We are not to hesitate to knock on her door should we need anything at any time. We will have a help staff tomorrow, but for tonight, we will be left alone to adjust to our new home."

Verity led us back to our apartment balcony and left us at the door.

"This gives me the creeps." Lucus had stopped shuddering at every new sight, but as he looked out at the ocean our living room view was open to, an expression of repulsion and loathing was on his face as he said, "It makes me feel trapped, closed in. I can hardly get a good breath. It is like a weight pressing me down. I thought the jungle was bad. But this …" He shrugged as if he could shake off the mantle of waves above us.

"I love it!" Reia touched the clear wall of our balcony as if she wanted to be out there in the water herself, with the Fish Children, the Obaskillian. "It is the most beautiful place I have ever seen."

"Well," said Rifkin, "with Pendyse as a friend, there's never a dull moment." He gave me a wink and a lopsided grin and ran a hand through his coarse red hair, then gave a one-shouldered shrug as if that explained everything.

Willobee's delicate eyebrows were pinched together with worry. "Are we safe, Pendyse? What if the dome breaks?" I saw a shudder pass over Lucus's body at Willobee's words.

I put my arm around her and pulled her close. "I think this place has been here a long, long time, Little Bee. I don't think you need to worry." Dray came over and put his arm around her from the other side, and Kid came and stood next to me but not touching me, alone and aloof. We watched the flow of the vivid green sea trees and grasses and fish in the currents, weaving among the ropy fronds. We all stood there, mesmerized by our surroundings, not saying a word for a long time, until Jorame broke the spell. "Come on, let's choose our rooms and put our things away," he said. "We have a whole year to appreciate the beauty of the Trillium Sea."

"Or grow to hate it even more than I already do," I heard Lucus snarl under his breath.

Evidently Reia heard Lucus too, because over her shoulder, she quietly said to him, "Everything has its own beauty, but not everyone has eyes to see it."

11

I looked away from them so they wouldn't see me smile. I had grown to love Reia and her sharp tongue. She could cut to the heart of a matter without a second word yet lose none of that tender heart she opened to anyone who needed a home. Her sharpness was never mean spirited. I was suddenly very glad she was with us. I knew I could count on her wisdom and trust her compassion to help keep me centered and balanced. I knew I would need that.

Inside our new home, there were nine suites and a large kitchen, dining and living space we would share. It was round, with a central column in the shared space. A spiral staircase rose up and wrapped around the column to a point about forty feet up to the ceiling, a graceful bowl-shaped roof over the three main rooms. The center of this high point was as clear as the dome wall outside. The narrow spiral staircase rose up to a small, opaque floored space at the top. It was a private space that couldn't be seen from the living room except for the round center, which was directly above the staircase. I suspected when the sun was up, light could come into the main living spaces from the clear roof dome above this small room.

We left our things in the communal rooms and went to look at the bedchambers. I didn't have a preference and let everyone else choose before me. Willobee clung to my hand and insisted that her rooms had to be next to mine. Jorame wanted the first one in line on the left of the long, curving hallway, to guard the rest of us, he said, and smiled, adding, "Closest to the kitchen, in case I get hungry. And the bedroom has an ocean view. I think I like that."

"I love the rooms on the left, down at the end of the curved hallway, the second to the last suite, with the ocean view," Reia said. "Did you see that view? I can watch the sea any time I want from both of my rooms."

"I'll take the suite across the hall from Jorame," Lucus said. "It has no ocean view, and that is just fine with me, and I can help keep a watch with Jorame. At least you ladies will be safe if anyone attacks us." He glanced around meaningfully at us. "We will be the first to go," he whispered glumly.

"Verity said it is a peaceful place and there are no such disturbances here," LaBo said, trying to reassure us all.

Lucus went to the living room for his bags and began making himself comfortable. As he did so, he said, "I will believe that when I see it. They did kill some of our people and took us from our homeland against our wishes. What do you think that was? Goodwill?"

LaBo moved into the space next to Reia with an ocean view from her bedchamber. The boys, Dray and Kid, wanted to stay together, and took the room next to LaBo, on the left side of the hall, the side with the ocean views. Rifkin laughed and said, "Jorame has the right idea. Show me the room closest to the kitchen so I can get up and eat a snack in the middle of the night without disturbing anyone."

"Sorry, I already have that one," Jorame grinned. "You'll have to settle for the one next door to Lucus. All the sea views are taken."

With Kid and Dray bunking together, that left a room empty between Willobee and Rifkin.

All this light banter was cover for the anxiety we were all feeling, I thought. We were in a situation we had not chosen in order to save our people. We would have to learn what it meant to share a wider world than we had once thought we lived in.

We collected our bags and disappeared down the long, curving hall to the suites we had chosen. Each had a private living space and equal-sized bedchamber, a bathroom and a wardrobe room. Our private spaces were a comfortable size and nicely appointed with everything we could possibly need. No one seemed to want the end suite on the left, so I took it. It had a view of the sea from the bedroom and was up against the side of the mountain. I had a stone wall in each of my rooms, which I really loved; it made me feel right at home.

Willobee picked the rooms opposite mine, across the hall. There was no view, but she liked the stone walls also. I understood how Reia felt. There was something soothing about the movement out there in the water, and I knew I would enjoy my sea view. But I felt quite at home with my walls set against the mountain itself. I ran my hand across the stone as if I expected it to respond and sing me its history. How long had the dome nestled against it? Who were the people who had lived here before me? I pressed the side of my face to the cool, smooth stone and listened.

The next thing I knew, Willobee was tapping me on the arm. "I'm done putting my things away." She cocked her head and frowned. "What are you doing? You haven't even started yet."

"I'm listening for the stone mountain to tell me its story," I said.

"Oh." Willobee pressed her small shell-shaped ear against the wall too, and listened. After a minute, she said, "I don't think it's ready to tell you."

That made me laugh. "Well, when it's ready, I'll share, or if you hear from it first, you can tell me." I ran my hand affectionately over the soft lilac hair that ran along the top of her head. "What's up, Bee?" Her perfect heart-shaped face looked up at me, her lavender cat's eyes huge and dark. Her tiny, sharp-edged nose seemed small by comparison.

"You've been in here a long time. I've been done with my unpacking forever. Everyone is in the kitchen fixing us something to eat. They said you and Ibera should come."

Ibera had followed me from living space to bedroom to bathroom. I wondered where she was supposed to go to relieve herself. There was no grass and no place to let her run. I'd have to figure that out before morning. At the moment she was asleep on my bed.

"Ibera, come," I called, and took Willobee's hand as we headed for the kitchen.

As we arrived, I heard Lucus say, "I do not understand why we are here." He glared at me as if this was my fault. "Why did they leave their people in Telling Wood? I know I did not want to come here!" he continued. "Their people probably didn't want to stay in our capital, either. How is this going to help create a peace treaty between these strange people and our people? I would rather work with the Sabostienie, as different as they are." He shot a glance sideways at LaBo. "No offense."

LaBo gave a half smile. "No offense taken. But I relish the chance to get to know these people, to find out how this," she indicated our surroundings and the view from the glass-fronted apartment and balcony outside, "came into being. They live under the sea, doesn't that intrigue you? Don't you find that fascinating? Don't you want to know how all this works?"

"Quite frankly," Lucus said, shaking his head, "no! It scares the hell out of me." He turned his back to the view. "Why would anyone want to live *under* the sea?"

"It's beautiful!" Reia said.

"It is hidden from the known world," Kid said. Reia smiled at him. He sort of ignored her, as if he wasn't quite sure how he fit in among these people.

"No, Kid is right." Rifkin said. "They might feel like it's safer than living where we live, I believe if our people had seen them before now, they'd have tried to kill them outright. If not for this place, they might not exist at all. So it seems like a smart move on their part. Like Kid said,

14

they're hidden. Hidden from the killers of different. Look what the Voice did when she and her people went to the moon."

"I think it's interesting who they chose to bring here," said Kid. "Don't you, Pen? Look at us: three children, three women and three men. Why us? They had our names before they came for us. Where did they get our names? How were we chosen, and who chose us?"

Since Kid had been released from the cell he'd spent the last few months in, he had not spoken much. But I sensed his keen awareness of the people and places around him. He had read voraciously while in the jail with the others who had come from Dunsmier Dakota to take over the capital, Telling Wood. He was a thinker. Even though he had tried to kill me when we first met, when he began to learn the truth, we had grown to trust each other. But he was still an aloof ten-year-old boy who was somewhat a mystery to me, but in some ways reminded me of me at that age. Even though I could feel his truthfulness, his thoughts were constantly guarded: he didn't let stray bits and pieces escape that inner vault. He was a thinker, but a quiet thinker.

What surprised me most was the instant bond Kid and Dray had formed, as if they had been best friends forever, or spirit brothers. Both were orphans in a sense, Dray for real, Kid by choice.

"Those are very good questions, Kid," I said. "Hopefully, tomorrow, when we meet the First Woman, we will get some good answers. I am sure each one of us has something to offer in this time and place, and something to learn, but being as we don't know what that is yet, let's eat and get some sleep if we can. It's been a long and stressful day, and who knows what tomorrow will bring?"

Lucus snorted. "Optimist."

We ate. Most of the food was unfamiliar, and tasted and looked different than what we were used to. Some of it we liked, and some we pushed away after one bite.

After that, when the others began to drift off to their separate chambers, I took Ibera out on the balcony. I didn't know what else to do but let her go to the corner and relieve herself. I would have to ask if there was any way to have a bed of dirt brought onto the balcony for her.

Just as Ibera and I were getting ready to go back in, Rifkin and Jorame came out to join me.

Rifkin came over to the glass bench I was sitting on and began to rub my neck and shoulders. I melted; I hadn't realized till just that moment how tense I was and that I had a headache.

"How are you doing, Pen?" Rifkin asked as he massaged my stiff neck muscles. "What are you thinking about all this?"

"When you're doing that to my shoulders, I don't think anything at all. I just feel," I said as I relaxed with a sigh.

Jorame gave a chuckle and sat down. Rifkin sat down on the bench on the other side of me. They took my hands in theirs, and we sat for a long time, just watching the sea as the lights dimmed in the glasslike dome until the only light left came from the living room behind us and the occasional neon blink of a fish outside the dome.

"Do you think we'll be OK?" I asked, squeezing their hands in thanks.

"Wonannonda is with you. You're with us," Rifkin said. "How could anything go wrong? Of course we'll be OK."

I felt so grateful for their warmth and presence. I knew they gave me strength, even if they might not know it. They pulled me up from the bench, and we went in for the night.

CHAPTER TWO
(Day Two)

As we made our way up to the highest curl of shell-shaped buildings, we all talked in low tones. Verity remained silent, however, until we got to where we would meet the First Woman.

Then Verity spoke, and LaBo translated. "There is only going to be a brief meeting with First Woman this morning, Verity says. We will each have time with her later. She wants to get to know us."

My curiosity was killing me. What would she be like, this woman who was their leader, our hostess? And what was the social structure of this city she led? What were the rules or laws of this place? What were the customs?

A young girl came to the door to let us in. "I am Iloura. Please follow me," she said.

I looked around at the others, my brows rising up under my curls in surprise at the English she spoke. I didn't know if this was the only thing she could say or if there was more. Iloura looked to be ten or twelve. Her hair was long, down to her knees, a pinkish pearly color that pulled at my attention with its unusual hue. Her clothes were the same shade of blue as Verity's dress, with white trim. I wondered if they were house or uniform colors.

The nine of us were led into an opaque-walled room that was twice the size of our apartment's shared living space. It reminded me of the council chambers where the Telling Wood throne still sat. Was this an audience chamber, a throne room? Or was it a council hall, or maybe all three?

A woman with the palest of silver-white hair that flowed to the floor in wispy, soft looking strands stood up from her large chair. Was it a throne? The First Woman appeared to be somewhat old, and somehow different-looking from the other Stella Mara, paler in skin tone.

Verity said, "Our First Woman, Ilantha," and gave a little head bow of respect.

She dipped her head again in a slight bow of silent greeting, then stepped back and waved me forward. "Pendyse Ra'Vell," she said, indicating me. Then she went down the row. "Kid. Dray. Willobee. Lucus Tallman. Reia. LaBo. Jorame Oath. Rifkin Steel." She stopped at the end of the line.

The young girl, Iloura, still standing next to me, said, "She is known as First Woman, or Ilantha." She looked down the row of my people. "Because you are our guests, you may call her Ilantha."

This implied to me that we were to become well known to each other. And I suppose that *was* the purpose of this exchange, but to call her Ilantha seemed far to intimate at this point of the acquaintance. I might be able to think of her as Ilantha, but I could not use her name, not yet.

It was very hard for me to judge Ilantha's age. Even though she seemed old, she also seemed quite fit. She was tall and lean, and dressed in a bright crystal blue. Her silver-white hair shone like the inside of a ghost shell from the northeast shores of Nueden. The First Woman was staring at LaBo with a fascination that lit her countenance; then her gaze moved to Willobee. Ilantha sat back down in the large chair at the head of a semicircle of chairs.

"Come here to me, Willobee." Some of us caught our breaths in surprise, not at the accent of her speech, but because she spoke English. "You sit here next to me."

Willobee looked at me. I nodded, and she went and sat in a small chair next to Ilantha and gave her a little head bow, which seemed to delight the woman.

"LaBo, please, come to this side. I am most curious about you," she said.

LaBo took the offered chair to Ilantha's left and sat down on a cushioned footstool.

"Please be seated," Ilantha said, and she indicated the other chairs. Verity, along with the rest of us, sat down facing her.

"Before I ask you questions about why you attacked my Fish Children, I will tell you who I am." Ilantha made eye contact with each and every one of us before she continued. "My mother was a Sabostienie from Well One."

Out of the corner of my eye, I saw Jorame give a small jerk of surprise at this statement, then settle back again in his chair. It was then that I realized her eyes were more like cat eyes than the large, round eyes of the Stella Mara.

"My father was the son of the First Woman who ruled Hadria for eighty years," Ilantha continued. "Father was on a scouting mission and found a Sabostienie woman washed up on the beach far from the Domed Wells, at the mouth of the river. It was forbidden for the Stella Mara to reveal themselves to the Sabostienie or the Others." She glanced at me as she said this. Her movements, hand gestures, even the way she held her head, were the epitome of grace and loveliness. She must have been a stunningly attractive woman in her youth, for even now her allure and power of presence were masterful.

"I grew up in Well One, speaking English till I was eight. My mother would take me on a cyna-cycle to the mouth of the river once a year to spend time with my father. We all kept our secret from both of our peoples. But when I was nearing my ninth year day we made our last trip to the Trillium Sea to be with Father. Mother told me I was to go with him to Hadria." She paused and glanced around the circle. "You may wonder why I am telling you this story. You need to understand me. For I am the open hand of Hadria." She swept her flat open palm around the circle, and then she clenched it tight. "I am also Hadria's fist." She looked around at us again. "I may be getting old, but I will let no one hurt my people." After this, she kept a stony silence for a while.

Then, smiling again, she settled back into her chair. "Leaving my mother was not something I wanted to do. But Father said Hadria needed me. And I had yearned to see the city under the sea for such a long time. Father's mother was dying, and they had no female children in the family line but me at that time. When they discovered Grandmother had the long, slow sickness, Father told her about me. She sent for me to come and train to take over the leadership beneath the waves."

She stilled, her eyes focused on a distant point in her life. I felt her there, at that sad memory. *Life has so many losses*, I thought,

19

wondering if she had ever seen her mother again. *We are not so different after all.*

Ilantha sighed and continued. "I came here. I trained. I learned. A new way of life, a new order, a new language. I grew to love all things Hadrian, and I especially love our Fish Children, the Obaskillian." She lifted her hands and looked up. "And it is beautiful here, don't you agree?"

We murmured our agreement, all but Lucus, who looked sullen and truculent. "My grandmother died when I was eleven, and I became the First Woman," Ilantha continued. "I have peacefully led the Stella Mara for sixty-eight years. I may have another twenty-five or thirty if your people don't kill me first, or start a war that will do us all to death."

We all sat in utter silence. How was I to explain to her and make her hear the truth?

"I have always had at least one person around me who learned English—thus my little Iloura, who has been taught both languages from birth—so I wouldn't forget how to speak it, for the First Woman before me, my grandmother, who taught me how to be the First Woman, was sure there would come a day when the people above the Steel Desert would attack us. And you," she turned a hard-eyed stare in my direction, "have proven her right."

I gave a small bow from the waist while still sitting. "Forgive us our error, First Woman. But we did not know you or the Obaskillian were down here." I moved forward in my chair, egger to explain. "We only just this year discovered there were people who lived in the Steel Desert and on the Blue Moon. We thought we alone inhabited this world. Maybe ignorance does not excuse our actions in your eyes, but we didn't know you were here. I can assure you, if we had known, we never would have emptied the Life Stealers into your ocean."

"We feared some of our own people getting their hands on them," Lucus snapped. "We thought if they were at the bottom of the sea, no one could get them, and we would all be safe. But your people dumped them back on us. Honestly, we did not know of you. You must know that is the truth if you have been spying on us for who knows how long." His tone was harsh.

"So, it is our fault you tried to kill us." The First Woman half rose from her chair, her hands balling into fists.

"No!" I held up my hands. "No, he wasn't saying that." I could sense Ilantha's anger boiling just below the surface. We had offended her. Thinking fast, I asked, "May I tell you a story, a true story?"

20

She gave me a slight nod, her posture stiff, unyielding, but she settled back in her ... throne? Did she consider it a throne?

"Maybe you know of the Wonannonda Tree," I said. Ilantha gave another curt nod. "Well, our people believed that the Book, the Tree and the Voice were our guiding light in life. But we were being lied to. For hundreds of years, the Voice lied to the people, turning them against women."

I saw the First Woman recoil at those words. "Yes, your treatment of women is despicable," she said. "And to think a woman was the cause of all that suffering for other women." She shook with outrage. "Wicked. Such a wicked woman!"

"The Voice," I said, returning to my story, "really having no love for any of the people, men or women, for hate had eaten her soul; the Voice who had pretended to be a man—Zee was her name—she and some of her guardsmen went to the Blue Moon and took some Life Stealers from an ancient starship. My friends and I tried to stop her. Zee killed the Father and Mother of the Sabostienie people."

At that, the First Woman gasped and clutched at her chest, but said nothing.

"I became her captive. Zee wanted my island home, and she intended to take it at any cost, even if the price was many lives. She didn't care how many. On the plains of Nueden, just outside Telling Wood, our largest city, she used one of those bombs on our own people for no other reason than to test the working distance of the device. I was there to witness this horror. Close to four hundred thousand men, women and children perished without warning. Horses fell in their traces, dogs dropped with their masters. The only sound was that of the dying. You cannot imagine ..."

Dray gave a sob. I looked at him; we both had tears in our eyes. I brushed mine aside, ignoring them. "Dray was there too." I indicated our small group. "We all felt the shock and horror of this act of depravity. Every one of us lost friends or family members that day." Pausing, I swallowed and blinked a few times, allowing no more tears to come. "We had tried to stop it, but we failed. Our people all over Nueden were in shock and afraid, but we moved forward in the best way we knew. We are trying to bring the people from all parts of our world together to become one people in peace, accepting our differences, appreciating them. We buried those bombs in the ocean to stop a war, not to start one."

21

Jorame spoke for the first time. "This is the truth. We had no ill intentions toward you or your people, as we knew nothing of you. And if the nine of us being here can help bring our people together in peace, then I swear an oath to you and give myself over to the process of bringing a lasting peace to our people. All of our people, yours and ours."

After that, we all swore to it. The children readily agreed with Jorame first; Lucus agreed last, reluctantly. I felt his reservations and fear, his doubt of the First Woman's goodwill toward us. I could sense his hesitation to commit to her without knowing what her intentions toward us were.

Then Ilantha said, "Verity and Iloura will show you around our city today; they will answer your questions. Iloura and LaBo can translate. For now, go back to your place and meet your help staff. They will not live with you; you will have your privacy. They will come to clean your rooms and prepare your meals. I will think on what you have said."

"Thank you," I gave her a respectful head bow. "The apartment is quite comfortable. I do have one request, though, as I brought Ibera, my Nar Hound." I saw Ilantha's eyes light up. "She needs a place to relieve herself. Maybe a large, flat tray of dirt or sand."

"Verity," Ilantha said. There was a short exchange of words spoken in their language, too fast for me follow any of it, and then she spoke to me again. "Please, you must bring her to me. I wish to see this land animal. I remember Nar Cats, the smaller ones that were pets in the Wells. I would like to met this … Ibera."

She stood, indicating that our first meeting was over. We all stood in turn.

"LaBo and Willobee will stay with me and have midday meal here. I wish to talk with them further," Ilantha announced.

LaBo took Willobee's hand and gave me a quick glance. I nodded and said, "That is fine. Will they be joining us for the city tour? Should we wait for them?"

"I will see to it they are back before you leave."

By the time we arrived back at our place, there was a long box of dirt in the area where Ibera had relieved herself the previous night. How had Ilantha done that so quickly?

"Look!" I heard Kid say to Dray. I looked up to where he was pointing. Shafts of sunlight slanted down, wavering through the ocean, and lit up the High Dome. In our apartment, the spiral staircase that led up to the small, twisting point of the cone was like a magnifier of the light, which spread throughout the shared living space with a movement that was alive in that shimmery way light through water has of dancing around a room. We were all caught in its spell.

***

After the mid-day meal Iloura had joined us when she brought LaBo and Bee back to us before our tour.

LaBo was translating what Verity said. "The High Dome has no businesses, only habitats … homes." She listened to Verity again. "All the merchants and stores, schools, science labs and things of that nature are in the Mid Dome. The Low Dome is where food is produced. Whether it is grown there or gathered from the sea, it is processed and packaged in Low Dome."

I didn't like not being able to follow all of what was said. Learning Sabostienie as quickly as I could should be my first priority, I decided. *And perhaps teaching English to as many of the Stella Mara as wanted to learn a close second*, I thought. It was beautiful to listen to, but it made me feel like I was in the dark with no way to turn on the light.

It was strange. I kept feeling as if Verity was not what she seemed. A feeling of deceit or something secret, false, seemed to lurk in her and tickled around the edges of my mind. I knew she would be someone to keep an eye on. Verity … I had a feeling that she might prove to be the opposite of the meaning of her name. This made me remember when I was on the Blue Moon in the Old Ship and Zarek was talking about the words that we held in common.

The main city dome, midlevel, was like nothing we'd ever seen or could have even imagined. The shapes were round, curving or rising, spiraled wonders. Many of the glasslike structures had sharp conical roofs or ceilings with stairs leading up to the highest point to take advantage of as much of the light as they could get. The walls could change colors on the whim of the people who ran the establishment, with some kind of mechanical switches. The buildings could become opaque as well. The Stella Mare didn't seem to care if their living spaces were open to the public or not. Even the businesses were like that. You could stand in the passageways and watch garments being made, or any of a dozen other types of things they used there.

"Venire," said Verity. "Ludus."

"She said come … to see the school," Iloura said, smiling at Dray and Kid as she took Bee's hand.

One of the larger grey, shell-shaped buildings, with a dull transparency, was at the end of one of the winding passageways. We stepped inside, out of the hustle and bustle of the many people in the byways. The large main room was separated into areas for different ages, and it didn't seem to have that many children in it, maybe one hundred among all the age groups, I saw with a quick visual calculation. Fewer in every age group as they got younger.

"LaBo, would you ask Verity if this is the only school, or are there others here, too?" I asked.

LaBo asked her and then answered me, "Yes, this is the main school. There are a few smaller private schools that teach the children from High Dome, and one work school for the children in Low Dome, where they teach them how to work at the jobs they will have when they are adults."

"That sounds like fun!" Kid said sarcastically. "Like Military League for those who can't afford Library."

"They also learn to read and write," said LaBo, "and as they reach puberty, they go into the factories to work. Verity says no one has to work more than four days a week. Four days working, four days off, with a holy day at the end where no one works, except for emergencies."

"What are emergencies?" Willobee asked, looking alarmed, as if she had picked up on what the word meant without it having to be explained to her.

"They are times when something unusual happens," LaBo said, patting Willobee's shoulder. "Nothing for you to worry about, Little Bee. Grown-ups take care of them."

Lucus, Rifkin and Jorame were in a shop just off the main promenade where they sold sticks you could read or listen to, which plugged into a small handheld device, somewhat like our readers. The First Woman had given orders that we were to have whatever we wanted, and they came back with a cloth bag full of things. "To help us with the language, and their history," said Jorame, handing them to LaBo with a grin. "You are going to be our teacher."

"Humph," Lucus huffed. "How can we learn this place? There is no order anywhere. It just goes round and round. What passes for streets just meanders; we'd get lost out here alone," he complained.

"Where is Reia?" He looked around in a sudden panic. "Have we lost one of us already? Has she wandered off?"

"No," I laughed, and he glared at me. "Really, Lucus, calm down. We are all perfectly safe. She is in that shop over there. She spotted a garment she wanted and went to get it."

"I do not like it when we are not all together," he said with a nervous little jitter.

Really, he was becoming worse than a mother hen. Willobee took his hand and said, as she smiled up at him, "Don't worry, she's on her way back now."

I looked around but couldn't see Reia yet. I wondered how Willobee could know this; then she looked at me and whispered, "I can feel her coming." And she nodded with another smile. Then Reia was walking toward us with a huge smile on her face, carrying a cloth bag big enough to hold several outfits in it.

"I'm hungry," said Dray.

"Me too," chimed in Kid and Willobee.

"We've been walking ever so long," Willobee said.

LaBo talked to Verity and then to us. "Verity said she would take us to the Garden for dinner."

The Garden was the most spectacular place. It was the only building that was long like a tube, with a curved, peaked ceiling and a series of cathedral-type windows of colored glass that the slanting sun shone through, splashing colors around the large room. The windows reminded me of the story tapestries in the Heart of Moon City. I studied them to see if I could get a sense of the place, but nothing earth shaking came to me. The Stella Mara people at the other tables stared at us with bold curiosity, a babble of comments among them, none of which I could understand. We were staring at them with similar interest.

There were tables grouped around small fountains and raised stone garden beds, with a long, narrow pool winding down the middle of the building. It looked like a stony brook meandering between the tables and flowerbeds filled with greenery, along with pinks, purples, blues and the reds of exotic plants. It was an altogether lovely place that I hoped to visit again.

When we were finished eating, Rifkin pushed back from the table and said, "Well, that was satisfying." He glanced around. "And a really beautiful place, too."

"For a city as large as this one seems to be," I said, looking around, "it doesn't feel like it has that many people in it."

"Verity, what is the population of Hadria?" Reia asked.

The exchange was made and the answer returned.

"Around twenty thousand. They keep their population small so they don't outgrow the domes. They only have one child, to replace themselves. A mated couple may have two. It is very similar to the Sabostienie. That way, it doesn't put an undue strain on the enclosed environment."

"That doesn't seem like a lot," Jorame said. "This place is quite large; from what I've seen, I think it could actually hold more people comfortably without stressing the system. But maybe they need the spaciousness of the passageways and buildings so they don't feel closed in. I bet in the winter, they don't get much real sunlight down here."

"Yeah," Rifkin said, looking up through the clear dome ceiling, "the light is already fading." He looked at his cell watch. "It's only two o'clock, and more lights are coming on in every building, and lining the domes too."

"Yes," Jorame said "but our cell watches are still set to our time back home. We are farther west than Ra'Vell Island here in Hadria: I would guess a lot farther. So the times won't be the same."

We all looked up, watching what light was left fade. Lucus sighed, an exaggerated, long-suffering sigh, his displeasure plain. "Who know what time it is here."

I thought the glittering points of light on many levels and through many surfaces were magical, and they set off the twinkle of reflections in Willobee's lilac cat eyes, which were showing more black than lilac right then. She had a look of wonder on her face.

"Oh, my. This is soooo beautiful." Bee took a deep breath and said, "I will have to show Uncle Zarek this as soon as they let us talk to home on our coms."

At the mention of Zarek, I closed my mind to the pain of his absence there.

I caught a glimpse of Verity out of the corner of my eye, and I got the feeling she knew exactly what Willobee had said. It made me wonder again. Could she be one of the ones the First Woman spoke English with? That made sense to me. Why wouldn't she speak English, if she were to be the next First Woman?

"The Low Dome will have to wait until tomorrow," LaBo said, "when it is at best light."

There was general agreement, and we talked among ourselves as we walked back to the elevators and back to our rooms. Even as I chatted casually with our people, I watched Verity with furtive glances from under my lashes, and caught her many times seeming to understand something before LaBo would repeat it to her. It made me feel uneasy. If she could speak and understand more than she was letting on, why would she pretend she couldn't?

CHAPTER THREE

By the time we got back to the apartment, we were quite tired from all the new experiences, and most of the others drifted off to their own rooms.

"What do you say we take a flight to heaven?" Rifkin asked me, looking up the spiral stairs. "Want to explore?" No one had been up to the little room near the skylight yet.

"Sure, why not?" I stood and stretched, then headed for the stairs. Rifkin followed right behind me. The stairs were wide at the bottom and narrowed as we wound our way up. At the top of the clear glass stairs that gave my stomach the wobbles was a small room with a blue floor and cushions ringing the space, the bowl ceiling going up another ten feet to a clear window about twenty feet in diameter. The room was only about nine feet in diameter.

"Would you look at that?" Rifkin grinned. "It's the first night of the full Blue Moon."

And because of the bowl shape of things, it was magnified right into the small space, making it light up with a soft blue-white glow, but the light was not powerful enough to go any farther than this tiny haven.

"No, not again," I groaned.

He laughed. "Yes. Again. It's your birthday."

My mind touched briefly on the image of Zarek's face. I had been with him on my birthday last year.

"And I forgot."

"I know you did, but I didn't. Happy fourteenth."

"Fifteen and a half in Old Earth years. Physiologically speaking," I laughed. "Remember?"

28

Rifkin pulled a small, folded square of black velvet cloth from his pocket and handed it to me. "Actually, it is from the three of us, James, Hanni, and me. We didn't have a chance to give it to you last year, as you were on the Blue Moon by then."

I pulled back the folds of velvet slowly, a corner at a time, until the silver of a chain shifted in the evanescent light of the moon. The chain was not heavy, but it was quadruple linked. "The four of us!" I said, a smile curving my lips.

"Exactly," Rifkin said. "Let's sit."

We got comfortable on a couple of cushions, and I kept examining the gift in my hand, still mostly covered in black velvet cloth. I gasped as I unwrapped it further to reveal the open, lacy work of a silver heart a little larger than a slingshot ball. Inside it was a … "That smells like a blossom from the Wonannonda tree on the island," I said in amazement.

"Look closer."

I did, and realized it was indeed a bloom from the tree. It was tiny, yet perfect, bright and new. It was white, and had a dazzle of faint color that swirled around the edges, implying a state of motion even in its stillness.

"But how?" I asked.

"The day it grew, when it shook the earth and rent the air with its cry of becoming, this dropped at my feet. I saw it fall, and then …" Rifkin stopped, bit his lip and blinked a few times. "Then Mark fell. And our world changed. When we went back that day to dispose of the … murderer and clean the ground, I found this blossom by my footprint in the dirt. I picked it up. I knew it was for you. But I didn't know how to give it to you." He settled back on the bright red cushion, leaned against the wall and looked up at the hazy light drifting through the ocean above us. He ran his long fingers through his coarse red hair and sighed.

"Then you were gone." Rifkin shook his head. "I tell you, the island went a little crazy that day." He nodded and looked at me with a wan smile. "That was as hard a day as the one when we sent Mark's spirit to Tomorrow Land," he said. "I more or less forgot about the blossom until Hanni saw it in my room, still as fresh and beautiful as the day it fell at my feet." A true smile lit his face then. "Hanni's the smart one. She said we needed to have a chain and heart cage made for it and to give it to you as a birthday gift."

"It is beautiful," I said, pulling the chain out of the folds of soft fabric and slipping it over my head. I lifted the woven cage and saw the blossom fully for the first time. "That smell is wonderful. How can this be? How can it still be fresh, as if it fell this morning?" The blossom rested inside the protection of the open weave. "It is the best gift ever." I leaned over and gave Rifkin a hug. "That will have to be passed along to Hanni and James when we get back."

He breathed deeply and nodded. "A whole year. How will we ever endure it, that long without sunlight full on our faces?" He sighed. "I miss it already."

"I know. It seems impossible there is even a place like this," I agreed. "What do you think of Verity?" He gave me a sideways look, eyebrows raised. "I mean, other than you think she's beautiful," I half snorted. "I already knew that. Come on, be real."

"Well, she *is* beautiful," he exclaimed, "it's pretty hard not to notice that! And I am being real. So what are you referring too?"

"Well, sometimes I feel like she actually understands English."

Rifkin looked up and nodded absently, stroking his cheek, making a scratchy sound on the day's worth of stubble showing, the corners of his mouth drawn down. "Well, I haven't noticed that, but I'll watch for it now that you've mentioned it."

Then we just leaned back and, without words, watched the passage of Blue's light as it faded from view. A very short span of light that illuminated the little glass room, a hole in the dome, that's how I saw it. I kept my hand on the blossom cage, which nestled between my budding breasts. I couldn't imagine still having to pretend I was a boy. *No matter what that revelation had cost me, I am so glad I can be who I am now, free of any disguise or deception,* I thought, *whatever that means, however I came to this self I am now.*

"The thing I know, Pen, is that the Wonannonda Spirit gave that to me to give to you," Rifkin said. "It is to remind you that the Great Spirit is with you, will go with you even to the bottom of the Trillium Sea. There is no place out of sight of that Great Spirit. That one never-dying blossom was meant for you. And you are meant for the people, a leader, a Mother if you will, to your people because of the love you hold in your heart."

We returned to silence. I couldn't help thinking of Zarek, the Father of his people. And yes, some people did call me the Mother of mine. Could I ever really be that, at my age, with so little life experience?

30

Zarek, I called to him in my mind, not expecting an answer. What had happened? Why had he broken off contact? I thought we were friends, maybe more than friends. I knew I loved him, and I thought ... Well, I just didn't understand what had happened.

Rifkin and I sat there, slumped against each other in the quiet dark, until I became sleepy and rose to go. I helped Rifkin up, and we quietly went down to our rooms and said good night.

***

(Day Three)

The next morning, after we met our new staff—chef, maid and kitchen help—we ate what we could of the meal they prepared for us. Verity showed up at exactly the right time to take us to Low Dome. We took another route through the Mid Dome part of the city, so we could see more of its beauties, she said. We walked through a park and stood below a twenty-foot waterfall and walked in small garden patches with exotically colorful plants in them. The people were polite and shy, and curious about us. Some tried to talk to us, and LaBo enjoyed asking them questions and passing along snippets of compliments, mostly to Willobee. Everyone seemed to be fascinated with the child. And she was fascinated with them.

"They have very clear heads," Willobee whispered to me after one exchange. Her small hand squeezed mine as if to reassure me.

"Thank you, Bee," I said, and had to smile. She could be so very grown-up that sometimes it was hard for me to remember she was only six. She had the grace and dignity of an adult at times. That had to come from the Father and Mother, her family connection to the leaders of the Blue Moon and the Domed Wells. It saddened my heart to remember that they were both gone out of our world. Willobee squeezed my hand again, looking up at me with sadness in her face. "I miss them too," she said.

That knocked me for a loop. Had she just snatched a thought, a feeling, from my mind? Then LaBo was asking, "Can the people pet the 'giant fur creature'? They want to know if it bites."

"No, Ibera only bites if someone tries to hurt us. You can tell them that," I said. LaBo repeated this, and the people looked mystified and asked questions in their language. LaBo translated, "They said, 'Why would we want to hurt you?' and 'You are our peace. Our protection.'"

"OK." Rifkin nodded. "Well, that was a bit awkward."

I caught a slight smirk on Verity's face, covered by a quick hand and a cough, at Rifkin's remark. More and more, I felt sure she could speak perfect English, just like the First Woman and Iloura and who knew how many others around here. What if they were all pretending not to so they could listen in on what we were saying to judge whether we were a threat to them or not?

LaBo was talking again, explaining something the people were saying. "They say they don't have 'misdeeds' here. They say it is the same as in the Wells and on the Blue Moon. They have strict laws about conduct. They have to, as it is a dangerous place to live …"

Lucus broke in on LaBo. "I knew it. This is no way for people with half a brain to live."

"Like they were saying, a dangerous place to live unless all the people follow the laws and rules exactly in order for everyone to be safe," LaBo finished.

We ate lunch at a smaller, open garden place just at the entrance tube to the Low Dome. As we finished up, Jorame leaned over to me and said, "We have company. Don't look now, but Verity's vanguard just grew to include five more guards. Could the Low Dome be more dangerous than here, do you suppose?"

"I don't have a clue," I whispered back, "but pass the word to everyone to be extra cautious. Lucus will love that. Maybe you shouldn't tell him. He's already cautious enough."

Serious as the situation might have been, Rif chuckled.

This layered a texture of apprehension on our natural curiosity-tinged fear of going deeper under the Trillium Sea to find out how the people of the Low Dome worked and lived.

It was midday on the surface of the ocean, when the sun would be at its zenith, and down here it was half light compared to the light in the High Dome.

"That doesn't make sense to me," Rifkin said to Jorame and me. "It seems like things would grow better up closer to the light."

"They would," Jorame answered. "See how much poorer the buildings are down here. Not nearly as ornate, or light-filled either."

"Well, we knew," I said, "that they live in a tri-class society, much as Nueden has done, just divvied up differently. Maybe there's not that much difference between a matriarchal culture and a patriarchal one."

Jorame nodded. "Egalitarian views directed by common consent is the way to get a society that will work together for the good of all. One not run by rules but by love and respect for all the people. To have egregious imbalances like this and like what went on in Nueden for hundreds of years will always come to ruin. They are against the very nature of Wonannonda's spirit of love and the worth of all persons."

"Yes!" I said. "A love of peace. A love of the people for the people, a desire to see all the people flourish. That is what I want. There is enough of everything, enough and to spare, if we would only understand that and share equally."

We moved down a long, wide, slanting tube to reach the main area of the Low Dome. Down and down we went; it seemed to take forever to reach the bottom, but when I looked at my cell watch, I saw that it had only been a couple of minutes. The level of light was certainly diminished down here. I had had the feeling that the people who had and the people who had not were divided by the middle dome. Now I understood why High Dome was most desirable: it was the light! The treasure of the realm under the Trillium Sea was the light.

In the first of what they called grow barns there were some open flats of dirt at waist height with strings of lights above them, growing some kind of yellow plants. I could see that the flats ran all the way to the end of this giant open space. Each one held a different-colored planting.

I noticed children working the beds of plants. They were sad-eyed children who moved with mechanical precision. "This is the final-stage school of the Low Dome children's education," Iloura said.

"This doesn't look like school," Dray said.

"No!" said Kid. "It looks like work to me."

I noticed there were more children here, working, than there had been in the one school we'd seen the previous day. It didn't feel right. Not only did the children look sad, they looked tired, run down. Almost … *sick*, the word popped into my thoughts.

Verity took us through two processing centers, and we were coming to the third open, warehouse-like structure when there was a disturbance in the crowd coming to meet us. A man was yelling something.

"What is he saying?" I asked LaBo as Verity hustled us away from there.

"Something about Low Dome starving while High Dome eats its fill," she said. Then she frowned as Verity's guards pushed the crowd back behind the walls of the open-topped building we had been going into. "I think he said something about the children dying, or not being born. I don't know. Not sure. It all happened so fast, and their accent is strange to my ear."

We were being pushed away, herded to the tube back up to the Mid Dome.

"They are going to feed him to the fish!" Willobee said sadly. "That is not how Father and Mother would treat a misbehaving child of theirs."

We all looked at Willobee, aghast at such a thought. Where had that come from?

But as I looked back at the entrance of the building, I could see the man being bound and carried off somewhere, and other men, women and children glaring at us as their friend was being hauled out of sight.

And I wondered, *what is the punishment for insurrection around here?* In Nueden, it would have been death. Was it the same here? We passed through Mid Dome, subdued. Verity had left us with her guards; now she caught up with us, and she seemed to be seething just under the surface, trying to keep it out of sight, but what I *felt* rolling off her was barely suppressed fury. There was a lot of mental chatter, seepage of bits and pieces of thoughts. I kept getting words from a male presence in English. *"Deep six the lot of them."* I kept looking into the faces of the people in Verity's party. Someone there could speak English, maybe more than one person, for some of the snippets of thought I heard were definitely mixed with English, a cacophony of two languages colliding like uneasy partners dancing on the wrong foot.

I didn't know what *deep six* meant, but it wasn't a good thing, not for those people back there, that much I knew. And I thought maybe that was why they had very little misbehavior in Hadria.

CHAPTER FOUR

We ate dinner alone, the nine of us, after the staff left for their homes. LaBo had tried to talk to the staff about their working conditions and those of the Low Dome, but they had just smiled and said everything was good for them. All of Hadria was happy, according to them. The more she'd pushed, the faster they moved to finish up and leave.

Verity came by an hour later to take us up the slope to the highest house in High Dome. We had an appointment with the First Woman, and Ibera was to be the main attraction.

This time, things were more casual. A woman was playing a many-stringed instrument shaped like a large fan with a rounded end that went around her neck. She used a brush to strum the strings. It was interesting music, and her singing was melodic. There was a table set up with desserts and pink, sweet drinks. Some of the families who lived in High Dome were there too, and we were to mingle with them in small groups. There were six new people who spoke English. Curiouser and curiouser. They helped keep us all distracted for the evening. I tried to mingle and still keep a watchful eye on my eight comrades. The boys took it upon themselves to be Ibera's keepers. They didn't stray from her side. Iloura was keeping the boys company, acting as their interpreter where needed.

I spotted Verity across the room, worked my way around to get behind her, and said in a low, whispered voice, mimicking the First Woman as closely as I could, "Nice party."

"Yes," she said, turning, "it is …" The smile faded from her face as she saw me and the First Woman behind me on the other side of the room. "So, you caught me, very clever of you. And I must say a very good imitation of the First Woman's voice. I don't think she would be please at your cleverness though." I felt a wave of tiredness envelope her at this point. She glanced over toward the First Woman. "I don't suppose I could get you to pretend this didn't happen? I really don't want her to know that you know I speak this language. I'm supposed to be the one who listens to your evil plans, if you have any, which I doubt, but she has become somewhat paranoid. We've had ... some problems with rebellious servers. Then the Fish Children brought her your bombs, and all the hells possible visited her dreams." She pulled me by the elbow over to a small niche where a couple of chairs were hidden from the part of the room where the First Woman was talking with Jorame. We sat down.

"If we are honest with each other, things will go much smoother," I said, "and we may even be able to help with whatever troubles you are having."

"Why would you?"

"We want to go home all in one piece. We want your people safe as much as we want our people safe. Why wouldn't we?"

Verity leaned out and glanced over at Jorame and Ilantha. "He is quite handsome. Does he have a mate?"

She was changing the subject. I nodded. "Yes. He's very mated," I said stiffly, somehow feeling affronted for Julka. "They will marry as soon as we go home."

Her attention snapped back to me. "Not you? I thought I saw a certain protective ..."

"Then you need to look closer. You haven't noticed that we all feel protective of each other."

"Truce, then. Let us try to be honest with each other." Verity looked at me for a long time. "We have something wrong here. And she," she tipped her head toward the First Woman, "Ilantha, can't see it. Won't see it. She wants to go on as usual. She won't listen to me. Our people are falling apart. And I don't know why." I felt the frustration biting at her. She continued. "She hasn't been down in Low Dome in years; she won't listen to how things don't seem right." She stopped and looked out at the small group gathering around Ilantha, Jorame, Ibera, the boys, Willobee and LaBo. I felt the heat of anger rising in Verity. She straightened. "Is that enough truth for you? You think you can help with that, when I haven't been able to budge her in five years? Ever since I became Second Woman, she has been deaf to me. Before that, her and her half sister, Lupa, loved me dearly. But now Ilantha seems only to see her end when she looks at me. And Lupa is up there," she pointed to the ceiling, "in that horrid, dry place you call home, and she can't help me with Ilantha anymore."

She stood up suddenly and marched off toward Jorame. I stood and followed slowly, and watched as she poured on the charm, and spoke through LaBo as if she didn't know English. She petted Ibera's long, sleek, white-furred back as she tried to work her feminine wiles on someone who wasn't interested in her that way, while Rifkin strolled up and kept trying to insert himself into her translated conversation with Jorame.

I said nothing as I quietly joined the group.

"I love this Nar Hound animal," Ilantha said, moving up next to me. "She is as large as some of the fish in our sea. But I quit going out to the open ocean a long time ago, so it is good to feel that animal spirit that lives inside her. That strength. I miss the wildlife out there." She looked wistfully up at the clear, glassy ceiling, to where there were creatures that glowed yellow in the dark waters, long, frilly, undulating things that mesmerized and fascinated.

"They are beautiful! What did you mean 'going out to the open sea'? You mean like the Fish Children?" I asked.

She laughed, a light, musical sound that caught the attention of most everyone in the room, as if this woman's laughter was rare.

"No. They are like other sea mammals, breathing air, but they have feet and can go on land when they want to, though they spend most of their time in the ocean. We have other methods for spending time in the open sea. Do any of you have an oxygen ball with you?" she called out to the room. I wondered if any of my people had caught her mistake. She spoke as if all the people there could understand her, and it appeared at least one man did, as he brought something over. All my people gathered around to see what an oxygen ball was.

Ilantha held it up: a mouth-sized, round, squishy, soft thing. "If you put this in your mouth, you can breathe for at least five hours out there," she explained. "You can swim with the Obaskillian, our Fish Children. They will take care of you and keep you safe from the more dangerous elements, like those neon-yellow Flag fish you noticed. The Flags can kill you with one flick of their long, whiplike tail that's so hard to see because you're watching the enticing lights on their frilly, flat bodies. The Fish Children have a sting of their own that makes the Flags

37

stay away from them, and the Fish Children are not affected by the Flags' sting. You'd be perfectly safe, if you want to go out there for a swim. It is an experience you'll never forget, I can assure you." And she smiled widely, her wrinkles happy brackets of parentheses around her statement.

I saw a look of amazement cross Verity's face, and I realized she was taken aback by this reminiscence of the First Woman.

Yes, this would be an interesting year ... if we all survived it ... and if I didn't worry myself sick about what was happening here and in Nueden that I couldn't see or know what to do to change things for the better. How could I possibly know? My hand went to the inexhaustible blossom around my neck, and I remembered it wasn't up to me to change the world. Just do my part, that was my job; my small part. I just had to figure out what that was.

***

Willobee and I were in a tunnel, climbing a steep rise with an occasional set of steps on the path. "Where are we going?" She asked in my mind. "We are searching for the surface of this problem," I said. "And you are going to help me."

I was suddenly wide-awake lying on my back, Ibera standing over me on the bed, nose to nose with me. She was staring at me, eye to eye. That long-distance mind connection with Zarek flashed through my memory. The snippet of dream that was there at the edge of sleep seemed somehow like that extraordinary event. But really, that interaction with Zarek had not been the beginning of something great ... it had been the end of it. That gave me the chills.

"What are you doing?" I scooted up against the headboard of the bed, took Ibera's face in my hands and looked deep into her eyes. "I wish you could talk," I said, and reached up to scratch around her horn. She shook my hand off impatiently and stared into my eyes again. "Or mind speak ... something," I said, staring back. "What are you trying to tell me?"

Ibera jumped off the bed and ran to the door. She pawed frantically at the handle, whining. Her hackles were up, which raised every hair on my body in alarm. The chills returned. I hit the floor running. I jerked the door open and scanned the other room, adrenaline zinging through my body. I grabbed a tall, thin but sturdy vase and dumped the water and flowers on the floor. Glancing around, nothing seemed out of place in my sitting room, so we ran to the door and I flung it open. Ibera ran across the hall to Willobee's door.

I pushed it open, and Ibera ran in snarling and snapping, her lips drawn back, her purple gums and sharp white teeth wet and dripping with the desire to bite someone. There was no one in Willobee's sitting room, so we went into the bedroom, the tall, sturdy vase held up over my shoulder, my only weapon. Ibera rooted around in the messy bedcovers, but there was no Willobee. I ran to the bathroom. She wasn't there either. I was awash in a sick feeling of dread. When I came back into the bedchamber, Ibera was scratching at the stone wall next to the bed and howling like a demented devil. I felt the bed and found it still warm to the touch. If she wasn't here, maybe she had gone to the kitchen.

"Come on," I called. Ibera didn't want to leave, but she came. I ran to the living room and kitchen. I made a quick pass through them and ran back down the hallway. I banged on all the doors as I went down the curved hallway. I yelled, "Wake up! Everybody, wake up!" Ibera added her voice in a long, wailing howl.

I banged on their doors again as I headed back toward the kitchen. I checked out the living space, every nook and cranny, then went to the kitchen and dining area and did a more thorough search. By this time, Lucus and Jorame were in the living room and Rifkin was pulling on his pants as he hurried out of his rooms. The women and boys came last, also pulling on clothes as they came.

"Willobee is missing!" I said. My voice was stone cold and hard, but there must have been fire in my eyes, because Jorame took a step back.

"I knew something like this was going to happen!" Lucus wailed. "Haven't I been telling you? But noooo, you all just wanted to..."

"Shut up, Lucus!" Rifkin snapped. "This is not about you. Has anyone been up the glass tower?" He said this as he was almost out of sight, running up the curving stairs. He came back down just as quickly.

"No?" I asked. He shook his head. I had never seen him look grimmer.

Ibera raced off back to Willobee's room, a full-throated howl rolling down the hall after her loud enough to wake all of Hadria. I ran back to Willobee's room, hoping that this was just a game and we would find Bee hiding somewhere, even though I *knew* we wouldn't. We all did another search, all eight of us crowding into her bedchamber, pulling it apart.

"Why is Ibera scratching at the wall like that?" Kid asked. We all stopped and stared at her frantic behavior. I called her away from the wall and went over to it. "Turn on all the lights. Rif, go get my cell flash from my desk." I began to feel around on the stone wall, my fingers going lightly over the surface. I couldn't feel any crack or indentation, or any kind of latch that was obvious. I felt around the side of the bed closest to me, remembering what Grandfather had said: "If you think there is a secret chamber, where would you hide a latch mechanism? Think!" I kept feeling, then Rifkin handed me my light and I focused its beam on the wall, going over it again to see if I could find a line or anything that would explain why Ibera would scratch right there.

"What is she doing?" Lucus huffed. "We are wasting time."

"Pen suspects there is a way into the mountain," Rifkin said. "If there is, she will find it."

I searched that whole wall, and I did finally see the thinnest of lines in the shape of a small door, but I could find no latch. I screamed my frustration, which made everyone jump back, some of them screaming too, in alarm.

"It's no use," I said. "I can see a thin line that could be a doorway, but there isn't a latch anywhere on this wall or by the bed."

"Then we take this to the First Woman," Kid said. "She has got to know these rooms. If you say there is a door there, then I believe you."

"Yeah," said Dray, "we will force her to tell us what they have done with Willobee and get her back. No one is taking our Bee away from us."

And as if Ibera understood what we were thinking, she ran out of the room and around the hall to the living room and stopped at the door to the outside—as much outside as there was inside a dome under the sea.

We ran as a pack up the slanted, curved pathway, Ibera in the lead. We banged on Verity's orange door and kept going, not sure she would or could hear us from out here. We reached the opaque blue door of the First Woman's council chambers, not sure where else to go.

"Does she even live here," Lucus snapped, "do any of us know?"

"There's one way to find out!" I said, and began banging on the door loudly enough to wake the Obaskillian out in the sea.

CHAPTER FIVE

When no one came to the door, I tried the handle, and it opened. We went in, shouting "Ilantha!" at the top of our lungs. Several guards appeared with weapon staffs at the ready. By this time, Verity was coming through the door behind us, dressed in a see-through shift, her nakedness visible beneath its gauzy length.

"What is the meaning of this?" she demanded. She raised her hand to halt the guards. The First Woman came from the back of the large chamber, wrapping a similar gauzy, ice blue garment around her self. I didn't care if the whole damned lot of them were naked I just wanted Willobee back with us.

"What have you done with Willobee?" I said, glaring at the First Woman. "We want Willobee back! Right! Now!"

Ilantha looked puzzled, then straightened. A look of horror crossed her face and she stumbled toward Verity. "They wouldn't," Ilantha said, "Would they?"

Verity's face held equal horror. Her hand flew to her mouth, and she said, "Not to a child! Surely not."

"She spoke English," Lucus said flatly, stating the obvious.

"You were right," Rifkin said to me, with a nod of his head toward Verity. I felt a little guilty that I hadn't told any of the others that I knew she could speak English. A pandemonium of questions broke out then.

Then Ibera howled so loudly that everyone shut up.

"What do you mean? Do what to a child?" I demanded. "Who are the 'they' you are talking about? Where is Willobee?"

41

"I warned you!" Verity said to Ilantha. "Those Low Domers were at their breaking point." She wrung her hands and paced the floor. "And now, if they've done anything to that little girl …"

"They wouldn't do that." Ilantha shook her head vigorously, back in firm control of her denial. "They love me. I'm their First Woman. They wouldn't deep six a child. They wouldn't."

"There is something wrong down there, I've been saying so for over a year now," Verity said. "You've deep sixed too many of their workers for speaking against High Dome when we should have been listening to them. But you wouldn't even listen to me; now see what has happened because of it. I tried to tell you trouble was com … "

"Shut up!" I screamed. I grabbed Ilantha's arm, and a guard raised a heavy-looking fishbone cudgel, ready to strike me with it. Verity blocked the guard and knocked the club from her hands.

"You will take us to wherever they would do this deep six thing to her," I spit the words out through clenched jaws. "And you had better pray to whatever deity you pray to that she is still alive, or …"

"Pendyse." Jorame placed his hand on my shoulder. "Pen. No, that is not our way. Not your way."

I released Ilantha's arm, coming to my senses, shaking off my anger. "Please, Ilantha, take us to that place now. Before it's too late."

Verity and Ilantha took the lead, their flimsy garments forgotten in our hast as we got on a couple of platforms and hurried through Mid Dome and down to Low Dome, a squad of guards joining us at the entrance. I kept wondering how they did that. How did they know what was going on? Did they also have a kind of mind touch that sent out orders to let people know where to be when they needed them? At the farthest side of Low Dome, we came to a tight knot of people gathered around the mouth of an exit tube.

"This is Ocean Lock Six. It is six fathoms deep—our deepest gate," Verity said. "This is where we bury our dead and punish our lawbreakers."

A ragged-looking woman was just coming back through the opening, wet from the sea. There was no one with her. She came in, dripping and proud of herself, her head held high.

The crowd parted for the woman. "Now you will listen to us," she said.

"What have you done?" Ilantha demanded in a shaky voice.

"Only what you have taught us to do through your own example," the woman spat out. "My child died in the processing house, hungry and sick." She glared at Verity, and a sly look crept over her countenance. I knew a lie was coming. "She knew. We told her what was happening. For years now, we have suffered for the good of our betters," the woman spat out and pointed at Ilantha. "But now I see you are no better than I am. I just killed a child, but you have caused the deaths of many children."

Ilantha looked stricken, her eyes wide, hurt rising off her like heat waves.

"You claim to love us," someone else shouted, "and speak of the rule of peace for the people, but we die and you do nothing. What kind of love is that?"

The woman who had come from the ocean spoke again. "You deep sixed my man yesterday because he dared to tell your 'guests' what was going on here. Your guards put him out to sea. Fed him to the fish. Now he sleeps with the Obaskillian you love so much, our own Fish Children, those of us who went out from Low Dome and became something else ... to get away from ..."

"So we did it to someone we knew would cause you to listen," a man yelled.

"She is gone!" the woman said in a high-pitched wavering wail, as if it broke her heart to say it, but I knew it was an act; I could feel it in my gut. I shivered with the remembrance of Zee, the consummate liar. "Just like my little girl who died because you didn't care what was happening down here," the woman continued. "Well, look around. Was that little girl from topside worth more than mine?"

I closed my eyes to the horror of what was being said, but the thought of Willobee drowned broke through my resistance. That much I knew was true, and the silent scream I sent out was for Zarek alone. If he could hear me, he would know his grandniece was dead and I was undone. Again.

When I opened my eyes and looked around, everyone was on the ground, holding their hands over their ears. I couldn't understand what had happened.

Jorame rose and came to wrap me in his arms.

LaBo was there too, and I heard in my mind, *She is not dead. I would know it if she were. Take heart. Believe. I think the Fish Children have her. And you'd better tell Zarek she's not dead.*

I looked at LaBo. "I didn't know you and I could..." I stopped speaking out loud, *...mind speak. Are you sure?"*

43

"Could what?" Rifkin asked in confusion, standing back to back with me protectively.

Tears were running down Dray's cheeks. "Did they kill Willobee? What did they do? Did they drown her?"

"Come on, let's get them!" Kid said, balling his hands into fists, his head lowered, body leaning forward, ready to attack while the people were still on the floor.

"No!" I clutched them both to me. "There will be no more killing. Jorame is right. Killing only makes more killing."

LaBo said, "She is not dead. I think she may be with the Fish Children." Loud enough so everyone could hear.

People began to rise from the ground. The Stella Mara there was general confusion. "What was that?" I heard people saying.

"It is not possible. I saw her float away. Out to the grass fields," sneered the mother of the lost daughter, now being restrained by the guards.

The First Woman was quietly weeping as Verity lifted her up. "What happened?" Ilantha kept asking. "What was that?"

"Leave her alone!" Verity snapped at the guards who were holding the mother of the child who had died. "Leave her alone, now. She has lost enough. They have all lost enough. Can't you see that? We must get to the bottom of this mess."

"You say that now, when it is too late!" the wet woman screamed. "You think that will change our minds? Do you think letting me live will stop ..." One of the other women grabbed the screaming woman and jerked her to the floor, pinning her down, and slapped her quiet.

"Come with me!" Verity said to us. And we followed.

We left that place and the people of the Low Dome behind and Verity took us to the place where we had come into Hadria only three days before. "We can call to the Fish Children from here. Sometimes they come to us when we call," Verity said.

We waited till the sun came up, but there was no answer from the Fish Children. We left guards with instructions to come for us if the Fish Children showed up there and went back to our apartment. Verity and Ilantha stayed with us there. They had the staff bring them their clothes, and they prepared for a hard day.

Verity had one of our communicators brought to us, and we talked with our people in Nueden. I didn't want to talk to anyone. I had LaBo talk to Zarek. She was the one who thought she knew Willobee was still alive. I had tried to contact him by mind touch and there had been no response. It disheartened me in every way. All I could see was Willobee floating in that Trillium Sea forest of fronds and sea grass. It filled me with a dread so deep it chilled my bones.

After that, I slipped up the glassy, spiral staircase and sat in the quiet light, opening up my senses to the world around me, feeling for Willobee, dead or alive. I searched the seas outside, and I searched inside the domes as well.

What I found first was the latch and the tunnels that led from her bedchamber and mine up to the surface of an island that was part of the stone wall that High Dome clung to. And coming out of that cave onto a purple-tinged white beach, I saw Willobee playing in the surf with some little ones, Obaskillian children.

She *was* alive … and she was with the Fish Children, just as LaBo had said.

Willobee! She turned and stared up at the cave where my inner self stood, looking down at her. *We're coming to get you!* Then I was opening my eyes in the small glass tower room, back to myself.

***

"I know where she is," I said as I came down the stairs. "She's on the island."

"What island?" Lucus leapt to his feet, ready to go there right this minute, if not the minute before.

"There's an island?" Reia perked up, as did LaBo, Kid, Dray, Jorame and Rifkin. "And Willobee is alive?" "Let's go get her." "She will be afraid." They were all speaking at once.

I smiled. "No, she is fine. She's playing with the Fish Children. The Great Spirit has shown it to me."

"You are like my sister Lupa," Ilantha said with awe in her voice, staring at me. "You have visions!"

Verity just shook her head in amazement.

Neither Verity nor Ilantha knew anything about the secret passageways to the surface. Ilantha said, "Those were only children's tales from long ago."

Everyone always seems to lose track of their tunnels, I thought, *and their histories*. It was obvious that at least some of the people from Low Dome had known about them, though, on some kind of limited basis at least. That was how they had stolen Willobee from her bed. Ibera knew it before any of us.

"We are going to get her!" I said. "Do you want to go with us?" I asked Verity and Ilantha.

"I want to go," Iloura said, and she took the First Woman's hand and pulled Ilantha to her feet from the chair. "Come on. You come, too. I have never seen the island."

"What will we need to take with us?" Verity asked. "Won't we need water and light at least? If we go by tunnel."

"Can't you take one of the ships to get her faster?" Ilantha looked frightened, agitated and tired. She shook her head. "I don't want to go."

"Yeah, well, we did not want to come here. But you insisted," Lucus challenged Ilantha. "Maybe you should know what that feels like."

"I am the First Woman, no one dares speak to ..."

"Please," Verity pleaded, "Ilantha, come with us. Come with us and see more of your world than High Dome. You've lost perspective with your people." Verity enveloped Ilantha in a loving embrace. "You need to come. It has been too long that you've allowed your grief to rule our home. Rexon is gone, has been gone for a long time now. We are still here. Can't you see us? Your grief has become the First Woman. It's time to take back your true authority, your heart for the people. Please, Ilantha."

At this, the older woman seemed to crumble, her resistance gone.

We gathered up what things we might need, and we all trooped down the curving hallway to Willobee's rooms. As we crowded into the bedchamber, I went to the foot of the bed. There were carved stone shells on the four posts at the rounded corners of the bed. I took hold of and twisted the one farthest away from the wall where I knew the door was, and the door began to grind open by pulling back, leaving a dark hole in the wall. Ibera let out a howl of excitement and shot through the opening.

"Follow the hound," I heard Rifkin say as he dove into the dark, the boys right behind him, Iloura keeping up with them. The breath of adventure followed them.

"I can't go in there!" Ilantha balked at the door. "It's under the ground. It's dark!" She shook her head. "No, I can't go." Her breath was short and choppy. "I already can't breathe."

46

"Well, isn't that ironic?" Lucus said. "We finally have something in common. These kinds of places take my breath away too."

"OK," I said, "both of you calm yourselves and take a deep breath. Then walk. Follow the light."

The tunnels were wide enough for three people abreast, but we tended to be more staggered in our line. The first passageway with a crossing tunnel we came to I believed followed the edge of the High Dome. At the end of the tunnel, there were steps that led down. These were all man-made tunnels, perfect in smoothness and size, precise in their dimensions.

"This is most likely the way to Mid Dome or Low Dome, or both," I said. "The people of Low Dome may have known about these tunnels for a long time, while the High Dome people forgot about them. At one time, this whole system may have been an escape route to the surface of the island in case of catastrophe … although I'm not sure how many people could access the tunnels before the ocean would inundate them, unless there is a system of locks."

At this, I heard Lucus and Ilantha both groan. "Remember, deep breaths," I said. "We are all doing just fine."

"That's easy for you to say," Jorame said. "You're familiar with tunnels. Your island is full of them. This is the first time underground for some of us."

"I was underground on Ra'Vell Island," Dray said, "and in the small village where the Voice and her men killed all those people. The ones that survived hid in their tunnels and caves. That's what saved them. Tunnels are good."

It was at this place in the passage that I knew I had seen a way up. I pictured it in my mind now as I began to search the walls. Soon the boys, Dray and Kid, were feeling for the second latch as well.

"What are we looking for?" Kid asked.

"A variation in the stonework. A latch, a divot, a protrusion of some kind."

"I found it!" Kid exclaimed. It was at the edge of the tunnel wall off the second step down.

"Go ahead," I said, "release the catch." I felt a surge of pride in Kid.

After the section of wall moved back into the recessed passage, one by one, we stepped through onto a stairway going up. I thought Kid might even have come to like me. Well, at least to respect me.

"I have to hand it to you, Ra'Vell, you are not a boring person to be around," Lucus said.

Kid gave a hoot at that. "Yeah, and if you pay attention, you might even learn something, Master Tallman."

At that, Dray and Kid began to laugh, and it echoed up the tunnel eerily. Jorame and Rifkin joined the laughter. Lucus only grunted.

Again I was aware of how close Dray and Kid had become. I wasn't sure what their laughter meant, but the fact that Kid thought Lucus could learn something from me was enlightening. It meant that his time in the jail with Norman, his father, and the captured soldiers, and his break from those men, and all the books he had read while there, had paid off for him, and for me as well.

Winning someone over to my corner is always good if it means less danger for me, and my friends, I thought. But even better than winning someone to my side was helping to set that someone free to become who he was meant to be, and I could see a fine blossoming in that young man.

We went steadily uphill, and the talking died down while people unused to such activity began to breathe more heavily. We had to stop several times for the First Woman to catch her breath. Her trembling body testified to the stress she was under. Jorame and Rifkin worked up a makeshift sling chair and carried her for a while between them until she wanted down "to walk on my own two feet," she said. Jorame and Rifkin were breathing hard by then, and even though I felt we were close to the exit, I knew we needed to take a longer rest for Ilantha's sake at least, if not for the rest of us.

As we sat on the rock floor in the shadowed light from the cell torches, we talked and partook of refreshment. After a while, the talk lapsed into silence and quiet breathing. I think Ilantha even took a wink of sleep, slumped against Verity. But the boys were getting antsy just sitting.

"How do you think the Fish Children saved her?" Dray asked.

The First Woman popped awake and caught her breath enough to speak. She said, "What? What did you say?"

"How do you think the Fish Children saved Bee?" Kid repeated.

"They carry oxygen balls in sealed tubes for just such occasions," Verity said.

The First Woman stretched and added, "For when one of us might get in trouble out there."

"Yes, that is true," Verity agreed. "If they were around and saw her in distress, they would save her. It's in their nature to save us air breathers."

"I wonder …" I began, then stopped, but decided to say what I was thinking anyway. "How often do you go to the island?"

"Well, almost never," Verity said. "There is a farm area on this side that is sometimes used for growing things, but it has been fallow for years now. On the far side of the surface is the old city. It is in total ruin, and has been for several centuries. There is nothing of use there anymore. No one ever goes there. I don't even think we've sent a ship around that way in a couple of centuries according to our records."

"How big is the island?" I asked. "I wonder if the Fish Children saved anyone else from being fish food?" I glanced at the First Woman. "And if they are maybe on the island?"

I saw a shudder pass through Verity and wondered which side of this question she might come down on. I noticed she didn't have her staff. Did either one of them have a weapon we didn't know about, and might we need one? If there were dissidents on the island, could we be in trouble if we went out there?

But I knew I had seen Willobee playing in the surf. She was all right. We would be too.

"I'm going to scout ahead a bit," I said.

Jorame stood and said, "I'll come with you."

At this, Rifkin and the boys also stood. Rifkin said, "You're not going anywhere without us."

"Not without us," the boys repeated.

"And if you think I am going to miss a chance to see the sky," Lucus said, "and breathe real air and touch real earth …"

"Not real earth!" Kid snapped, as if offended anyone could forget after having heard it once. "This is New … Eden, remember, not Earth. Nueden."

"Oh, for Great Tomorrow Land," Lucus snapped back rolling his eyes. "Don't be so literal minded. You know what I meant." He said this looking around at all of us in the dim and shifting cell lights. "Didn't you?"

I noticed everyone was already standing, "OK, then. Let's move out. Rest time is over."

Not far down the tunnel, maybe ten minutes, we came to a dead end.

"We're trapped!" The First Woman and Lucus said at the same time and in the same panicked tone, which made the rest of us laugh a little bit before we stifled it.

"What is so funny?" Lucus snapped.

"For you to think someone would go to all this trouble building a tunnel and not put an exit door at the end?" Verity herself was trying not to laugh, but her laughter kept escaping her control.

"Verity!" Ilantha ordered. "Stop that at once."

We all went quiet, and I realized that the laughter had held a note of nervous tension to it. I was the only one who had even a hint of what might be out there.

"All right," I said, "let's look for the door latch."

CHAPTER SIX

I heard a click, and part of the wall began to grind with the sound of stone on stone. Looking around, I saw Dray's face alight with satisfaction at being the one to find the latch this time. "Good job!" I said. He swelled with pride at the praise.

It felt like forever for the door to make so much as a narrow opening, and it was still moving back. Most of the others had contorted through to get to the other side before the door was fully open. Once through, we found ourselves in a small, cave opening out to a beautiful expanse of smooth, curving beach not far below.

At the head of the path stood Willobee, waiting for us in the sun, as naked as a newborn, her pearly white skin with a troubling rosy glow to it.

She was smiling, pinkish green seaweed tangled in her long lilac hair that was stiff with seawater. Then I was on my knees and she was in my arms, and everyone was clustered around us. I took off my coat and wrapped it around her. "Where are your clothes? You'll get burnt to a crisp in this sunlight."

"The mean woman took them," Bee said.

At the end of our reunion, we all turned and looked out on the purple-cast ocean. The Trillium Sea. Slowly, one by one, we picked our way down the side of the grass-tufted, ancient path to the beach. I heard a collective breath drawn in as we all took in the beauty and serenity of this place.

I turned and looked around us. Rolling hills, then a range of various-size mountains rose up on all sides of this secluded, protected beach. On the higher level from where the cave was, were the farmlands Verity spoke of.

"Where is the ruined city from here?" Ilantha asked.

Verity looked around. "Well, this is the northeast side; the gardens are over there in the terraced areas south of here," she pointed to the foothills and the rising mountainsides, "and the ruins are on the southwest side of that mountain range. This isn't the season for gardening, but some of the Low Dome people used to live up here a few decades back. See those little houses at the side of the cliffs? On the opposite end from where the cave is?"

"Why would your people make a tunnel that didn't go straight to the city they once lived in?" asked Kid.

"And if you could live on this island, why did you go underwater?" Dray's hand made a shield over his eyes as he looked out over the ocean to where Hadria rested below the gentle swells.

Verity shrugged. "This is the better side of the island for practical purposes. The other side is very beautiful, but the city was never meant to be permanent. We are told it was our science center, where we mapped out the whole island."

"But that is a good question, Kid," Jorame said. "I see where you're going with it. There might be another tunnel that intersected with the main line at some point that goes under these mountain to the ruins."

Willobee and I walked a short way off, and I asked in a whisper, "Where are the children you were playing with?"

"Oh," Willobee grinned, whispering back, "I told them you were coming for me, and they went into the sea."

"But how?" Ilantha wanted to know. She had followed us and heard our whispers. "How did you tell them? How did you know we were coming?"

"I just knew," Bee answered. "Come into the water." She took LaBo's hand and pulled her to the edge of the shoreline, and a wave broke over Willobee's feet. LaBo bent to cast off her shoes before she waded into the surf. Then everyone took off their shoes. A sudden festive mood enveloped us, and we played at the edge of the water for a while. Now and then I saw the head of one of the Fish Children pop up and watch us for a bit, then disappear again below the waves.

"What an absolutely lovely place," I heard Reia say to Lucus as they walked down the beach together, arm in arm.

"Better than where we've been," he answered her. "Maybe we can come back here when we need a break from that oppressive place."

Willobee had slipped out of my coat and was running naked in the waves, letting them pick her up and push her toward the shore.

The boys began to disrobe, and that's when I called everyone back to the sand. "If you do that, soon we will all be naked and in the water, and we still have to go back through the tunnels. By the time we get back, we will be so tired we'll wish we hadn't played so long."

And besides, I thought, *I want to talk to Willobee alone, and that can't happen here, with all these people around watching us. And listening.*

Willobee came out of the water and put my coat back on. "You're right, we should get back," she said, and took my hand, and we started back toward the cave entrance.

"Wait," Dray said, "I'm not ready to go back. Can't we spend the night?"

"We could build a fire," Kid said in a pleading voice. "We can sleep on the sand, around the fire."

I stopped, turned and sat down in the sand. The boys came and sat with me.

"Do you have any firer starter? Any wood?" I asked. "Or bedrolls?"

"Well, maybe it will be warm enough without a fire," Kid offered.

"Not tonight, fellas," Lucus said as he and Reia walked up and sat in the sand with the rest of us.

"Loath though I am to say it," Lucus said, digging a stick into the sand, "we would need to plan such a campout and have all the gear put together. But maybe we could bring some things and leave them here in the cave, or in one of the little shacks up on that ridge; then any of us who wanted a night under the moons could come here once in a while." He cast such a longing look at the water and then at Ilantha, as if asking for permission, that the First Woman laughed at his open desire to stay on land, even as I felt her desire to be back under the sea.

"To spend the night, or even longer," Rifkin sighed. "Now that would be an adventure I could appreciate."

"Besides," Ilantha said, "as enlightening as this whole trip has been for me, my old bones rebel at the thought of sleeping on the ground. That is fine for you young people. I am just relieved to have

Willobee safe and back with us, and now all I want to do is go home, sleep in my own bed and forget this whole thing happened."

I caught a determined look flash across Verity's face before she said, "There has been too much forgetting. We need to start remembering what it means to lead our people."

***

The time going back seemed shorter than the time it had taken us to find the beach. We saw Ilantha to her door, and then headed to our place. Once we were back in our apartment, we started eating the food the serving staff had left for us. While we were eating and talking, the young people planning a trip back to the beach, Verity sidled up to me and asked, "Everything happened so fast; how did you know about the tunnels?" She stared at me intently. "And how did you know that Willobee was still alive and with the Obaskillian? And what happened at Lock Six that dropped us all," she gave me a calculating stare, "except for you?"

I knew these questions would surface, but I was hoping it wouldn't be till tomorrow or the day after. I still hadn't decided what I would say, what I wanted to tell her. And I wanted to talk to Willobee first, before anyone else thought to question her.

"You know where I grew up," I said with as frank a look as I could muster. "My island is riddled with caves and tunnels. It was the only way I could think that someone could snatch Bee without us knowing. Ibera knew. She kept scratching at the rock wall. I should have known then too, but it was only after I had time to think, to let my intuition work, and Wonannonda, that I believed we could find her."

"How did LaBo know she was alive and with the Fish Children?" Verity kept picking at the puzzle in her mind, and I could sense her doubt at my answer.

"LaBo and Willobee are very close," I said. "They have a special bond."

"Oh," the Second Woman said, "I see." Then she frowned. "You seem to have a special bond with her as well."

Willobee came over to us just then and took my hand. "I'm very tired. May I sleep in your bed with you and Ibera tonight?"

Verity knelt down in front of Willobee and gave her a hug. "I am so sorry that one of our people did that to you." She pushed back the lilac hair that hung loose over Bee's sunburnt forehead and asked, "You said you talked with the Fish Children. How?"

Willobee gave a little shrug. "They sent me pictures. And I sent them some." Then she yawned and shook her head. "That's all. I don't know. I'm tired now." She kissed Verity on the cheek and turned, pulling me along with her.

"We can talk tomorrow," I said over my shoulder as we left and moved down the curving hallway to my suite. Verity stood staring after us, a look of troubled contemplation on her face.

"We will," she said, barely above a whisper, as we passed out of her sight. But I felt her still standing there, staring, even when we got to my rooms. I knew there would be more than a few questions tomorrow.

I sent Bee to shower and went to get one of her nightgowns. Once we were all ready for bed, we got in and sat leaning against the headboard, my arm curled around her shoulders. She looked up at me with a most angelic smile, her purple cat eyes bright, face pink with too much color. I worried about the damaging effects of the sun on her sensitive skin and eyes. I pushed her clean damp hair back, ran a finger down the sharp ridge of her small nose and kissed the tip of it.

"Now tell me what happened," I said.

You're like Father and Mother, aren't you? And like my Uncle Zarek, too.

Yes! Kind of. And I knew it to be true, even as I thought it to her. *Maybe not fully, yet, but I will be!* I answered her in mind speak, not at all surprised we could communicate this way.

Verity has listening things in our rooms, you know, Willobee said.

No. I didn't know that.

Yes. In all the rooms! Bee said into my mind, nodding. *I can feel them in my head.* She tapped her forehead with an index finger. I cast out my searching thoughts into the rooms, trying to see or feel what might be a listening device, but didn't know how to spot them, what they would feel like. Bee joined my mind, and she showed me where to find them.

When I turned again to this amazing child, she wore a peaceful but tired expression.

"Ah, look at my poor dear," I said out loud. "She's fallen asleep already."

Willobee looked up at me and grinned.

I would have to make sure everyone else knew about the listening devices … tomorrow.

You're smart, Willobee thought at me, nodding.

So are you, my little one! Now tell me how you got to the beach.

Willobee began her story in her room in the middle of the night. *I was asleep. I woke up scared and someone grabbed me and poked me with something sharp, and I was asleep again. I tried to call for you to come help me. But I couldn't get out of my head into yours. We had never talked that way before. Uncle Zarek said you could, though, so I kept trying.*

No, I think you got through to me in a dream, I said. *That's what woke me up, that and Ibera growling in my face. Anyway, keep going.*

When I woke up, I was down in the Low Dome with a bunch of scary people. They were all angry, yelling at each other. Some wanted me for fish food and some wanted me for trade with the First Woman, to make her give them more food. A lot of them are sick Pen, and their children are dying. It is so sad. I was scared. I felt … I don't know exactly. Sad. They are all so sad and angry. She was quiet for a while.

There is something wrong here, Pen, she finally said.

I know. I have felt it too.

They made me get naked. They were going to feed me to the fish. That angry woman took me out to the floating trees. I held my breath for as long as I could as I swam for the surface.

She began to cry, and I rocked her in my arms until she stopped.

It was just like what Ilantha did with that woman's husband. She wanted to make him feed the fish, but the Fish Children saved him. They save all the ones that get fed to the fish. They are just like me. They don't like to see people get drowned.

What do you mean?

That's the way they get rid of troublemakers down here. In Moon City, we talk, we just talk and talk and talk, until everyone understands everyone else and can feel what it means to be everyone else. I think that works much better, don't you?

I hugged her close to me. *Yes, so much better, Little Bee.*

Did you know my parents worked in the algae farms in the Celestial Sea? They were scientists.

No.

I knew how to swim before I knew how to walk. That's what my family always says. There was an accident at the farm, and my mother and father drowned. I thought I was going to them when that hurt angry woman left me in the floating trees. But then there was a Fish Man who came and sent calm to me just when my last bubbles went up, and he pushed an oxygen ball in my mouth.

After a pause, Bee continued. *I wish Mother and Father had oxygen balls when the accident happened to them. They would still be here if they had had oxygen balls.* She gave a shuddering sigh and snuggled tighter against me. *It filled my whole mouth. It felt very strange, but I could breathe again. And he showed me pictures of the beach and took me there. His family was all there, and we had a good time. The end.*

I chuckled as she yawned and closed her eyes. "Pen," she said in a sleepy voice, "I'm sorry I Rectified you on the Blue Moon that time."

"Shhh, now." I kissed her forehead. "Go back to sleep. You're safe now. We're both safe."

***

I lay there thinking far into the night, not used to sleeping with anyone else, it was hard to drift off, as Willobee would move or snore, or say a word in her sleep. I never knew it could be so hard to sleep with another person before, but it gave me time to think.

I had wondered what had happened to Willobee's parents. I knew she lived with her greatma and greatpa. So where were her grandma and grandpa, then, if they were her great, great grands?

My thoughts turned to my own grandfather, what he had meant to me, and how I knew he loved me, even though he seldom ever said it. *What was it about him that informed me of his love?* I wondered. *How can I be that kind of person too?* I think it was that he always had time for me, to listen to my questions, to talk to me like I was a grown-up. It was respect as well as love. I wanted to be able to give that to Willobee, and others. I wanted to bring that calm she spoke of with the Fish Man. I wanted to meet this man and see if we could send to each other.

Could the others also learn mind touch, Verity, Ilantha, the people of Hadria? The Stella Mara were hardly that different from the Sabostienie, and if they could mind touch, would that be a good thing or not? If they could sense the truth of what we speak, as I can sometimes when I get in that mind space, which was happening more and more often, would that help them with their own people? If only the Stella Mara could learn to let go of their class system way of thinking, even though they say they don't have one. At that I laughed at myself, how ridicules I am. Can my own people let go of their class system? That was still a question we had only just begun to explore ourselves. Many of us were trying. It sure wasn't going to happen overnight. I wondered what was happening up there right now, with the group calling themselves the Natural Order. What if something happened to one of the Hadrians like what almost happened to Willobee?

Thinking that made me shudder. Even as reasonable as Verity seemed to be, I had sensed an angry impulsiveness in her, too, that I didn't know how to gauge. It reminded me of my brother Pelldar and how he used to say I was impulsive; and I had been angry because of what had been done to Mark. So I could understand those feelings; they had also stemmed from a sense of helplessness and an injustice I didn't seem able to change.

My hand went to the silver chain and the forever blossom that hung around my neck. I closed my eyes and prayed.

"Give me rest in the love that is in all and through all. Help me see and understand."

CHAPTER SEVEN
(Day Four)

Verity, Ilantha and I were in Ilantha's private chambers, a lavish, colorful place. Comfortable chairs and tables were grouped around the room for easy conversation. Beautiful art from the sea and smaller objects of blown glass, of elegant charm and exquisite shapes, were all surrounded by the dome closest to the sunlit surface. Even the side of the island could be seen from here, at least the part under the water, and a distorted, watery view of a cliff that rose up out of the sea and into the open sky.

"When I was a young girl," Ilantha began, "I used to hear that the Father and Mother of my mother's people could do something called mind touch. No one in my family could do it, and none of us ever met the Father and Mother. So I asked my father if it was real. I remember Father telling me it was a myth, something the Sabostienie played at to keep the people docile and controllable." She paused and took a drink of the sweet pink tea that had just been served. "But now, with Willobee and the Fish Children, I wonder about that myth. Is it only a myth?"

"Willobee said that the Fish Children and her exchanged pictures," Verity said. "Do you know anything about that?" she asked me. The two of them watched me closely as I took a drink of my tea, giving myself a few seconds to collect my thoughts and coach my face, as there were more things than thoughts that could be read by others.

"When you brought back the Life Stealers and dumped them at our council chamber doors, you said the Obaskillian could sense what they were made of somehow," I said. "Iloura told me that the Fish

59

Children speak in sound waves that we can't hear. Maybe they can also talk to each other in pictures, or meanings; I don't know. You speak to them yourselves in hand pictures, and somehow you understand each other."

"Yes, but in a very simplified, limited way," Ilantha said. "They are like children, and not very bright children; they wouldn't understand anything more complex. They are simple creatures. Just children, really."

"You sell children short by saying that," I said. "They are often smarter than adults give them credit for. Just because they may not have the words or capabilities to speak like you in adult terms doesn't mean they are less intelligent. As a child, people often misjudged me about what I knew and what I could do—maybe not those who knew me well, but other adults did, all the time. Something the Sabostienie have taught me is to listen to the experiences of others even when it is slow going. You have to spend the time to hear what they have to say in their own way before you pass judgment on their intelligence, their actions, needs or deeds."

A long silence followed. I wondered, being young myself, if that had been presumptuous of me, or if I had overstepped my own ability to express what I thought was the true worth of children. But surely not, as Ilantha herself had only been eleven when she became leader of the Stella Mara. So she must know I spoke the truth. Or had she forgotten?

"Who are the Fish Children?" I asked. "Where did they come from?"

Verity shifted in her chair. "They came from the Lower Dome. The people there have always been those who serve, the workers who go out to the sea to forage and work the farms for food for all of us. The longer some of them stayed out in the sea, the more they changed, until their skin became thicker, iridescent, and their feet and hands became webbed. Every generation, they became more adapted to the ocean than to the domes. Eventually, they lost their ability to verbalize in our way. It took hundreds of years, of course, for those first changes to happen. But now, even though they give birth on the island and can breathe air, they live mainly in the sea. Even so, they would drown if they couldn't come to the surface when they need to. They are us, or were Stella Mara before they became Obaskillian."

"That is why we love them!" Ilantha said, "They are us! Don't you see? They were willing to change so completely so we could live in this beautiful city. The few sacrificed themselves for the many."

"And we love them for it," Verity said. "They still serve us."

"Are you sure of that?" I asked. "Maybe you serve them! You seem to be the ones locked up, and they seem to be the ones who are free. Maybe they became what they are to get away from Low Dome, like that woman said. It seems you have some problems down there."

The two women exchanged a glance. Ilantha's pinch-mouthed expression was disapproving, and Verity steamed with anger for a split second, then an emotionless mask rose up into place as they turned back to me. I could no longer sense Verity's anger, but I knew it was still there behind that placid exterior. Did that mean she suspected me of mind touch ability of some kind and was deliberately building a wall around her emotions, starting with her face, just as I had done only minutes before?

"That woman is a liar and a troublemaker," Ilantha snapped. "You can't believe what the servers of Low Dome say. They lie all the time. They are weak-minded people who don't know what is good for them."

"I have eyes, and a brain, Ilantha," I said. "No one had to tell me there is trouble below. I grew up in troubled places. I know what it looks like, the shape, feel. The thoughts of the poor are written on their faces and in their body language."

"Our lives here are perfect!" she snapped. I felt the turmoil of emotion rolling out of her, and a vast grief I could relate to. Her words didn't match her feelings.

The silence stretched out for so long that we sat in discomfort and stared at each other, hot spots of color suffusing the two other women's cheeks. They were both trying hard to control their emotions now, while I was trying to intuit what they were feeling and why they were feeling it?

"Maybe once it was perfect," I finally said, "but something is happening here that you are not willing to look at. And it has been my experience that when a leader goes blind and deaf to the people, all the people, bad things happen."

"I beg your pardon!" The First Woman's face became an even brighter shade of light green. "How dare you speak to me that way! I am ..."

Verity shifted in her chair. "It's only what I've been telling you ever since ..."

"Don't you dare! Not now. Not on this of all days." The anger whipping off Ilantha was raw and corrosive. They began speaking their language, too fast for me to even pick out a word here or there from my meager store of Sabostienie words. The sound of it all ran together like flowing water over stones, like music, one note after another in a liquid burble of sound, like an angry song that had been sung many times and known by heart. It was a discordant jangle of emotions too private to be shared with me, a stranger, I suddenly realized.

Popping to my feet, I said, "I'll be going, then," and set down my colorful cup with a clatter as I moved toward the door.

"No!" Ilantha said, "Wait." I felt the effort it took her to subdue her ire. I could feel that she was trying, so I turned and walked back to my chair and sat down.

"You are right." Ilantha's words were barely audible, emotion taking her breath away for a moment, and then she seemed to wilt before my eyes. "We have disagreed over this for so long that I have become like the side of this island," she admitted, a small, self-deprecating laugh huffing out of her. "But no one knows what it is like to lose someone who is part of you."

The wound in her heart was like a raw gash her life's essences bled from. I could even see the face of the man her grief was broadcasting into my mind.

"Verity doesn't understand," Ilantha continued. "She has never been in love. She has not yet bonded with a mate. Some never do." Did I detect a slight accusation in those words, in Ilantha's feelings about that? "She does not know what love is."

Verity drew in a sharp breath. "I have loved ... you. Lupa. Keto."

"It's not the same." Ilantha shook her head. "My pain ..."

"Your pain is no more nor less than the woman whose husband you deep sixed the other day," I ventured softly.

The First Woman shook her head violently. A cascade of silver-white hair shimmered like a waterfall over her shoulders and down to the floor in front of her. "You're so young. You don't understand either. What could you know of love and loss?"

This was not what I had expected when they had called me to meet with them this morning. *What do I do now?* I wondered. *What do I say?* Then the image of Mark rested in my mind, Mark and all my lost loved ones who had traveled to Tomorrow Land. I felt the grief that welled up, now a part of the very fabric of my soul. My understanding of loss went deep.

"When I was born, my family reported me as a male birth," I began. "They raised me as a boy. I grew up as a boy, I was taught as a boy. Girls were not valued in our country, not as people, only as objects to be owned and used, just as I sense boys are not equally valued here, except maybe for you and your Rexon. You seem to think woman are superior. I believe male and female are of equal value and worth, and should be equally respected. I believe those who live at the bottom of society, the poor, the workers, people with less, are not worth less than those at the top of society. I have read a great deal and studied this out, and it seems to me that when we get out of balance and there are those who have too much and those who have too little, not even enough to survive, let alone thrive, from day to day, that is the pot that brews the poison that will kill us when we're least expecting it."

Ilantha shook her head with the tiniest of motions. Verity's intense regard of the First Woman seemed to be hopeful.

"Let me tell you my story," I said.

They both gave slight nods. "Please do," Ilantha said, and settled back against the cushion of her chair as if she was ready for a long story.

"You are not the only one who has ever loved and lost the one you love." Leaning forward, I reached out my hand and took one of Ilantha's, looking deep into her eyes that were a mix of both Stella Mara and Sabostienie, the pupils slightly elongated, but not as sharply drawn as Zarek's. "I say this not to discount your loss but to acknowledge it. The fact that we feel these loses is to say we understand what is important in life." I took a deep breath and settled back into my own chair.

"Love is love. It may be different with every relationship, but I'm sure the love Verity has for you is as meaningful to her and as important as your love was for your mate.

"I have loved and lost many: mother, brother, nephew, all murdered, my nephew Mark before my very eyes. I killed the man who did it, trying to stop him from killing Mark. He was not the first man I had killed protecting my friends. As a boy, I had been taught how to fight and use weapons. I have given up weapons in place of the Rectifier. Death is such a permanent solution to problems that are sometimes temporary, problems that might be solved with a little more time and a little more talk. Once they're dead, you can't bring people back for a conversation. You will never understand them or be able to come to some kind of agreement that could work for both of you."

"Maybe some people just need killing," Ilantha whispered.

My thoughts turned to Zee, the Voice. I felt my eyes mist over. "But sometimes no matter how hard you try, there are some people who … will not … who … have turned inward to the point that any love they ever had for their fellow beings has gone dark, leaving a black hole in their soul in place of a heart. Sometimes they can find no true relief or comfort anywhere. Power and death become their only companions."

I let the tears come as I told them of the day in Forest Deep when I discovered what the Voice really was, a murderer and a false Voice speaking from the dark. I told them of Michkin, Pelldar, Mark, my grandfather Charthandrew, and my great-uncles and how they had died one by one and been taken out of my life—my father, too, though I had discovered he was not dead after all. I told them of finding my sisters and losing them, one to a horrible death, the other to the one I loved, my best friend, when he felt betrayed because I was really a girl and hadn't told him.

I talked for a long time, the tears drying my cheeks stiff. I told them of Ra'Vell Island and the caves, and Telling Tree's death and rebirth, of the Great Spirit of Wonannonda, and of the Blue Moon and meeting Zarek. I told of our efforts to stop the Voice and the king, and our failure, and the result of that failure … so many deaths, and the pain that all our people felt because of one false leader.

I also shared the joy and love of friends and family: John and Wydra, my half-brother, Lodar, James and Hanni, all of them, all the people I loved, those living and dead, and how they all were woven into my life. As the stories spun out, I saw a tapestry of all my short years spread before them.

"And really, all of that is why I'm here," I finished. "I agreed to come, to save them if I could. I want no more death. Not for them and not for you or your people."

Verity's eyes shone with unshed tears, and she was biting her lower lip as if to force back words that wanted to come out.

Ilantha was pale, her face in shadow, as if the daylight had fled from my many words. "I don't know how you still stand," she breathed. "How could you endure so much?"

"Because life is precious, and I choose to live it. I intend to bring as much good into this world as I can in my lifetime, short or long." I shrugged. "I just want as many people as possible to have what they need, and give what they can, and be a part of all that."

At that, Verity leapt from her chair and ran from the room.

Ilantha and I stood up in alarm at Verity's sudden departure.

"Is she all right?" I asked. "Should I go after her?"

"No. I've been pretty hard on her lately. She has been pushing for change, and I've ... not ... Well, I have not wanted to be ... present, let alone suffer through changes I don't want," Ilantha sighed, and in a weak voice, she added, "I see I have been wallowing in my grief these last seven years, letting things fall apart around me ... not in here," she indicated her sanctuary away from her world, "but out there," She waved her hand in a loose manner. "Out there, I have been ignoring everything. I have to admit that now, at least to myself." She looked at me then and gave a half smile. "My sister, Lupa, was right about you."

"What do you mean?"

"She said we needed you here. That you would find the sore spot and uncover the infection."

"I don't understand." I frowned. "How could she know anything about me?"

"I may be the head of my people," Ilantha gave me a feeble smile, "but Lupa is the heart of us. Everyone loves Lupa."

"Ah," I said. "So, she listens to people ... and loves them. Is that what you're telling me?"

Ilantha's smile lightened and was childlike in its sincerity. "Yes. That would be Lupa." She glanced around the large, lavish room, and sighed. "This place is empty without her. I miss her something dreadful, and she has only been gone a few days. And I can hardly bear it." She gave me a searching stare. "Lupa always seems to know things. She brings light into every room she enters."

"I hope I get to know her."

"She is the one who chose the nine to go to your Telling Wood city, and she chose the nine of you to come here."

"How did she make that choice?" I asked. "How did she know who to pick? And why?"

"Lupa talks to our Mother Spirit, who guides our people. She spends time in the Silent Chamber, and when she comes out, she knows things. I have never been there myself; I've always been too busy," Ilantha said and gave a dry chuckle. "Or too scared. Lupa spends hours in there. It is her sacred place. She found it when she was very young, only a child of six. I had been First Woman for five years by that time. Everyone in High Dome was frantic at her disappearance one day."

"What happened?"

Ilantha laughed, a true laugh. "She just showed up and said she found the World Mother and they had a talk." We sat in the approaching dark and laughed together at the wonder of children.

"You see what I mean about children," I said.

"Yes! I had forgotten." A dreamy smile rested on Ilantha's face. I felt we had really connected for the first time, like there was something solid between us now.

"Is Lupa the only one who goes there?" I had a sudden strong urge to see this place for myself. "Do you think she would mind if I spent some time in the Silent Chamber?"

Ilantha searched my face with her intense silver-blue gaze. "Do you mind being naked?"

"What do you mean?" A shiver of fear passed through me at the thought of revealing myself in that way, at the memory of keeping myself covered in the disguise of being a boy, on the one hand living with the fear of my secret being revealed and on the other what a luxury it was to be naked in the shower or bath, and how timid I still was about even other girls or women seeing me naked. I was surprised to discover how uncomfortable I still was with being openly female. Even now, I am comfortable with who I am on the inside, but still have the tendency to want to hide my body.

"That is a hard question for me," I finally said.

"I thought it might be," Ilantha said. "But Lupa says no one can enter the Silent Chamber taking anything with them. That's what she says. That's what she does. When you can go as your bare, honest self, you may enter the Silent Chamber."

CHAPTER EIGHT
(Late Afternoon, Day Four)

As I left the chambers of the First Woman heading down the gentle sloping spiral curve to our place, Verity stepped onto the path to walk with me.

Silence was our companion until we reached my door.

"Why did you leave in such a hurry?" I asked.

Her blue hair hung loose, long and wavy. She twisted a thick hank of it around her left arm in an absent-minded way, but her eyes held mine with an intensity that I couldn't look away from.

"You made me cry." She blinked. "I have never cried. To be First Woman, you have to be strong. You have to be clear headed, you have to be powerful and you have to be ..."

"Heartless?"

"Well ... No! Of course not."

"Tears don't make you weak," I said, "and sometimes they can clear your mind. It is quite true that they can sometimes make you feel powerless. I know that: I was afraid of tears too. Afraid if I let them come, they might never stop." I was remembering the little room I was in with Mother's sister, Alice, when I discovered Mother was dead.

"All my growing-up years, where I came from, tears were the realm of women. Men were not allowed tears. I'm surprised to find here that woman are not allowed them," I said, gently touching her arm. "There's no shame in tears. I have discovered they are salt from the healing sea."

Releasing the coil of blue hair from her arm, Verity walked over to the bench and sat down. Following, I sat down next to her. Even though her eyes were dark rimmed, pupils large, the black crowding out any color, I marveled at her pale, pearly, light-green complexion, so smooth and beautiful, framed by her vivid blue hair.

"There is so much pain in the world, Pendyse," Verity said, staring out at the ocean. "Sometimes I can barely live with the concept of it all, let alone the reality. I see the problems and maybe some of the solutions, but they often overwhelm me, and even as Second Woman, my sphere of influence is limited. I follow the orders of the First Woman, even though sometimes they're too harsh for my liking. And she hides. Sometimes I want to hide from it all myself, like Ilantha has. And for me to have the power to change things as they need to be changed … would mean Ilantha would be gone … and I can't bear that thought either. She has been a constant in my life, and always good to me."

She swallowed, giving me a searching stare, then looked away again. We sat in silence for a time, watching the swaying green forest streamers on the other side of the dome wall.

"You have lost so many loved ones," Verity said finally, and turned to me, shaking her head, her eyes brimming with sympathy, "yet you seem so open to the possibility of life with more loss. How do you do that?

"I'm not sure." I shrugged. It was my turn to stare at the sea forest and fish. "And it's not because I don't feel it. Sometimes the sorrows of my life overwhelm me, to tell you the truth, but like you, I have a responsibility, a job to do, something I was born to be! And I've come to have faith in life itself, the Great Spirit that flows through all things. Inexhaustible. And I see that life is not all about loss. It's about … generosity, too, and love." I shook my head. "I don't know." I shrugged again, feeling silly, thinking, *I am so young; what do I know?* But I did know. "It is just there … in me." I tapped my chest. "It won't let me to give up, even when I've wanted too."

Verity gave a little laugh. "You sound like Lupa, Ilantha's sister. You seem wise beyond your years. I bet it is not the first time you've been told that."

"I had to be preternaturally aware of who I was and what was going on around me all the time in order not to give myself away, to reveal that a girl's body was beneath the boy's clothes I wore." I gave a small sigh, looking down at what I was wearing now. "What I still tend to wear. What I am most comfortable in."

Verity grinned. "We'll have to get you some sea silks and change that, at least here, for the time being."

"Now you sound like Wydra, Jorame's sister, and one of my best friends." I laughed. "She just got married to the man who had been married to my mother. John. He's sort of like a second father to me."

Quiet washed over us with the movement of the Trillium Sea, and again we sat in companionable silence for a time, watching the rhythms of ocean life.

"What was that like, to choose to make yourself one of inferior standing?" Verity asked, breaking the silence.

I shook my head. "In Nueden, men are dominant, not inferior. They are thought to be superior. Here, it is women who rule. But I believe both men and women are of equal worth, as in the Wells and on the Blue Moon. And I didn't *choose* to pretend I was a boy, my parents chose that for me, in order to keep me with them. I chose to keep it up so I wouldn't be put in a Women's Palace or House. And so they wouldn't be punished for breaking the law. And my past has made me who I am, has helped me see the equal value of both men and women. To believe in the equal worth of all people, that there is no one inherently better than another, not because of gender or position or wealth. The only thing that makes us different are the actions we take to make this world a better place for all to live in … or not."

A school of silver and magenta fish darted among the sea fronds. "I have some friends who are male," Verity said, after a time, "but even at twenty-five, I have no close male friends. None I would want as a permanent mate. I haven't really had time to find a mate, even though the sisters urge me to have a child as soon as I can. I have tried, with no luck. In the past two years, I've lost two babies. I may not be a fertile bed for a tiny pearl." She shrugged and turned to look at me. "Besides, I don't really understand men. The only one I know well is my brother. And now Keto is with Lupa, one of our nine. He did not want to go." She sighed. "We are no longer close. When we were small we were, but not anymore. I believe he is a good man, though."

Even as she said this, I wondered at the tinge of the opposite emotion I felt coming from her in regard to Keto. She didn't believe he was a good man, she hoped he was, but I felt the slight fear in her mind that he might not be and it overshadow her words.

"Our mother died when I was too young to remember her. She never mated either one of our fathers," Verity said. "My father was from High Dome but I never knew him. Keto's father was from Low Dome. Mother served Ilantha. The sisters were fond of our mother. When Mother died, Lupa and Ilantha, not having any children of their own, raised us. I was schooled in High Dome, and my brother, Keto, was schooled in Low Dome in the grow barns but lived with me here in High Dome. It was too great a contrast for him. It always left him unsettled. But Ilantha and Lupa are the only family we've ever known. Keto has some resentment about the schooling. Even though Ilantha put him in charge of Low Dome, he's never been quite happy with his position in life. He thinks he should have been taught in High Dome as I was, and given a higher position because I was. But what Ilantha wants is law here, and he should have felt honored, as no man has ever been put in charge of any dome before."

Verity smiled sadly, shaking herself. "As we say, Ilantha is the head of Hadria, but Lupa is the heart, and I think you two will be fast friends when you meet."

"I am beginning to believe that could be so." Smiling, I nodded and said "Ilantha was telling me about her, that she picked the exchange groups."

"Yes. Lupa and I have spoken many times about the problems here in Hadria and in the heart of Ilantha. Lupa has worried a great deal about her." Verity took a deep breath and stood up, smoothing her long mother of pearl sea silk robe. It shimmered beneath her hands.

"What an amazing thing," she said as she straightened up to her full height, of almost six feet, I guessed. "I am feeling so much better. You must be right. Tears can heal. But I don't think I'll make a habit of it. I have far to much to do."

"I'm glad we could talk like this," I said. "Maybe you and I can be friends, too."

"I'd like that." Verity smiled and impulsively gave me a quick hug. "It's time we give your communicators back on a permanent basis so you can talk to your people any time you want," she said, giving me a long look, "and so you and Lupa can get to know each other. I think we all need you and Lupa to know each other."

***

John answered my call. I figured it might be a mealtime there, even though it would have been hard to know what time it was even here if not for my cell watch, which was still set to Telling Wood time.

70

"Thank Creator," John said. "You're safe."

"We are," I agreed. "Things here were a little dicey for awhile, when we thought we had lost Willobee, but we have her back and we are all OK and together," I said, looking around at the faces of the others of our nine gathered in our common living space.

"Hey, James," I heard John snap, "call everyone back to the table. Pendyse is on the com."

I could hear James and his brother Ferris in the background yelling for Rifkin's father, Heronimo, who must be there visiting, to come back, along with our other friends, Zarek, Wydra and Julka. As we heard them gathering, I could see them in my mind's eye coming to the plank table and finding a place on the benches, John's communicator front and center among them all as he said, "We are here."

"So are we," I said. "We've been given back our personal communicators and will be able to call home now any time we want. And you can call us, too."

"It's great to hear your voice," James said, and there was a general babble as we all greeted each other, exchanging a few words with our friends and families.

"Little Bee," Zarek said, "are you all right? Did they hurt you?"

"The mean one tried to, but the Fish Children saved me," she answered. "I had fun with them. They are good people, Great-Uncle Zarek."

Then we had to tell the whole story of the Obaskillian and the deep sixing as a punishment for causing trouble, and how it came about that the man's wife wanted revenge and took Willobee and deep sixed her.

"That's horrible!" Wydra said. "What a horrible thing to do to your own people. Having had a few talks with the one called Lupa, it seems impossible to believe. I adore her. She is wonderful, Pen."

"It's unbearable to think of you there with such cruel people," John said, which made me smile, remembering who he used to work for. "This business of deep sixing folks is very troubling."

We discussed it for a while, what we knew of it and what headway we might be making as peace ambassadors between our people. Eventually, my friends wished me a prosperous fourteenth year. I told them of the gift Rifkin had given me. We talked about our apartment and private rooms, and about being under the Trillium Sea.

"You should see this place, Father," Rifkin said. "I don't know how it works, the domes, the air, the recycling of fresh water, the removal of waste, and all the many systems of the place, but I want to understand it all. It is beautiful here. I wish you could all see it."

"Maybe someday," said Zarek, "we will all be one people again, and anyone can go there as a visitor."

"Wydra," Jorame's voice had a pensive edge to it as he spoke his twin's name, "I've been wondering, do you remember how our stepmother used to tell us about the child she lost to the sea when we were children?"

"Oh, yes, I remember it well, our lost Sabostienie sister. To the day Isola died, she never got over the loss. She grieved the death of that child, Sister, was swept out to sea." Wydra paused, "Why do you ask?"

"Do you remember what her name was? Everyone just called her Sister." Jorame questioned. A shiver went down my back as I watched him holding his breath. Was it a tremor of premonition? Or was I picking up some deeply held emotion in him?

"Well," Wydra said, "Isola didn't often use Sister's name, and it has been over sixty years now, but I think it was something like Ilandiea, or ..." They both spoke at the same time "Ilantha."

"Yes!" Wydra said. "You remembered; Ilantha. Why do you ask?" she said again.

"I think the First Woman is our lost sister. Our stepmother's lost daughter."

Suddenly everyone was talking at once, a babble of voices, questions, one voice drowning out another, over and over, until Rifkin's loud whistle silenced everyone. "OK, friends, let's start again, and talk one at a time," he said.

"You never told me you had a sister," John said to Wydra. I could hear a smile in his voice, as if he were delighted to learn something new about his wife.

"Well, it wasn't like we ever really knew her," Wydra replied. "We were young when our own mother died and Father married Isola. She used to talk about Sister, tell us about her, but it was a long time ago. And now Father and Isola are both gone, so we can't ask them. Jorame, are you sure? How can that be? She died, was taken by the sea. At least, that is what Isola told us."

"She *was* taken by the sea!" Jorame said. "Or at least her father took her to Hadria. His mother was the last First Woman, before Ilantha, and that First Woman only had a son." He pulled on his ear absently.

72

"Strange as it seems, I think she could be our stepsister. I have no idea what this could mean for our future, but I think it will be interesting to find out,"

"Jorame, I want to talk to her," Wydra said. "Can you arrange it? I think we should talk to her together."

They agreed to set up a time with Ilantha and Lupa, the four of them, along with John, me, and Verity.

We continued to share things that were happening in both places, and finally set another group meeting for two days away and some personal times between different ones of us with our own personal coms.

"Hey, Bee, can we talk a bit longer?" That was Zarek, and my heart gave an extra thump ta da, still not ready to let him go. But he wasn't mine. I had to remind myself of that. I wasn't his. He didn't want me after all. *How could he?* I thought. *I am only a child to him, in his eyes not much older than Bee, his great-grandniece.*

"May I take the communicator to my room to talk to Zarek some more?" Willobee asked.

I could feel the delight and joy radiating from her, and even from Zarek all that distance away. No one objected, and she skipped off to her room with my com.

I grabbed my journal and headed up the glass stairs to the little room to be alone and catch up on my writing of current events, and to think.

***

I was just finishing my journal entry when I heard someone coming up the steps.

Jorame poked his head around the curved entryway. "Mind some company?" he asked.

"No, not at all, come in." I smiled at his raised eyebrows and patted a cushion next to me. "I imagine you and Julka have been talking now that we have our communicators back."

His smile widened. "You know it."

"What does she think of you maybe inheriting another sister?"

"She thinks it might help with negotiations if Ilantha is our sister," he said, and then he frowned. "What's up with you and Zarek? And don't tell me, nothing! I saw what was happening between the two of you. Before Julka and I … got together … I thought maybe the two of you were going to …"

"Stop," I said, laughing. "Please, no matchmaking." Looking at my hands folded on my journal, letting my shoulder-length curls fall to hide my face. "Zarek and I are just friends." I felt the tremble in my voice and the sting in my eyes. I had just poured my hurt out on the pages of my journal, and didn't really want to talk about Zarek.

"So," I said, lifting my head and giving Jorame a real smile, "what have you and Julka been talking about all this time?"

Jorame laughed. "All right, I get it. But when you want to talk, I'll be here to listen. I won't push, but I know something is wrong, and I want you to know you're not fooling me about the way you feel about our 'friend' Zarek." He gave me a very intense look his lips a tight line, and nodded. We sat quietly for a while; then he said, "Do you really want to know what Julka and I talked about?"

I nodded. "Of course. I care about you both." I placed my hand on his for the briefest of time. "But not the mushy stuff, please." I laughed. "You know, I saw the moment the two of you connected…in the Chamber House at the council meeting the first time the two of you shared your council table. Your hands touched, and I felt something pass between you."

"Hmmm," he said, and gave a dreamy little smile. "I hope you don't mind me saying this, but before that moment, I thought I was madly in love with you."

"I was afraid of that, and I think I would have welcomed that love before I met …" I suddenly realized what I was saying. "Well, anyway, I'm glad you found her. I like her. She's perfect for you. You're perfect for her. I can see it in the way you move together, touch each other." I paused, getting my wayward emotions in check. "You could mind touch from that first time your hands brushed together, couldn't you?"

Jorame nodded and gave a huge grin. "You know, she is the first person other than Wydra who I've ever been able to instantly do that with. And Wydra doesn't really count, as I can't remember a time when we didn't mind touch. That twin bond, you know." He settled back against the wall and looked up at the light of the evanescent half moon. The moving waters cast shifting water shadows over his face. "She pierced my heart and mind, Pen. And now…I can't imagine life without her. And the most amazing thing is that she feels the same about me." He glanced my way. "And you know the strangest thing is that we can feel each other's emotions, even this far apart. I know if she's having a good day." He sighed. "We will marry as soon as this time here is over, even though we know it means we will never be able to have children."

"What do you mean? Why wouldn't you be able to have children?"

His brows lifted in surprised. "Don't you know? Humans and Sabostienie can't produce offspring together. But it's something we are willing to sacrifice to be with each other."

"Oh, I'm sorry. No. That isn't something I knew or ever even thought about."

"Yes, even though there are some who willingly cross over that divide, like our father with Isola, but she had a daughter and he had us. They didn't have to be a childless couple."

"Well," I said, "If you really want children, Nueden has an army of orphans. I'm sure no one would mind if you raised a few of them as your own."

"Now that's something I hadn't thought about. Julka might like that."

We talked for a while longer, and once the light had completely vanished, we went down to the kitchen for a snack.

At Jorame's door, he stopped and turned as I was about to head down the curving hallway. "You know I will always love you Pendyse, just … differently."

I turn to face him. "And I you." I smiled, heading down to Willobee's room to check on her before I called it a night.

CHAPTER NINE
(Day Five)

"Do you think it would be OK if we could go look around Mid Dome?" Dray asked. "Just Kid and me on our own?"

"Well," I paused to take in their hopeful faces. "Verity did say we could shop at Mid Dome when we wanted to. I can't imagine why you couldn't; you're old enough. Just don't go near Low Dome. We still don't know what is going on down there, but you know it could be deadly." I paused again and whispered, "Check out everything you can. See if you can get a fix on what the people are like, what they are thinking about us, about what is going on in the domes overall, anything you think might help us understand them and communicate on a better level. Anything we can learn about them will be helpful. But be polite, and don't get in trouble."

"Rifkin and Lucus are going on a tour of the working systems for the domes," Kid said. "You should talk to them too, when they get back." Kid glanced over at my hound. "Do you think we could take Ibera with us?" His eyebrows pinched together. "No one would dare try anything funny with her around." Kid's sharp features and whip-thin body were tight as a spring.

"OK, what are you two planning?" I asked, suspicion tickling the back of my mind.

"Oh, nothing," Dray said innocently. "Really, we just want to go to Mid Dome and look around. Check things out. On our own, you know, without … adults."

"You think of me as an adult?" I chuckled, thinking of when I was their age, such a sort few years ago, getting up to one kind of trouble or another with James, Hannratti and Rifkin. "What kind of mischief are you up to?" I gave them a lopsided grin. "Come on ..."

"Honest, Pen," Kid grinned back at me, relaxing as if he already knew my answer, "we won't get into trouble."

"Say yes," Dray wheedled. "Please, Just for a couple of hours. We'll do everything you say."

"And we will stay away from Low Dome," Kid said. "Won't go near it."

"You will be in meetings all morning with the First Woman and that bunch," said Dray, "We will be back before lunch. Pleeeese."

"All right," I said, with some reluctance. I whistled for Ibera. "You take good care of Dray and Kid." Ibera looked over at the boys and back at me. A shiver ran down my spine. I knew she understood completely. Why that would surprise me, after what Ibera and I had been through together? But our bond was still a new thing for me, and sometimes I could hardly believe how strong it was. She was only a year old, after all. I knew no harm would come to them with Ibera along. I couldn't say as much for anyone who might try to harm *them*. Looking at the three, Ibera included, I said, "You be good. Behave yourselves; we are guests here. What freedoms we now have can be taken away. You understand that, don't you?"

Dray and Kid nodded, and Ibera's eyes told me everything I needed to know about her part in the trio.

***

"What's this about?" Ilantha wanted to know. We had enlisted Verity's help in setting up a meeting with Ilantha.

"We wanted to talk to you," Jorame said, "my sister Wydra and I."

"Oh?" Ilantha lifted her chin, just so. "I can't see why."

Nervous looks were exchanged between, Verity, Jorame and me; then we looked back at Ilantha.

"What is going on, Verity?" she snapped. "You all seem jumpy as jitter fish. Tell me at once."

"I think you're my sister!" Jorame blurted out.

"That's preposterous," Ilantha huffed. "You're a young man, I'm an old woman. Besides, we look nothing alike, even if our ages didn't already make it impossible. Why would you think such a thing?"

"Was your mother's name Isola?"

Ilantha froze in mid-motion, Jorame holding her gaze. "Who told you that name?" She bit the words out after an indrawn breath. She looked over at Verity. "My Second doesn't even know my mother's name. Lupa doesn't know my mother's name. How do *you* know my mother's name?"

Jorame relaxed then and leaned back in his chair, smiling. "I think you're my stepsister. And I'm older than I look. Can we call Wydra now?

"Well," Ilantha looked at Verity, "get on with it! I want this mystery cleared up at once!"

We had Wydra, John and Lupa on the com in no time, and greetings went around.

"Lupa, what is all this?" Ilantha said, irritated. "You must know it can't be true!"

"Oh, dear sister, I do believe it is," Lupa laughed. "Our family has just expanded. Let them tell you how."

A long pause ensued as Ilantha looked at each of us. I felt a subtle longing surface in her, a desire to know what had become of her mother, the woman she had never seen again once she'd come here to Hadria. I was right about that, I was sure of it now.

"All right," Ilantha breathed. "Tell me."

"Isola was our second mother," Wydra said.

"Our mother died," Jorame added. "We lived in Well One. We were small children when Father met Isola. We all liked her. She was gentle and kind. Father married her soon after they met. She was a wonderful Healer. A loving and generous woman."

"Yes, that was certainly true of my mother when I was a child." Ilantha smiled as tears glinted in the corners of her eyes at Jorame's words. Nodding, she said, "Yes, I remember that about her. She worked at the healing and birthing center in Well One. It must be the same Isola; how could there be two? Tell me more. Is she still alive? Could that be possible?"

There was a brief silence, and then Wydra spoke softly. "She told us how she had lost a daughter to the sea. We always thought our stepsister had died. Drowned. What else were we to believe? Our mother, Isola, loved her first daughter very much. She nearly died of grief before she met Father and they bonded. She talked about our sister who the sea took, how she never saw her again, not even in her dreams. Sister's image had been taken from her, too. But not the memory of her sweetness, and her adventurous spirit, not her name, *your name*. It was the last word Mother Isola spoke before she died."

The shimmer of tears rolled down Ilantha cheeks. Verity took the First Woman in her arms, cradling her, rocking her, and tears wet the cheeks of both women. When they dried their eyes, Jorame continued.

"Father and Isola were married for forty-seven years," he said. "They weren't all that young when they met, but they had a happy life together. We are so sorry to bring you the news of her death. Our father died a month later. He couldn't bear life without her. They could mind touch, and he said he felt her waiting for him. So he left too."

Ilantha groaned as if in pain. "Oh, I wish Rexon and I could have known each other's thoughts, shared our feelings that way. We were so close ... but that would have been lovely. Like what they used to say about the Father and Mother of the Sabostienie people." She stared into Jorame's eyes. "So it's true then, people can really do that?"

Our secret is out now, I thought. *For good or ill.*

Jorame looked at me and blinked, as if for the first time realizing what he had just revealed.

"Yes," he said, "some people can mind touch. Not everyone. It is no different now than when you were a child." I felt he couldn't help himself as he glanced in my direction. "Some people are better at it than others. Born naturals to the mind touch."

Ilantha and Verity didn't seem to notice the telling look and fell back into conversation.

The four new family members continued, and Verity, John and I listened quietly. I felt amazed at how the barriers came down as laughter rose up and story after story spilled out. Lunch was forgotten, and time lapsed into midafternoon.

When the visit was over, Ilantha was exhausted, and Verity helped her to her room to lie down for a nap. We went back to our place.

Rifkin met us at the door, talking about all the things Lucus and he had seen while they were out. "You have to see the water refinement station, Pen. You will marvel at the way it works and how it powers the place with light, too. And the ..."

"Wait, wait, let us get inside and sit down before you tell us everything," I laughed. "Could you be any more excited?"

"It's like the first time he was in the Wells," Jorame laughed with me. "I can see he …"

"Where are the boys?" I cut in, throwing myself onto the couch, realizing how tired I was, tired enough to take a nap myself. Closing my eyes, I pinched the bridge of my nose and then rubbed my temples. "I thought they would be out here listening to all the wonderful things you two have seen today."

Jorame looked around. "Are the others in their rooms?"

"They must be." Lucus shrugged. "We just got back ourselves. And Rifkin is right. We are going to see the labs tomorrow and learn a bit about how the doming works. That will relieve my mind. At least, I hope it will." A disgruntled look flashed across his face. "Or it will send me up to live a hermit's life on the island."

"Have you guys eaten anything?" Jorame rubbed his stomach. "We skipped lunch, we were having such a good time talking. Ilantha is my sister, just as I thought. It is beyond incredible. Just as if Wonannonda planned all this." As Jorame was saying this, I realized I could only sense Reia, LaBo and Bee in their rooms. I had no sense at all of the boys' presences, or Ibera's. I leapt up off the couch and startled everyone as I ran down the hall to the boys' suite.

I knocked and shouted so loudly that Reia and LaBo came out of their rooms, just as the men rushed down the hallway to join us.

"What is it?" LaBo asked. "What's the matter?"

I turned the door handle and went into the room. "Kid! Dray!" I called. No answer. Futile though I knew it would be, I called again. "Boys! Dray! Kid!"

"Great Creator, where could they be?" Fear laced Lucus's words. I cast my senses wide open, his fears stabbing at me like a hundred little knives in my gut. I sailed out of there and down to Willobee's room. The other five right behind me. Before I could even knock, Bee opened the door.

"Don't worry!" Bee said, her hands patting the air in front of me like a little mother reassuring a panicked child. "They are all right. They just can't come home right now." She invited us in. All seven of us crowded into her sitting room, and she said again, "You don't have to worry, they are all right. Trust me. I've been watching them."

"What?" Lucus frowned, puzzled.

I was pretty sure I knew what she meant. "You're watching them?"

She nodded. "Well, in a way. So please be quiet so I can feel them again."

We all sat down where we could and kept quiet. Bee sat down on the floor, cross-legged, right in the center of us, and closed her eyes. I joined her, taking her hands in mine.

"They want you to know they are sorry, Pen," she said.

"For what?" I barely breathed the words, trying to put myself into search mode like Zarek had taught me, trying to follow Willobee's mind touch link with the boys.

"They made a friend. And the three of them snuck into Low Dome. And they are sort of stuck in a hidey-hole," Bee said.

"How does she know that?" Lucus asked, looking from one of us to the other.

"For one so young," LaBo said, smiling, "she is a gifted communicator. Shhh, just listen."

I closed my eyes. *Bee?*

Yes, Pen. Come on, I'll show you where they are.

I could see the passageways of Mid Dome flash by. It was like being a pair of bodiless eyes in a wandering mind, linked to a six-year-old adept. I knew we were following a path the boys had taken. We flew by the marketplace, the school and into Low Dome. We finally stopped in a tight and absolutely dark place. I heard quiet breathing and felt the presences of three children, hot and sweat-sticky. There were three child-sized bodies and Ibera. It was Dray, Kid and another child, a girl around their age. Then I became aware that they were listening intently to voices coming from the room next to them. And I moved my eyes and mind and my hearing over to that space.

In a dim room the size of my bedchamber, five women and two men were yelling at each other. Anger permeated the atmosphere. The woman who had tried to feed Willobee to the fish was there. "I'm telling you, we need to strike now," she said. "If we wait, it will all fall apart."

"All our planning and preparations," one of the men said, "will be for nothing. Ursa is right. We have to do this now, in two nights' time, or we lose the advantage of the highest tide of the year. It's the only way we can have enough pressure to break through the locks between domes. You already know that."

"But what about Keto? We can't do this without him," the second man said. "He has access to the docking bay, we don't. How will we get out without him?"

"We are dying here anyway," Ursa said. "If everyone in Low Dome has to die in order to kill that greedy monster in High Dome, then so be it. We can't wait another year for Keto to return and save us!" she snarled. "We have to save ourselves. And we don't have much time to decide. We can get out with oxygen balls. That damned surface child did it. She lived. So can we."

"I'm with Tazz on this, Ursa. I can't abandon our people here to an inundation. That is too cruel, even for you." The other man said.

"Me? Cruel?" Ursa said. "That monster has taken everything from me. My man. My daughter. My father. You are all weak, spineless idiots." Hatred twisted Ursa's face into an ugly mask. "We will all die down here, and it will be your fault!" With that, she rushed out of the room without a backward glance.

The heat of anger went with her, and the others silently drifted out of the room one by one, until my essence was the last one left floating in an empty space that suddenly felt too large for comfort. I shifted over to the other side of the wall and found Kid, Dray, Ibera and the girl sliding the wall panel aside and coming out of the closet storage space, leaving through the same door as the others and going down a long, dim hallway. Was everything dark down here? The girl guiding them moved soundlessly. They were good little sneaks. There wasn't even a sound from Ibera's claws on the moss-like carpet on the floor.

Willobee caught me up in her link and swished us back to her sitting room. I felt dizzy at the speed of our return and had to sit for a bit with my eyes still closed just to catch my breath.

I knew the boys and Ibera would be back soon. I hoped they could tell us more about what that was all about. Inundation. I didn't like the sound of that one bit. Not one little bit. But it sounded like we at least had two days to stop them or evacuate Hadria. What had those people been talking about, planning, and why? And what was Keto's involvement with them?

Verity would have to be told, but how to explain what I knew and how I knew it. I would need to think on this. I wasn't quite ready yet to reveal my ability of seeing and hearing outside the normal range of things.

I opened my eyes and met Willobee's gaze. "It's all right, Pen, they will be here soon," she said.

I can send them to your sitting room so you can talk to them alone first before they talk to anyone else. Bee's words touched my mind, and I gave her a slight nod and got up.

"OK?" Lucus jumped out of his chair to his feet. Jorame and Rifkin stood also. Lucus wore a pinch-mouthed expression, and I could feel indignation rolling off him in waves. "Were you all off mind traveling or something?" He was perturbed, feeling left out of the loop, glaring around at everyone, grooves of suspicion lining his eyes and mouth, as if he thought we all had been absent from this room, everyone but him.

Jorame started laughing, which offended Lucus even more and set the women fussing over him to calm him down. "I'm sorry Lucus, it's not about you; it's her." Jorame pointed in my direction and said, "She does that. She goes off, and when she comes back, she knows things." He looked at Willobee with narrowed eyes. "And apparently so does our Little Bee."

Rifkin shook his head, holding up his hands. "Hey, not me. I can't do that, if that's what you're thinking. I only travel the usual way, with my two feet ... well, sometimes on a cyna-cycle."

Reia helped LaBo up from the floor as she said, "Come on, Lucus. Let's take a walk before dinner. We'll be socializing all evening. I know how much you like that. We need to stretch our legs. And I suspect you will want to talk to the boys when they get home." She looked in my direction.

"I'll go to the kitchen and see that the help has started dinner," Rifkin said, "so we can eat as soon as the two of you get back."

I went to shower, change and wait for my hound to come home, dragging the boys behind her. I would not only have to talk to them, but to Verity, and Ilantha too, and my housemates as well, eventually. I did not look forward to Lucus hearing the news that I'd overheard someone plotting to inundate the domes. I didn't think the woman Ursa could do this on her own, whatever it was, and the others didn't seem to want to go through with it, except for the one man who hadn't been named. But what if they changed their minds and did join in on the scheme they had been planning with Keto? At least I had two names to give to Verity tonight. No, three: Keto was involved in this too. We would be meeting with the educators, Healers and the dome scientists in the Gathering Hall tonight. It had to be tonight.

You can tell them you know this because Kid and Dray and Samra heard it, I heard Bee whisper in my thoughts, and I smiled.

You are a smart one, Little Bee. Keep this up and you will one day be the Mother of the Blue Moon.

A quiet giggle passed through me as I entered my rooms. *Not me, that's you, silly,* Bee said.

As odd a response as I thought that was, I let it pass, not knowing what to reply.

***

I twisted my hair up off my neck and swished it around in a bun with a couple of combs, but my curls were untamable. I was wearing a sea silk confection of blues and greens that, when I walked, mimicked the movements of the sea grass outside my window. Verity and I were almost the same height; she was maybe an inch or two taller than me and full breasted, with rounded hips. Like Wydra, Verity had excellent taste in woman's fine things and an eye for sizes. How did they do that? Come up with such things at a moment's notice? I didn't care a whit about fashion except as a disguise, but everyone else seemed to think fashion was the thing that defined a person.

Verity had sent the dress over for me to wear to the gathering that evening. We were meeting in the same place where I had tricked Verity into speaking English. I don't know how they thought they could keep the fact that they all spoke English from us. There were some folk here, like in the Wells and on the Blue Moon, who didn't even know their own language any more. I guess someone would have slipped up sooner or later if it hadn't been Verity. And now I was going to have to tell her, and Ilantha, too, about what I had overheard.

Dray, Kid and Ibera were due to return any minute, and I was ready for them. They wouldn't know what I knew about their confinement in the little room unless Bee had told them. I sat down and got relaxed and cast my senses out to scan Willobee's room, and to my surprise, I could sense that the boys and Ibera were near, actually in the tunnels. I reached out for Bee's thoughts.

I'm here, she sent my way. *They will be coming through my wall soon, from the tunnel.*

Why the tunnel? I asked. *Are you a silent partner in whatever they were up to?*

Well, one of the girls from our kitchen staff told them they needed to see something in Low Dome, but they knew you wouldn't let them go there. I went with them, sort of. The last thought was a bit of a mind mumble.

Did they know you were there?

Well, I think Kid might have. He is really easy to talk to. And he knows how to shield really well, so I don't have to worry that I'm prying into his thoughts. Dray just lets everything fly. I try not to listen, but ...

Don't worry about that now. We'll work it out. Is there anyone else you can mind touch with? Like LaBo?

Yes ... her and Reia. But they can't always talk to me or even hear me sometimes. But I can always hear them thinking when I want to listen.

There was a pause, a space of waiting, for I knew Bee wasn't finished.

And Rifkin, sometimes, but not sending, only hearing. I really like Rifkin. And sometimes I hear Lucus. He's funny, though; I hear him only when he is really scared. Then he has a very mixed-up mind, and I can't understand anything he thinks. He really, really, really hates it here. Except for Reia. And you, you are easiest of all. I bet I could talk to you even if you were on the island and I was down in Low Dome. You are so clear, like my Great-Uncle Zarek. I know something about him, but I'm not supposed to tell.

Something about Zarek?

The boys are back, got to go. I'll send them to you. OK?

Don't tell them anything. Just send them.

85

CHAPTER TEN
(Early Evening, Day Five)

The knock on my door was barely audible. I let Kid and Dray in. Ibera came in, wagging her tail and nose bumping me for praise that she'd brought them back all in one piece. She nuzzled against me, wanting a scratch around her horn. I gave it to her, making the boys wait while I did that.

"Do you have something to tell me?" I said finally.

Kid nodded, solemn as a priest. "And you're not going to like it!"

"Why don't we get comfortable? I think this could take some time." I indicated the chairs, and I curled up on the small couch facing them. "OK. Spill it."

"Well," Dray began, "we made friends with a girl who works In our kitchen. Samra."

"She told us something bad was going to happen," Kid said, taking over. "That there was some bad stuff going on in Low Dome. The people down there are dying, Pen."

"You went to Low Dome?" I gave them a stern look.

"There's a sickness in the plants," Dray said, "all through the grow barns, and the people are getting it now too."

"They have to send the best of everything that grows up to High and Mid Domes, and there isn't enough of the clean stuff any more for them too," Kid said. "It isn't right, Pen. If one should suffer, they all should suffer, isn't that what you say?"

"No!" I shot back. "It is more like all should have the same good fortune, not suffering. But … I suppose all things being equal it might mean the same thing." I would have to put that away for later thought.

"They're dying. And the First Woman won't do anything about it." I could feel Dray's anger rising against Ilantha.

"Maybe she doesn't know how bad it is," I said.

"No, she knows." Kid almost sneered. "The people down there, and a man named Keto, have told her many times, or at least they have told the Second Woman for sure. Why aren't they doing anything?"

I frowned. "Are you sure? It's hard to fool me, and I haven't felt that kind of evil in them. And why would they do that? These are Ilantha's people."

"Why did the Voice kill *her* own people?" Dray said. I nodded. He had a point, and you couldn't always tell at first glance what a person was on the inside. And we'd only been here for five days, not even nine, a full week.

"The people of Low Dome want to live on the island," Kid said, "but the First Woman thinks they won't keep serving the High Dome any more if they go up top."

"OK, where are you getting this information from?" I asked. "Who is Samra, and where did you go today, and why are you so late getting back?"

They gave each other a look. Kid shrugged. "I know we have to tell you everything, even if we get in trouble. It's a matter of life and death for all of us."

"We met Samra three days ago," Dray began. "We noticed how none of the grown-ups here would talk to any of you grown-ups about the important things. So we made friends with her, and when she was in our suite to make our beds and clean our bathroom, we talked to her."

"Once we knew she could speak English," Dray added.

"She began telling us over the next couple of days that she was afraid of the people in Low Dome. She thought they were going to do something awful to the First Woman and everyone in High Dome," Kid said. "Yesterday, she told us to meet her at the Education Center in Mid Dome, that she had something to show us in the grow barns. We met her, and she led us down service passageways to get into some of the deep working areas down there. Her father lives in Low Dome; Samra and her mother live in Mid Dome. She took us to a place at the farthest edge of Low Dome and showed us the beginning of a spider's-web crack in one of the grow barns on an outside wall of the dome." Kid paused. "A small crack, but the beginning of a fracture, in a city under the water."

"We will talk to Ilantha and Verity tonight," I said. "Continue."

"They haven't had a healthy birth in Hadria in over three years. The babies die, if they are born at all," Dray said.

"How can that be?" I felt shock tumble through me. "Surely they would notice something that life altering to their city's future."

"Well," Kid said, "it's true. Have you seen any babies here?"

"Samra says it is all hush-hush. The Healers don't even know what is happening to cause it. No one is supposed to talk about it," said Dray.

"Especially to us," Kid said.

"We were in a room where the woman who tried to kill Bee has secret meetings with some Low Domers" Dray picked up where Kid left off. "Samra said there was proof that they are the ones who are trying to make the crack break open with some kind of explosive device they used to use on the island to clear out the rocks and trees for up-top garden space. We were going to steal it so they couldn't use it. But when we got down there, it was already gone. We heard people coming and had to hide in a storage space off the main room."

"Could you hear what they said?" I asked. "Could you see them?"

"We could hear most of it. It was a thin panel door. The woman called Ursa was very angry and was screaming at the others. We all heard that," Dray said.

"I was the only one who could see anything," Kid said. "There was a thin crack in the door panel next to me. I counted five woman and two men. I heard the name Keto, who doesn't seem to be here in Hadria right now, which leads me to believe he is one of the nine in Telling Wood. And the two men were Tazz and Ajax. Don't know which is which; I couldn't tell. Ursa, Rabeen and Opheara were the women's names I heard. No one spoke the other two women's names."

"Ursa was the one who tried to kill Bee," Dray said. "I'd remember that voice anywhere."

"She's going to cause trouble, that one, one way or another." Kid nodded. "The Second Woman should have let the guards deep six her, or lock her up, or something."

"Yeah," Dray agreed. "We think she is Keto's mother."

"No," I said, "Keto is Verity's brother. They had the same mother. Ilantha put him in charge down there three years ago. And I think he is what's wrong with Low Dome. I have a gut feeling about him, and it's not a good one, but I'm going to follow my instincts. I will have to warn our people in Telling Wood to watch out for him."

We were quiet for a while, "OK, enough for now," I said, "except for one other thing. You both lied to me. I knew at the time you had something going on. But I didn't know how serious it was. A little harmless fun is one thing, but what you did was dangerous. I understand that sometimes you guys will have to follow your instincts too, but I want you to promise me you will never lie to me again. If you are going off on your own, you tell me your full plans first. Do you understand?"

They stood up, chastened, nodding. They both said, "We promise."

"Then go get cleaned up, put on your best clothes for the gathering tonight and come eat dinner. You must have missed lunch too. Oh, by the way, Ilantha *is* Jorame and Wydra's stepsister. So be nice to her until we understand what is really going on here in Hadria. Your Samra could be very mistaken about who is to blame for the condition of things in the grow barns and processing houses. Don't jump to conclusions." I smiled then. "You did good work. We know more now than we did. This information will save lives. Just include me in your plans next time. I might say no, or I might go with you."

I held the door for them. Ibera saw them out into the hallway. When she came back in, she went straight to the bedchamber, jumped on the bed, stretched out and closed her eyes.

***

There were about thirty people in the Gathering Hall when our nine got there. The men here dressed as colorfully as the women, in robes and form-fitting bodysuits, their hair as long as some of the women's. They looked much as the Sabostienie people did, except for their full heads of hair, which was more like my people.

I searched for Ilantha and Verity. Spying them by the dessert table, I headed straight for them. So did Jorame, who captured Ilantha's attention while I took Verity by the arm and led her away from the knot of folks who were talking and laughing next to the table.

We walked all the way over to the dome wall with a view of the ocean. I sat down on a seashell chair, saying, "Please, can we talk?" She sat down in the matching chair next to mine.

89

"Something's wrong!" Verity said, watching me closely. "You're tense. I can tell. It's not because of the dress, is it?"

"No." I smiled. "It's beautiful. And the flat-soled shoes are sensible. Thank you."

"What, then?"

"Have any of your guards been keeping an eye on Ursa since she tried to kill Bee?"

Verity stiffened her spine, sitting up at full attention. "Yes … well, not on an hour-to-hour basis. So I guess that would mean no."

"Do you have any kind of lockup facilities for rebellious people like her?"

"No. You know what Ilantha does to people who cause trouble, to lawbreakers. Fish food, it's our way to keep order, it has been for millennia. Maybe lately it's been used more often than it used to be, but …"

"We now know that the Obaskillian save the people who are deep sixed, when they can," I said. "Where are those condemned people? Where do the Fish Children take them? You say deep sixing has always been the way Hadria deals with trouble?

"I know the punishment seems harsh to you, but …"

"What if the Fish Children have been saving people and taking them to the island all these years?"

"Well …" Verity pondered this possibility, then shook her head. "I can't imagine such a thing."

"Did you know the people in Low Dome are dying at an alarming rate these past three years? And there's something wrong with the food."

"What are you talking about, Pendyse? Who told you this?" Her tone was defensive, "Why would our food production even be an issue for you? And what business is it of yours?"

"Verity, I'm not accusing you of anything, it's just that …"

"What, then? Tell me!"

"There is trouble brewing in Low Dome. They are sick and dying."

"There has always been the long, slow sickness in Hadria. We have one or two die every year in Low Dome, a few in all of Hadria. There is nothing new in that. If it were worse than that, someone would have told me. Keto would …"

"Keto. The people in Low Dome believe he has told you, and that you and Ilantha don't care if they die or not."

Verity jerked to her feet. "That's a vicious lie, Pendyse! I want to know who told you that."

"Please, sit down. I will tell you." I moved my chair closer to hers. "Our boys, Dray and Kid, have made friends with a girl who cleans for us. Samra is her name."

"Yes. I know her. She is a good server. More intelligent than most, and observant."

"She is afraid that Ursa is going to try to kill the First Woman ... and you," I took a deep breath. "And all of Hadria, for that matter, by an inundation of the ocean."

Verity didn't move. She sat like a stone, just staring at me, stunned.

"Ursa, Tazz, Ajax, Rabeen and Opheara are planning something for two nights away, when the tide is highest, for maximum devastation to Hadria," I said, and shook her by the shoulder. "Did you hear me?"

"That can't be right," Verity said. "Why? Why would they do that to all of Hadria? It would mean their deaths too."

"Keto had meant to take them out the ship bay airlocks, but he isn't here, so they have been storing up oxygen balls as a contingency plan. Are you having trouble with your birthing's?" I asked. "Are the babies dying?

Verity's eyes opened wider, if that was possible, the black pupils enveloping her vivid blue irises, making her look even more alarmed and foreign than before. "It's not true. I don't know why Samra would lie like that to Dray and Kid, but that just isn't true."

I shook my head. "Verity, you told me yourself you have lost two pregnancies, and I know you've been worried about the problems in Hadria, you told me so yesterday. I know Ilantha has been denying there is anything wrong here, but don't you do it too. A problem buried is a bomb waiting to explode. Isn't that why we're here? Our nine?"

"But why wouldn't Keto tell ..." She gave a shudder and a low groan, and she doubled over. "Oh Great Mother, what have you done, Keto?" She jumped to her feet, grabbing my arm. "Come on, we have to talk to Ilantha right away."

"Wait." I pulled her to a stop. "Not so fast. We don't want to start a panic. That's why I'm talking to you first, in private."

With her free hand, Verity rubbed her forehead, and cupped her hand over her mouth, a look of horror crossing her face. We sat down again.

"When he was younger, he used to say he hated her," Verity said. "But I just didn't believe him, because I loved her so much. I couldn't see how he could hate her; it didn't make sense to me, it didn't seem real. And then he quit saying it, and I thought things were different, were all right. I believed he outgrew those feelings of resentment. But sometimes I would catch a look on his face that would make me shiver. I didn't want to think that of him. He's my brother, my only blood kin in all of Hadria."

"Ursa hates everyone in High Dome," I said. Closing my eyes, cupping my elbow with one hand, I tapped my forehead with the fingertips of my right hand, thinking. "What if Ursa and Keto teamed up to conspire against the powers that be because they think they've been treated unfairly? And maybe they have been. That's usually where trouble starts. I have to tell you, they have some kind of explosive device, and there is a crack developing in Low Dome."

Verity tipped her head back and gazed at the ocean above the dome ceiling. "You've been here five days and you've already put your finger on the pulse of Hadria and found it slowing and near death. And I've been asleep at my station. I don't deserve to be Second or First Woman." She lowered her head, her eyes meeting mine. "Could Keto have been poisoning the food supply in some way that would cause the babies to die? And the people to get sick?" she asked.

"I don't know. But I suspect it could be done. I do know that hate can twist a mind in ways you wouldn't recognize as human." I was thinking of the Voice, Zee.

"But we aren't human," Verity said. "We are Stella Mara."

"That's just another kind of human," I said. "Sabostienie, Stella Mara, Obaskillian: we are all pretty much the same, it seems to me. So we look a little different. We all need food, water, shelter and love. And when hate gets into the mix and we don't have enough of all these things, fear, anger, hate becomes a killer, Verity. The poison in the system."

A moment of silence built between us, and then I said, "Now, what are we going to do about it?"

"I'm glad you said we." Verity fixed her gaze out in the ocean somewhere in the distance and took a deep breath. "There have been some who have, for a long time now, wanted to live up top, to grow our food there on a permanent basis. What if we let them?"

"Well, I'd say that is a fine place to start. But you will have to think twice about letting Ursa go with them. She could be a poison that

92

would kill any good done by letting them onto the island. I don't know if you could convince her that you and Ilantha didn't know about what was really happening in Low Dome these past few years. How do you think we should approach the First Woman with this?"

"Hmmm. She is going to want to smash them and grind their bones to make fish feed. That is likely going to be her first reaction. To be honest with you, the thought crossed my mind too."

"I know she has a heart for your people," I said. "It may have been buried in her grief for Rexon these past years, but maybe if we tell her that the people are dying … that they're sick, and hungry … maybe that is the way to start."

Verity nodded, thoughtful. "Let me do the talking."

"Wait." I touched Verity's shoulder, stopping her. "Do you keep records of production in the grow barns?"

"Yes." Verity's brow furrowed. "Why? How can that help us?"

"Could there be two sets?" I asked.

"Yes, there are two sets, one for us to keep here in the Hall of Records and one they keep in the Low Dome Record Room. So what is so important about keeping two sets?" Then the light dawned on her. "Oh, that would be clever: show us a record that made things seem like all is well so we wouldn't do anything, know anything. Ursa and Keto show the people below records that made it clear the production is down and the people are sick and dying, and make them think both records are the same. That would make it look like we don't care."

I nodded.

"How could he do that?" Anger flashed in her eyes. "He's my brother. We may not have been close for years, but I still love him. Doesn't he care about me at all?"

"We don't really know what he has done … yet," I said. "Why don't we have your guards check the Low Dome Records Room right now and see what they can find? Where is the Hall of Records here in High Dome? Could we go there?"

"Yes. Of course we can."

"Do you think we could slip away and do that before we talk to Ilantha? The more information we have, the easier it will be."

CHAPTER ELEVEN
(Evening, Day Five)

Verity spoke into a shell ring she wore, and I realized for the first time that it was a communicator. I had thought maybe the staff she carried sometimes might have communication capabilities, but she didn't always have that with her. So now I knew how things happened around here so quickly. Was it somehow controlled by voice command or touch? I would have to ask about that in the future, when we had more time.

"Captain Saeela, bring ten guards and meet me at the Hall of Records immediately," she said into the ring.

We followed a spiral passageway to a staircase that wound down to the floor below. This reminded me of the Heart's Library on the Blue Moon. As we approached the door to the Hall of Records, eight women and two men in the sea-blue uniforms of the Hadrian Guard came from the opposite direction.

"Good!" Verity said. "You're here. I want you to go to the Records Room in Grow Barn One and collect up all the record sticks for the past five years. I also want you to detain Ursa, Tazz, and..." Verity turned to me and asked, "What were the other names you were told?"

"Ajax, Rabeen, and Opheara," I said, checking out the guards, watching for any odd reactions or emotions.

"Yes!" Verity confirmed. "Bring them to the main docking bay in Mid Dome and lock them in one of the empty storage units there. Once you've done that, inform me where you've put them and stand guard, ten of you. Send Private Vabril to us here with those records. And keep your power staffs armed. These people may be dangerous."

"Yes, Second Woman Verity." Captain Saeela placed a fist over her heart and gave us a slight head bow, then turned crisply and marched out with her crew.

"Now we find the truth." Verity went to the records area for Low Dome. There was a wall full of the sticks like the ones we had seen on our second day in Hadria, for the readers similar to ours. Instead of flat, coin like disk books, theirs were stick books. She chose the last five years' worth of sticks, ten sticks in all, and carried them to a standing desk. I came up next to her to watch. She slipped one of the sticks into a round slot and pressed a key on the finger pad. "This is the most recent one from Low Dome," she explained.

Verity pushed another button, and a large screen slid up from the back of the desk. An image appeared on the screen, and she flipped through pages quickly on the face of the screen, evidently knowing what she was looking for.

"Nothing!" She gave me a sideways glance, and went back to scanning. "Not a single thing here about any real problems in the Low Dome. Not production, no unusual deaths, nothing other than a few minor squabbles between some of the workers that Keto seems to have solved justly."

She switched sticks a couple of times and kept reading.

"Can you tell if Keto made these reports?" I asked, curious.

"Oh, good question. Let me check. They have to sign each report with an auto marker."

She flicked through some pages and stopped on the last one in the report. She looked puzzled. "That doesn't look like Keto's signature." She flipped through some more pages on the screen. "It could be?" She did more checking, flipping pages back and forth. "But it doesn't look right to me."

"Could it be a forgery, someone else trying to make it look like his signature?"

Verity pulled out a small scanning device from a drawer and held it up to the screen over the signature. "Well, it isn't his signoff. So yes, it's a false report by someone from down there." She gave a sigh of relief. "It's not him. But how could someone else get reports passed up the line if they don't have his consent?"

More page flipping. "I don't understand," she said, shaking her head.

"If the pieces don't fit, move them around a bit," I shrugged, "and see what shakes out."

Verity stopped on a page. "This is from almost three years ago." She read out loud, "'Ursa helps me from time to time with the record keeping, as she knows all the ins and outs of all the grow barns, having been in charge before I came down here. She's been very helpful.'"

"Check his signature on that report," I said.

She did. "It's genuine." She looked at me, puzzled.

"So, if this one is genuine and the more recent one isn't, do you think he might have just given over the reporting to Ursa?" I asked.

"That wouldn't surprise me. He always felt that work was beneath him," Verity said. "It was Ursa he replaced when the First Woman sent him down there. She has hated Ilantha ever since. Ursa has been a troublemaker and blowfish spike in our side from the first day I can remember ever meeting her. Actually, come to think of it, I don't remember a time when she didn't hate Ilantha even before that."

"It doesn't sound like she held family connections against Keto," I observed.

"Why would she, if he let her retain the power and only acted the figurehead for Ilantha's sake?" Verity took the stick out of the reader and put in another one. "I'll try one from the fifth year back. I noticed that in the most recent report, that is not his genuine signature, and the body of the record has some odd phrasing that doesn't sound like Keto's speech patterns at all." She stopped on a page and, as she read to herself, she was shaking her head. "It's the same pattern as the most recent ones; the use of the word 'topside', for one. Keto would have said 'island.'" She checked the signoff. "This is definitely Ursa!" Verity held up the authenticator device and checked it again.

"Ursa must have just kept doing the reports and signing his name. And no one here in this office bothered to check the signature." Verity shook her head. I felt anger begin to simmer in her.

"It looks like it," I said.

The door to the records room opened and one of the two male guards came in with a pouch of sticks in his hands.

"Ah, Vabril, there you are," Verity said. "Do you know if Captain Saeela has the people I sent her after detained in the bays?"

"Yes. They are in docking bay storage room Theta. We put the two men in the one next to the women; they're in Beta."

Vabril handed Verity the pouch of sticks and left to return to his guard pod and duty.

Verity slid in one of the new sticks. "This is last month's report from Grow Barn One." She went to the beginning of the report. As she read, she nodded. "Then it is as you suspected. This record says they have had twenty-eight children and thirty-seven adults die just in the last month alone, and the First Woman, as usual, didn't even acknowledge their deaths. And that they have reported over and over with special requests for medical aid in the grow barns, with no response from the First or Second Woman. 'We die and they make us fish food because we dare to make a noise about it,'" she read aloud.

"Now we go to Ilantha," I said. "Will we be able to show her these differing accounts there in the Gathering Hall?"

"I'll make sure of it. I'll take a portable reader." Verity put the reader and the sticks in the carry pouch and slung it over her shoulders, making an odd, out-of-sync picture of a beautiful woman in a sapphire form-fitting dress that shone like fish scales or the deepest dark of mother of pearl with a rough-looking work pack on her back.

We headed up the spiral stairs and around the curving hallway. At the Hall entrance, Verity stopped. "I think we should talk to Ursa first." She looked at me, hesitating, then made up her mind and turned back the way we had come. We went to the elevators and down to Mid Dome and to the docking bays.

At Theta bay, Verity saluted the guards and asked to be let in with a power staff. The guards unlocked the door, and we walked in. Ursa stood rigid and defiant, while Rabeen and Opheara and two other women were sitting on the floor of the empty room. Why were they here? Neither one of them were the two nameless women I had seen in the small, dim room. These two sat apart from the others. They were strangers to me, and I didn't know how to tell Verity the guards had netted two who might or might not deserve to be in this room with Ursa.

Verity paused in front of Ursa. "We should have fed you to the fish!" Verity said in a voice I hardly recognized as hers. "You tried to kill that little girl from Nueden." She glanced in my direction. "If it hadn't been for her and her people, we would have shown you no mercy."

Ursa sneered. "Do you think that will make me grateful to that topsider?" She spit at me. I stared at her with a squint to my eyes, feeling the vile hatred roll off of her in waves. She even hated the women who were incarcerated with her. Ursa's thoughts shouted, *They are weak, spineless. Too much empathy and compassion. Too much love! But I am strong. What does love get you? Pain! Nothing but pain! My baby is gone. My man is gone. I will never love again. I am steel and stone, and I will crush you foolish people.*

I crossed my arms over my chest and tilted my head slightly, staring at her. "What was it before the loss of your baby and your man that made you hate so fiercely?" I asked.

She nearly jumped at the shock my words sent through her, as it had been her child and her man she had been thinking of at just that moment. I smiled a knowing smile. It made her shrink back a step as her glare at me intensified, as if she had just picked out a new target to attack. She was such a good sender of thoughts that I was curious to see if she could receive as well. *You think you scare me.* My expression followed my thought to her.

She screamed and fell back against the wall. "What was that?" She looked at Verity, then back at me.

I knew a woman who killed four hundred thousand of her own people. My people. I pushed this at her. *Hate eats the hater, Ursa.*

The woman jumped and screamed again. "What vile evil is this?"

Verity looked puzzled and shook her head. "I think we may need to call the Healers to come and sedate her. She seems a little out of her mind."

"You would be too," Rabeen said from the floor where she sat against the wall. "She has lost everyone in her family in a month's time, but what do you care for that?" the round, dark blue-haired woman flung at us. And if verbal daggers could cut, that one might have hit it's mark with me for poking the troubled woman—what had Little Bee called her? *"... the hurt woman"*... if I hadn't known there had been hate in Ursa's heart long before the loss of her family. The records showed it had been there for at least three years, and longer even than that, according to Verity.

"No!" Verity shook her head. "That woman has hated us for a long time, a very long time. It didn't start a month ago."

I squatted in front of Rabeen. "Can you tell us why?" I glanced over at Opheara and the other two. "Can you? Do you also hate the First Woman and Verity?"

"Why should we care about them?" Opheara whispered. "They don't care about us." She began to cry, which caused a chain reaction with the other women, who began to cry also.

"You only think that because that is what Ursa has been telling you," Verity said. She removed the pack from her back, opened the pouch and pulled out one of the sticks. "She has been sending us false reports about how things are going great down in the barns."

Ursa leapt to her feet. "That's a lie, don't you listen to her!" she screamed, and turning, she tried to attack Verity, who shocked her with the power staff, knocking her back against the wall.

"Try that again and I'll knock you out," Verity warned. "You know what I'm saying is true, and it is you, and maybe my own brother, who are to blame for the deaths in Low Dome. We would have been there with help if you hadn't been sending us false reports. So whose fault is it that your child died and your man is gone?"

The women stared at Ursa with dawning horror, and I felt a wave of guilt join the hate that ate at the broken woman, intensifying the hate because the fault had been pointed out.

"So," I asked, "where is the bomb?"

"You know about the bomb?" Rabeen paled. "But how? There were only a few of us ..."

"Where is it?" Verity knelt down in front of Rabeen. "Save us all, and you will see how much we do care. We are all one people. I will talk to the First Woman and will get to the bottom of this. I will recommend that she clear out the Low Dome of any disease while you are moved to the island."

"It's a lie!" Ursa wailed. "They hate us, they won't let us live. It's a trick. They'll feed us to the fish. Don't tell them anything." She pointed a shaking finger at me. "That one is an evil spirit from up top. Don't trust them." She gave a shuddering breath, clutched her chest and fell to the floor.

I bent down and felt for her pulse. "Call for the Healers, Verity. Hurry. Her heart is hammering like an angry stonemason."

In less time than it had taken us to get down here, the Healers came with their bags and their potions. We all watched as they ministered to the woman on the floor. They scanned her vitals, and one said, "It's her heart. We need to take her to the infirmary immediately."

"All right," said Verity, "but take four of the guards with you. This one is a dangerous woman who plots no good for all of Hadria. So watch her."

***

99

"And then what happened?" Lucus was leaning forward in his chair. Kid, Dray, Bee and I were telling them our story from the day before, with a few small deletions for Lucus's sake. We were all gathered in our living room after eating breakfast together so I could tell them what was going on and why.

"We all noticed that you and the Second Woman were absent from the party," Lucus said.

"Even the First Woman noticed the two of you were gone," Jorame added.

"Verity and I came back after the gathering was over," I said. "We brought with us a woman named Rabeen. She had agreed to help us find a bomb ..."

"A bomb," Lucus lost his weakly held composure and leapt to his feet, looking this way and that as if he might find it in our apartment. The others made a general babbling background noise.

"Sit down, Lucus," I motioned him down, and he fell back in his chair. "We found it. It was the only one they had, and now we have it. We took the woman Rabeen," I looked at our three youngest and nodded at them, "to the First Woman, and she told Ilantha everything she knew that was wrong down in Low Dome. Verity and I told her that the records had been altered to meet the scheming plans of at least Ursa and maybe Keto too, and maybe a few others. Rabeen and Opheara said they didn't know about the altered records and felt completely betrayed by Ursa. I believed them, and now things are changing."

"That's good!" said Kid. "That's very good, as those people deserve better than they were getting. They are the backbone of Hadria and should be given the best, as they keep this place alive."

"That's what Samra told us, anyway," said Dray.

Kid agreed. "It's always the same wherever you go. The working poor have to eat dirt, while those they serve eat the best of everything."

Dray nodded.

"Not on the Blue Moon." Bee said, smiling. "Everyone eats food there. No one eats dirt. We should tell Samra that things are going to change now,"

"I bet she already knows," I said, and patted Bee on the shoulder. "Ilantha and Verity are dealing with the problems that have surfaced in Low Dome and have been moving the people up to the island all night long."

"Is there anything we can do to help?" Rifkin got up and began to pace. "Help them get settled, maybe help put up buildings, like we did in ReMaid? What kind of building supplies are available to use right now, do you know?"

"That would be great," said Bee. "We could all go up and help." *Maybe I could see my friends from the sea*, she thought to me.

I smiled at her. "I think that would be appreciated," I said, and lifted my hand up close to my mouth. I now wore a shell-shaped ring like Verity's, and I tapped its side and spoke into it. "Verity, how are things going? Do you need any help putting up shelters? Or can we help take care of the sick? We could give some of your people a rest while we take their place in the work. All of us would like to help."

"At this point," I heard Verity's tired voice say from the tiny speaker I wore in my ear, "it couldn't hurt. Things are coming along slowly. We have been using the evacuation protocols, which we have never had to use, and quite frankly, we are finding many flaws in the process. If this were a real emergency, I'm afraid we would be in trouble. Come on down to the Theta bay and I'll send a ship to pick you up and bring you out."

CHAPTER TWELVE
(Day Six)

"Pendyse." Captain Saeela gave me a salute and gave a small head bow to our nine. "Second Woman Verity sent me to collect you and take you up to the island. Are you ready? My transport is not far." She eyed Ibera, wearing a touch of worry on her face. "Is the animal all right with other people?"

"She will be no problem," I said.

We followed Saeela to the ship that was boarding the last stragglers from the Low Dome. They were a tired-looking bunch of people carrying bundles and bags of things over their shoulders or on their backs, waiting in line.

"Here, let me help you," I said to an old woman I thought looked as if she was about to fall over while trying to lift a heavy bag. I picked up the large bag and a smaller bundle by her feet, and Rifkin helped her board the ship. She was very old. Rifkin nearly had to lift her up the steps and inside.

"Thank you, young man," she said, out of breath, and sat down in the first available seat. "This is everything I own, and I have no idea where we are going." A tremble filled her voice, and Willobee patted her arm and said, "It's a nice place. You'll like it. Once you rest up, you and I can take a walk in the surf. Would you like that?"

The old woman smiled. "Thank you child, I think I would. But I've been up all night and can hardly keep my eyes open. I think I could sleep, somewhere, anywhere, for a day or two before I do any walking. What is your name, Sweetling, so I can find you tomorrow?"

"I'm Willobee, but my friends just call me Bee. You can call me Bee. Or Sweetling is OK too," Bee said with a smile. "I like that!" This precious child from the Blue Moon gave the old woman a huge grin, and followed us to our seats.

The craft was only half full. Making a fast calculation, I figured a transport this size could only carry about fifty people, certainly not enough to save the close to six thousand people I was told lived in Low Dome. *So how many ships this size do they have?* I wondered. *And how many of the eight thousand Low Domers have died over the last three years? And what is the true count of the population of Low Dome? Or all the domes?*

Once we were sealed in, the ship lifted off the floor of the bay and moved slowly toward the air lock. I tried to count the ships we passed that I thought were the same size or bigger. Once we were inside the lock with the doors closed behind us, the lock filled up with water. I watched Lucus taking in big gulps of air as if he were about to go under water himself. Seeing him in council sessions, no one would have guessed what a fearful person he was. When he was with his fellow council members, he was a confident fellow … when there was no threat in sight. Remembering my fear of what he might do to my friend Wydra at one time made me smile. Now I only feared he might panic and upset the people in the transport.

The sea doors began to open. "Oh, oh, oh," was all Lucus could say.

Bee and the boys had their faces pressed to the windows. "Oh, look at that fish," Bee said. "It has legs."

"That is the Sun Dog Fish," Captain Saeela said. "They are one of our stranger-looking fish. They can't really use their legs." She shivered. "Ugly things."

"Oh, no," said Bee, "not ugly at all. Just odd. And sometimes odd can be beautiful."

"Would you like to see the Great Sea Tree?" Captain Saeela asked the kids.

They all nodded eagerly.

"The Great Sea Tree is sacred to our people," she said. "When you see it, you will know why. It is almost at the end of the island in a coral field, but with this ship, we can be there in just a few minutes."

I heard a man from Low Dome say, "I've never seen it. Have you?" to the woman next to him. She shook her head and said, "I've never been outside Hadria before."

A low, murmured conversation washed back and forth between the twenty or so folk from Low Dome.

The ship followed the underwater side of the mountain, and then began to turn broadside. Everyone on board came to the windows to see this great wonder.

It was a coral structure with limbs and a trunk the size of a large mansion. It branched out like the Wonannonda tree on my island, like the old Telling Tree before it died, only this was underwater, and sunlight was streaming through the Trillium Sea in patterns that hugged and caressed the arms of this rough-textured tree. Glints of many colors sparked off its gnarly branches, the most gorgeous purples and jewel greens I have ever seen, along with every other color in the visible spectrum.

After a collective indrawn breath, there was a silence that held a quality of the holy, just as I had felt in the presence of Telling Tree, and the awe I felt when the twin offspring of Telling Tree grew so fast that day on my island.

This Great Sea Tree held us all in this one breath. And I knew it carried the same spirit as the Wonannonda tree. At that moment, I felt again the kinship of all the people and nature of this world, as I had before. The truth of it reverberated in my heart and soul, in my very blood.

I looked around at the tired faces, now lit with a wonder and awe that matched that of my own people. I wanted to hold this moment forever, to keep it always fresh in my mind. I touched my heart blossom necklace as if to place the image there for safekeeping.

"Pretty spectacular, isn't it?" Saeela said in quiet reverence. We all agreed.

Slowly, the ship pulled away and headed back toward the Hadria end of the island and the beach we had been to when we went to find Bee. We came up out of the sea and landed on the fields above the beach, where the camp was being set up.

"I think we have more people topside right now than are in Hadria," Captain Saeela said, "as many of the Mid Dome people have come to help, too."

"I see Verity and Ilantha." Jorame pointed to a long white tent on the cliff side of an open field.

"That is the Healers' tent," Saeela said. "Well, I am on my way to the tent crew to raise a few more tents. Who would like to join me?"

To my surprise, Lucus was the first in line to follow her. Rifkin, Jorame and the boys fell in line without a word. I felt the lingering spirit of the Great Sea Tree with them, with us all. LaBo, Reia, Bee and I went to the medical tent to help there.

When we arrived at the entrance to the Healer's tent, Verity came to meet us. "The First Woman has worn herself out helping all night. I'm putting her in the tent next to mine for a good long sleep." She rubbed her eyes and yawned as she pointed out the two tents.

"It looks like you could use some sleep yourself, Verity. Why don't you stay with her for a while, too?" I said. She nodded and went to lead Ilantha away from the work.

From the doorway, I spoke to them both. "Don't worry, we know how to do this. After the killing of four hundred thousand, we saw some illness in the people as we made our way through cleaning up and burning our dead. We can follow instructions, and ease and comfort the sick. Things will be all right till you get back."

They boarded a small personal craft that sped away down the bank, onto the beach and up to the far side of the land closer to the cave. I stood there marveling at the technology these people had, and that of the Sabostienie as well. They'd been here a few thousand years longer than we had, and they had not only kept much of their history and knowledge, they had added to it, improved it. Why had we let it all go? To follow what—the dream of a perfect system, a perfect society, a New Eden? How had we lost so much and not even achieved the Eden our first ancestors sought?

A woman garbed from head to toe in pale blue of the Healer craft came and handed me a pair of paper-thin gloves.

"Put these on," she instructed, and handed me a full bedpan. "There is a pit in back of the tent where we have been emptying these. There is a tub of lye and disinfectant there. Toss in a shovel of each, covering well the waste you toss in, and make another trip, then another, until you cannot stand another bedpan, then find me and I'll switch you over to another job."

I hunted out the trench in back and delivered the waste and did what I was told. I sanitized my hands and put on a new pair of gloves, then made another trip. With every pass through the tent, I would stop at a different person and speak with them if they were awake and looking bored. I became acquainted with quite a few of the Low Dome people, and we even shared a laugh or two before I got sick of bedpans and went in search of the head Healer to do something new.

There were twenty Healers and a helping crew of as many, if not a few more, who did the menial work while the Healers administered medical prescriptions of one sort or another, depending on what was needed. I couldn't help but wonder about the benefits of the Purple Tea that had healed me of all my aches, cuts and bruises after I'd been Zee's captive.

There were maybe a few dozen people in all, at different degrees of illness. I'd been told we had had about thirty die who were too far gone to save. The Med-tech Healers were trying to keep anyone who exhibited symptoms of vomiting and diarrhea, or anything they thought was abnormal, away from the general populace. The strange thing was that by the end of the day, most of the people who had lived were feeling so much better. What liquids the sick could keep down and the fresh air seemed to be working wonders, along with the medicine the Healers gave them.

Things were slowing down, and the sun was dropping behind the mountains to our backs. Groups of white tent tops dotted the curve of the half-bowl-shaped valley tucked away above the beach. I stood at the head of the trail Bee had gone down some hours before to look for her friends from the sea.

"There she is," LaBo said, and smiled. "That one will be great someday. She is the spit and wiggle of the Father and Mother, after all."

Laughing, I spotted Bee running in the surf with an Obaskillian child. A shriek of pleasure lifted on the sea breeze, and I could *feel* that pleasure. I could *feel* that bond of friendship. *How strange,* I thought, *that two such different children can connect like that.*

"Isn't it great?" said Reia as she stepped up next to LaBo and me. She took in a deep breath. "Oh, look there is Willobee playing tag." She laughed, and we joined her. Contentment settled upon us, and we sat on some rocks to rest and watch Bee play. Before long, Rifkin, Jorame, Kid, Dray and Lucus trudged over and joined us at the edge of the path down to the beach.

Dropping to the ground, lying back in the grass, the boys were half asleep with exhaustion. "We did good work today," mumbled Dray, and he reached over and slapped hands with Kid.

"We did!" Kid responded, and let his arm fall over his eyes in repose.

The men sat down around us, and we all just watched the ocean roll in and sweep out, the boom and shush of the waves against the cliffs lulling us as the sun went down behind the mountains to our backs.

We sat.

After a while, Verity came up to us. "We have a small ship ready to take you home," she said as she sat down behind me.

I turned to face her. "Did you get any sleep?'

"Yes." Verity yawned and stretched.

"When did you wake up?" I asked.

"A few hours ago. I was over working on tents." She gave Rifkin a crooked grin. "You people know how to work," she said with a rueful chuckle. Then she became serious. "The Healers think those folk were poisoned. But some of them are already up and about."

"That is terrible," Lucus growled into the Mother Moon-lit dark. "How can someone do that to their own people?" His tone was judgmental.

"How is that different than one of our own poisoning thousands of people's minds and then killing them?" Rifkin asked.

"Well ..." Lucus seemed at a loss for words and closed his mouth.

"Let's just agree, whether it is the stomach or the mind," I said, "it should never happen. Never again."

"And," Verity said, standing up, "if I have anything to say about it, it won't." She dusted the sand off her hands and began helping me, and the others up. "We have a cleaning crew down below, and they have found some interesting things there that prove the Healers right about the poisoning." She glanced at Lucus. "Sad to say, but now we know how to medically treat our people. And what to look for." Verity gave a heavy sigh. "What I just don't get is how could that woman, Ursa, poison her own child? And blame us?"

We walked single file down to the beach and the waiting craft. We called Bee to us, and watched her wave good-bye to her friend as he dove into the sea. She came running to us with too much energy for the end of a busy day. Until Bee had gone to play in the surf, she had been a goodwill visitor in the healing tent, and everyone seemed to adore her sweet and spicy nature.

It will be good to have a hot shower and climb between clean sheets and sleep for hours, I thought.

107

Once on board a smaller craft than the one we had arrived in, Captain Saeela at the helm once again, we dipped below the waves.

Bee yawned. Now, with the enforced cessation of motion, I could see the droop to her eyelids. A welling up of love for this child enveloped me.

She turned to me and said, "I love you too, Pen." And almost in the same breath, she said, "Can we go see the Great Sea Tree again, Captain Saeela?"

"Sweet Bee," Reia said, patting Bee's knee, "it's dark. You wouldn't be able to see anything."

"Well," Saeela said, "then you will enjoy a surprise. We can take a pass by, if you'd like."

The children all seemed to wake up at that, and before we could even blink, we were there. This was a smaller but much faster ship than the one we had been in coming up to the island. And the fact of the tree's night beauty was bedazzling beyond surprise.

The phosphorescent glow of the giant coral tree was mesmerizing. And again we held our silence. A sense of peace and the rightness of life flowed into me.

Later, as we pulled into the air lock, Lucus said, "I must admit, the Great Sea Tree is about the most amazing thing I think I've ever seen."

Reia laughed and took his hand, holding it all the way to where we debarked.

CHAPTER THIRTEEN
(Day Seven)

I was the first one up around high light in the domes. I was rummaging around in the kitchen, making us something to eat, wondering where our help staff was, when Reia came sauntering in.

"Where is everyone?" she asked.

"We all slept in, I guess." I yawned and stretched. "Yesterday was a long day."

"But a good one," she said, sort of dreamy-like.

I looked at her more closely. "You seem particularly happy this morning. What's up?"

Reia smiled. "Oh, nothing, really." She twirled over and came to lean on the counter near where I was cutting up sea fruit. "It was just such a good, good day yesterday. We, or you, helped solve one of the problems here. We have our com links back. I got to talk to my daughter Klea last night. And ..."

"And what?"

"Well, I know this is going to sound strange, but I think I'm ..."

Just then, the three men in our party straggled into the kitchen.

"I'm starving!" Rifkin announced, and yawned. "Where's the food?" He looked around as if it would materialize at his hungry wish. "Where is our kitchen staff?" He straightened up and now looked wide awake.

Kid and Dray came banging through the front door as LaBo and Bee were coming down the hall.

"Get dressed!" Kid shouted. "All of you! Hurry!"

"Pack as much of your things as you can stuff in you bags, now," Dray ordered. "They are evacuating Hadria."

"*All* of Hadria!" Kid snapped.

"But why?" Reia asked, bewildered.

"That damned woman escaped," Kid said, "and the bomb is missing."

"What?" Lucus began to wail. "What?"

Reia ran to him. "Don't worry. We will pack and be gone in no time." She pulled him down the hall. We all ran after them, and we were back in the shared quarters in less than five minutes with as much as we could carry. Unfortunately, we didn't have an air pallet.

Ibera was by my side, ready for anything, alert and on guard.

"They said to meet them in the docking bay area. They are leaving from bay one, where we first came in on our arrival." Dray led the way out the door.

I ran up next to the boys. "Where did you hear this news?"

"Samra," Dray answered.

"We were supposed to meet her in the Gardens this morning for breakfast. We waited a long time, and then people began to run; everyone was running," Kid said. "You know something is up when people are looking panicked and running around like fools."

"Just when we thought we'd better go get all of you, Samra came," Dray said.

"OK," I said. "Let's pick up the pace, people. We don't want to be left behind."

We didn't run, but we moved fast and efficiently, heading for the elevators.

How could this happen? I wondered. *Someone must have helped her. Even in the infirmary, there were guards with weapon staffs watching her.*

Verity met us at the bay doors. "Good, Samra got to you. I was about to call you, but it's been absolutely crazy here. Quick, load up." She pointed to a small, sea blue-green, sleek machine. "That one." Verity kept pointing, hurrying us along. "It's Ilantha's personal flagship."

We all boarded. A few of Ilantha's staff and her guards were already on board. Captain Saeela was at the helm. We found seats and shoved our bags under them, and then we were on the move.

My com buzzed. I fished it out of my bag and pushed the speaker button. "Yes!"

110

"It's John." I sensed a shift coming, from bad to worse. "I hate to tell you this."

Everyone in the ship was quiet, tensely waiting for John's next words.

"We have some bad news of our own," I said, "but you first."

"We're not sure how it happened, but the Dunsmier detainees we were holding … escaped. They killed a few of our guards and stole one of the Stella Mara Stinger ships." He paused with a heavy sigh I felt in my own chest.

"Go on!" I said fatalistically. "What else? Who did they kill?"

"Captain Gregson. The head guard," He cleared his throat. "And guards Thomas, Robert and William."

I remembered the talks I'd had with Captain Gregson. He was a good man. I didn't really know the others well, but I had met them. I had talked to all the guards at the detention center at one time or another.

"Are you in your apartment?" John asked.

"No. We're on the First Woman's flagship. Hadria is being evacuated. We have an escapee of our own and a bomb threat."

"Oh. Is everyone with you, our nine?"

"Yes," I said, feeling something horrible coming.

"The Dunsmier solders took one of the Stella Marans. A man named Keto … and Rifkin's father was here talking to Gregson …"

"No … no, no, no, no, no," Rifkin was shaking his head, tears already springing from his eyes.

"I'm so sorry," John said. "There's no easy way to say this. They killed Heronimo too, but they both put up a fierce fight and took out five of the escaping men. They killed Heronimo's hound Violet too, but not before she crippled the man who killed Heronimo. The man isn't dead. We still have him."

I slumped in my seat. There was a deathly silence, except for the sound of Rifkin's grief. Bee went to him and placed her hands on his temples and whispered something in his ear. He quieted, but the tears didn't stop. I knew what she had whispered: "Save your tears for the living." And she had sent him peace, wrapped him in peace. Rifkin knew of their death rituals and what those words meant to Bee's people. He gave Bee a watery smile.

"Pen, are you still there?" John spoke into our quiet. I wondered what Ilantha and Verity were thinking about Keto being taken.

111

"Pen," he repeated.

"Yes. I'm here." I looked out into the Trillium Sea as we shot out of the air lock. Then I looked around at my people. There was a blurring of the edges; it was as if I couldn't distinguish who were my people. They *all* seemed like my people.

My heart ached for my friend Rifkin. I also suffered the loss of his father with him, he had been my friend too, the Nar Hound master, Heronimo ... and Violet, the Nar Hound we had saved together, and our guards, all our dead who had been taken out of our world. Good men all.

I came back to myself to hear John saying, "... they are massing to the north and the southwest."

"I'm sorry. What did you just say?" I was now riveted to his words.

"The Natural Order is marching on Telling Wood."

"What of the Stinger ship, and the man Keto?"

"According to witnesses, Norman boarded with him and a few of Norman's men. The rest walked out of town to the south under the cover of the dark just before dawn, we suspect to join up with the Dunsmier contingent of the Natural Order. The ship went that way too. That's all we know."

"So they have a ship now, too, one that could destroy any one or all of our capital cities," I said.

"It would seem so," John said. "It looks like that war we hoped to avoid is at our door."

"How far out?" I asked.

"Maybe a week at the least."

"Send Wydra and Lodar to the Wells," I said.

"I already tried. Wydra won't go. But Zarek took Lodar and many of the youngest children to the Wells. Hanni and her family went with him to help take care of them all."

"Good." I looked at Verity and Ilantha, who were watching me and listening. "I hope to come and join you soon," I said. "We are on our way to the island. I'll talk to you when we set up. Give Wydra our love. Tell James to keep his Sleeper close and ... well, what is there to say to Heronimo's family? I don't know. Just ... tell them ..."

"I know." John sounded choked up himself. "If you don't call me, I'll get in touch with you."

He broke the connection, and I stared at the com in my hand. Now I would have to face the facts of what was before us on two fronts.

Just as we pulled up onto the beach and were preparing to leave the ship, there was a percussive sound, and the ground shook and a mountain of water sprayed up from the ocean from around the area of Low Dome.

"Oh, Great Mother!" Verity screamed. "There were people still down there!"

"Hadria." Ilantha put her face in her hands and wept. "What have I done?"

"No! This is not your fault." Verity took Ilantha's hands away from her face. "Put the blame where it belongs." She looked around at all the silent people standing by their seats. "You might as well say it. I was the one who spared Ursa's life. Now she has blown up Hadria. This is my fault."

"Oh, get over it!" Lucus snarled. "The fault lies with the person who pushed the button. Don't take that from the one who wanted to kill every one. That wasn't you." He blinked a few times, but then, to my surprise, he continued. "I may not have liked living down there, but this is devastating, even to me. To think that someone could have that much hate in them ... Well, that just isn't right. Ursa is as vile as the Voice was. Maybe not on the same scale, but to the same degree, she is as wicked as that one. So don't you be taking on blame for what that woman did. She did it, not you."

I felt surprised, but grateful to Lucus. *Reia must be rubbing off on him*, I thought. It was pretty much what I would have said if he hadn't. *There is always enough blame to go around, so why take more than your share?* I thought.

The people who were already on the island crowded along the cliffs and on the beach. Weeping and wailing carried on the wind as they pointed to the debris as it began to surface in the boiling cauldron the explosion had produced.

Everyone was stunned at the events that had brought such a rapid change from the hope of yesterday to the despair of today. That would be what Brontis, our Ravenwood Castle keeper, would call war.

"Remember this day. This is what war begins with. This is what war looks like," I spoke softly, but Rifkin put his arm across my shoulders and gave me a squeeze. His eyes were red-rimmed and his hair stood on end, as usual. How I loved this sweet friend. I squeezed him back. We touched foreheads. "I'm so sorry, Rif," I said.

"I hope Samra got out," Dray said. "She said she had to go get her mother."

"How could this happen?" Kid was pasty white, his mouth a pinched circle of anger. "How could someone born here do this to their own city? I know with my head how, but with my heart, I don't understand."

I went to the boys and encircled them in my arms and drew them close. They leaned into me and clung to me as I clung to them.

Everyone left the ship and moved onto the beach. As we were headed up the path to the cliffs, three large ships came out of the Trillium Sea onto land. We all cheered. People were jumping up and down, shouting. Each ship held more than a hundred people. These were the largest ships the Stella Mara had for just such an event. Evac ships.

Captain Saeela ran to the captain of the first ship to land and flung herself into his arms when he came out. People poured from the large loading doors, greeting family and friends who had come up before them.

The two captains came over to Ilantha. "Captain Venree reporting." He clenched his fist and held it over his heart. "We were the last to make it out of the lock, but there are two more ships in there. The bay's air lock doors to outside were damaged in the blast. But they're working to get the air lock open. Low Dome is gone, but the locks between Mid and High Domes are still holding. And we still have communication links with the people trapped inside the bay area."

"That is good news," Verity said, her shoulders relaxing a bit. "Good news. Not all is lost. Maybe we can save the two upper domes."

Captain Venree looked away from Verity and the First Woman, and I realized he wasn't telling them everything.

"What else?" I asked.

He turned back to us. "The blast ... killed some of the Obaskillian that were nearby."

Bee bit her lip and her chin trembled, but that stoic soul didn't cry. "I can't find my friend and his family, Pen." She had her palms up to her temples, and she shut her eyes tight. "He's gone. So is his father. They're all gone." She opened her eyes and walked to the edge of the surf. The other eight of us from Telling Wood went with her to the water. We watched as the sea bubbled and boiled where Low Dome used to be. We saw many floating dead fish and even a few Stella Mara people, but none of the dead we saw were Obaskillian. Some women and men were going out to retrieve the bodies of the Stella Mara floating in the water.

"How do you know the blast killed Fish Children?" Ilantha wanted to know. "Did you see them?"

Captain Venree pressed his lips together and nodded.

"Where are their bodies, then?" Verity asked, a hand shading her eyes as she searched the sea surges.

"I don't know. But I saw them tumbled and tossed by the blast. We felt it in the ships. It's a wonder the three of us didn't crash into each other." He looked down at his feet. "If I could have, I would have brought them to you, First Woman. But we barely survived ourselves."

"If they are truly dead, the sea will bring them to us … in a day or two," Verity said. "Come." She motioned for everyone to follow her up to the cliffs. "We have much to do before night falls."

"Well, I guess we get to camp out on the island," Dray said in a flat, dull voice.

"This isn't the way I thought it would happen," Kid said, the edge of anger still in his voice. "I thought there would be a lot less people here when we camped out."

"Be thankful we are all still alive," Lucus said.

Jorame had picked up Little Bee, and LaBo led the way up the path. We, and all the people from the evac ships, looked like a long, bedraggled, zigzag line up the cliff path. But I felt hope hover over us like a giant winged seabird protecting her chicks.

CHAPTER FOURTEEN
(Day Eight)

The beach was lined with ships glinting in the sunlight as the tide rolled out. Some time during the night, the last two ships from Hadria had managed to get the bay's outer air lock doors open and make it to the beach. Because of the dark, the evacuees had stayed in the ships, sleeping as best they could. Now, as the sun rose, the camp was stirring. The people were searching for family and friends, and regrouping accordingly. There was some jubilation going on, even though many seemed frightened of the outside.

Kid and Dray ran up to me as I stood watching people find family and friends.

"We can't find Samra," Kid said, tight-lipped.

"Her mother is not here either," Dray added. "Samra would never leave without her mother. If she couldn't find her … or if something happened …"

"There are thousands of people here," I said in exasperation. "I'm sure they are here somewhere. They will show up."

"No!" Kid said fiercely. "I feel it in my gut." He hissed, clenching his fist near his belt. "They are not here. You have to do something." His hands motioned around his head. "Like Little Bee can do. We know you can, too."

"Please," Dray said. "Please help us find our friend."

I sighed, feeling the weight of so many needs of all these people, and now this too.

"All right," I said. "Do you know where Bee is? I need her."

116

Ibera bumped my hip with her nose. I absently rubbed her head around her horn.

The boys ran off and came back with Bee and LaBo.

"What's going on?" LaBo ran her hands protectively over Bee's shoulders.

"It's OK, LaBo." Bee smiled up at her. "They just want me to help find our friend Samra. Come on, let's go to the cave. No one is there, and we can be alone." Bee looked at Ibera eye to eye. "She can guard us while we're out."

The people don't like the cave, Bee said to me privately. *They think caves are for Lupa. They think you are like Lupa, only maybe dangerous.*

But … why would they think that? I asked as we wove our way between tents and campfires, heading to the cave at the north end of the beach, Ibera at my heels.

Rabeen has been telling everyone who will listen that you can get inside heads.

Can you tell if she had anything to do with Ursa's escape?

Bee sighed. *Maybe!* She paused on the path, looking at me. We all stopped. *I don't know.* Then she shook her head. *No. I don't think so.*

"OK, let's pick up the pace," I said.

Once we were in the cave, the five of us, and Ibera, sat on the smooth, cold, sandy floor. "I want you to relax and slow your breathing," I said to the others. "LaBo, I know you and Bee can mind touch …"

"Not all the time," LaBo said. "I am not always able …"

"Just try," Dray said. "We will too. We will do anything you say." He was looking at me in such a pleading fashion that I reached over and squeezed his hand.

"We will do everything we can," I said, "with Bee and me together and you three to support our going out and our coming back. You can keep us tethered." I looked around and nodded at each one in turn, then closed my eyes. "Bee, are you ready?" I asked.

"Yes, Pen."

Let's go, then.

We joined hands and breathed together, clearing our minds and relaxing into the silence. I even felt the alert presence of Ibera with us in the connection with Bee. Then we moved out, my little guide and I …

and Ibera? Bee's heart beat a light, steady rhythm. I sensed her smile. We hovered above ourselves.

You think I have taught you things. Bee's mind touch was just a whisper at first, and grew a little louder. *But you have taught me more. You taught me how to* see. *I didn't know we could do that until you; now I can do it too, and I'm getting better at it. I have found my friends, the Fish Children. They are on the other side of the island. I was looking in the wrong place. Did you know there is a tunnel through the island under the ocean? They use it as a shortcut to the other side.*

I am very glad to hear they are safe, I said. *We will talk later about the sea tunnel. Are you ready to search for Samra?"*

I need to tell you: there are Stella Mara people over on the other side of the island, just like you thought. And Ursa's man is one of them. They live in the old wreck of a city there.

Really? That is interesting. But for right now, we need to focus on Samra.

I felt Bee lift up out of the cave, and I was pulled with her. We went to the bay air lock area first. We looked all through the bay area, then we moved into Mid Dome. It was empty, cavernous and empty. We felt no life essences there at all. Our questing senses were drawn upward to High Dome. That is where we found them, Samra and her mother … and Ursa. Samra and her mother were tied up in the beautiful shell chairs Verity and I had sat in as we talked about the possibility of two different records being kept to fool her and Ilantha. Ursa was pacing, a fevered gleam in her eyes, lecturing them.

"You have interfered with me and my life for the last time," Ursa snapped. "You may be my half sister, but my mother was always better loved than yours. Better loved than any of the other women. Better loved than Ilantha herself. And our father always loved me best. I was the first. His favorite. And just because my 'friend' forced you to help me escape from the infirmary doesn't mean I will let you go." Stopping in front of Samra's mother, Ursa shook her head in disgust. "Your pandering to the First Woman makes me sick."

"I did it to save you," Samra's mother sobbed. "Don't you understand? You can get away now. You can be free." The truth I heard in the woman's head was that she had done it to save Samra, her only child, the granddaughter of Rexon I realized.

"Free!" Ursa scoffed. "What do you know of free? You are a slave to that hagfish who stole my father from me. You worked for them. I would have gutted the hagfish the first chance I got. You got to spend time with him that I didn't. That should have been my time. You kept Father's secrets. But I have secrets of my own." Ursa smirked, and a wicked glint sparked in her eyes. "He built me a house on the island. I can go there anytime I want. Right up the tunnel. We used to meet there, Father, Mother and I. It was lovely." Then Ursa whispered through clenched teeth, "Until you ruined it. He died because of you."

Samra's mother moaned. "Why are you saying this?" She was shaking. "You know it's not true. You just want to hurt me. OK, you have me, go ahead, hurt me if you want. But please, let Samra go!"

"No! Mother don't say that!" Samra cried.

Bee, can you try to mind touch with Samra? I asked. *Tell her we are here and that we will come and get them. I'll go in with you. I have a message of my own too. But you speak first.*

"You are pathetic," spat Ursa. "You and your little hagfish daughter. Two troublemakers." She turned her gaze on Samra.

Hold back, Bee, I warned. *Too much attention on her right now.*

"I have a surprise for the two of you," Ursa continued. "In the house you don't believe is there are more explosives. Our first attempt may not have done the job, but the second and third will." She gave a saucy little head motion and grinned. "And you will have the best seats in the house to watch it all go kablooy." She made a sound and motion with her hands like an explosion, and walked over to the dome wall. "Although I have to admit I will miss this place … maybe a bit. But at least *she* won't have it any more. And I'll get *her* in the end. She isn't even one of us. She's a topsider, for Mother's sake."

Ursa kept talking, attention distracted.

Now, I said.

Samra. It's Bee.

Samra tipped her head as if she were listening intently. She carefully looked all around, as far as she could turn her head, as if she were looking for us.

I felt a woof of a *Gruff* and knew without a doubt Ibera was with us too. How could that be possible?

Samra, I am here with Pendyse. We will come and get you. She wants to talk to you now.

I thought Samra was hearing us, but there was nothing coming back in a mind touch way. Then she said, "I hear you!"

Ursa spun around and stared at the girl intently. "I'm glad someone's listening. At least one person in your family has some sense.

119

If your mother had listened to me years ago, maybe this wouldn't be happening to you right now." Ursa tipped her head this way and that. "Too bad!" She walked over to stand in front of Samra and studied her. Samra was holding her breath. I slipped in when she exhaled. "But it's too late now."

Samra, this is Pen. Dray and Kid sent us. We know where you are. We will come for you.

Samra nodded, all the time staring up at Ursa, her eyes round with fear.

"I'm sorry," Ursa said, and shrugged. "For all the good that will do you, when Keto and I blow this place out of the water. You ... will be fish food."

Tell Ursa, 'Your mate is alive and ...'

I suddenly felt a tug back to my body. Bee and I pulled apart. Bee quickly said to Samra, '*... the Fish Children can find him.*'

Then we were speeding back in a flash. And my com link was buzzing in my hip pocket.

It was Wydra.

"Pen. The man Violet crippled is awake," she said. "He thinks he's been out of it for days and that their two army divisions are at our doorstep. He's bragging about how smart their leaders are in the Natural Order and says that there is nothing we can do about them now. He says we will all burn, and that there is nothing we can do, because you're gone and they don't think you can know anything about what is happening up here. But he doesn't know we have com link ability."

"And he told you all this?"

"Well, some of it. Zarek helped pick out a few stubborn pieces."

My eyebrows rose up under the messy curls on my forehead, surprise lancing through me.

We all sat still as stone as we listened to the rest of what Wydra had to say.

"The man Keto helped them break out. Keto is the one who killed Gregson in order to get the keys. He promised to take Norman south if he would make it look like they forced him. And Keto killed the Stella Mara guard where she stood watch over parked Stinger ships. He is coming your direction. He also did something to disable the remaining ships. None of them are working now."

"Yes. I have an independent source who just made it clear to me that Keto is here on the island." I stood in one fluid motion and headed for the beach and Verity. "I have to go," I told Wydra. "Things to deal with of an urgent nature. Lives are at stake. Thanks. I'll com you back when I can."

I clicked off and shoved the com back in my pocket.

"Come on," I said to the others. "I'll tell you on the way what we heard and what we saw in High Dome. Samra and her mother are tied to the seashell chairs in the gathering room. They have more explosives and plan to blow up both domes, along with Samra and her mother."

***

When we stepped out of the cave, it was raining hard. Visibility was next to zero. I had never seen such a downpour. We were all soaked to the skin in seconds. But at least it wasn't cold rain. It took three times as long to get to Verity's tent as it had taken us to get to the cave.

"Wait for me in the cabin," I yelled above the noise of the rain. "As soon as I talk to Verity, I'll come for you. Tell Rifkin and Jorame what I told you. Be ready to go when I get there." The boys and LaBo peeled away and headed for the wreck of a cabin my eight and I had been given to share for the time being.

"Verity, are you there?" Bee and I yelled above the din. The tent flap lifted, and she let us in. Once inside, Ibera shook herself, and Verity turned away from the indoor deluge.

"What is it?" She stood tense, tight, as if the rain had already set her on edge. She looked around at the small quarters and sighed, brushing the droplets of water off herself.

"I remember now why we don't live on the island. It rains. A lot ... Especially on this side! But it usually is short lived, a quick burst of rain like this maybe once a day this time of year. That's why this place is good for growing crops."

She sat down on her cot and motioned us to sit on the other one. We did.

"You look grim, even you, Little Bee, like you're the bearer of bad news." Verity rolled her eyes as if she just didn't want to hear anything more that wasn't something good. She looked tired, and her shoulders slumped in resignation. "All right. Go ahead, make my day."

"Where is Ilantha?" I asked. "I don't think she should hear this, at least not right now. No one else should," I whispered. Bee sat next to me, nodding. And she did look grim. I turned back to Verity and promised myself I would see to Bee's state of mind when things had slowed down some.

Verity rose and poked her head outside and looked around. "No one else is around. I imagine everyone took shelter when the rain started. Ilantha is staying in her flagship. She would never come out in this. Don't worry. What's the problem now?" she asked.

"Well," I said, "do you want the bad news or the good news first?"

"Oh, come on. Don't play with me!" she snapped. "Bad news. Get it over with."

"I just had a com talk with Wydra. One of the escapees who was injured and left behind has come to and, not knowing or thinking that our people could get in touch with us, revealed that Keto has come home ..."

"But how could he get here? Swim?" I felt anger surge in her.

"No!" Bee said in her sweet, innocent voice. "He flew one of the Stingers you left to protect your people. He killed one of your guards to steal it."

"That's not possible." Verity blinked.

"Yes. I'm so sorry to tell you this. He helped those men escape, and they let him go for a ride to their main body of solders," I said, holding her gaze with mine. "Then he came here and helped free Ursa."

Verity put her hands to the sides of her face, stunned. "But ..." She shook her head. "But how can that be? How can you know that?"

Verity! I could hear Bee say in a soft but commanding voice. *Verity, can you hear me?*

Verity was staring at Bee. Her hands fell to her lap, and she nearly fell off the cot. "Yes," Verity said, and Bee and I both felt the shock that rippled through our friend.

Please don't be mad at me, or Pen, Bee continued. *Sometimes we can talk to people in their heads. Only some people can hear us; most can't.*

I could hear Verity think, *Oh, Great Mother, it is true. The mind touching.*

"Yes," I said. "I'm sorry we didn't tell you sooner, but there's been no time ... and at first, I wasn't sure I could trust you. Before we talked and then found out about the records. I wanted to tell you then." I looked down at my folded hands. "The Sabostienie would think it quite rude to look into someone's thoughts without permission, but these have been such stressful times ... and I'm relatively new at this myself. So I apologize for our rudeness."

If you can hear my thoughts, then I must be able to speak to you in like kind, I would think. The emotion I felt now from Verity was a blast of revelation and elation.

Yes. Bee and I said at once. *We hear you.*

Suddenly we were all jumping up and down and hugging, Ibera howling and leaping around. I scooped Bee into my arms, and the four of us nearly fell over the cots trying to dance around the small space.

"I can see why you wouldn't want Ilantha to hear this," Verity said at last.

We all sat down again. There was a buzz in the air, a new vitality. "No," I said, "that wasn't the part I wouldn't want her to hear." Bee and I looked at each other. "We can go places and see things sometimes if we let go of our bodies. It's how I found Bee on the beach."

"I knew it," Verity grinned. "I knew there was something more to that whole story. And the thing that knocked us all to the floor at the Deep Six Lock. That was you." She became more serious "You ... in grief. That was a scream. I still can feel it in my dreams, or nightmares. That was raw power." She was looking at me with something like awe.

Then she began to laugh. When she stopped, she said, "We put listening devices in all your rooms to see if we could hear what your wicked plans might be. And all along, you didn't even need mechanical ears. You could just tune in to the thoughts of any one of us." She began to laugh again.

I sat there, not knowing what to say. I felt no anger toward us, or threat in her laughter.

"Don't you see how ironic that is?" Verity said.

"But it doesn't exactly work that way," I said.

"I want to learn how it does work." Verity reached across the space between the cots and took a hand of each of us. "I want to understand it, and the two of you. Everyone."

"Why?" Bee asked before I could.

"Because I want to be the kind of leader the Father and Mother were." She looked at Little Bee when she said this, then at me, and said, "The leaders you told us about that you so admired. I know I won't measure up to them, but I can head in that direction, just as you are trying to do, Pendyse, Willobee. Now finish your telling, and we will make plans."

"Ilantha is not going to be happy about what we heard," Bee said, shaking her head. "I'm not sure why, but I know it will upset her."

"Rexon had more than one wife," I said, waiting for the explosion.

"You mean mate. We don't call them husband, or wife, for that matter," Verity said. Then she drew up her brows and squinted her eyes at us. "You mean before he and Ilantha ..."

"No ... I think it was during. And not just one extra mate; it could be many. I don't know what the standards for such things are here, but Ursa made it seem very secretive. Ursa said she was one of his daughters and Samra's mother, too, and Ursa implied there were other women with his children."

We quickly told her the rest of what we had seen and heard.

"And Ursa said there were more explosives in this house Rexon built for her on the northwest tip of the island? And that my brother Keto is there right now?" Verity asked.

"Yes," I said. "Well, not exactly. But where else would he be?"

"First things first. Let's rescue Samra and her mother, Lilith."

Bee gave a sigh of relief. "Good."

"All right. How do we do that if the air lock to Mid Dome isn't working?" I asked.

"The tunnels, of course," Verity beamed at me. "Thanks to you, we can make use of them again. But we need to hurry. It will take us some hours, and we don't know how long it will take them to place the explosives in the domes."

"Maybe we can stop them," I said. "We can get Kid, Dray, Rif and Jorame to go get Samra and Lilith. You, Bee and I can go see if we can find this house. Oh, I just realized I saw an image of it in Ursa's mind. It's by a lake and a small falls, and the house is surrounded by trees. Maybe an orchard."

"It's not far! We can go there, with our eyes and minds," Bee said, closing her eyes and reaching out for Verity's hand and mine.

Just breathe deep and slow. I spoke into Verity mind, but I knew Bee was listening also. *Are you ready to try this? Don't let go of our hands. I know it is too soon and without any practice, but necessity may be the best teacher. Remember, don't let go of our hands, no mater what you see.*

"OK." Verity nodded and closed her eyes. We all linked in and took a few deep, calming breaths, Ibera lying on the floor between our feet. I felt her join us in quiet breathing.

After a while, we drifted up, slow and cumbersome, as if we were still in our physical bodies, but we were floating above them, sitting there in a tight little circle, holding hands. After a bit, we moved outside, through the wavering rain and up the mountain, moving faster now, like a ring of shining flowers in the wet wind. We sped over the mountain until we were on the other side, where there was no rain. We swept down into a beautiful valley with a large lake, almost as large as the lake below Ra'Vell Island. At the northern side of the lake was a small falls that sang down a gentle decline from the lake to the sea. The house was like nothing I had ever seen before, all glass and tall wooden beams making a sharp peak. It was not a very large place, but had spectacular placement. A flat wooden deck with no walls strayed out over part of the lake and the beginning of the falls. Behind the house, past the trees, in a wild grain field was the stolen Stinger Keto had used to come here in.

I know where this lake is, Verity said quietly in our minds, as if she were afraid it would startle us into breaking our bond. *I can find this place again in a Stinger of our own.*

Let's see if they're home, I said.

We came closer, and I noticed the wooden deck was wet. The rain had been here too. There was a device like what stonemasons used in our quarry to set off a blast to sheer the stone apart, and a detonator. They were soaked. I wanted to laugh but didn't, as that might disturb our new traveler. Unless they had more explosives, they would have to dry these devices out to make them work. And sometimes, I knew for a fact, water could damage these kinds of devices beyond use. I knew this because of my family's quarry business.

We passed through the glass wall and into the house. It had multiple levels and not many inside walls. I heard voices and steered us toward the sound.

Entering a large bedchamber, we saw a messy bed, low to the floor, placed in the middle of the far wall. Keto was lying back on the bed as if he had sat down at the foot of it and just fallen back, his arm over his eyes. The heat of his anger rose to engulf us. Ursa stood at the threshold of the room.

"But it wasn't my fault!" she wailed.

Keto shot off the bed and onto his feet like a spring uncoiling and was across the room and in her face in the space of a breath, his shaking fist clenched next to her head.

"Are you blaming me? You fool woman!" He turned and paced away from her. I felt it was to keep himself from striking her. That was a point in his favor. "Wasn't it you who left the explosive devices and detonator out on the table? I know I told you to box them and take them inside," Keto shook his head, "but no, you had to have some fun first." He glanced at the bed. "You're getting too old for me. Old and forgetful."

What about the mate she is so fond of? Verity hissed in my mind.

Keto spun and came back toward Ursa. She flinched. "Well, it wasn't my idiot sister who left them out there. It was you." He barked a cruel, hard laugh. His eyes were cold, but his heart was full of a very hot, unreasonable rage. "She never should have allowed the hagfish to close me up in the lightless Low Dome. She will regret that."

Ursa sidled up to him, crablike, and caressed his face. "They both will. You'll see. They will get what they deserve. It will all dry out in a day or two. It will all happen just as we planned."

Then they were kissing, not a gentle, loving kind of kiss, but savage and punishing.

CHAPTER FIFTEEN
(Day Eight)

I've learned enough. I want to go. Verity spoke in our minds, and Bee quickly pulled us back to our waiting bodies. We snapped apart like dry twigs and sat as silent as stone for a few minutes, all of us adjusting to our present realities.

"Well," I finally said, "I think we have a bit of a reprieve. Time to go get Samra."

Then we heard people talking just outside the tent flap. Ibera woofed and wagged her whole behind. My hound dashed outside when she came back towards the tent she was followed by Reia, Lucus and LaBo. We went out to meet them, as the tent was far too small for six people and a Nar Hound. The rain had let up and was now just a fine mist that made the air wet and warm. We greeted our people.

"Where are the boys?" I asked.

"What do you mean?" Lucus's brow furrowed. "They went to get Samra and her mother, like you told them to."

Verity and I looked at each other, shaking our heads at the same time, like a couple of mothers just realizing they had a pair of errant children at a very inconvenient moment.

"I thought they would be all right," Reia said. "Rifkin and Jorame went with them."

"All right, then." I gave a sigh of relief, and said, looking at Verity, "That will free us up to do what we have to do. Will one or two of the Stingers and a few guards be enough?"

Verity pursed her lips, thinking about it. "No. Let's take five ... as many guards as we can take, just in case there are other people

127

guarding the house or the Stinger Keto came here in. I will hand pick them, only those I've worked with before and know well enough to trust with my life."

"What's going on?" Lucus demanded. "What do you need guards and the Stinger ships for?"

"LaBo," Verity turned to the tall woman now holding Little Bee's hand, "will you take Bee and your friends to stay with the First Woman, Ilantha, please? Pendyse and I have some urgent business to attend to, and we would like to make sure you are all kept safe." She looked directly at Lucus. "Especially Ilantha." Verity reached out and put her hand on his shoulder. "This has been a very trying time for her, with all the changes and the fear for Hadria and her people."

"And it could get worse before it gets better," I added under my breath.

Lucus rolled his eyes at being left out of the loop of explanations, but he seemed pleased to have been given a job. He fidgeted and swelled with importance even as he looked irritated. I could feel the mix of emotions roiling in him. He felt he had been personally asked to keep the First Women safe, and it made him proud, but I could see he felt put upon all at once.

But he said, "I will see to it," taking Reia's hand and LaBo's arm to guide them toward the beach path, heading for Ilantha's flagship.

"Ibera, go with them. Keep them safe." I gave her a nudge with my mind, and she loped after them.

Verity and I headed to the southern upper ridge where the Stingers were parked on high ground and where the guards had a temporary guard station overlooking the Hadrians' whole camp.

"I wish we had my cyna-cycle right now," I said as we worked our way through the lines of tents going up the incline of the multi level farmland. "We'd be there already," I said, breathing a bit heavily.

"What's a cyna-cycle?" Verity squinted at me, shading her eyes from the sun that was burning away the mist as she looked at me curiously.

"You don't know about cyna-cycles?" My brows lifted in surprise. "Well, where to begin?" As we paused for a breather on the rise, I told her about the fantastic mode of travel I had only come to know about a little over a year ago, finishing with, "So they are kind of like your sea and airships. I couldn't tell you if they operate on the same principles or not." I shrugged. "They are sort of like your air platforms that you move things and people around on. I'll take you to the Oasis

Wells, where Ilantha was born, and you will see how they are used. What useful machines they are. I have a few on Ra'Vell Island myself, but the Wells are closer to here." I paused. "I think. I'm not sure where here is in relation to Nueden on the whole. Hmmm, I hope I'll get to correct that at some point."

We continued on up the road of hard-packed dirt, now soupy with a thin layer of mud.

Verity smiled at me. "You are an unusual person, Pendyse. You seem to have an insatiable appetite for information of all kinds." She shook her head and said, "But now is not the time; we need to pick up the pace. Can you run?"

We had just reached the top of the rise, and I could see the blue tents of the guard station at the far end, past the Stingers. I said, "Can I run?" and shot away from her in a sprint that soon slowed to a trot. She joined me, and we covered the distance in no time at all. We burst into the main headquarters tent, and the nine women who were there jumped to their feet in alarm, snapping to attention when they realized it was Verity, with their fists over their hearts and with respectful head bows they saluted their commanding officer.

"Where can I find Captain Saeela?" Verity took a deep breath, and, looking at each of the nine guards standing before us, she pointed to five of them in turn. "You, you, you and you two. Come with me." The five came to stand next to us. Verity turned back to the remaining four. "Call in replacement guards for the ones I'm taking. We will be in the air with five Stingers in thirty. Call all guards to alert. I will be back to explain before we leave." She gave a brief salute. "To your posts."

Outside the tent, Verity asked, "Where is Saeela, do any of you know?"

"I believe she is with the First Woman or her mate. I can contact her if you'd like, have her come in." said one of the guards.

"Hmmm," Verity said. "I will go pick her up myself. I will tell Captain Saeela and Ilantha about Keto then. Ilantha may already be aware that something is going on."

"May I ask what is going on?" The same guard wrinkled her brow in puzzlement.

"My brother Keto is on the island, and he is the one who orchestrated Ursa's escape. I know where he is, and we are going to get him. Tell no one what we are doing. We could have betrayers among us."

The five women gave each other grim sidelong looks from the corners of their eyes, nodding. Verity gave each of the five two names and sent them out to find the guards she'd asked for and bring them to the Stinger field.

I remained quiet as she used her ring to contact Saeela. "Captain Saeela, I need you to come with me. I will pick you up in a Stinger in five. I'll be picking up Pendyse's animal, Ibera, too … Leave that to me … I will talk to you and the First Woman when I pick you up."

With that, we went to a Stinger and climbed in, Verity and me in the two front seats.

As we rode down to the curve of the northernmost edge of the beach where Ilantha's flagship was, Verity told me a little bit about the Stingers. "This is a Switch Stinger. The one Keto stole is also a Switch. Captain Saeela knows how to use a Switch to shut down another Stinger." She paused in thought for a moment. "Apparently so does Keto. Where he learned this, I can't guess."

"But it's worth thinking on," I said. "Something I haven't told you about my strange ability is that I can often tell when people are lying or telling the truth. Even when I can't exactly hear their thoughts, I can feel their emotions. I can feel the truth or the lie of it."

Verity glanced at me. "I bet that comes in handy. But it must be limiting to intimate relationships."

"I grew up in a culture where trust can be tricky. I think my instincts were already keen to body language and tone of voice, but this is … more than that. It is …" I shook my head. How could I explain it? I didn't even understand how or why I could do these things myself, but I trusted my own inner senses about this. "And, yes, I suppose it could be a drawback to making friends. But …"

"Don't worry," Verity said, "we'll use it if we need to."

We pulled up on the beach next to Ilantha's flagship and got out.

There was a small crowd gathered around a large fire in the center of logs that had been placed around the flames. I was flooded with memories of hunting trips I had been on with my brother Pelldar, my father, my grandfather and my great-uncles. A warmth not entirely due to the heat of the fire washed over me. I pictured Grandfather Charthandrew smiling as he built the fire up.

"Pen," Verity said, shaking my arm. "Pen. Come on. We should get on with this. Where were you just now?"

"Memories of other campfires, hunting with my family," I said. "It seems like a lifetime ago." We walked along the flagship to the fire and the group of people. "I guess in a way it was."

Captain Saeela and Captain Venree, her mate, were the first to greet us. A few guards had rigged up some sticks in Y shapes and had some fish skewered on a cross stick to cook.

"How did they get the wood to burn? It must have been wet," I said.

"The power staff!" Venree said, smiling. "It has many uses. Are you hungry? It should be ready soon."

Saeela and Verity glanced at each other. "No, but thank you," Verity said. "Captain Venree, we don't have time. I need to talk to you," she indicated Saeela, "and Ilantha in her ship." Turning to me, she said, "I want you and Bee with me."

Venree gave the heart salute and head bow and returned to the fire and fish fry duty with the other guards, leaving Saeela to her business with the Second and First Women.

"Do you think you can show Ilantha how you know the things you know?" Verity asked me.

Saeela looked at me with curiosity but said nothing, just kept pace with us as we walked up to Ilantha.

"Well, what is this new trouble?" the First Woman snapped irritably. "Tell me now."

"Let's talk in your ship." Verity glanced around and gestured toward the flagship door. Ilantha swept toward it in a most regal way.

Bee was watching us. Well, I guess most everyone there was watching us. *Bee, come with us, we need you,* I said. She was on her feet and next to me with her small hand in mine without a word spoken. The First Woman frowned but didn't say anything. Once we were inside, Verity closed the door.

"Well?" said Ilantha.

"May we sit?" Verity suggested. "There are some things you need to know."

We all sat around a small table that was command central for this ship when it was on a mission.

"You wondered about mind touch, Ilantha. You even spoke about it the first day we met."

"Yes?" Ilantha smiled at Little Bee. "You're Sabostienie. Are they going to tell me you can mind speak? That would be a treat with all these horrible things going on."

A look of such powerful concentration came over Bee's face that I knew she was trying to speak mind to mind with Ilantha. I gave her a power boost, joining minds with her.

I can!

Ilantha jumped in her seat. "What was that?"

I can speak to your mind. And I think you can hear me.

The First Woman began to cry. "He was wrong! My father was wrong. I was wrong."

Saeela looked around the circle, frowning. Verity gave her a slight shake of her head.

We have a story to tell you, Bee said. *Will you listen and try to hear what it all means? I don't understand it all, but I know you can; you must, you're the First Woman.*

"Yes. I will listen to your story," Ilantha said.

"What story?" Saeela asked.

"Pen, try her," Verity said.

"What? No!" Ilantha shook her head vehemently. "She can't mind speak, she's not Sabostienie."

Saeela, can you hear me? I said. No response.

Saeela. Bee spoke, and Saeela turned in amazement to her.

Then Bee and I spoke at the same time. *Saeela, listen to our story!* The woman's head snapped around to look at me, eyes wide, then she looked back at Bee.

"I heard you. I heard you both. I don't understand how, but I did." She looked at Ilantha. "I heard them. And you heard them."

"No. I heard Bee," she said, looking at Saeela. Then, turning toward me, she added, "But if you say you heard Pendyse, I believe you. She is more like my sister Lupa every time I learn something new about her."

She looked at me and smiled. "Please continue."

CHAPTER SIXTEEN
(Late Afternoon, Day Eight)

"When we get there, what if he fights back?" I asked Verity as we flew wide out over the northern Trillium Sea to come up behind the house by the lake, shielded by the copses of trees between the lake and the house.

"I have seen his true self. There is no going back from that. And I'm sure he *will* fight back. He won't just give up and let us take him in." She spoke quietly. Sadness laced her voice with regret and longing for a brother she felt she had never known but had only imagined. Even though I could detect the sense of loneliness and feeling of betrayal, there was no taste of bitterness in her emotions, or of revenge.

"Have you thought about what you will do if we can't take him by surprise?" I asked.

"Only my most trusted people know where we're going. I'm sure none of them would tell him, even if they could inform him somehow." Her ire peaked, and she cursed, "Damn the whole lot of them! Anyone who has a traitor's heart."

"Still," I said, "we must be prepared. Maybe we should hold back three of the Stingers for a second landing."

Verity turned and looked at me. "Where do you get these ideas?"

"It's just a feeling I have."

"All right." She switched on the com link and called out to three of the pilots. "Hang back out of sight until I call you in. If you don't hear from us in three spans, come in hot. Don't leave a stick of that house standing."

"What if you're in the house, Second Woman?" one of the pilots said. "What if you're hurt?"

"If I'm in that house and I don't answer back, it will be because I'm dead. Follow my orders and burn the place to the ground. No quarter for the enemy."

The two ships coming in behind us tucked close in to the land and sat down with a quiet whoosh of air as they settled.

"I have a reading on Keto's Stinger. I am disarming it now." Verity tapped out a long code of numbers, and I saw a blue, blinking light go red, then blink out altogether. She grinned.   "Done!"   She said this over the com for all to hear. "And lock down your ships. I don't want someone flying off with one of them," she added. Then she said, "Come on, let's go get our traitor. Take him and anyone with him alive if you can. If not … well, if worse comes to worst, do what you have to, to save Hadria and to save yourselves. You all know what's at stake."

We came to ground and climbed out of the Stinger. I couldn't help feeling awe at the beauty of the landscape. The lake was a sparkling indigo, with mountains rising to the east and south. The flat plain on the western side of the lake stretched out green with waist-tall grass with purple heads for as far as the eye could see to where the land dropped off down to the ocean in the northwest.

The grass rippled green and purple, imitating the lake pushed by the wind. Our three ships were half buried in the tall grass. Only the tops glinted in the sunlight, like bubbles of collected water held by the tall grass.

We were damp to the waist from our trek through the grass. I turned my attention to the wild grove of trees ahead that curled like a crescent wave around the south and west side of the house, and realized they were fruit and nut trees with full, round crowns of greens, pinks and purples, the largest trees I had ever seen in an orchard. Neither fruits nor nuts were ripe yet, but the scent and sight of them reminded me of my home on Ra'Vell Island.

"Pendyse, you take the lead." Verity gave me a bit of a push forward. "You are far more used to being on the ground than we are." Ibera moved as quiet as my shadow beside me into the wild, overgrown orchards, with Verity and Saeela and the four guards with power staffs at the ready in a V formation following us. I had no weapon—well, no cold steel, no slingshot and no bow—but Ibera was only two steps away. I felt the bond rise like mist between us, that strange, mysterious link we had when danger was near. The six people behind me were making so much noise moving through the trees that we'd already lost any element of surprise. If Keto had a watch out on the deck, they would have surely heard us by now. Even though we had only seen Keto and Ursa in the house didn't mean they were the only ones here.

I stopped. Turning, I put my finger to my pursed lips and held up my hand for everyone to stop. Looking in the direction of the house, I scanned the ground beneath the trees. Leaf and tree debris from many years made a thick carpet beneath the orchard, and except for what little rain reached the ground through the heavy canopy, it was dry. I noticed scuff marks in places. I listened. It was far too quiet now that we were all still. Verity moved up beside me.

"What is it?" she whispered, scanning the area as I did. "I don't see anything. Why did you stop? At this rate, we won't even make it to the house in three spans. I'll have to call …"

Ibera began to pace in a semicircle in front of us, agitated, looking up in the trees. I looked up too, and so did Verity.

I spoke in a hushed voice. "Spread out. Watch." I pointed up. "In the trees." I sent my senses up into the canopy. My attention went to the trees closer to the house. There were eight people spread out above us in the direction we were headed. Looking to where I sensed them, I turned and held up one hand, fingers splayed, along with three fingers on my other hand.

One of our guards stepped up quickly to the Second Woman with her power staff raised. I moved just in time, rolling Verity to the ground as the guard swung the staff at her head and caught Saeela a hard but glancing blow on the shoulder. Saeela screamed in pain and rage.

"They know you're here!" yelled the guard who tried to hit Verity. "Help me!" She screamed as I swung a branch at her, cracking her square in the face. She fell like a stone, blood running from a broken nose. Saeela gave her a shot with her power staff. I didn't know if it was a kill shot or not.

All at once, the trees erupted with their yield, man-and woman-sized fruit that was rotten with betrayal, and we were right in the thick of that jam.

And they had power staffs too. I grabbed up the fallen guard's staff. "How do I use this thing?" I yelled and shook it at Saeela.

She turned it on. The head of the staff glowed a faint violet, and there was a buzz in the air around it I could feel all the way down in my bones. "Just point and push this button." She pointed. "But don't try to use the firepower at close range; it can backfire."

I hated using weapons I didn't understand. I carried the staff and the broken branch into the fray.

Three men and thirteen women had dropped from the trees, I had miscalculated, each one with a glowing power staff.

One of the women was Ursa, and one of the men was Keto. He wore an insane grin that marred his good looks as he moved toward Verity with hate in his eyes. More the fool he: he only saw her as his warriors circled ours.

"Sixteen of them, nine of us; back to back!" I yelled as Keto and Ursa closed in on Verity and me.

After Verity shot Ursa with a power blast that knocked her down but not out, Ibera jumped on the fallen woman and pinned her to the ground, holding Ursa by the back of her neck. Ibera was waiting for my command. Ursa could be dead with one bite. "Hold her!" I shouted, blasting a woman who was about to fry Ibera. Then I rushed at Keto just as he and Verity shot each other. Verity went down hard. Keto also fell, shuddering as if he'd been zapped with a ball of lightning. I jumped on his back, dropping my weapons, jerking his left arm and right ankle together and snapping the electric cuffs on him. Grabbing up my staff and bouncing to my feet, I ran over to Verity and felt for a pulse. Nothing. Lightning balls of purple, black and red were zapping around like Dragon Bugs from the Blue Moon.

"Saeela!" I yelled.

Saeela looked over and saw Verity on the ground. The power blast she'd been aiming at one of the male attackers missed. She came running. The guard at Saeela's back used her power staff as a club and cracked the skull of the man Saeela had missed, nearly taking off the top of his head. He was down and I was sure he wouldn't be getting up again.

Saeela and her guard knelt beside Verity.

I had no time to watch or think about my friend; I had to protect her.

The sounds of blows connecting with flesh and bone and the screams and the zap of power staff shots were awful. I wanted to be anywhere but here. One of ours had fallen, fried to a blackened mass of twitching flesh. With a glance, I saw that two of our guards had three women attackers down on the ground and were cuffing them, as I had done to Keto, before I engaged with the last three attackers standing.

They were running straight at me. I blasted the two women, who were a foot apart from each other. They fell beside our fried guard, as dead and blackened as she was. I felt sick.

I thought of Zarek, and everything I'd hoped for, what I wanted for this world. So, this was glorious war. I hated the death. I hated making death. The smell of it, the useless waste.

But I wanted to live. I wanted Verity to live.

The last man was swinging his staff at my head, and I held up mine to block his blow, which reverberated down the handle of my staff, buzzing my fingers. I nearly dropped my staff. He hooked his staff under the glowing head of mine and jerked it out of my numb hands. I looked desperately around for the branch I'd had earlier. He was holding his staff above his head, ready to swing down on me, when Ibera hit him square in the small of his back.

Snap! The sound of that crack and the scream that came with it resounded through the orchard as he fell forward. I dodged out of the way.

Giving the scene a quick survey to make sure our attackers were all down, I went to Verity, who was very pale but half sitting, more like leaning, against Saeela's guard's lap. I didn't know how they had brought her back. I'd been so sure there was no pulse, so afraid there was none, but I was relieved beyond words to see I was wrong.

"I can't tell you how glad I am to see you awake," I said, kneeling beside Verity. "Are you all right?"

"I will be," she said, rubbing her chest. "I can't say that about Ursa." She glanced at the woman. "She won't be a problem anymore. When that man who's still screaming was about to kill you, Ibera snapped her neck and then hit him at a full run. I've never seen anything like it."

"Has anyone notified the other Stingers not to blow up the house?" I asked as an afterthought. "We might need it with all these prisoners and wounded."

"The other ships are already here." Saeela pointed behind me as they landed next to the trees. "My guard, Reeada, commed them." She indicated the woman Verity was leaning against. I didn't know any of the guard's names because we'd been in the air before the niceties could be exchanged.

Out of the ten of us who had entered the trees, three were dead: the traitor and the two guards who'd been burned to death.

Saeela's arm was still painful, but Saeela's guard didn't think anything was broken. The other seven had minor burns, cuts and scrapes. We were better trained ... and perhaps lucky.

Of Keto's people, ten were dead and maybe Keto too; I wasn't sure about him yet. He wasn't currently conscious, at any rate. The man Ibera had hit surely had a broken back. He wasn't moving except for a shudder now and then. He had quit screaming, for the most part. I think he was in shock. The other four women were cuffed but alive and crying bloody murder by the time our other pilots and guards got to us.

"Pendyse," Verity said, and tried to heave herself up to a sitting position. Saeela's guard helped hold her up. "Take five of our people and check the house and surroundings." She was almost as white as a Sabostienie from the effort she made to sit up.

"When you com us," Saeela's guard said, "we'll move the Second Woman to the house where she can rest easy. She can't be exerting herself at this point." The woman spoke like one of their Healers.

"We'll put him ..." Saeela nodded slightly toward the man Ibera was still watching, "in stasis and move him there as well, along with the other live ones." She indicated Keto and his four loud women warriors. So he was alive. I almost thought *That's too bad*, but I checked myself. What would Zarek say about such a thought?

After having someone check on Keto and talking to the recently arrived guards, Verity chose the five she wanted to go with me on a tour of the place, and we left.

"Spread out!" I said as we came to the edge of the trees. "But be careful. These people could have set traps. Look for wires, fresh dirt where they may have planted explosives of some kind. Watch every step."

"I knew Ursa," one of the women said. "She was a nasty bully, but she didn't know anything about bombs." I read the nameplate on her uniform: Zinneeta.

"Well, she sure learned somewhere along the way," I said. "She was the one who blew up Low Dome, with Keto's help."

"Oh," was all she said and moved her attention back to the ground.

We went slowly, foot by foot, and reached the back of the house intact. I felt they wouldn't booby-trap their own living space, their headquarters. I thought we could relax a bit as we circled around to the deck. But I was leading, so I'd be the first to go if I made a mistake, which made me all that much more cautious again.

I stepped up onto the deck. The explosive device that had gotten drenched by the downpour was still sitting where it had been when Verity, Bee and I had made our mind link and come here to see what was going on. I approached it while the others held back, not coming onto the deck but looking at all the surfaces for anything that could possibly be dangerous, even checking underneath the deck.

Being as I grew up around explosives because of our quarry and the stonemason trade my family worked in, I could see the device had been partly disassembled to dry. But it was a different kind of device than I had ever seen before, and I didn't want to touch it.

"Do any of you have experience with explosives?" I asked.

"I have some." The tallest and darkest green woman I had seen among the Hadrians, with hair as green-black as it could get and still be considered green, stepped up onto the deck. She looked without touching any of the parts laid out.

"I could put it back together for you," she said, looking at me with one eyebrow cocked.

"No, thank you. I'd just as soon no one touch it right now."

The woman's brows furrowed in puzzlement.

"What?" I asked.

"That disk with the wire attached ... I've never seen anything like that in one of these before." She stretched out her arm to touch it.

I knocked her hand away. "Don't touch that!"

She looked startled. "Why ever not?"

I checked the nameplate over her heart. "Aaru. If there is any kind of trap here, it will be in something that looks harmless." I looked at the disk and wire. "I'd like some time to study that before anyone puts a hand on it. I'd like to see the rest of us live through all this."

Aaru nodded and stepped back. "I'd prefer that too. Thank you."

"All right! Let's search the house," I said. We carefully went through each room, and the lower level too, and found no deadly weapons or killing devices of any kind. That one bomb and those power staffs may have been all they had. I knew there was a tunnel entrance in the subterranean level of the house, but I would look for it later. I had posted guards in that area in Verity's absence, and for right now, it seemed safe there.

"Aaru, would you com Saeela and tell her we've finished checking the house and to bring the others up?" I asked.

She did, and I sat on the bench that lined the deck on the waterfall side to enjoy the familiar sound of singing water. I closed my eyes, relaxing into meditation, and immediately heard Bee in my thoughts.

Pen! I've been trying to reach you. We're being attacked. I can feel they are trying to get to Ilantha. I'm taking her underwater to my friends.

Can you tell how many are attacking you?

I'm not sure; maybe twenty. They are killing people. Her sending was outraged at that.

Ilantha's guards should be able to take care of that few.

No! I think some of them are her guards. We are almost to the ocean. I got her out just in time. I could feel it coming. No one knows where we are. I'll bring her to you.

That's a long way underwater.

There are caves and tunnels underwater too; the Fish Children know them all. Don't worry. I am with friends.

Blessings to you, then, keep in touch. I'll be waiting.

I hope Willobee is right, I thought to myself. *But what can a six-year-old know of deceit and betrayal?*

I heard that, came to me loud and clear. *I know how to sense a lie, Pen. We'll be all right. I've got to go now. They're waiting. We're under the Trillium Sea.*

I knew I would not have an easy moment until Bee was here with Ilantha.

CHAPTER SEVENTEEN
(The End of Day Eight)

I sat there on the bench, keeping an eye on the bomb, as the sun began to fall behind the orchards into the Trillium Sea. Violet diamonds danced over the lake. The mountains beyond the lake were variegated purple and blue. The sky turned so vivid a beauty that it took my breath away as full dark blinked out the light and blanketed the land.

True Dark was upon us, I realized. It had been so hard to keep moon time when we were under the ocean. I sat in the dark, thinking, until I heard Saeela and the others coming around the backside of the house, power staffs lighting their way. Verity was on a stretcher; so were Keto and the man with the broken back. The four women were shackled together, legs and wrists in a ring. Keto and the man with the broken back were cuffed to the legs of their stretchers.

The guard who helped Saeela with Verity confirmed what I was already sure of, yes, the man's back was broken. That was what Nar Hounds were known for after all. Their horns were bone breakers, and she did what she was bred to do to save me.

Ibera lay at my feet, a full-grown war hound, a mountain of a dog, panting, tired but watchful, eyes on guard for my safety. I felt a rush of love for my purple and white companion. She looked up and whined, then her tongue lolled out and she smiled, I scratched around her horn and ears while all our people came up on the deck and into the house.

I left Ibera to watch over the bomb parts and followed Saeela and her guard, Reeada, as they took Verity to the largest bedchamber, the one we had seen Keto and Ursa in, and put her in that big bed that could fit four grown adults. She looked small and defenseless. Her eyelids were fluttering with the effort to stay awake.

"Can I talk to her?" I asked Reeada.

"You can, but she probably won't remember anything you say. I gave her a restorative. It will make her sleep for eight to twelve hours. It also heals. She needs that time. You may not realize it, but she was dead for a few seconds. But thanks to you, we were able to apply lifesaving measures. I was so afraid." Reeada took a deep breath and looked away.

"I gave the same restorative to Keto and Jussip, the man with the broken back." She gave me a look over her shoulder. "I know him. He used to work in the recycling facility. I never would have thought he'd be part of *this*, whatever *this* is. And Sava, she was my friend ... anyway I *thought* she was my friend, but ..." Her large, dark-green eyes glistened in her light-green face. She turned away from me again.

She was hurting, and what could I say? I know what you're feeling? What good would that do? Would it even scratch the surface of her pain? Her "friend" had meant to kill us all, and I hadn't seen it coming. What good would my platitudes be, even if they were heartfelt?

She walked out of the room, leaving Saeela and me alone with Verity, who began to lightly snore. I debated with myself whether or not to tell Saeela that Ilantha was on her way here, and decided not to. I wanted to talk to Verity first. I would sleep on the outside deck next to Ibera. We had split up what blankets we could find, and there were barely enough for us each to get one. I used my coat as a pillow and curled up with Ibera for warmth. I kept thinking, half afraid to sleep, but I knew Ibera would wake me if anything unusual happened.

Then I remembered the inn we'd stayed at in the Fingers when John and Wydra got married and how the Obaskillians had come into the room and Ibera had slept through it. How had they done that? Would they, could they be a danger to us? To Little Bee and Ilantha?

I thought I wouldn't be able to sleep, but I was so tired. It had been a long and exhausting day, and I had forgotten to ask Bee if Kid, Dray, Jorame and Rifkin had come back yet. And had they found Samra and her mother? Were they all safe, my people? Lucus must have been beside himself with the disappearance of Bee and Ilantha, unless Bee had gotten in touch with LaBo. I hoped she was able to do that. I didn't want Lucus to panic. He shouldn't have to worry if they were safe.

But are they? I was even to tired to search for them.

Even though worry plagued me, soon my eyelids drifted closed, and sleep carried me away.

***

(Morning, Day Nine, one full week)

A noise woke me in the dark. I lay still, listening. What had it been? I felt for Ibera. She wasn't there. I sat up without making a sound. There it was again: the tumble of a stone and a small plop as it went into the water at the bottom of the twelve-foot waterfall, then more sounds, this time of someone scrabbling for footing. I heard Ibera whine down at the bottom of the falls by the small pool. Then I sensed the shape of Bee and Ilantha and five Obaskillian men carrying Ilantha up the steep embankment to the deck.

In less than a flash, I was there to help. Bee, wet and wrinkly, was in my arms the minute she saw me. I couldn't stop hugging her. She kissed my cheek and giggled. What a brave child she was.

"I'm OK!" she said. "We're both OK."

I picked Willobee up and carried her the rest of the way, Ibera leading with her keen eyesight in the grey light of morning. The Obaskillian men carried Ilantha in a webbing of some kind and sat her down on the deck. I gave her my hand and helped her sit up.

"Well, that is the most undignified way to travel I've ever experienced." The First Woman pulled herself to her feet, wet, shivering and exhausted. "As grateful as I am to be alive, I hope never to repeat *that* trip again."

She turned to the five Fish Children and thanked them with hand signs and words.

They understand us fine when we talk to them, Bee whispered in my mind. *They have very good hearing, even better under the water. They know everything!* I smiled at the praise she was giving her friends. She skipped over to the largest man, and he bent down and gave her a hug, his long arms and large webbed hands wrapping her in a tender, protective embrace. When he stood up, the six of them were limed in the first light of day. I could tell they spoke with each other; I could sense the exchange but couldn't understand it. Then the five web-

143

footed seamen stepped off the deck and melted into the shadows and as they returned back under the falls.

Ahhh, I thought, remembering my falls at home. These didn't have the scope of my falls and tunnels, I was sure, but were big enough to bring Bee and Ilantha to me. I'll have to check it out. But right now …

"I need to dry off. And sleep. I am exhausted. What is this place?" Ilantha looked around as the sun peeked over the tops of the mountains, illuminating the outline of the house.

"Here, use my coat. I'll find you some clothes inside." I turned to Ibera. "You stay on guard." Ilantha wrapped herself in the sleep-warm coat. Taking Ilantha by the arm, I led her and Bee into the room where Verity was still asleep.

Saeela and Reeada were also asleep, at the foot of the bed on a mat, sharing one blanket. When we came in, lighting the way with a power staff, they both began to stir. Then Saeela jumped to her feet when she realized the First Woman was there and dripping on the floor.

Reeada used their blanket to wrap Bee in. I went to the cupboards lining one of the walls and began looking through them for the stack of clothes I had seen there last night when we were all looking for bedding.

I pulled out something that looked like a man's dress robe. It would be too big, but at least it would be warm. Bee was drying herself after stripping off her clothes. *I have to find something for her until her things dry*, I thought. Saeela and Reeada were tending to Ilantha's needs as they asked her how she'd gotten there. As they finished drying her off, I wrapped the dress robe around her shoulders, covering her nakedness.

She pulled it tight about herself, and then gasped, "Where did you get this?" She turned to face me. "Where did you get this?" she repeated savagely. "This was Rexon's." She shook a long sleeve at me. "Why is this here?" Her distress was palpable.

"It was in the cupboard over there," I said lamely.

She ran over to where I had pointed and began pulling clothing out. "This is his. And this. Why are they here?" Ilantha began to cry, great, shuddering sobs. We were all at a loss to know what to do. Then I remembered the restorative. "Reeada, do you have more of the restorative with you?"

"Yes! I'll get it." Reeada rummaged in her kit, went over to Ilantha and gave her an injection.

"No … I want to know why … what is this …" Ilantha shook the front of the robe weakly, "doing here." Weeping and pacing, she kept repeating, "I don't understand. I don't understand."

Saeela and Reeada guided her to the bed and tucked her in next to Verity. They tried to remove the robe from her, but she clung to it, pleading, "I want to know. I want … to know." She was drifting, drifting down into sleep.

"She doesn't really want to know," Bee said, taking my hand and leaning against me. "But she already knows," Bee said.

I looked down at this strange child, my eyes filling with tears. Bee squeezed my hand. "It's OK to cry," she said. "When she wakes up, we can talk about it. She won't be so tired."

Bee picked up a shirt and put it on, then crawled up between Verity and Ilantha and went to sleep.

The three of us left awake let go of our tension and left the room.

"What was that all about?" Reeada asked.

Wiping my eyes, I said, "I think I know, but am not at liberty to speak about it right now. Maybe when the two, or rather three, of them are awake …" I shook my head. "This is not going to be easy. Ilantha is going to need people around her who will support her, now more than ever."

I took the two wet blankets they had picked up and were still holding. "If you two will hunt up some breakfast, I will hang these out to dry and go on patrol around the house," I said.

By the time I was ready to leave, others were waking up and moving into the kitchen and dining area.

Aaru came up to me and said, "They said you're going on patrol. I know you have Ibera, but I'll go with you if you want to leave her with the bomb."

"I wish Jorame was here," I said. "He could encase the damn thing in a force field and we wouldn't have to worry about it for awhile." I tapped my fingers on the table were the bomb still sat, undisturbed.

"I know Ibera would like a run," I said, "if you wouldn't mind staying."

"Not at all." Aaru smiled.

I felt for any falsehood in the woman and sensed none. But did that mean there was none? I felt shaken up from the trouble with

145

Ilantha this morning. Could I trust Aaru? Could I trust my own senses right now?

"Remember, don't touch any of those parts," I said. "I still haven't had a chance to …"

"I know." She broke in. "I'll keep it safe. And I won't touch anything." She shook her head.

Ibera was already at my side.

"That is one amazing animal!" Aaru said, still shaking her head slowly. "I would not want to be on the wrong side of those teeth or that horn."

I heard her say in her mind, *I've seen the results of that!*

I nodded in agreement. I picked up the power staff I'd been using, and Ibera and I went off the end of the deck and around the corner of the house.

"Come on, girl, we'll check on the ships first, and swing around and come back by way of the lakeside," I said.

We cut loose and ran. It felt great. I weaved through the orchard, avoiding the place where the killing had happened. I didn't want to see it. The run was all too short. I climbed up on top of one of the ships out in the grasslands and surveyed the landscape for as far as the naked eye could see. Nothing looked disturbed or out of place from what I remembered from the previous day.

I slid off the ship and, attaching the staff to the harness on my back, freeing my hands, I ran like a child, zigzag through the grass, my fingers brushing the purple heads, Ibera bounding beside me, barking and biting at the grass. When I stopped, I was near the lake and she was still zigzagging in leaps and bounds. She was a good head taller than the grass, but when she leapt into the air, she came all the way out of the grass, then disappeared inside it again.

When she came to find me, I was sitting on a large rock overhanging the water. I watched her find her way down to the water's edge and drink. I drank from my canteen, resting on that rock till my breathing came easy again. I relaxed my body. There were so many reminders of home there: the calming shush of the lake, the mountains, the grasslands. I got up.

"Come, Ibera. Come on, girl, time to head back."

In spite of the fact that I knew it was not going to be easy to tell Ilantha that Rexon had more than one woman and who knew how many children, I knew the truth had to be talked about. And even though I knew this was going to break her heart all over again, somehow I felt my spirits lift. Life was full of change. It was the power behind the scenes, always moving, always pushing us toward something new.

We ran along the lake's edge again, but this time in a slow jog, my eyes feasting on everything nature had to offer. We came around the far end of the orchard and up to the house. There were steps on that side of the house leading up to the deck from the lake and falls. I took two steps at a time ... right into a new calamity.

CHAPTER EIGHTEEN
(Day Ten)

Aaru was lying on the deck with Reeada working on her head. Another guard I didn't know the name of was also down and twitching like a fish on a hook. The bomb parts were scattered all over the deck.

"What happened?" I knelt down beside Aaru and saw a long, bloody gash on her forehead.

"It seems we had more than one traitor among us," Saeela said, giving the twitching woman a toe in the ribs.

"Shouldn't someone do something for her?" I asked. "She might be able to tell us if there are any others."

"But would she really tell us?" Reeada snapped. I felt a flare of red-hot anger rise up in her.

"Who's with Verity and Ilantha?" I said, then jumped to my feet and ran into the house, Ibera at my heels.

I breathed a sigh of relief to see the three of them, Verity, Bee and Ilantha, sleeping peacefully. I set Ibera to guard them and went back outside.

Aaru was sitting up, holding a damp towel to her forehead to stop the bleeding. The woman who'd attacked her had stopped moving, and I went to check her. The nameplate said Gale. She was dead.

"She hit me with my own power staff," Aaru said. "She came out to bring me something to eat. I thanked her. I thought it was so nice. She set the food down and picked up my staff. I didn't pay much attention to what she was doing. The next thing I know, I'm lying on the deck, and she's got the bomb parts in both hands, and she's shaking like she's being electrocuted. I didn't know what was happening to her; I didn't understand why I was down. But now I know you saved my life

148

Pendyse, when you said not to touch those things." She put her head down between her knees, breathing raggedly. "Ahhhh, my head hurts. I feel like I'm going to throw up."

Aaru rocked back and forth for a time as we all stood around wishing there was something we could do for her.   After a bit, she strightened back up and quit rocking.

"I think the pain med you gave me is kicking in," Aaru said to Reeada. "And the bleeding has almost stopped." She lifted the towel away from her head.

Reeada checked the wound, turning Aaru's face this way and that. "That thing right over there." Reeada pointed to the disk and wire object Aaru hadn't been able to identify, which now lay inches away from the dead woman's hand. "That's a device the Healers use for a bad heart. Someone amped that one up to kill."

"Evidently no one told her," Saeela said. "I don't understand what is happening!"

"A revolt," I said, sitting down beside Aaru. "They happen when leaders don't talk to their people. Trouble brews when no one listens to each other."

Looking at the bits of the disassembled bomb, I asked, "Aaru, can you tell me which of these pieces won't blow up if I smash them?"

She looked at me, startled. "Well, that one for sure, and ..." she looked around at the scattered parts. "That one. But why would you want to smash them? There are more of them in the hydro facility. Not like this one," she pointed at the biggest piece. "The blaster on this one is many times larger than any I've seen. I'm sure I could put it back together, though."

"You're not doing anything till I stitch up that gash on your head," Reeada said, pulling thread through a curved needle.

"Maybe they use these larger ones somewhere else in the domes," Aaru said. "I don't know." She pointed again to the largest part of the disassembled device. "That's the blaster. Right there."

I pick up a large stone I thought must be used to prop the door open, brought it down with both hands and smashed the first part she had pointed out. Then I did the same to the second one. Again and again, I smashed the parts to rubble. Jumping up, I threw the blaster as far out into the lake as I could.

"No one else is going to die because of this device." I kicked the bomb debris off the deck and went inside, leaving the others all staring after me as if I were a madwoman. *Maybe I am*, I thought.

I went to the bedchamber and lay down on the sleeping mat at the end of the bed. Ibera came and licked my face. I kept telling her to stop, but she wouldn't, her long, wet tongue giving me a good washing until I buried my face in her silky purple ruff. When she was done trying to get at my face, she plopped down beside me. I curled around her, thinking about home and what might be going on there.

A revolt.

Certainly a revolt, from both sides ... Which one was in the right? I know what I thought. But does anyone ever see themselves as being in the wrong?

How can I get everyone to talk? I wondered. *Talk first before spilling blood. Is it too late already? It certainly is for my friend Heronimo, Rifkin's father.* At the thought of that big man dead, my heart squeezed painfully. With everything that had been going on here the last couple of days, I hadn't thought about what might be happening in Telling Wood. Now I felt an urgency to be there. "I need to be there!" I said aloud.

But if things hadn't happened the way they have, Hadria would be gone, along with Ilantha and Verity and all the others I've met, I thought. *And we would never even have known they were once here. On the other hand, Heronimo might still be alive.*

Are there others like the Sabostienies, the Stella Mara and the Obaskillians? What does this world really hold hidden from us? How many others might be out there?

Change. How much can people take in, even when it's needed? Even when it would make life better for everyone, easier for more people? But really, do we have a choice, or must we just roll with the turn of our Earth? Planet? My thoughts spun off in a dozen directions. *I want answers, solutions.*

Real communication. If being here has taught me anything, it is that we must talk. Everyone must have a voice in our decisions, even when we don't like what the other is saying. Even more importantly, we must learn to listen to each other; truly hear each other. And maybe that starts with me. How can I make a difference in this?

And as I looked through the prism of possibilities and impossibilities, I fell asleep thinking, *Please, let someone else do this. I can't; I don't know how.*

***

I woke to someone shaking me. "Pen! Wake up." Bee shook me again. "They're coming!"

Jumping to my feet, crouching in a fighter's stance, I blurrily looked around for attackers and something to fight them with.

No! Bee said in my sleep-fuzzed brain, *not* them—*our friends. Rifkin, Jorame, Lucus and Reia and LaBo. And Iloura, Samra and her mother are coming, too.* Bee was spilling over with excitement; her mind seemed to buzz with overlapping thoughts. *Dray and Kid are coming. Did you know they are going to be Argonauts?*

What are you on about? I sat back down on the mat and rubbed the sleep from my eyes, yawning. *Are the Obaskillians bringing them too?* I was thinking of another soggy entrance.

No, silly. They are coming on Ilantha's flagship. Saeela's mate is bringing them. They stopped the fighting. For now, things are all right again. They left their strongest captains in charge.

I looked at the bed where Verity and Ilantha slept on, and rose to my feet. "All right, then," I said. "Let's go greet them." I took Bee's hand and told Ibera to stay on guard.

Most of our people were out on the deck watching the flagship land on the other side of the small falls. There was a narrow, rocky place for crossing at the top of the falls between the lake and the falls.

"They'll have to get wet if they land there," I said.

"They wanted some separation," Saeela said close to my ear, "just in case we have more revolter's among us. We can't have them hurting the First Woman once we move her over to her ship, can we?"

"No. We can't." I shook my head. "She is quite safe where she is right now, though. Ibera would die before she'd let anyone hurt the First or Second Woman. And I can tell you, we would all know about it by the first howl. No. No one would even be able to get in the room before she would be on them. I'm the only one who can enter at this point. Not even Bee would go in there with Ibera on guard duty." I turned and smiled at Saeela. "If anyone attempted to take a weapon into that room, Ibera would know. She can smell cold steel, like the power staffs, one step beyond the threshold, she would give a warning growl, there would only be one. Death follows." I paused. "That is the kind of guard duty I set her too. Ilantha and Verity are perfectly safe here."

151

"Here they come!" Little Bee clapped her hands. "Look, Pen."

Kid and Dray came stepping from rock to rock across the top of the falls, grinning from ear to ear, calling "Pendyse! Willobee!" hurrying the last half of the way, hardly splashing at all as they came.

Dray was the first across, moving as if he'd been born to walk on wet rocks. He grabbed Bee and whirled her around as she shrieked in delight. When Dray was done, Kid did the same, but with somewhat more reserve and style.

The next thing I know, Rif was doing the twirling and it was me up in the air.

"Put me down!" I cried. When he did, I cuffed him on the shoulder like we always used to do to each other when everyone thought I was boy. He grinned and punched me back. Soon all my people were on the deck, crowding around Bee and me and the new arrivals. Hugs and words flowed sweet and easy among us, with relieved laughter at being together again.

Even Lucus came and gave me a quick, embarrassed hug. Then, stepping back, he said, "See, everyone is safe and sound," then dropped his gaze. "Well, uh, I understand Little Bee and her friends brought the First Woman here to you." He nodded. "Well I'm glad she's safe too."

Suddenly, Ibera set to baying like a banshee, which silenced everyone to an abnormal quiet. Arguing voices rose from the bedchamber, the waterfall next to me imitating those voices in a murmuring gurgle of quarreling.

I strode through the house to silence Ibera and find out what the First and Second Woman could be yelling about.

Entering the room, I said, "Ibera!" and commanded her with hand signs to sit and be quiet. She immediately complied. In the aftermath of her baying, the two arguing voices sounded deafening. Both women were crying, sobbing as they screamed the same thing at the same time to each other: "You should have told me!"

Then they realized I was in the room and Ibera was no longer baying. Their stricken faces turned toward me. Ilantha's face was pale, her lips pinched. Verity gave a shuddering, indrawn breath and wiped the tears from her face with an angry swipe of her hands.

The three of us stood as if transfixed in the moment. Then we all took a deep breath, and Ilantha sat down on the bed, and then immediately leaped to her feet and moved over to a nearby chair.

"That was his bed!" She pointed an accusing finger at the offending piece of furniture. "He slept there with other women."

I didn't want to correct her at that point. At least she knew what she was facing. Her precious Rexon had not been faithful, maybe had never been faithful. She had spent the last seven years grieving for something that may never have been real at all, at least not for him. Now there was a new grief she would have to live through. I felt it all. The pain was so intense I thought it would buckle me; and then Verity was on her knees and crying in Ilantha's arms. They clung together like two lost souls adrift on the sea. But the pain shared by two was half in volume, and I could breathe easier again.

"I'm so sorry," Verity said. "I'm so sorry I had to tell you."

"I know." Ilantha patted Verity's head as it rested upon her breast. "I'm sorry too. I'm sorry you never knew him as your father. I'm sorry I never really knew him. I'm sorry I've wasted so much of my time and energy on something that has led us all to this time and place."

Ilantha looked around the room. I felt her noticing little details that cried out the maker's name. Rexon, Rexon, Rexon.

"He built this place!" She shook her head. "How could he have done this and I never knew about it?"

"How could you know?" Verity's muffled voice asked.

"He loved to work with wood. He spent a great deal of time looking for the right kinds of wood. Now I know all of it. I loved him from the day I first saw him. I loved him to distraction." The First Woman kissed the top of Verity's head. "How long ago did he start sowing seeds of dissent? Did he ever love me as he said?"

I wondered what she meant. Was Rexon Verity's father? That would explain a lot. She hadn't known her father. And what had happened to her mother, really? Was she another of Rexon's women whom Ilantha had found out about?

Ilantha looked over at me and gave me a weak, quivering, watery smile. "Yes," she said, "To all of your questions."

You heard them? I asked in my mind.

Verity sat back a bit. Both women turned more fully toward me, and Verity said, "I think we both heard you."

"Come here, Pendyse," Ilantha said, and motioned me over. Verity rose, and we moved two of the chairs over closer to where Ilantha was sitting.

"Let me tell you what I know about Verity's birth," she said.

153

CHAPTER NINETEEN
(Day Eleven Morning)

"Rexon wanted a child," Ilantha said to the crowd gathered on the deck. Everyone listened with rapt attention to a new strand of Hadrian history.

"I can tell you I did not know he already had several: many daughters, and maybe sons too, according to what Pendyse told Verity she overheard Ursa saying. Ursa thought she was the first of his daughters." Ilantha paused, nodding at me. I felt sorrow swell up and nearly engulf her, but she took a deep breath and moved on with the second telling of her story. "I thought we were true life mates," she said. Her voice trembled a bit.

"Rexon fooled us all. All those women." Ilantha's eyes closed, and the thought came to me, *I wonder what he told them.*

"He fooled me.

"We had tried to have children for many years. But I proved barren," she glanced around the group, "as are too many of our women. I thought Rexon loved me in spite of my inability to give him a child. I was past time for bearing when …

"Anyway, I thought that was what he wanted. But maybe what he really wanted was having many women and the power that being my mate gave him. Twenty-five years ago, he came to me, crying, and told me he had made a terrible mistake and had slept with Verity's mother. He said it only happened once, but that she carried his child. I was crushed. I couldn't understand how he could do that to us; do that to me. Not only did I have to suffer not having a child of my own, but he had made a child with another woman. A woman I knew and liked. A woman I respected and trusted. A much younger woman.

"Rexon promised he would never do that again … if he, if we, could keep the woman and her child close by so he could watch her grow up. How could I deny him the child he seemed to want so desperately, even though he couldn't claim her as his own because he was my mate? He said it would shame me, and he couldn't bear to see me hurt. So I agreed to keep quiet."

Ilantha drifted in memory for a few moments before she took up the story again. "I don't think he was ever who I thought he was." Ilantha, the First Woman, the leader of these people, brushed a tear from her wrinkled cheek.

"My sister, Lupa, was the only other living soul who knew Verity was Rexon's child." Ilantha took Verity's hand. "As you grew, I saw more and more of Rexon in you." Blinking to keep the tears back, she continued. "I grew to love you for yourself. I loved you as if you were my own. It was only natural to take you in after your mother died."

Venree, Saeela's mate, asked, "Is Keto also the child of Rexon?"

Ilantha looked at Verity. "We don't know. Of course, we talked about the possibility."

A woman asked, "How many do you think there are? And could any of them be in danger from these … people … like Keto and Ursa?"

"Or could we be in danger from them?" someone asked.

"At this point," Verity answered, "There is no way of knowing. But I want to meet and get to know anyone who thinks they might be Rexon's children. I wouldn't mind having more brothers and sisters." A thought was sent to Ilantha and me, *Being as Keto has deemed me such a disappointment as a sister.*

"I'm glad Ursa never knew you shared the same father," Ilantha added. "She might have been more focused on getting rid of you early … Oh, excuse me." She looked at Samra and her mother, Lilith. "She seemed to be set on doing away with any siblings. You were the ones she knew about and went after."

"No." Lilith bowed her head. "I think she and maybe Keto knew about others. She tried to use me to hurt you. But I always found ways around her … until just recently."

"Well, I am so glad our new friends were able to save you both," Ilantha said, and she indicated me.

Everyone turned to where I stood by the steps leading to the lake edge, and a round of spontaneous applause broke out. I raise my hand and pointed, the noise abated. "Jorame, Rifkin and the two who wouldn't give up, Kid and Dray, were the ones who went and saved them," I said, and that started the applause all over again. Ilantha spoke when it became quiet and attention returned to her.

"I hope you can forgive me for keeping what I knew from you, from all of you, but I thought it was something just between us, Rexon and I. I had no idea he … I can see now how it has had a detrimental impact on all of us," Ilantha said, looking into each face. "Forgive the years I have languished in grief and not taken the care of my people as I should have.

"I want things to be different from now on, more open, as I see what harm can come from secrets and lies.

"Pendyse tells me we must all begin to tell our stories, to listen to how we feel about things as they happen and as they have happened to us in the past. It might be the only way we can heal the wounds that have divided us. As much as you love my sister, Lupa, I tell you our young guest, Pendyse, is very much like her. Lupa has been telling me for years I need to pay attention to the voice of the people, but I have not been good at listening. I've been good at demanding and keeping the status quo. I've been good at remembering the wrong things and forgetting what is important.

"Now there are people who are dead and others who have spent their lives in the bitter pursuit of resentments because of secrets. People trying to take what I should have been mother enough to give to all of my children, not just to Verity. I have loved you, but I have not loved you well enough.

"I have stumbled.

"We have stumbled.

"Please let us try again … or if you choose, I will step down as First Woman and Verity can lead you in a new way, a younger way of viewing the world.

"Even if that is your will—for Verity to be First Woman—I am not saying this is going to be easy for any of us, but can we try? To live up to the Mother Spirit, to be one as the Sea Tree is one with the ocean, to be one people again, like the sky and the land is one."

The answer came from the woman who had asked about other children. "My name is Anka. I think I might be a sister," she said to Verity, and began to lay bare her life.

Verity had thirty-eight guards left from the ones that had come with her. Thirty-one were women, seven men. Some began to tell their stories. They talked and listened to each other until the sun was nearing the sea.

Everyone helped put together a meal. At this point, we were mostly quiet, digesting the stories we'd heard along with the food we shared.

I felt that people were thinking of what it was they really wanted Hadria to be like, how they wanted to live together in ways where all people got what they needed.

Most of them had agreed, while sharing, that there was much good already about how they lived. They agreed that they did not want to disaggregate their community, but admitted that more could be done to let people choose how they wanted to live their lives, what jobs they wanted or what they wanted to learn. The people were tired of things being decided for them by just a few elite. All agreed there had to be some basic rules to keep order, the simpler the better, something for further discussion tomorrow or the next day, or next month. This was not going to be a short process or a quick fix. And they had to figure out what to do about the immediate problems of the city of Hadria and the displaced Hadrians as soon as possible.

Saeela and her mate stayed with the guards and prisoners in the house while Verity, Ilantha, Iloura, Samra, Lilith and my eight, along with Ibera, crossed the falls to Ilantha's flagship to spend the night.

Rifkin and I were the first on watch beside the falls crossing, along with Ibera.

We talked about our fears for home. He poured out the painful loss of his father, Heronimo. We cried together as good friends will. Halfway through the night, Lucus and Reia came to relieve us. Ibera stayed with them.

Lucus and Reia had become a couple. Life goes on, even in the midst of disruption. Maybe even because of it. *Strange thought.*

Yawning, we went in to get some sleep.

As I was about to sink below the waves of sleep, I heard Zarek's voice in my head, saying, *I am so proud of you!*

But I must have been dreaming.

***

(Day Twelve)

"YOU!" Keto spat at his sister, Verity, and glared at the First Woman. "You vile monsters." He jerked on the chains that held him secure to the wall along with the other three prisoners.

"I don't understand." Ilantha shook her head, looking troubled. "I gave you a home, I loved you, and you call us monsters. Why?"

"Think about it!" Keto snarled, lips twisted in loathing, I could feel the contempt rolling to a boil in him. "You don't love me, you never have! You love her! You never gave me one thing I asked for." He glared at Verity, only a couple of feet from him, her hand raised toward her brother as if she longed to touch him, soothe him. He lunged against the chain and slapped her hand away, hard. Verity jumped back out of his reach. She too shook her head. The pain I felt in her had nothing to do with the welt that was rising on the back of her hand.

"And now I find out you are one of Rexon's get," Keto said. "Wouldn't that have been news for Ursa? That my own dear mother was one of *his* women? Ursa kept denying it, wanted me to believe her mother was the only one, until we found Lilith, then another. We found eight of his women. But she kept saying her mother was his favorite, she was his precious." He laughed. "I bet that pinches a bit," he said to Ilantha. "It certainly bothered Ursa. She wanted to kill them all, but we found some of his women useful, as they had been treated badly by our Rexon. Hadn't they? You would know about that!"

Keto's blue-black hair lay lank on his shoulders. His fine clothes were disheveled and dirty from the fighting two days before and a couple of nights on the stone floor. His blue eyes, the same shade as Verity's, were hot with his unreasoning hatred.

"You killed me," Verity said.

"Too bad you didn't stay dead." He slumped against the wall and slid to the floor, feigning nonchalance I knew he wasn't feeling.

"If you had been a better shot there would have been no coming back at all," Verity said. "I only knocked you out,"

He laughed again. "I knew you couldn't kill me ... sister." He stopped laughing and sneered, "You're soft. You are no kind of leader. You'll drag all Hadrians to their death at the hands of our enemies."

"What enemies?" Ilantha asked.

Keto looked in my direction, locking his venomous gaze on me. *That pink-skinned bitch and her kind,* he thought, but he said nothing.

158

"The only enemy I see here is you," Ilantha said, turning to leave. "An enemy is one who wants to hurt you. That is what you have done. An ally is someone who helps you in times of trouble." At the foot of the stairs, she turned back and gave Keto a cold stare. "I won't forget which one you and your friends are, and the pink-skinned *woman* and her kind are my allies and my friends." Then, with great dignity, she climbed the stairs out of sight.

The look on Keto's handsome light-green face was priceless. Not only did he have a loud mouth, his thoughts were so loud even Ilantha had heard them.

Verity and I followed the First Woman, leaving our prisoners to stew in the turmoil of their own thoughts.

I spoke to Verity's mind. *I bet that will freak them out. They won't know what we can pluck from their heads.*

Verity laughed as we went up the stairs.

***

It was hot in the direct sunlight. We were at the edge of the orchard, overlooking the lake, where we all agreed was the right place to bury the dead.

We had carried the bodies of the fallen, friend and foe alike, and planted them in the earth. This was the only time I have ever seen such a thing done. We carried stones to place at the heads of the graves—that was what Kid called them, graves—and stacked the stones up, making small mounds, and etched their names in a stone we sat on the top of the little *pyramids*—also a word we were unfamiliar with that Kid used.

"I read about this in one of the Old Earth books," he had said.

Everyone worked together to get this done. Ilantha had the prisoners come and watch as we honored all alike. The man with the broken back was still on his stretcher, held in stasis by meds but conscious of his surroundings. The others, shackled uncomfortably together, kept quiet for a change, giving us no trouble.

Verity asked for the Mother to receive the dead, that they might all become part of the Great Mother, and the Sea Tree.

We went back to the house for our last meal together in this place, everyone in a somber mood. We gathered in the great room after we had eaten.

159

"I have talked to Captain Saeela's second in command at Beach Camp," Ilantha said, "and she informed me that people have been working on the main air lock door all morning, and it is functioning at one hundred percent now. Some of the maintenance crews and their guards are going back to assess the damage from the Low Dome explosion."

"Is it totally gone, then?" someone asked. "I grew up there."

"Yes." Verity nodded. "It will have to be rebuilt. If it's what everyone wants."

"But what will we eat over the next few months?" another woman asked. "We got eighty percent of our food from what they produced there."

"Eat the purple-headed grass." Dray stood by a window that looked out at the crescent edge of the orchard, overlooking the sea cliffs and the grass that grew right up to the cliff line. "The people of Isuladune make bread and a lot of other things from it. They call it wheat."

"Harvest it," Kid said. "Cold store it. Use it when you need it. That's what we do in Dunsmier Dakota."

"And I'm sure my friends, the Fish Children, will help you just as they always have." Bee smiled up at the worried guard. "And we will help too." She gave a little nod, as if that settled the matter. I noticed Ilantha cover a small smile, and I felt a wave of adoring love leave her and wash over Little Bee, who looked at Ilantha and smiled.

The First Woman stood up. "I'm going home. I'm very tired. I haven't had a good night's sleep since this all started. I bet none of you have either," Ilantha said and there were a few tired laughs. "For now, we will close up this house and all go back to Beach Camp. I for one have had enough of fresh air and open sky for a while."

"Go pack up whatever you need to take with you," Verity said. "The prisoners will travel with us on the flagship."

"Meet you on the other side of the mountain." Ilantha gave all in the Great Room a heart salute and a head bow. The people returned it to her and began to leave.

Once everyone was gone and only Ilantha, Verity and I were left in the great room, the First Woman took a slow circle around, looking at the place.

"I see him here. In the wood," she said. "He loved working with wood. In the fifty years we were mated, he would often go topside to gather special pieces to bring back to a shop he had in High Dome. Isn't it funny? He was an engineer, he knew how to build things." Ilantha ran her hand over the handrail of the stairs that led up to the bedchambers. "He must have built this place during those trips. And there must have been people who helped him. And I never knew it."

Verity wrapped an arm around the older woman's shoulders, and Ilantha wrapped an arm around Verity's waist.

"I give you this house," she said to Verity. "It is yours. I don't want to come back here for a very long time. Maybe never. But you deserve to have something beautiful from your father. It's just too painful for me to see so much of him here. In the wood, and know he was never really mine."

CHAPTER TWENTY
(Day Thirteen)

By evening, a swarm of guards had passed a mind scan by Ilantha, Verity, Jorame, LaBo, Bee and me. Even though Kid and Dray hadn't shown any true mind touch ability—yet—they both had an excellent sense of intuition, and they sat in on the parade of guards as we listened to them tell what they hoped to see for the future of Hadria. The ones who we didn't have a clear sense of we left to work topside on organizing the hospital and food centers for Beach Camp.

Along the ridge, where there had been farmlands in the past, we could see some permanent buildings going up. In the few days we had been gone, a community had started to take form.

"It's really beautiful here," I said, looking out to sea, talking to no one in particular.

Verity smiled and gazed out to sea also, toward where I imagined Nueden was. "Yes. It is. I realize I haven't appreciated the island and what it has to offer Hadria until now."

"It sure seems like the people are taking to the land," said Kid, "but there are a lot of complaints that the light hurts their eyes. Bee tells me that when the Sabostienie have to work in the day, they wear big shade hats."

"Someone should tell them," Dray added. "Or make some to show them how."

"It's true." Jorame smiled at Willobee as she giggled and wrapped a woven mat on top of her head and pinned it with a thin stick, all lopsided. It stuck up like a one-pole tent.

We had just finished going through a group of scientists and crew members who were essential to the working of the domes and sent them with the guards to get the place back up and running smoothly.

"We should be able to go back home tomorrow," Ilantha said, and sighed. "I'm so ready."

"I'm staying right here at Beach Camp," Lucus said. "Reia and me are staying on the island if you don't mind."

I looked at Reia. She had loved the beauty of the underwater city. Was she really feeling fear about going back there? As I watched her, I realized it was out of respect for Lucus that she was choosing to stay with him topside. Dare I say love? Life is strange. Who would have paired those two?

"That is your choice," Verity said. "We won't force anyone to return to Hadria."

"Know you are welcome there any time," Ilantha said. "I can't provide the luxuries up here that you would have in your apartment, though, but if this is what you want, you can be my eyes and ears up here."

"We can do that!" Lucus nodded. "I think that is something that comes naturally to me." He took Reia's hand as they sat on a sun-bleached log and stared into each other's eyes.

"Come on," Kid said. "I think I'm gonna be sick."

Bee and Dray jumped up. Bee's hat flew off in a breeze, and the three children ran off down the beach chasing it. "Let's go find Iloura," I could hear Kid say. "And Samra," the other two chorused.

Rifkin, Jorame and LaBo sat a short distance away, watching the waves roll in. They were talking, but I couldn't distinguish the words from the murmur of the tide as it came in. I couldn't hear what was being said, so I turned back to Ilantha and Verity.

"I have to go back," I said. "I hear the call of Lupa's cave."

Ilantha and Verity glanced at each other. "We were wondering if you had forgotten," Verity said, and smiled.

"With everything that has happened," Ilantha added.

"I was wondering how long it would take you once we got back on this side of the mountain. Not even a day." Verity's blue eyes stared at me with a bit of a squint. "And when you come back, we must talk to your people in Telling Wood," she said. "We have work to do there. You have helped save my people; now I must do the same for you."

Ilantha nodded agreement. "The others can come tomorrow. We'll go tonight."

***

Ibera and I sat at the mouth of the cave.

I thought about my life and how the culture I grew up in forced me to take the mental shape of a boy. How much I had worried about the changes my body would go through as I became a woman and about how I would hide myself from the horrors of discovery. I felt so grateful I no longer had to worry about that, at least.

What do I feel about my body now? I wondered.

I think it is a good body, I decided. *It does what I tell it to, most of the time.* I grinned, taking a deep breath. Then I sobered, remembering the fight, the dead. *Sometimes it does what I need it to before I tell it.*

It's becoming exactly what it was meant to be. Strong, healthy and womanly.

Ilantha had said you can't take anything into Lupa's sacred cave you weren't born with. You have to go willing to show who you really are … with nothing to cover falsehood, pride or vainglory. She had said you have to go in naked and let the Mother Spirit show you your authentic, original self, and let that be what clothes you on the inside.

Undressing slowly, I folded my clothes in a neat pile a piece at a time. The last thing I removed was my forever blossom necklace, laying it on top of my clothes. A draft from the tunnel glazed my bare skin, making me shiver.

Kneeling beside Ibera, I buried my face in her purple ruff and breathed in her clean dog scent. I didn't have to tell her to guard my things. I knew she would.

It was time.

The call was persistent and strong. It tugged at my heart.

I moved into the small cave entrance, unashamed and soulfully naked.

Soon I was on my hands and knees, crawling. It humbled me to enter the presence of deity on my hands and knees. The smooth floor seemed to go on forever. Eventually, I came to a place where I could no longer even stay on hands and knees. The cave became a round throat with a slight decline. I was being swallowed by the Holy, and I felt a feather of panic brush over my bare skin.

Down on my naked belly, the cold stone felt like silk beneath me. I slid along using my hands and feet to pull and push with, my head

164

and backside barely clearing the smooth top of the narrow tunnel. Breathless, I paused, fearing I might not be able to get back out.

But then I remembered Lupa, a child of six, being called here for the first time, and I breathed in an amazing cool, sweet scent of Telling Tree, which encouraged me to continue.

At last, I arrived at a small, round room large enough to stand up in, but I didn't.

The phosphorescent glow of a sparkling white light dusted the walls and ceiling. It was simple, but at the same time, the most beautiful place I had ever been. I realized I would never be able to describe what it felt like to be in this room, enveloped in light.

I sat on the smooth floor and crossed my legs, resting my shaking hands palms up on my reddened knees, empty, ready to surrender myself and receive what I had been called here for.

No words came to me that I might say, so I kept silent, listening.

An image of Zarek's smiling face rested in my mind. I brushed it away impatiently. I was sure that was not what I was here for. But it came back even stronger. So I sat with it, my heart swelling with love and loss, until I remembered the words his voice had spoken. Had it been a dream? *I am so proud of you.*

But wasn't that a dream? Wishful thinking?

The hushed stillness in this sacred space caressed me.

Who are you? What are you? I cast out a mind quest.

You already know me, Pendyse. The voice was not discernibly male or female. It was both at the same time, yet neither. *I am Way Maker, Truth Teller, Path Finder, Parent. I go by many names and images of creation, comfort and correction. I am perceived by the need and understanding of my children. But more than any other name I go by, my name and my image is Love.*

An image of Father, Mother and all my loved ones lost and living visited my perceptions, and when they had gone, my face was wet with tears.

I am in all that loving.

A warmth embraced me, infusing me with a strength and capacity to receive even more. And with every breath, I felt myself expand to meet this larger love.

Even at the bottom of the sea, I can find you. You are precious to me, my child. As are all my children. You will always be welcome to come back here, but you don't need to, as I am everywhere: your Telling

Tree, Rush River, Ra'Vell Island, the Great Sea Tree, the wheat in the fields, the mountains and lakes and the people.

Especially the people, the infinite, invisible, intimate presence continued. *I will always be as close to you as breathing. Let your breath remind you, I am.*

But there is so much I don't know.

The sparkle on the walls and ceiling intensified, and I heard laughter.

Do you think a flower is born in full bloom?

I thought about that.

It's a seed first. The voice said. *Then a shoot, and then a flower, bit by bit,*

"Oh." The sound of my own voice startled me.

Even a flower at the end of its life doesn't understand all of what it is and will become, and neither can you. Accept what you can do. More understanding will come.

I sat in comfortable silence for a time, thinking of all the people I knew and loved and how that group had grown. I thought about what I wanted for them and even for people I didn't know but felt a kinship with. This loving settled on me and in me. Seeing my naked self from outside myself, I realized there was a glow of that love at the core of me, like the walls of this cave. Was that what I was meant to be? Was that my authentic, original self? Love? Sanctuary?

Go now! The voice urged. *Your people need you. Some need more time as seeds in the ground; some will need to be rectified to the new realities that are coming. It's time!*

I felt the slow withdrawal of the presence and immediately wanted it back, like a greedy child at the breast being bereft of its immediate supply of sustenance.

A tickle of a whisper said, *Don't worry, I am still here. Remember, I am with you always.* And I felt an extra thumping in my chest, like someone tapping me there.

I breathed in and out a few times.

"OK," I said, and began my journey out of the cave.

***

My eight, Ilantha, Verity, Saeela, Venree and a few others were gathered on one of their largest transport ships, going over the plans for the trip back to Telling Wood one more time.

LaBo, Bee, the boys, Lucus and Reia were staying here with Ilantha. I was leaving Ibera on guard, the boys in charge of keeping her fed and watered.

Jorame, Rifkin and I were going in the flagship to Telling Wood with Verity.

"We can take all the transport ships and a few others, just in case the army is bigger than your people think. We can move maybe twelve hundred people at one time," Venree said, "if they don't want to talk about how you can all live together peaceably."

"If they try to put up a fight, we will simply put them to sleep and transport the lot of them to one of the habitable islands hundreds of miles away from Hadria," said Saeela.

"And leave them there to fend for themselves and live as they say they want to," finished Venree.

"That seems like a fair solution," the guard Aaru said, "If you don't want to kill them, which we could do."

"But we are all choosing to do things differently," Verity corrected. "Putting the rebels to sleep and moving them will be good enough."

We all nodded, looking at the computer image of Telling Wood one last time. *We've gone over and over our plans,* I thought. *What could go wrong?* But I knew things are never as simple or as easy in real life as what you plan them to be. You have to expect the unexpected.

"We all go in cloaked on the northeast side, close to Forest Deep, between the forest and the city. There is plenty of room there, and they won't be able to see us when we land and let down the cloak shields," I said, pointing to the spot on the map. "There is plenty of cover from the forest while we debark and move into the city."

"John and Wydra say the army divisions are massed on the northwest side of the city," Jorame pointed them out, "and the south central side. Unless they've managed to slip into the city under cover and are spying on what the city is doing to fortify, they won't know we've even come in."

"Unless ..." I mouthed under my breath, "Expect the unexpected."

Jorame glanced in my direction, a bit of a frown on his face.

"Now that all our ships have been modified per Zarek's instructions and with your help, Jorame," Verity said, "we can land undetected and keep the ships safe while the Stingers equipped with wide-sweeping Rectifiers put the soldiers to sleep. If they won't listen, we can move them to their new home and they can talk to themselves when they wake up."

"Along with Keto and his bunch. We have around thirty or so at present in holding," Ilantha said, "but maybe they should go to their own island, as I'm not sure they wouldn't be killed by your bunch, Pen, just because they're different."

I nodded, knowing the truth of it while hoping I understood the reference to Rectifying some of my people in order to give them time to think before war tore us apart.

"Well, OK then. Time to fly." Rifkin grimaced. "Let's go home, Pen."

He was thinking of his father, gone now, and the brothers he wanted to see, and his mother, along with his father's kennel of Nar Hounds. A hundred of them had been pressed into service keeping guard day and night around the main entrances of the city.

"Everything is ready." Verity put her hand on my shoulder. "Shall we go?"

We lifted off the beach, fifty ships of varying sizes, over half of them Stinger ships.

All of Hadria was on the cliffs to watch us leave.

Ilantha had loyal and faithful people in control of the progress being made on the island. I turned my thoughts to our mission in Telling Wood.

***

Telling Wood was built on high ground and walled, with nine wide gates that used to be open all the time but were now closed due to the Natural Order troops camped in the fields just outside the city. It wouldn't be easy to besiege. Maybe they were having second thoughts. *Maybe there can be a peaceful resolution to this*, I thought, even though doubt waged war with hope.

The troops had been camped there for a couple of days now and done nothing, made no moves, according to the watchers on the walls. That suited me fine, but what were they waiting for was the question. What were they doing while waiting? What were they thinking?

The watchers said they didn't even have siege engines. How did they intend to breach the city walls?

John told me Wallace William Waldorf was the leader of the Natural Order, which didn't surprise me. He was one of the very richest men of Nueden, whose ways were cast in stone, literally: he was another quarryman, the owner of Black Stone Quarry. He wouldn't be an easy enemy. To hear tell, he had been incensed when he'd heard that his quarry's black stone monoliths that sat behind the Telling Wood throne, which bore the Code, the Creed and the Law, had been sanded down. The Council of Nine had voted them removed from the Chamber House after the mass murder by the Voice. They had been her rules, her laws and the people didn't want them anymore, all but the few who ran with the Natural Order.

"Wally," as all his followers called him, was someone Father had told me to stay away from, a man he never liked and didn't trust, even though he was a fellow quarryman. "He's a bombastic, sneaky narcissist," Father had said. "But never think he's stupid just because he's a loudmouth who says mean and stupid things. Wally's as clever as a field fox."

Wallace William Waldorf was the only man I knew who had three names and was proud of it. I had seen him in the crowds on festival days in Telling Wood. A certain type of people loved him and followed him around like he was king. In fact, Wallace William Waldorf always liked to remind people he was in King Edward's lineage. He liked to brag that he was the best, the smartest, the richest … you name it and he would say he had it mastered better than anyone else.

Wally was a short, round man with outsized hands and a red-orange fringe of hair that he combed over a bald spot. He wore a thin, reddish mustache with large gems braided into the two long streamers that hung down upon his barrel chest. Those gems would wink in the sunlight and catch people's attention.

Look at me! Look at me! I always thought they shouted.

169

The Steel Dick had been one of his adoring fans. That alone had been enough to make me stay away from him, even if Father hadn't warned me about the man.

Wally was the antithesis of everything my father stood for.

Now it looked as if I would have to meet him face to face and try to negotiate a peace agreement. I wasn't looking forward to that.

The flight was long. Many of us dozed until we arrived at Forest Deep.

CHAPTER TWENTY-ONE
(Evening, Day Fifteen)

Night cloaked us as we debarked the ships. Once we were near the northeast gate, the shields were turned on again to keep the ships unseen, at least from a distance. Nothing could hide them from someone who ran into them by accident.

The smell of the forest was a rich, sweet pinkpine smell that grounded me to home but at the same time made me tense, knowing what I was coming home to.

Then the gate opened and John and Wydra were there to meet us, along with Julka and James.

"Great Creator, it's good to see you!" John said, and Wydra enveloped me in a hug. Then John hugged us both at the same time.

James and Rifkin slugged each other playfully. Jorame and Julka greeted each other with no words at all, in each other's arms.

Guards hushed us and urged us through the gate. We had sixty-three people with us, and we hurried to get the gate closed and barred behind us.

John, Wydra and James had brought with them five work-sized cyna-cycles. I was very glad to see them, as I knew how far it was to my home, where most of these people would be staying. Some of them would spend the night at John's boarding house.

Platforms were extended. "Don't worry," Verity said. "I think this is like our air carriers."

"Just step onto them." Saeela did so to demonstrate. Venree stepped up next to her.

Verity got on the platform with John and Wydra and me, along with about ten others, everyone grabbing onto the person next to them as John made a jerky start. "I see you've been practicing," I said with a chuckle. "At least you didn't spill us."

At John and Wydra's too-large house that had been turned into a boarding house, we dropped off about thirty people with their gear. Wydra had seen to it that there were people there to show the newcomers to their rooms.

"Thank you for your hospitality." Verity rested a hand on Wydra's shoulder. "My people thank you."

As we continued on to my place, I noticed that work had been done in the fourteen days we'd been gone. Things were looking good. And even with the army camped outside our walls, the people seemed purposeful, not downcast. They seemed confident. And even though there were families who'd left Telling Wood after the tragedy, there had been new people who came in to work and rebuild our nation's capital.

"John, how many people would you say are in Telling Wood currently?" I asked.

"Maybe four times as many as are out there in Waldorf's army. Oh, I'd say, a little over four thousand, men, women and children. Once the people heard you were coming with allies, everyone perked up. As Waldorf's men came on us a few days ago, this place had the stench of despair about it because so many have taken the pledge."

"What pledge?" I asked.

"Not to lift arms against another. Many thought they would die or be swallowed up into the old ways by the Natural Order. But now everyone's outlook has changed, thanks to you. And you, of course," he said, and nodded to Verity.

Four thousand seemed like a lot after the horrendous event of the Life Stealer bombs that ripped through nearly the entire population of four hundred thousand people. I shuddered at the memory.

"Are the Life Stealers still under shield at the Chamber House?" I asked.

"Oh, yes! And under guard day and night," Wydra affirmed. "No one's getting close to them."

We pulled up in front of my home and went inside. The aroma of a fresh-cooked meal made my mouth water.

"What is that delicious smell?" Saeela lifted her head and took in a deep breath.

"Let's go find out," John said. "A certain cook came in yesterday when he heard you were going to be here. He said you had to be fed properly and that no one else could do it."

"Chet!" I yelled as we entered the dining area. "Chet, I'm home."

The round, apple-cheeked man came out of the kitchen, dusting flour from his hands. "A feast for sore eyes," he said, coming toward me, arms outstretched. His embrace left white handprints on my back, I knew, but I didn't care.

"So, so good to see you," I said. "And I can't wait to see what you have for us."

We spent the next few minutes on introductions all around, then sat down for a meal to remember. Most of our guests seemed pleased with it. But I remembered how, only fourteen days ago, we were eating strange food, some of which we liked and some of which we thought was … well, not edible. It made me smile. I felt almost happy, and certainly grateful to be home.

We talked till well past midnight, people getting to know each other. I got to talk to Lupa and all of their nine. Cyrus was a boy of seven, smart and sweet, who left early for bed after dinner, along with Lodar, but Cyrus kept showing back up. I knew exactly how he felt. At his age, I'd always hated being shuffled off to bed when the most interesting things were happening.

At last, I crawled into bed and slept soundly till morning.

***

(Day Sixteen)

Wydra and Verity were dressing me. As if I couldn't dress myself. But they had a certain look in mind for my meeting with Wallace William Waldorf and wouldn't be put off. Even though I wanted to wear my comfortable, regular clothes, they wouldn't hear of it.

I had known Wydra and Verity were two of a kind, and they had become instant friends. I almost envied their relationship's easy beginnings. But it did please me.

Once again, I was pinched into a skintight body suit, black and plain, with long sleeves and a high collar up under my chin, a sheer,

173

purple-silver tunic that fell to the knee and ridiculous calf-high boots that had two-inch platform soles with three-inch heels.

"He's a very short man. Don't you think this is a bit intimidating?" I said doubtfully.

"No," Wydra said. "I heard somewhere that Wally loves tall women. I want him to think he can sway you. That his great prowess can woo you."

"I don't know," I said, with a wobble to my walk, "how impressed will he be if I fall at his feet?"

"Don't worry, I've never known you to be clumsy," Wydra said. "Besides, he thinks all women are stupid anyway, so he won't be looking at your brain."

"We want him distracted so you can get a gauge on what they are thinking," said Verity. "While he's looking at your ... style ... and grace."

Lupa came into the room where I was being made into ... what, a trap? Was this right?

"Look what they've done to me, Lupa," I said. "I hardly feel like myself."

"But you do look beautiful!" Her smile was so serene that I relaxed a bit. "Here, John gave me these. Said they were your mother's. Chet brought them with him when he came. He was sure you were going to need them."

She pulled out the emerald collar necklace and ring. I took the necklace and fastened it around my neck. And the ring, I slid on my finger. I was feeling choked up and couldn't speak.

"You know, when you are facing an enemy, you must look your best on the bargaining floor and your most fierce on the battlefield," Lupa said. "This is a bit of both." She reached up and adjusted my black purple sheened curls over one shoulder.

"Now, I would like to speak with Pendyse alone," Lupa commanded with her gentle eyes on Verity and Wydra. "We have matters to discuss."

"Well, we've done our part," Wydra said.

Verity smiled and nodded. "And look at her. Regal. And strong."

They left the room.

"And close the door, please!" Lupa's raised voice brought Verity back.

She grinned in at us. "You know me too well, Lupa," she said, and closed the door.

174

"Sit down, dear," Lupa said to me.

"I don't know if I can, this thing is so tight, Lupa." But I did sit, and found the material had give after all.

"I am glad you went to the Mother," she said. "Although we call IT that, the Great Spirit is more. I know what you shared with me last night has great meaning for you … and me. I always wondered why it was so easy to communicate without speaking out loud. Then I met Zarek." She laughed. "He has shown me how to do that with other people."

We are becoming one people! Her mind touch was gentle but firm.

I nod. *I see it too.*

We must bring others in as they are ready. She clasped my hand, and the grip of her tiny hand was strong and sure. *You have many gifts. You have been forged in the Spirit. Trust that link.*

I will do my best.

"I had a dream last night." Lupa's eyes clouded with worry. "I saw panic, and fear. Families running to the Zap Station." She shook her head. "But I can't say what it means."

"Did you feel this was … imminent?" All at once, alarm prickled up and down my spine. "Have you talked with Zarek about this?"

"No, I'm telling you."

"OK. Will you tell him too?

"It may just be because an army is camped outside these walls. It sets us all on edge," Lupa said.

"You just told me to trust that link. *This is something, Lupa.* Not just about the possible siege. I think we should listen to your dream and have Zarek and John start moving families out in a calm and orderly fashion. Get people down to the Zap and off east and west, just in case. What can it hurt if it is just an exercise? In fact, we can call it an exercise."

"Ilantha told me so much about the exodus from Hadria and the horrible potential for what could have happened there." She wrung her hands, unaware she was doing so. "I just don't want something like that to happen here too."

I looked at my cell watch. "It's about time for me to go. Please tell Zarek and John, Wydra, all of them. They need to start moving people out of the city, I'm sure of it. As many as they can stuff into those Zap cars."

Lupa stood, tucking a strand of lime-green hair behind her small, shell-like ear. She nodded, and I rose and embraced her. *I love you already, my beautiful friend.*

As I do you.

Her smile grew sure and radiant. *Yes. I knew it. The Mother chose well with you.*

***

"Remember, this button will put them to sleep if you need it," Verity said and handed me the modified power staff. "But it will no longer kill anyone. We've modified all of them back home too," she said for the benefit of all my friends ready to see me off. "If you keep this one on, we will be able to hear every word said."

"And this button," Saeela said. "When you turn it on, you will have a shield like the one Verity had when you first saw her. They won't be able to see the body shield. But nothing can penetrate it." I flipped that switch and she demonstrated by trying to give me a good whack with a staff. It bounced off the shield about two feet out from my body.

Zarek brought out the new cyna-cycle. Sleek black. No designs, all business, no curlicues. It was beautiful. Made for speed. I would have loved to just get on it, set the cloak and ride right past the army, all the way out to Isuladune.

I sighed. I caught a small smile cross Zarek's lips. My heart skipped a beat. Was he reading my emotions? I longed to talk to him, but ... but ... Instead, I just said, "Thank you, Zarek."

He nodded, face grim again.

I climbed onto the cycle. "On," I said. I rose two feet off the ground and without another word they opened the gate and I headed out.

We had sent Wally a message wrapped around an arrow shaft, saying that I wanted to meet with him outside the northwest gate near his camp. We had spies who knew which camp was his.

Norman, Kid's father, was his captain in the other camp to the south. I wondered if they had spent any time talking about me—to be specific, about my ability to hear thoughts. I didn't want to be rude, but we needed to catch what we could. It might mean life or death for my people.

Then I remembered Wallace William Waldorf was also a child of the Parent. How do you love an enemy? Can you make an enemy a

176

friend? Maybe. But my thoughts flicked to Zee, the Voice, and I shuddered. There was no way she would have ever chosen to become a friend. She'd lost her True Self centuries before we met.

I took a deep breath as I pulled up in front of Wallace William Waldorf's camp. A wall of men were standing to receive me, wearing fighting gear, with bows and arrows, spears and swords and hard, angry looks. The hate I felt emanating from them was all because I was a woman. I still didn't feel quite like an adult, although I was certainly of marrying and childbearing age by Nueden standards. For both genders, fourteen was considered adult enough.

There was no trouble figuring out which one was Wally. His presence leapt out at you, bigger than life, even though he was of diminutive stature. A broadsword was strapped to his very round middle, his girth not being diminutive. He wore a gold metallic robe with white fur trim. His clothes and mustache were bedecked with gems and gold beads that sparkled in the sun, but all I could see was the black aura that surrounded him, as real as the black stone dust from his quarry.

My heart sank.

CHAPTER TWENTY-TWO
(Afternoon, Day Sixteen)

Zarek. I sent him the black-shrouded image of the man I saw before me. I didn't expect an answer, but got one.

I'm here. I'm with you. I see him.

My eyes widened at Zarek's response. Wally must have thought that was meant for him, because he gave me a flirty, lopsided grin, as if I had been impressed by his magnificence. I sucked in air and straightened my spine, stretching to my full five feet, nine inches holding my somewhat military stance. With the extra three inches my boots gave me, I was six feet tall to his … maybe five, five.

You keep him busy. I'll scan for stray thoughts.

"Some of my men said you were a looker," Wally said. "I see they were right. I remember your father. Too bad he's dead now."

I didn't correct him.

"Tragedy, really." He smirked. "He was always a good competitor, with his Rose Stone."

I knew he cared nothing about my family, not as competitors in the stonemason and quarry business or in any other way. I didn't say anything.

"I remember your mother, too," he continued. "I wanted that piece, but your father got to her before I could. You certainly are her spit and image."

His gaze traveled down the black-clad shape of my very visible body and back up again, pausing at the V of my legs and then moving on up to my breasts, now well defined by the tight bodysuit and on display through the silvery-purple, gauzy tunic. The look in his eyes made me

178

want to cover myself with my hands. I forced them to remain where they were, at my sides, holding the power staff firmly in my grip. My feet were set apart in a fighter's stance.

"Although your family always had some real funny ideas," Wally said. "Mostly about women and ed-u-ca-tion." He said it like that, spreading out the syllables as if they were nasty words, too dirty to cross his lips, as if the words education and women in the same sentence left a bad taste in his mouth.

The horrid little man stepped out of line and paced in front of me, but not too close. After all, I did have something I could club him with. He stopped about four feet away. "Can you speak? Or are you struck dumb by my brilliance?"

"Yes!" I said, "I can speak very well ..."

Watch what you're saying, Zarek cautioned.

... as I was one of those women who got an education in spite of men like you, I finished my thought so only Zarek could hear.

"I will enjoy showing you what a woman is for. You are beautiful enough to be my queen." He smirked. The thought nearly gagged me. "You even have a scepter. You want to be my queen don't you?" His eyes made the journey down my body again. "But you'd have to be re-educated to your new station in life."

Such I tempting offer, I thought.

"That might take some physical work. You look pretty cocky to me." One sausage-like finger went to his lips. "Oh, that's right, you're a changeling, aren't you? Grew up as a boy. How did you pull it off for so long?" He nodded and made a little semicircle around me. "To save your city, would you bow to me? I can see you as one of my wives. Maybe even queen."

Fat chance, that! Zarek sounded indignant at the idea. My heart leapt and I smiled, not thinking of my audience.

"Oh, you like that idea, do you? I could give you the world. And you would give me some fine, handsome, strong, **tall** sons."

Then I felt and heard some of the thoughts of his men. *Yeah, and when he tires of you like he does all of his women, I'd get a shot at you, me and half his army. You're just my type.* And, *Never mind that skinny bitch; there are plenty of fresh women behind those walls.* And, *Too tall for my tastes. She looks like she could fight back. No thanks. He can keep her, and welcome to her.*

179

It went on and on. A smile was plastered to my face to keep me from searching out the thinkers of such thoughts and putting them to sleep just on general principle.

Bombs ... I heard someone think. *If Wally can't have this city, he'll level it along with everyone inside. This bitch can't fool him with her phony smile.*

I hadn't been listening to Wally's droning voice, but then I heard him say, "Is it a deal?" All my rehearsed words were gone, my tongue stuck to the roof of my mouth. I didn't know what deal he was talking about.

He wants to marry you. He'll let everyone live if you'll give him the city without a fight. Not just the city, he wants the whole damned country. Plus. The anger I felt coming from Zarek was strange. Never in the short time we had spent together had I ever felt such anger in him.

"What do you say?" Wally asked.

"Let me think about it," I said. "Maybe I'll be able to sweeten the deal. You might give me a crown, but I could give you the moon." I was so glad he couldn't hear my thoughts, because I was thinking I'd die before I gave him anything. "I'll give you my answer tomorrow. Same time, same place."

"What?" He looked put out at being put off for even a day. I realized no woman had ever had a choice with him before, and he wasn't happy about my answer.

Numb and feeling as stupid as he said women were, I climbed on the cycle and zoomed away before any more could be said.

We have to move the people out of the city. Fast. Before morning, I sent to Zarek.

***

The city was a hubbub of activity. Zap cars were being filled, and Verity had the transporter ships come in cloaked, one ship at a time, and gather up as many people as a ship could carry, then another and another till they were all filled.

"Where do you want me to take them?" Captain Saeela commed me.

"The closest city east of here. Then come back as fast as you can for more."

Rifkin and James ran up just as the sun was setting. "Some of our guards and war hounds discovered a man swimming downriver to the south," Rifkin huffed, out of breath. "There is a hole in the river grate. We've got spies among us. We know that for sure now."

"A woman was found in the Song Tower by the Chamber House." James said, "She was trying to send a light signal message to the north, straight up the north ridge, directly up Ridge River. There must be someone up there too, waiting."

"I think we stopped her before any message was sent. But we can't be sure. We need to deploy the Stingers as fast as we can," James gasped, still out of breath from running. "Put the whole damned lot of them to sleep before someone gets the message to blow this city sky high."

"We have no idea who has the trigger, or where it is." Rifkin's breath came fast and hard.

James nodded. "Or where the bombs are."

"Does anyone know how many people are still left in the city?" I asked.

"John says about half," Rifkin replied. "Maybe two thousand or less.

"Tell John to get on the next transport along with Lupa and her crew. I'm giving you the responsibility of seeing they comply and of keeping them safe," I said to Rifkin. He gave me a curt salute and ran off toward my home.

"James, come with me," I said.

James jumped on a work cycle that was parked by the Chamber House. I climbed on the fast black cycle from earlier in the day.

After some searching, we found Verity and asked her to deploy the Stingers. "Put the two army divisions to sleep now," I barked as I got back on my black cycle. James followed on the large work cycle, and we sped through the still-too-crowded streets to his home to make sure his remaining brothers and their families were ready to leave. When the Voice had bombed and burned much of the city, half of his very large family had been killed, and I wasn't going to let that happen again.

"Get your family out of the city and as far away as you can." I spoke to him through the helmet communicators. "Go to your Montana Resort homes."

"What about you?" James said. "I'm not leaving you."

When we pulled up in front of his home complex the family had been rebuilding, some of his brothers were milling about, helping the wives carry things to where several cycles were parked out in the square, their extended pallets being loaded with all kinds of things the wives wanted to take with them. I was amazed at such stupidity in the face of likely or at least possible death, and my incredulity at the menfolk allowing it sparked a tirade from me.

"Things can be replaced. Lives cannot. You should know that better than most. Those cycles' pallets are for people, not things. Take the bare necessities and move it!" I shouted. "We have no idea how much time we have. Get out of here. Now!"

I was back on the black cycle and speeding away from James and his people. "Make them move!" I said into the helmet com. "Take them out the southeast gate and get them as far away from here as you can by morning. I don't care what you tell them. Give them a good scare if you have to."

"Yes, boss," James said with a grin in his voice. "Great Creator, I've missed you."

I laughed. "Just be safe. OK? Now get out of here. I'll be following you soon. I have to go check on something."

In the public square, another transporter was loading people on board. I saw that the streets were emptying out. A few people didn't want to leave their homes and property, and I couldn't convince all of them to get out by any means available. Some of them didn't believe Wally would really destroy Telling Wood. I heard someone say, "It is the capital, after all." And, "If he wants to be king of Nueden, he must have somewhere to be king from." "He isn't all bad," someone else said.

"Yes!" I replied, "He is! And if you stay here, you're likely going to die." As I left the knot of people, I hoped they would listen. I didn't want to be an alarmist, but they hadn't seen that black miasma that gathered around the man. There was such a thing as evil in the world, for I had seen it in Zee, the Voice, but I just never realized how far it reached or how deep it went.

I pulled up in front of Chamber House and hurried inside.

The guards were there, six of them, equipped with Sleepers, swords and knives. No one was getting past them.

"It's almost morning," I said. "You need to leave. There's a transporter out there now."

"But who will keep these Life Stealers safe?" one of them asked. "And out of the hands of another madman?"

"Or woman!" another of the guards said.

182

Just then, a guard came running in, yelling, "The Chamber House has explosives all around the building. We just discovered them on our outside patrol. What do we do?" Panic was in the guard's voice.

Even though my heart was hammering and my ears felt like they were burning with sound, I still remained calm on the outside. "Leave! All of you, leave; get anyone you can find and get out of the city at once."

"What are you going to do?" someone asked me.

The sound in my head reverberated the information I wanted, needed, if these guys would leave and let me focus. "Just go. I need you to go." Good and faithful solders, they hesitated only a moment then followed orders.

I sat down cross-legged in front of my small table where the Life Stealers were in their shielded box. If this building came down, what would happen to the shield for the Life Stealers? Would it hold? With so many of those white spheres inside the box … I tried to focus on who might have the trigger or the multiple triggers for the bombs spread through out the city and where those people might be.

I felt like I was about there when Zarek rushed in. "What are you doing? We've got to get out of here!" he cried.

"But I can almost see where …"

He jerked me to my feet and pulled at me. "It doesn't matter. It's too late. We have to go." He clasped my hand, and we ran outside to the black cycle. Zarek swung me onto the cycle and got on in front of me, and we snapped on our helmets and raced for the southeast gate we knew would be left open. He skirted the outside wall, going so fast we flew over Ridge River and blurred past Captain Norman's sleeping camp. Natural sleep or otherwise, if the killing of this city crushed loose those Life Stealers, they would all be as dead as the city. Maybe all of us would be! Who knew how far that many Life Stealers would reach? Maybe all of Nueden.

Why are we going west? I asked Zarek.

I am taking you home to Ra'Vell Island.

We were already past the place the Voice had tested the first Life Stealer before we heard the first explosion go off. We kept going. Zarek poured on the speed until we were pulling up out of the bowl valley, twice as far away from Telling Wood as I had been that first time when one Life Stealer took nearly four hundred thousand lives. Zarek pulled to a stop at the edge of the valley, and we turned and saw explosion after explosion in the distance. Fire lit the night sky. Dawn came without notice, rivaled by more plumes of flame reaching for the ghost of Mother Moon in the dusky morning sky.

Even if there might be no one there to push the buttons anymore, the heat itself would finish the job. Our capital city was engulfed in flames and destruction, two thousand years' worth of history destroyed in a few hours.

We got off the cycle and sat in the grass. I wept. Zarek held me, rocking me gently. I kept weeping, inconsolable, fear for the people palpable in every sob. Did they all get away?

Then we saw what I was waiting for in the center of the city, the biggest explosion of all.

Chamber House.

A wave of distortion rose up and shimmered in the black cloud-filled air and fell back to city streets. It was happening again.

"At least we'll die together," I said, sure we weren't far enough away, nor would we have been even if we'd kept going on the cycle at top speed. I thought that many white spheres must be powerful enough to wipe us all out.

Zarek drew me closer and cradled me against him in a tight embrace as we watched the city burn from forty miles away. We waited for what would come.

And we waited.

When the sun was directly overhead, we decided we weren't going to die that day after all and began trying to get in touch with our people through the cycle's long-distance communicators. I also tried the ring Verity gave me. Nothing worked.

CHAPTER TWENTY-THREE
(Day Seventeen)

"I have failed them?" I said after a very long period of silence between Zarek and me.

"No! Anyone who is still alive is alive because of you," he said.

We have to go back.

No! I'm taking you home, where you will be safe.

"Zarek," I said out loud, and faced him. "We haven't even made contact with anyone yet. I need to know how bad it is."

"Or how successful you were at getting people out. I understand."

"And to see if anyone can be reached from there. Have you found Wydra or Jorame by mind touch?" I looked off toward the still-burning city. The flames were dying out in some places now, or diminishing enough so I couldn't see the fire anymore from this far away, only the black billowing smoke.

"No," Zarek admitted. "I've been trying. But don't know what direction to focus on."

"We have to go back," I repeated.

His large, luminous purple eyes and catlike pupils were narrowed to fine slits against the sun's glare. His pearly white face, tinged a slight pink, shone in the light of high noon.

"You're getting too much sun," I said, simply drinking in his presence, not knowing when this might end. I noticed again that he had cut his long braid off at the nape of his neck and now wore his hair loose to ruffle in the breeze.

I wanted to cry over the loss of it, a disproportionate emotion compared to what had just happened to our capital city. But I had loved his purple braid.

Hair grows back.

How strange, I thought. *I have longed for this touching of minds, and here I am on the rim of the world, over forty miles out from Telling Wood, with so much fear for my people, and he picks out of my mind the worry over the loss of his braid.*

"I cut it off when Jorame, Wydra and I pledged to quit drinking the Purple Tea," Zarek said.

"But you're the Father now. What about your people?"

"Life is not lived in a box, Pendyse. Everything around us is changing. And everything we do now will change the world around us too." Zarek looked at me with such longing in his eyes. *I guess I was making an attempt to fit in with your people.*

"Why did you stop being my friend?" I looked away from him, not wanting him to see the hurt in my eyes, even though I knew he could already feel it, as I could feel his longing.

He took my face in his hands and turned me to look at him. "You're so young. You should have a chance to live your life and fall in love, and have a family …"

My mind instantly flashed back to something Jorame had said about humans and Sabostienies not being able to procreate together, and some things became clearer to me at last.

"What if I'm OK with not having children?" I said. "What if I'm already in love and will never think of anyone else in that way? What if you're it? The only one in all the wide worlds I want to be with? What then?" I tilted my face up to his, steel in my gaze.

"I would say you're young and …"

I kissed him hard and felt a corresponding feeling flare from him into me and back again. The kiss deepened.

You love me! I thought fiercely. *I can feel it. I may be young, but I'm not a child. I may not know what I'm doing, but I know what I want.*

He pulled back from me, still holding my face cupped in his hands. "I know. I just wanted to give you a chance for a normal …"

"Ha! I've never had normal, and you know it. You're just being a coward."

That made him stop and consider.

"Maybe," he admitted. "It does scare me how strong my feelings are for you. How I know where you are and what is happening to you at all times. How I'm always afraid that light, which is your life, will blink out because of men like Waldorf or Keto. How could I live with that loss?"

I began to laugh. When I could speak, I said, "Then don't squander the time we could have. Life is short. And for you, it just got shorter if you're not drinking the tea anymore. And if there is one thing I know from living what life I've already had, it is that loss is not something we can ~~avoid or~~ plan for or avoid. It happens, so we might as well take the good with bad and do the best we can. How could you even think to live with the loss of never having ... us? That's a loss I don't want to live with."

We turned, sliding into a silent, easy embrace, side by side, my head tucked against his small, shell-like ear, to watch the burning city die. The skies became black with smoke and ash and a falling haze, the wind pushing the black cloud north into Forest Deep and up Ridge River. We stood watching for a long time, basking in the light of each other, not wanting to move back into the world.

But then we knew it was time to go.

Together, I think we can do something good in this world, we thought at the same time. Then we laughed at the synchronicity, the mutuality, what we had missed about each other, as we climbed onto the cycle and headed back toward Telling Wood.

***

(Late Afternoon, Day Seventeen)

As we neared the camp of the army division to the south, we saw all their tents and equipment still standing where they had been when we'd sped past them as they slept. The tent flaps were screaming in the high winds, as if the wind wanted to scour everything clean and be done with killing. The horses and dogs and men were unrecognizable, just twists of flesh and bone, not even enough to gather and burn ... or maybe too much.

"I think there has been burning enough," I said. "Let the carrion birds have them. They will go to Tomorrow Land in the belly of sky flyers. That will have to be good enough." The camp was full of large red and black birds pecking in the stink, flapping their wings like the tents in the wind.

187

"So this is what comes from too many of the white spheres exploding in one place," Zarek said, eyes full of sadness. "Waldorf was caught in his own scheme. What he meant to have happen to others, he did to himself. Didn't his spies tell him about the Life Stealers? Couldn't he have put two and two together and figured this might happen."

"At least we will never have to worry about any more of those horrible inventions."

"No." Zarek's tone was flat, his voice brittle. "Nothing like that will ever be made again, if I—if we have anything to say about it."

The city was as unrecognizable as the camp we surveyed. No building remained standing or whole, and fires still burned here and there. Fire and rubble, and craters from bomb blasts, were all that remained of this once fair capital. The only living things that kept moving through the city were Ridge River and the wind.

Zarek and I stood at the edge of what had been southeast gate, staring at the ruins.

"It's as if the river and the wind wish to wash this land clean of all reminders of the life it once held," he said.

"As if the river and the wind know the shame of the acts done here," I added. "So this is what war creates. I've already seen to much of it in my life."

"Rubble and refugees." Zarek nodded.

The scope of it was far more than I could take in. We turned toward the Steel Desert and Montana Lake and rode until we couldn't see anything of Telling Wood. We stopped and tried to contact any of our people. Still nothing.

We ate some of our food supplies from the cycle and stretched our legs for a bit before we headed southwest toward Montana Lake and Resort town.

The sun will be setting soon. Zarek's gentle mind nudge woke me from a drowse.

I answered in kind, *We'll have to make camp or continue on to Resort Town. That's where I sent James and his family.*

Let's keep going, he said.

I knew what he was feeling. The dark made the land feel even more empty than it felt in the daylight. I snuggled against his back. "Do you want me to take over for awhile?" I said into the helmet com.

"I'm good."

"I know that! But do you want me to let you rest for a while?"

188

Zarek laughed. So did I. It was hard to believe we could still laugh.

Not long after that, we began to catch a glimmer of lights now and then as we climbed into the mountains, following the lighted path. Montana Lake was at an elevation of over five thousand feet, and the mountain was full of steep ravines and lighted bridges.

"These are solar lights to mark the way to the resort town at night. Years ago, a few traveling parties were delayed past dark, and there were a couple of incidents where a horse team and wagon went over some cliff areas on the path," I said, feeling a little edgy. "Maybe we …"

"Don't worry. This isn't a horse or wagon." Zarek turned up the casting light to full illumination to make me feel better. "We have a panel of sensors, and I can get readings of the land mass around us without a problem. And my eyesight at night is excellent."

I smiled, remembering my walk through the dark tunnels in the Heart of Moon City with him and Mergel. I started to ask, "How's …"

"Mergel is fine," Zarek said. In fact, he is still with your father and sister, Panda, in Well One."

"Planning roads?"

I sensed him smile and settled down to drowse some more. I hadn't slept in two days, except for catnaps here and there. I wondered how Zarek kept going. *I'm pretty sure he couldn't have gotten any more sleep than me*, I thought. Then I was drifting.

***

(Day Eighteen)

When I woke, it was to sunshine and the loud and raucous voices of ravens arguing.

I sat up and realized I was in a thermal sleeping bag, with an empty, rumpled bag next to me. The song of a brook nearby made me wish I had a toothbrush. I got up, looking around for Zarek. The cycle was there, even though he wasn't. I dug out a canteen from the kit on the side of the cycle and went down to the brook.

Zarek had a fishing line in the water and a few small fish on a catch line, cleaned and ready to cook.

"How are we going to cook those?" I asked. "We have no pan."

He turned and smiled. "You're up. When I couldn't go any farther last night and was afraid you'd fall off the cycle, I stopped. You were snoring."

"Noooo!" I elongated the *o* in disbelief. "I don't snore!"

"You were so far into sleep that I moved you over to the grass, laid out the sleeping bag, rolled you into it, and closed it, and you never opened an eye."

I stretched and yawned. "I feel pretty good for sleeping on the ground."

"Yeah," he said as he took the fish and carried them over to the cycle, "me too."

There were some flat, roundish rocks there that looked red-hot. Zarek lay the fish on the hot stones, and they began to sizzle. "Oh," I said, impressed.

"Breakfast." He grinned up at me from his kneeling position. "You didn't think I was going to make you eat them raw, did you?"

I shrugged. "The Stella Mara eat some fish raw," I said matter-of-factly.

Zarek sat on the ground, leaned against a log and patted a place next to him. I sat down. "Tell me about them!" He took my hand in his and laced fingers with mine. "Tell me about Hadria."

We talked while the fish fried. I told him of the most recent things that had happened as we warmed ourselves beside the stones, a dual use for the heat cooking our breakfast. A cycle that could heat stones was a good thing to have in the wilderness, as the shadows from the tall trees made it a little chilly under their boughs.

When the fish was tender and flaky, we ate, talked and licked our fingers. When we were finished, we washed up in the brook.

It was as if we were the only two people in the world. I stood for a long time soaking in the scent of the air and the sigh of the gentle wind dancing with the branches above our heads. The musical accompaniment of the clack and rub, the creak of the swaying limbs was all so comforting, as if reassuring us that all life could be this balanced and peaceful. I sighed.

"I know," Zarek said. *We will come back here someday and stay for a while.*

I nodded. *But now we have to focus on the future.*

One small step at a time; we will do the first small thing, then the next small thing. Help where we can and do what we can, and soon the little things will add up to the big things. Small steps. We don't have to do this alone. In fact, we can't. It belongs to all of us, if it belongs to any of us, both the successes and the failures.

I nodded. "Yes, I do know that." I went to him. We embraced, and he kissed me. We lingered.

"I'm sorry," Zarek said, finally, and brushed the curls from my forehead.

"What for?"

"Being such a fool. For hurting you as I did." He shook his head, "I just thought ..."

I kissed his cheek. "Then stop that and just feel for a while. Do you know what you want?" He nodded. "Can you tell what I want?"

He nodded again and gave me another long kiss. We were both trembling with the power of our mutual bond now that it was no longer denied.

"I will always be there when you call," he promised. "I will never block you out as I have done these past few moons cycles. Never again."

"How did you do that, anyway?" I asked. "You will have to teach me that. I couldn't get through to you at all. It felt so ... I felt so ... alone."

"That's what I am most sorry about. It was killing me to see you hurting like that. You are my heart and soul. I thought I was doing it for you, but ..."

"Heart and soul," I repeated, lacing our hands together and staring into those amazing eyes. I felt at peace, at one with him and myself, like I had felt with the Father-Mother-I Am, in Lupa's cave. And remembered the words I had heard Zarek's voice say as I fell asleep on the Hadrian island: *I am so proud of you.*

Yes, that was me! He mind spoke to me. *I couldn't help myself. I think I was beginning to realize it then, that I was and would ever be miserable without you and you without me, so why was I doing it? But it took seeing you again and trying to resist the pull you have on me.*

Peace gathered around us.

Heart and soul! We bathed in that thought together. It felt like a mind touch kiss. It reminded me of how our hearts had beat in a syncopated rhythm when I was first learning a different way to see and hear, a new way to be in this world: mind touch, a new way to communicate. Maybe this was the first language, true speech, mind to mind, heart to heart.

"Time to go." Zarek sighed and kissed my forehead.

"I don't want to leave." I looked around, "This place feels so special … a holy place."

We allowed ourselves a few more minutes of soaking in the colors of the forest, the sounds of bird and brook, making this place a part of us, taking it into a deep, hidden sanctuary within where we could keep the best of the world, those perfect moments that might sustain us when times were hard and less than perfect.

Then we stowed the sleeping bags and filled the canteen after drinking our fill.

I was still wearing the very rumpled and torn outfit Verity and Wydra had poured me into two days ago. "I wish I had something else to wear," I said as we got on the cycle.

"We're maybe two hours from the top and Mountain Resort. I'm sure you can find something there more to your liking … but," Zarek looked over his shoulder at me, "I think you look fabulous." And the corner of his mouth curled up along with one thin, arched brow. "I like it. Black suits you. Especially with that slivery and purple thing over the top." He slipped his helmet on and waited for me to do the same.

He turned to the front. "On," he said. And we rose a couple of feet off the ground and moved back onto the trail leading up the mountain.

CHAPTER TWENTY-FOUR
(Day Eighteen)

We arrived in Mountain Resort a little before noon to find not only James's family there, but all the Stella Mara people as well. Their ships were encamped beside the lake at the north end of the city, near the road entering the town.

"We felt you coming," Lupa said with a beatific smile. "Verity and I. And we all prepared a meal in your honor. Your warning and quick thinking saved a lot of people."

James and his brother Ferris, who had been my savior more than once, came trotting over. James hugged me. Ferris slapped me on the back. Suddenly we were engulfed in people glad to see us alive and back in their presence. Mountain Resort had nowhere near the population of Telling Wood, but it was not small, the city itself wrapped around the northeast curve of Montana Lake. The city was well designed, with wide streets and beautiful views of both the mountain peaks and the wide expanse of water. Montana Lake was the largest in Nueden, so large you couldn't see the other side, or even guess where it might be if it weren't for the distant peaks of the mountains that ringed the lake. Mountain Resort and the lake sat in a bowl of mountains inaccessible except by the one entrance road.

The sea of people cheering and clapping was a bit overwhelming to me, and I reached for Zarek's hand among the swell of the crowd. In all that mass of people, our hands connected, and I breathed easier.

"We are glad to see you made it." John said as he and Wydra squeezed their way up to us.

My little half brother, Lodar, climbed me like a pole to get his arms around my neck and his legs around my waist. "I was so ascared I might never see you again," Lodar said, and pressed his warm cheek against mine. "We saw the exploding fires from the ship when we left. We were miles and miles away. But the sky burned so big we could see it from a long, long way off."

This dear, sweet little boy made me realize the trauma this would cause to all who had witnessed and lived through it. It would produce fruit. What kind depended on how we, as a nation, dealt with the trauma in the days that would follow. I knew I would never forget it, and Lodar would never forget it either.

As would none who fled Telling Wood and lived to tell the tale.

Our capital city was no more and would never be again. It was a graveyard, a city of the dead now. Telling Wood would only be a ghost in our memories, and of those who were fortunate enough to escape, many now were homeless in an uncertain world.

***

John and Wydra and the Stella Mara nine were staying in a large house that James's family owned. James and his brothers and their families were set up in the next three homes on the same street. The overflow that couldn't be accommodated within the regular means of the city had been given tents and supplies, and they were currently located at the south end of town, at the lakeshore.

Zarek was staying with James, and I was in John and Wydra's house. Jorame and Julka were there too. Rifkin's brothers, wives, children and mothers were scattered between these four homes. I invited Verity and Lupa to stay with me until they left for Hadria. Lupa's adopted grandson, Cyrus, was in Lodar's room with him. They were of an age and were already fast friends. Verity's guards and ship's captains were scattered throughout the city. Mountain Resort folk who were curious about the new people, both Sabostienie and Stella Mara, were clamoring to have them stay at their homes or inns. Those of the vacationing mind-set hoped to make connections so they could go to Hadria, the city under the sea, and the Blue Moon.

There were some Resort families in mourning because they had loved ones who lived in Telling Wood who hadn't made it to Resort and were now assumed dead. But despite that, there almost seemed to be a festive air about the town, which seemed incongruous to me. But then, the city folk hadn't seen what I'd seen.

Maybe it's just a sign that life goes on; life picks up the pieces and keeps going, I thought. *Maybe it's best that life continues on as normal a path as possible under the circumstances.*

It seemed that this resort town didn't mind opening its doors, hearts and minds to visitors or refugees. It had lived by expanding and contracting for centuries according to the seasons, and the townsfolk were generous and welcoming by nature.

Many of our friends had just finished the shared evening meal and were gathered in John and Wydra's great room.

"We lost a ship." Verity spoke with a quiet respect for the dead. "Captain Elisma and her two guards, along with their passengers, over six hundred people. The ship was overfull and too late to get out safely. The bombs had begun exploding in different parts of the Telling Wood. The people who thought they wanted to stay suddenly decided they didn't."

"It was so loaded down it nearly foundered getting over the wall," Lupa said, and closed her eyes. "That Life Stealers soundless wave caught them some ways out of town, and the ship fell like a stone from the sky." She paused, then said, "I felt it!" She opened her eyes and looked straight at me. "No one should ever go inside that ship. Let time and nature bury it."

Now it is a can of bone meal, Pen. Verity spoke to me privately with a haunted look in her eyes, then said to everyone, "Let it be a silent witness to the horrors of what a few can do to the many when they have selfish, and hateful intent in their hearts."

"Or ignorance and indifference." Jorame's mouth turned down in disgust. "That can be just as bad."

"Wallace William Waldorf had a shriveled soul," Zarek pointed out, "which caught him in his own wicked plans, but we must all guard ourselves against pride, arrogance and greed, as he is a perfect example of what the end result of such things are."

The image of the curlicues of flesh and bone the carrion birds had been feasting upon flashed unbidden between Zarek and I. Bodies literally turned inside out. The utter horror of it, no one should see. No one should even go to that place till nature had carried away all signs of the human carnage.

195

Don't worry. No one wants to go back there. I think no one will for a very long time. Zarek's words soothed my troubled thoughts, and I focused on the conversation at hand.

"What I don't get," said Ferris, "is why Waldorf set off the bombs in the first place."

"Yeah," James said, "didn't he know the Life Stealers were in the Chamber House? I mean ... he had spies in the city. How could he not know?"

Brent, Rifkin's oldest brother, sighed heavily. "What if he did know? What if he didn't care how many people he destroyed, even his own men, as long as he could disrupt the forward movement of the unification of the humans, Sabostienie, and Stella Mara?"

"That might sound like something Wallace William Waldorf would do," Ferris said, then shook his head. "But I don't think he'd be willing to kill himself in the process."

"What would be the point?" James agreed with his brother. "It's pretty hard to cause trouble if you're dead."

"When you and Zarek came back through Telling Wood," Brent looked square at me, and I could tell something was seriously troubling him. "Well, when the cyna-cycles first started showing up in the city, I happen to know someone who sold Waldorf one. Is there any way he could have gotten away before his two camps were put to sleep?"

You could almost hear the gears grind with all the silent speculation and fear at this possibility.

"It was a fine cycle, too." Brent looked to the ceiling. "It had cloaking abilities; a big work machine. I tried to buy it myself, but the guy said it was for a special customer. He let it slip, bragging, that it was Waldorf himself. Got a lot of tokens for it too, and extra to keep it quiet. So ... did you happen to see a work cycle in the camps?" Brent looked at Zarek with hope.

"No, I didn't." Zarek shook his head.

I agreed. "Nothing. But we were only near the southern camp. We didn't go back to the one where Waldorf had been," I said.

After a long and thoughtful silence, Ferris said, "The only two cities we haven't heard from are Brendle Georgia and Dunsmier Dakota. Waldorf owned a huge amount of Georgia and Iowa," he said for the benefit of those who might not know, "including his Brendle Snow Lodge in the mountains of Georgia and the Black Stone Quarry just outside Numark, Iowa. Not that far from Telling Wood to reach either one of those cities on a cycle."

The possibility of that man still being alive chilled my heart.

Quarrymen always had access to explosive materials because they worked with stone. Slabing stone was not easy work. And now it was known that Waldorf had had a cycle that could cloak. *Not good! Not at all good!* I thought. *Where is that cycle now? Could Waldorf still be alive?*

"Norman, Waldorf's second in command, came from Dakota," Ferris said. "Even though we sent messages to both cities about the catastrophe, we've had no word back, and that's a problem, because the spokes of the Zap having collapsed at the hub in Telling Wood means Ravenwood, Re-Maid, Ra'Vell Island and Rose Rock village are cut off from the rest of the country until we can re-establish connections with those last two cities."

"We had our contacts in Numark, Mugar City and Ravenswood, block the Zap tunnels so no one from those two cities could come in unaware." John stirred the fire again as he spoke. "That should stop any possible retaliation for now."

"But we can com them, and go by cycle," I said, "They are not totally cut off."

"No," James said, grimacing. "But very few of us have cycles yet. So few have them that it isn't practical to think that is a good enough way to get between the east coast and the west side of the country as far as commerce and travel are concerned."

"True!" John said. "We wouldn't be able to trust those two Zap Stations to allow cars through to the west side of the country, at least not until we know what is going on there. They may have their stations blocked against us, for all we know."

"Then we have to go to Dunsmier and Brendle and secure those stations." James stood up as if ready to go right that minute.

"We will be going back to Hadria in a few days," Verity said. "What if I left a transport ship and crew here to accommodate travel and trade between the cities for the time being?"

"Yes," said Lupa. "We will be back and forth, I'm sure. We have an alliance to build."

"But you have your own problems to deal with," I said, giving Lupa and Verity a sympathetic glance. "I know your people need you … Is there anything we can do to help there?"

Verity smiled. "I'll let you know. Keep the ring; we can always talk by the coms."

197

"Then why couldn't we reach anyone after the blasts began and the Life Stealers exploded?" asked Zarek.

"We decided it must have been some aftermath effect," Brent said. "Disturbing the air waves."

Julka looked as if she had something to say, but in her quiet way didn't want to interrupt. "Julka, what's on your mind?" I asked her.

"Just that the Wells have already started increasing production of cyna-cycles, knowing the need with the capital city being … well, with it being gone and the Zap only being able to travel half of the outer rim of the Fast Track at this time," Julka said, holding a two-year-old on her lap. This beautiful child Jorame and Julka had saved from being left behind in that city. I shuddered at the thought. They were trying to find her family, if she had one, if they'd survived. Some of the broken families that had made it to Mountain Resort had no idea where they might find the people whom they had connections with.

"Has anyone thought of a way for families to find each other if they've been separated?" I asked. "The diaspora was so chaotic that I'm sure there must be many children like Merry here," the little girl's long blonde hair swayed as she turned to look at me with solemn big blue eyes when I said her name, "like she was separated from hers," I finished.

"Dave Steel, one of Rifkin's brothers, has started a registry for lost families. He's put someone in charge in every city we've heard from," John said, adding a stick of wood to the fire in the fireplace, stirring up the coals until the wood caught.

"Good!" Zarek and I said at the same time. I nodded and asked, "Has anyone heard anything from Hannratti's family?"

"You mean my cousin, Hanni?" James said with a bit of a scolding smile.

"Yes. Her new name; Hanni," I repeated.

"They are in North Harbor," Ferris said.

"Ah," I nodded, "that was where her family went to hide when I took the cousins to Ra'Vell Island a year and a half ago. Good, they will know people there. They won't be alone. There are some good people in that city."

"So the registry is working!" Zarek paced the floor. "That was very quick thinking."

We talked late into the night, hashing over plans, ways and means to reunite the country, making our way around the gaping wound at its heart.

198

You may think no one will go back to Telling Wood, I said to Zarek alone, *but we may not have a choice. We need to know if there is an abandoned cycle at the northwest camp.*

Yes. And I can see we will need to repair the Zap hub. He sighed. *But let's leave that for another discussion. We have other more immediate things to tend to.*

Like finding out if Waldorf survived! I said with a shudder. *We need Little Bee, and anyone else who can help support casting out search lines, like Verity, Bee and I did to find Keto and the island house.*

CHAPTER TWENTY-FIVE
(Day Nineteen)

The morning was crisp and cool. Winter was coming, and there was the feel of snow in the air. A crowd of folk bundled up in warm clothes, were headed toward the building the townspeople had let John use as a command center.

Verity shivered in the puffy coat someone had given her. It covered her from chin to ankle. "I've never been so cold," she said. "How can you live in such places? Beautiful as it is here, I'd never make it through a winter. And Wydra said this isn't cold, it's just cool." Our breaths were visible, which amazed all the Stella Marian's. Cyrus and Lodar were huffing and puffing just to make the adults laugh.

I shrugged. "At this elevation and time of year, the cold is to be expected. We might even get some snow before the day is out." I scanned the sky for snow clouds.

"What is snow?" Lupa's natural curiosity was piqued.

I smiled. "You'll see. Anyway, I hope we get some snow before you leave."

We walked up the steps of the large, old, stone building, a concert hall of very famous proportions, a fine old edifice. Many talented musicians, actors and singers lived in Resort. Creative, artistic folk gravitated to this vacation town, just like they did to the Fingers of Mugar, only at the opposite end of the landscape spectrum.

Mountain Resort had always been a little looser with the Code, Creed and Law because they had no representation, and thus not as many eyes on them, either. Maybe that was what made these people different than those of other cities I'd spent time in; they seemed happier and freer.

200

The leaders of the city, the Stella Mara nine, Verity and her captains, and my group of people from Telling Wood were gathering for our first council meeting since my return from Hadria and the destruction of Telling Wood. I estimated that there were several hundred people in a room that could hold triple that. I had heard the acoustics here were excellent, as good as the council chamber's had been, but I'd never had the opportunity to experience them for myself.

Once we were all seated and quiet, I began, speaking in my normal low-timbered voice—low for a female, anyway. I didn't want to have to shout for everyone to hear me. "I've heard from thirty-three of the thirty-six council members," I said, surprised at how well the building's acoustics carried my words, maybe even better than the Chamber House, which was no more. "They agree we should reconvene, perhaps here in Mountain Resort, if you," I spoke to the city leaders, "will allow us to share use of this building for the duration of our need while we figure out what our agenda must be for the coming year. We must assess the damage done and the ways to reform our leadership base and get the nation on its feet again."

I had to give myself a mental shake at how odd it felt that people listened to me, looked to me for some word of authority. My reputation was much larger than I felt my ability to lead was. *How can I ever meet the expectations of these people?* I wondered, and I couldn't help questioning again what I was doing at the head of this meeting.

You're doing what you were born for Zarek encouraged me. *You're doing what you were trained to do. What you were educated to do. You may not have known that at the time, but it's so. You're leading!*

"That is agreeable to us and our people," Bryson, the town Father, said. "You have brought more excitement and potential to our city than has been here in a very long time, and we are glad to have you."

Yes, it is true. Zarek grinned at me. *Good acoustics.*

***

Several hours later, coming out of the meeting just before noon, we found an inch of snow on the ground, and a light, powdery drift coming down from the darkening sky.

"Oh," Lupa said, looking in delighted amazement at the white and purplish lacy stuff. "Snow." She raised her hand to catch some, only to have it melt on her fingers. Verity laughed at Lupa's dumfounded puzzlement. "Well, you try to catch some, then, if you think it so easy," Lupa laughed.

Verity raised her face to the sky and opened her mouth. Soon they were twirling around with their mouths open. Many of us joined them laughing and twirling like children.

"So this is snow!" Verity stopped, dizzy, and sat on a street bench. Lupa sat down next to her. "My people will never believe it. It turns into water on your face and hands."

"How strange," Lupa said in delight. "Snow is hard bits of rain. How do you make it do that?"

Zarek and I laughed. "It is nature …" I said.

"… who makes it do that!" Zarek finished my sentence.

"It is cold!" Verity shivered.

"The cold is what makes rain turn into snow," said Wydra, smiling and pointing to the front yard of their house. We moved down the street to where Lodar and Cyrus were throwing snowballs at each other, squealing with laughter when they hit their target. Even though Cyrus was almost three years older than Lodar, they were much the same size, well matched for a snowball battle.

We adults watched for a while, our guests in the grip of their first snow. In no time, Verity and Lupa joined in with the boys.

I remembered my childhood friend, Quill, my brother Pelldar, my nephew Mark, all my friends whom I had ever had snowball wars with—so different from the real thing. With a snowball war, all you had to do at the end of it was go indoors, dry off and get warmed up.

Zarek put his arms around me from behind. I leaned into his warmth and closed my eyes … and got a snowball in the face.

We joined the battle.

***

(Day Twenty-two)

Wydra, Lodar, James, Ferris and Rifkin were leaving with the Stella Mara.

Lodar was upset when he learned his new friend was going away. John thought it might be a good thing to let him go with Cyrus, but Wydra wouldn't hear of it. Not without her. So they were both going.

Jorame and I were staying.

"Ferris is a builder," John said to Lupa and Verity, "a very talented builder. When we get things sorted out here, we will send stone for your public building at Beach Camp."

"Verity will be in charge of that," said Lupa. A small woman, she smiled up at Ferris. "You two can plan the layout together. I love this mountain city. Maybe you can make it with wide streets like this. And square blocks …" she tilted her head in thought, "or maybe round ones. Do you think you can do round ones?"

"I've been to Blue Moon." Ferris raised his eyebrows. "Wait till you see that place, if you like the idea of curving streets."

"Maybe we can do a little of both," Verity said, and gave Ferris an appraising stare. "Maybe, as we make plans, we can take a trip to the Blue Moon and you can show me what you mean."

She was leaving us two of the transporters and two of the Stingers with two crews each, so they could switch out for down time.

Farewell hugs were exchanged, and the ships were boarded, with the addition of thirty townsfolk going to Hadria, and they were up in the air and gone over the mountaintops in a heartbeat.

John sighed. "I hate to let them out of my sight." He rubbed the stubble on his chin. It made a raspy sound. "But in a way, I'm glad to see them out of harm's way."

"Harm's way?" I said, giving him a puzzled look. "This is probably the safest city in the country right now. Only one way in and one way out, at least on the ground."

"I don't think for a minute we have seen the last of Wally Waldorf." He lowered his head and his voice. "I want them out of his way if he surfaces somewhere to cause trouble."

Pen, we have to make another try at finding that cycle, Zarek voice's whispered in my mind.

I nodded to them both. "OK," I said hesitantly.

"John, they need you here to keep the command center going," Zarek said, and placed his hand on John's shoulder. "Keep watch on the road into the city. You will be our liaison person, and now that the coms are working again, we will report in to you every evening."

203

"I thought to take a more personal part in the hunt," John said, a little disgruntled. "I know you're right, but I've always been a great finder of hidden things."

So … we go alone. I spoke to Zarek with my eyes as well as my mind. Our eyes spoke volumes all by themselves.

Yes … we go alone.

***

(Day Twenty-three)

We were ready to leave the next morning. All evening, we had done what we could to prepare for whatever circumstances we might find in the ruins of Telling Wood.

"Remember, com me every night," John said. "Keep the cycle cloak on at all times, and when you have to be out in the open, keep those personal shields up and do that mind thing you two do. No talking where someone might hear you." His hand waved about as if it was lost in his effort to say he cared for me and Zarek, and he couldn't look me in the eye for fear of revealing how alone he felt with Wydra and Lodar off to Hadria, and now us too, when he wanted to do more than watch over the command center.

"I know." Embracing him, I could hardly keep dry eyes myself. "We will all talk every night. And they will be fine."

John nodded. "I already talked to both of them a couple of times since they arrived. Wydra said Ilantha's people named the island Hadrianna and are already excited about building a town where Beach Camp is." That made him smile. "They seem to have their few dissidents in hand, as they are talking about what it is they seem to want and what can be done to help them achieve their needs."

"Maybe we can be as fortunate," Zarek said as we climbed onto the cycle. "Maybe we can all go and see their new city together."

"As soon as I can," John said, clapping Zarek on the shoulder, "I'm going to see that place. Wydra says the underwater city is amazing. You two be careful, you hear?" He gave us a hard stare and walked away toward the command center.

"On," Zarek said. "Helmets." He switched the cloak on, and I knew from experience that our sleek black cycle and the small pallet that carried our supplies were now invisible to the onlookers who had

204

already made their good-byes. The small crowd was breaking up as we pulled away from town.

We flew out of Mountain Resort over the road that was barely more than a wide path. I leaned into Zarek's back, taking comfort in his presence. My arms encircled his chest, and he patted my hand that rested over his heart and laced his fingers with mine. We felt the combined beat of our hearts. I knew we would be all right, no matter what we found. We were together again, truly together for the first time.

The new climate suits were now a mottled green and brown, less visible when we were off the cycle and not cloaked. We had personal shields, but so far, no personal cloaks existed. And I didn't think I wanted such things to exist. Knowing even one cloaking cycle was out there in the hands of people who sought to do us harm was more than enough to worry about.

In less time than it had taken us to make our way into Resort from our special camping place by the brook, we were past it and on our way to the Ruins.

A few hours out from the Ruins, we decided to stop and see if we could locate any sign of or indication of the direction we should check for Waldorf's work cycle, or Waldorf himself.

We made camp in a small thicket of trees that had a creek nearby. We stayed cloaked, but sat near the creek for the pleasant song of it. We sat cross-legged with our knees touching and clasped hands, much as we had done the very first time we'd tried to make this kind of connection. I had grown in my ability, so had Zarek, and we instantly stretched out toward what used to be a city but was now just miles of rubble. With the shape and size of a work cycle in mind, we carefully felt through the north and south army camps and anywhere nearby. We searched for any sign of a living person in the vicinity. No matter where we went, the two of us were together in that bond of eyes and ears, our senses going out while our bodies remained seated, our hearts beating a slow rhythm as one.

But we found nothing and no one.

John, eager to talk to us to see what we had found so far, contacted us as we were preparing dinner. We spoke in low tones. Just because we were cloaked didn't mean we couldn't be heard if someone where clocked nearby. The babble of the creek would be good to drown out low voices, we thought. There was nothing really to report, so the conversation was brief.

That kind of mind travel is wearing, so we ate and slept, recuperating for what had to be done the next day.

CHAPTER TWENTY-SIX
(Day Twenty-five)

We didn't talk much, but when we did, we followed John's advice and only spoke mind to mind. Nearing our destination, a glow encircled us, that I could see and feel, the Presences I knew from the cave and the Tree.

Do you feel that? I asked Zarek.

Yes.

I spoke to the Presences, knowing Zarek would hear too. *Help us do right and bring the people together.*

We arrived outside the Ruins around noon on the second day out from Resort. The open expanse felt less than comforting. Somehow, in just the few days I had been in Resort, I had grown to love the mountains and the many pines of greens and pinks. I missed the place. I missed Ra'Vell Island too. I wanted to go home and see my friends there. I missed Ibera; I had left her in Hadria to keep guard over the children, and now Lodar and Wydra too.

Even though Zarek was with me, the person I loved more than breathing, I felt haunted by the separation from all those other people I loved, who were scattered all over this world and the Blue Moon. I wanted to serve the greater good for all the people. I wanted them safe and happy. I wanted this even for the ones who didn't want to see me safe and happy.

Don't fret. We care for them from a distance till we can care up close, Zarek whispered into my thoughts. *Remember, we are not alone in this.*

It's impossible to have everyone you love with you at all times anyway. I know that wouldn't even be a good thing, necessarily. It's just that things seem so uncertain right now.

Don't be afraid!

Then where should we start the search to make things a little more certain? I asked.

We circled the southern camp. There was little left of the human or animal remains. The wind had tattered what it couldn't knock down or blow across the grasslands. We parked and recloaked the cycle as we did a thorough grid search. There was no hidden or cloaked cycle we could find, with a physical, eyes on search, so we moved on.

In less than an hour, we made our way up to the northwest camp and gave it a thorough walkthrough, feeling for the cycle as we went, crisscrossing the entire camp as we had done before. It was much like the first camp, as if an angry wind had scattered things about in every which direction.

Even though there were no visible dead lying about and the smell had dissipated, carried off by the whirlwind, I supposed, I stood where I had stood the day before the destruction and remembered each face in the crowd of soldiers and even Wallace William Waldorf, and felt a weight of sorrow at the waste of life in an unnecessary conflict. We could have worked something out. We still could, I was sure of it, if only we could all be open enough to listen to each other and make plans accordingly.

After a thorough search, Zarek said, *It isn't here,* and came over to where I stood. We dropped our personal shields, and he hugged me. *Let's go check the Zap Fast Track station and find a place to spend the night. It will be dark in a few hours.*

I took a deep breath. *I know we have to go inside, but I really don't want to.*

If there were any other way ... But we couldn't see anything last night when we tried with our mind search.

We just stood there like that, clinging to each other, for a while, until I could face the Ruins.

At the northwest gate, we found it blown off its pair of two-foot-long steel hinges, two twisted, jagged crumpled sheets of metal. We carefully maneuvered on roads and streets where we could and over slabs of fallen walls where we couldn't find passable streets. It was hard to imagine or remember what it had looked like before, or even where we were within the city, it all looked so different.

208

We finally came to something we recognized, the center of the city where the fountain still stood unharmed, that grotesque statute of the trollish man with the world on his back and all that empty space around him where we had burned Old Town in our efforts to clean up Telling Wood after the first time someone had turned loose a Life Stealer and there were dead bodies everywhere. It seemed that this time, even though it may not have gone more than fifteen miles, the soundless force of the blast had been so great that people had exploded along with buildings, like individual bombs.

Why not this monstrosity? I thought. *Too bad!* That statue was one thing in all this wasteland I wouldn't have minded seeing blown to bits.

I heard Zarek laughing as we pulled up to what was left of the burned-out Zap station. We got off and recloaked the cycle, then activated our personal shields as we had done at both campsites.

There was no sound anywhere in all of that mess. Dead quiet. It was eerie. I had a bad feeling about the Zap Track tunnels. All but one had collapsed entrances. The one entrance that hadn't collapsed was held up by a Zap car that hadn't made it out of town. The stink was unbearable. I fled, gagging, Zarek right behind me.

At least now we knew where the missing Zap car and those people were and how badly the hub was damaged. It might take a few years to clear the rubble away and repair the lines to all the major cities. I sucked in a lungful of air when we got out to the surface.

At least it was quick. There's no lingering with the white spheres, I said, thinking of what Lupa felt when one of their transporters fell from the sky because of the Life Stealers.

Zarek was as shook up as I was. *Let's get out of here.*

He nodded and took my hand, and we hurried to where we knew our cycle was hidden, leaving the station to look for what might be left of my home, which I knew was nearby now that I was oriented. Dusk made the task more difficult, but we found where we thought it should be and found only more rubble. But there was one corner of the garden wall still intact, and we moved the cycle against it. Cloaked and shielded, we set up camp.

We commed John and told him what we had and hadn't found. I talked to Will on Ra'Vell Island and told him we were coming his direction and that we would stop and see how the people of Isuladune were doing.

We ate cold camp rations and slept as we could.

The Ruin of Telling Wood was a haunted place, difficult to sleep in.

***

(Day Twenty-six)

I woke up with sunlight in my eyes and rolled over to find Zarek in his sleeping bag, his head covered. I sat up and stretched, yawning. Climbing out of my bag, I went to rummage up something to eat, stepped on a stone and nearly twisted my ankle. I looked down, and amazement suffused my whole being. There at my feet was my mother's small sculpture of a mother and baby, the one John had carried off with him that first time I met him. I knelt and picked it up. It filled my hand, whole and complete. I bit my lip in ecstatic joy and clutched it to my chest, weeping.

Zarek sat up, wide awake, and clambered out of his sleeping bag.

"Look!" I spoke out loud. "Look what I found."

He came to me and wiped the tears from my cheeks. He knew what it was. He knew where it had been on the fireplace mantle where John had returned it. He knew what it meant to me and to John and Lodar.

"I can't believe it," I sobbed. "In all this broken stone, all this mess look what I found."

Wonannonda has blessed you with a gift. He took me in his arms. *Shhh, a blessing is nothing to cry about.*

These are happy tears. My head beneath his chin, I kissed the hollow at the base of his throat. *This makes me happy. And being with you makes me happy.* I felt bathed in euphoria and believed the world had just righted itself somehow.

Our mood lighter than it had been since we'd left Resort we ate, then packed up and worked our way out the southwestern gate and headed toward Ra'Vell Island.

By noon, we were at Isuladune. That peaceful little village had not heard of any of the events that had taken place over the last month, and its residents were eager listeners to all the news.

We stayed overnight and rode away well fed in the morning, cutting a path through the tall purple grasslands.

210

An hour or so before sundown, we pulled up and stopped on the landside of East Gate Bridge. I smiled up at Zarek as we dismounted the cycle and decloaked. Zarek spoke to Will and asked him to open the gate for us. Just as he was giving the order, I yelled, "Wait!"

"What is it?" Will, on guard, answered back over the com.

"Something is not right!" I scanned the landscape. Zarek followed suit. We joined in that way we had experienced before, and there it was ... Wallace William Waldorf's work cycle, following us on the grass path we had made.

Waldorf's cycle flashed into being, its cloak dropped to reveal the man astride the machine.

It wasn't Wally.

He set down not far from us and got off the cycle.

"Who are you?" I asked, looking around. "Where is your Father?" It could only be a son of the man who had put Telling Wood to ruin. He might have a few inches on Wally Sr., but this was absolutely a Waldorf. The unfortunate young man looked just like Walace William Waldorf, round form and red hair and all, right down to his outsized hands.

"So, you know who I am." His smirk was an exact replica of the one I had seen on Wally's face when he thought I was interested in him as a mate. "And the answer to your question of where he is?"

He took a step closer to us and stopped, just a few yards away. "Dead! Deader than dead." His eyes went as cold and bright black as the stone from Black Stone Quarry. "I've hated that man for years. I've waited and watched and copied his every move ..."

"That's too bad," Zarek said, and I knew the com link was still open and that Will could hear every word. "If you hadn't done that, you might have become someone."

"Get on that cycle and ride out of here now before I kill you," Waldorf snarled at Zarek.

"And why would I do that?"

"You'll do what ever I say to save Ra'Vell from the same fate as Telling Wood."

My blood felt chilled, and I reached out to snare a thought or feeling, only to see walls, big, black stone walls in this man's mind.

"That's right, sweetie," Waldorf said. "I see you trying, but you can't get into my head. Wally didn't listen to the men you messed with.

He said it was a lie, a trick you played on them. He was stupid. I'm not. I heard what they were saying about you and prepared myself."

Zarek and I were dumbfounded.

"So what is it you want?" Zarek gave me a little push toward our cycle.

"No. She stays. You go."

"I can't do that." Zarek shook his head.

"OK. I thought you might say that, you purple-haired, white freak. So I've arranged for some fireworks to show you how serious I am about this. I was never going to let dear old Father have her, **but I surely will**. She's mine, not yours. And if you don't go, the next one will be inside Ra'Vell Town."

He pushed a button he had concealed in the palm of his hand, and this end of East Gate Bridge exploded in a twist of metal that screeched partway down the cliff side to land on a rock shelf about ten feet down, where the shredded feet of the structure stopped it.

"Damn." He peered over the edge. "It was supposed to go all the way down into the river! I never was as good at positioning explosives as my older brother, you captured him swimming into the city." He gave us a lopsided grin. "He's dead now too."

We could all hear Will and several other men screaming over the wrist com.

"Throw that thing over the cliff," Wally Jr. bellowed at Zarek, who slipped it off and threw it out over the river.

"Now, you're going to get on that thing and not cloak. I want to see you till you're out of sight the natural way," he said to Zarek. "And you'd better not come back. If I see so much as a dust cloud, I'll blow this town all to hell."

"What makes you think I'll leave?" Zarek said. "You've already wrecked the bridge. It's not like you can get over there now."

Wally Jr. stepped back and flicked the tarp off whatever it was on the cycle pallet that made the tarp stick up like a tall tent. It was some kind of catapult with a very large explosive device in the cup, aimed at the heart of my village.

"You will ride away and leave this woman to me." He blew me a kiss. *This man is even worse than his father*, I thought.

"I knew she was meant for me the moment I laid eyes on her." He stared at me all dreamy, and hungry at the same time, as if I was a dessert from Chet's kitchen. "That was when I knew it was finally time to be rid of the old goat for good. Father had to go. I was his most trusted son. There were a lot of sons, some not trusted at all. I put up with more dung from him than any of them, so I could position myself to his right in everything. I was his spymaster. They brought me the reports of what was happening inside the city; that's how I knew to get out of there before all those bombs Father placed throughout the city went off and brought the white death or whatever you call ..."

At this, Zarek glared at the man, threw himself on the cycle and sped away, heading toward Rose Rock Village down by the lake. I was stunned. *Not even a good-bye.*

"Well, how rude." Wally Jr. chuckled in amusement. "Not even a good-bye," he said, mirroring my own thoughts. "I guess he wasn't as keen on you as you imagined." He grinned, watching Zarek go.

"My name, by the way, is Robert. But you will call me Rob. I'll call you Pen. Pendyse is far too formal between husband and wife, and besides, it's a man's name, and you won't need that any more. I'll show you how to be a proper woman, a good wife. That is one thing Father taught me well and something I did agree with him on. Maybe we can name our first son Pendyse. That would be more appropriate, don't you think?"

I walked a ways off after Zarek's departure. Robert followed me.

"I don't understand what you think you've accomplished by blowing up my bridge. You certainly can't take possession of my town if we can't get to it." I stopped and turned toward him, shrugging my shoulders. "I don't understand you." I was near as angry as I'd ever been at anyone, but I wasn't sure who or what I was angrier at: this odious little toad of a man; Zarek, for leaving me without a word; or the whole damn unfairness of being put in this position again. *Like father, like son,* I thought, so furious at him for trapping me like this and putting people I cared about in harm's way once again.

What is it with these crazy, morally corrupt people who have no real power as I see it—the power of love—so they have to resort to force and coercion instead to get what they think they want?

"Ah, ah, ah," Robert scolded, wagging a finger at me. "That's no way to think about your future husband."

Shock shivered through me. Had he caught my emotions or my thoughts? If he could block my thoughts, could he also hear them?

His grin widened.

213

CHAPTER TWENTY-SEVEN

I shook my head. "Is that all you know—force, intimidation?" The emotions that welled up in me next were anger were sorrow and compassion for his impoverished soul had just been. "Have you never, ever, known love? Any kind of love?"

Robert's face went rigid, and I felt a rage roiling in him that was old, nearly as old as he himself, from somewhere early in childhood, I thought. I saw his nostrils flare and his eyes widen as he tried to put up that wall against me, but I now saw the chinks in the wall and knew how I could break in. I knew I could do it, if I wanted to be like him. But I didn't. And I let him know that, my mind wide open.

"What was it?" I asked. "Did he give your mother away to his men?" My eyes began to tear up at the thought of what horror that would have been for a small boy. "I heard that's what he did with most of his wives."

Robert rushed at me. I didn't flinch, as I was shielded. He raised his large fist to punch me in the face and slammed into the invisible shield around me. He jerked his bloodied fist back and cradled it against his chest, screaming, "What the hell did you do to me?"

"I did nothing," I said. "You saw...I was just standing here. It was you who meant to do something wicked to me. And if this is what your father taught you about being a husband, it is no wonder his women would prefer death or being with his men to being with him. You learned to hate him because of it, I think, *and here you are being just - like - him.*"

"That's not true. I am nothing like him." Robert's mouth turned down, and he blinked rapidly. "That's not right. *Women must obey!*" he yelled, spittle flecking my shield. "It is the natural order of things. I know

214

it. It's my turn now." He turned away from me, licking the oozing blood from his knuckles.

"It's my turn," he repeated, softer but more deliberately. "My turn. And I want it all."

"And that's the way you think you will get the love you want? I know you want to be loved, but love doesn't come by force."

Robert spun around again and glared at me, holding his fist as if it was a wounded pet. *You will love me!* His thought screamed into my mind, making my head ring.

"No," I said softly, shaking my head. "Trying to force love only blocks it. Force produces resentment and hate, you know that already. Love, true love, has to be given, Robert. It can't be taken."

"*You will give it* or I will destroy your town and its people."

"And once they're gone, what then? What will you use to hold me?"

Furious, he turned and walked over toward the catapult machine, but in midstride, he slumped to the ground, asleep.

A Stinger decloaked a little way off, and Zarek and the black cycle became visible right next to me. He jumped off, wrapped me in his arms and held me so tight I could barely breathe. He buried his face in my hair and whispered, "I was so afraid you would let down your shield and go away with him to save the village before I could put everything into motion. I knew he would hear my thoughts if I tried to warn you. Are you all right?"

"I'm OK." I lifted my face to his and kissed him. *We're OK.* I clung to him for a while longer. "We're all right."

"Then let's get him over to the island and lock him up," Zarek said. "The transporter is here too and can take us and the cycles over to the island. Or maybe we should take the Waldorf cycle to Rose Rock quarry to see about defusing that thing somewhere out of harm's way so there is no possibility it can hurt anyone if it blows up. That is, if someone can figure out what the trigger is or where it is. Maybe we should strip the little man before we lock him up. Find out what he has in his pockets."

"He was headed toward the catapult. I think the trigger device is on the pallet or on the cycle," I said.

We loaded up the transporter, and Will sent one of his men over in the Stinger to take the work cycle to Rose Rock Quarry.

I was going home.

***

I was sitting at the long dining table after the best breakfast Chet had ever made me. Funny how he kept showing up in places I didn't expect him. He'd come with the transporter and Stinger and their crews from Resort.

Alone in the huge, open room, catching up on my journal accounts, I was just finishing up when I heard Will and Zarek out in the entry hall.

It was great to be back in my own castle, on my island.

Things felt different to me now, though. True, it did feel like home, but less like my island and more like Will's. He had done a great job in my multiple absences, and the place was thriving. It was odd, like seeing Ra'Vell for the first time, or with new eyes. *Maybe I should give the island to Will or the people collectively*, I thought. Who knew what my responsibilities were going to be or where they would take me next? There was so much to do. We were convening a council meeting at Resort in a week, so nine short days was all the time I would have here.

Zarek and Will came in, and I closed my journal and stood up.

"We are going down to the prison to talk to your future husband," Will joked. I shook my head but grinned in spite of myself.

"Want to come along?" Zarek took my hand and kissed it. I blushed, a funny reaction to a kiss on the hand, but Will was watching intently. I felt a sudden pleasure radiating from him about what he was seeing and blushed even more.

"Yes, I'll come," I said, ignoring my own reaction. "I'd like to talk to all the prisoners here. Have they been treated well?"

"They've been fed three meals a day and have been given reading materials to keep them occupied. You know, the Old Earth disk books. They listen to music. They talk," Will said. "We listen to them talk."

"So what do you think?" I asked as we headed for the spiral stairs down to the cells below ground where we kept the men who insisted on trying to take Ra'Vell Island for themselves. "Will you be glad to be rid of them?"

Will pursed his lips and said, "Yes, but that is not the question. Are you sure you want to take them with you?"

"We think we have to," said Zarek. "We want them to take part in the council meeting, along with some others we are currently gathering up from Dunsmier and Brendle."

"They will be in restraints, but they will have a voice, and a choice in their future." I looked at Will with appreciation at his concern for our welfare.

Once below, we came to the long, curving hallway that led to the locked wooden stockade door with a small barred window about head high.

"Are you men all decent? A woman's coming in!" Will said, and gave me the keys.

I unlocked the door, hearing no complaint. This section was also a curved, wide hallway, with niches in the rock and steel bars along the wall facing the hall between the cells. The cells were about ten by ten, and each held a shower, a toilet, a sink, a cot and a table. Gene was the first man on the left, with his fifteen men strung out along both sides so they could see each other and talk, more or less, face to face. Robert Waldorf was in the first cell on the right as we went in. He was awake and hissed when he saw me, like a caged wild animal.

"You! You did this me! You *woman!*"

Gene, directly across from Robert, laughed. "'You woman'? That's the best you can do?" His men gave out whoops and insults as well.

"Agggh!" Robert screamed and rushed at the bars, reaching out as if he wanted to rip my head off. Maybe he did. It felt a little like that. He had most likely never been locked away for misdeeds. Maybe he'd been beaten, but he'd probably never been restrained before.

"I'm sorry," I said, keeping my distance. "I know how it feels to be held against one's will."

At this, Gene howled with laughter. "And if I'd known then what I know now, we would have had some fun, wouldn't we, boys?" The men shouted out more demeaning names and howls of laughter.

"Your men sound in good spirits," Will said as we walked down the line, holding to the center.

"I want to see the woman!" one of them yelled. "We have not seen one in months, not since we was put in this hole."

I had dressed carefully that morning, being aware this visit might be on the agenda, and made sure all my clothes were comfortably baggy and concealing. My hair, after a year and a half of growing it out,

217

was long, well past my shoulders and hung in thick black curls: that was about the only thing they would consider feminine, that and my face. Even without paint or tattoos, my face had become so like my mother's. People always said she was beautiful. I always thought she was beautiful, but it was hard to think of myself that way.

You don't mind if I think of you in that way? Zarek gave me a look and a small smile. *Don't worry about these men. They know you bested them, and they sort of respect that about you.*

Well, maybe, I said, looking at Robert, *except for him. He's a cesspool of hate. He's going the way of the Voice, Zee herself, if he doesn't turn around.*

I hear you! Robert glared at me. "You are not worthy to be my wife," he said aloud.

I walked down the line greeting Gene's men, nodding to them. Some made rude comments, which I ignored, but most were more respectful, though I felt some of that was mockery.

At the end, one of the men shouted at Robert, "You must be blind, Robert Waldorf, or as crazy as your old man to think this one unworthy of your ugliness."

I had an image of a screaming little boy reaching out while his mother was being dragged out of their rooms, never to be seen again, before the black stone wall was firmly in place again. It broke my heart. Everyone has beginnings. And the way we react to them makes us who we are. And what if we can't help ourselves?

"I'm not here to discuss my worth or lack of it," I said. "I've come to tell you to prepare yourselves for travel. You are all going to a Chamber council meeting."

"You've been told what has happened to Telling Wood ..." Will started to say.

"Yeah," Gene grumbled, interrupting him, "and we know who's to blame for that one."

"It was my father's fault," Robert protested. "I did not do ..."

"Never mind who's to blame" Zarek cut Robert off. "That is not what this is about."

"You will be going with us in the airship," Zarek began.

I jumped in, "And there will be others of like mind with you from Brendle and Dunsmier. We will hear your concerns and whatever you want to tell us. We will listen, then we will give you some choices. Be prepared to make them. What you won't be allowed to do is make war on peaceful people. You won't be allowed to kill us anymore. And we don't want to kill you. And so, if we can come to some kind of agreement about how we can all live together in peace, we will do so. That is our goal."

"You think I am a fool!" Robert said from the other end of the line. "I'd have to be to believe that. You plan to get us all together in one place and kill us."

"We want everyone to be safe," Zarek said, by my side. "You have all proven by your past actions that you can't be trusted not to try to hurt us. We are not the aggressors. We were not camped outside your cities. Nor have we attacked anyone. We have defended ourselves when we had too. We want you to be free to live your way, and we want to be free to live ours."

The denials and complaints and rattling of metal cups against the bars made a racket, and Will held up his hands and said softly, "If you don't quiet down, you won't get supper."

The grumbling died down, and Will continued. "Most of you have been here a few months. We have not killed you, even though we knew what you meant to do to us."

"Haven't you been treated well?" I asked.

"If you weren't killed here, why would we move you somewhere else to be killed?" Zarek said with exasperation. "It's true some people may not be able to adjust to the changes that are coming, but everyone will be given the opportunity to join communities of people who follow more of the old ways."

"We just want you to be thinking about these things," I said. "We will be leaving at the end of the week."

"Hey," Gene said, hanging casually on the crossbar of his cell, after we'd passed him on our way out, when we were at the stockade door. "Where are you taking us?"

"I think we will leave that bit of information until we are on our way." I said.

We left, and I locked the door behind us and handed the keys over to one of the two door guards. Their Nar Hounds were standing beside them. As we walked away, we could hear the rumble of voices as the men began to talk.

CHAPTER TWENTY-EIGHT
(Day Twenty-eight)

Zarek and I spent the evening in the company of Will and Tearveena, and the three children remaining at home. Quill was in Re-Maid along with his older sister, Onamie, and her husband, Paul.

Charm, Jillio and Max entertained us after dinner with all kinds of accounts of the goings on around Ra'Vell Town from the perspectives of a twelve-, seven- and five-year-old. Brother Swayne stopped by after the kids went to bed, and the five of us finished the evening off discussing island business.

The week went quickly, and before I was ready, it was time to leave.

Good-byes are always hard. You never know when you might be back again. But good work had been done, and the island was legally firmly in Will's hands now, along with the people of Ra'Vell Town. I retained the rights to Ra'Vell Castle: everything else now belonged to the people, under Will's leadership.

Brother Swayne was flying with us, and the prisoners to Resort. The other council members were already gathering there.

"Come on," Gene wheedled, "tell us where you are taking us. We have a right to know."

"You gave up your rights when you came against us with murder in your heart," Will said, and gave Gene a small shove toward the transporter. Will's Nar Hound ruffled his upper lip, showing purple gums, and emitted a low growl, his head lowered, his horn pointed toward Gene, who relented and stepped into the transporter. The men shackled together had little choice but to follow.

"I will not get on that damned machine!" Robert was straining against the chains and spitting out his words like a crazy person. "I will not. I am not going."

"Teeth," Will said, "help him up."

Teeth nipped Robert on the rump. The little man howled in mortal terror and jumped up the step and into the airship.

"Please, take your seat," I said, putting a gentle hand on his back. He jerked away as if I had burned him and hurried off at the request of his chained fellows in their hurry to get out of the reach of Teeth and the other hounds on board. As many hounds as prisoners, and as many guards, were coming with us. Each guard had a personalized Sleeper as well as a hound.

Once we were all seated and ready, the captain of the ship lifted off the ground. Some of Gene's men gripped their seats as if their lives depended on holding on.

Gene grinned. "If I had known this was even possible, my life would have been very different," he said. His eyes shone with a childlike glee at being airborne. He was trying to get a look in every direction, even rising from his seat to stare out the windows on the side of the ship where the guards were sitting. Then his breath caught, and he said, "You ... have a Telling Tree here." His gaze fixed on that image, along with all of his men's and Robert's, for as long as it could be seen; then they looked at me with something like awe in their manner. Gene said, "I do not understand how ..."

Then he fell back into his seat and just stared out his window as Ra'Vell Island receded into the distance.

"The Creator has forsaken us," Robert wailed, sliding his arm under his runny nose. Great tears slid uncontrolled down his cheeks. "We are lost. Doomed. Forsaken ... this is not fair."

"Oh, for God's sake," Gene shouted, "shut up! Let us enjoy the view without your sniveling, you big baby."

"You would never have talked to me that way if my father was ..."

"But he's not," one of Gene's men snapped, "You killed him. Remember?"

How could I feel any more sorrow for the little man? No matter what he did or said, men like these would never give him respect or listen to him. *The things he wants most—love, respect, power—are somehow just out of reach for him,* I thought. Glancing over, I saw a look of venomous hate flash from his eyes toward me. The distaste of the pity I felt for him was written on his face in that hate. I held his gaze and tried to send him something better. Hope for a new life. He looked away.

It took such a short time to reach Resort. The men hadn't even had time to become overly restive before we were landing. When we hadn't fallen out of the sky right away, most of the men had settled down and watched the land pass below us.

"Hey," Robert said, "that's Montana Lake."

All the prisoners were pressed against the windows, watching, as the Transporter set down at the designated landing field at the edge of the city.

"Good choice," I heard Gene say to some of his men. "Very defensible." He shot me a look and said, "Was that you?"

"A joint decision for now, the council hasn't made it final, not yet," I said. "Are you ready for your first council meeting?"

***

(Day Twenty-nine)

There was a new, small table and a gavel placed at the right edge of the semicircle of larger tables where the council members sat. The council guests were on the famous stage of the concert hall, which we were borrowing from the Resort citizens. We had gathered up two hundred and eighty people who said they were part of the Natural Order or who had some known part in the destruction of Telling Wood. We were here with them to determine their fate among us.

I was surprised to learn that Lucus Tallman had resigned his seat to a nephew in order to stay in Hadria during the building and planning of the new town on the cliffs. Reia and Lucus were also planning a wedding. I smiled at the thought as I banged the gavel to call for order.

I stood to address the people gathered there. A hush rippled across the crowed until it was so silent you could have heard a leaf fall. I took a deep breath and started.

"As you all know, this gathering is to determine several things, including what city we are going to make our capital city now that Telling Wood is gone and what to do with the Natural Order and those who have shown themselves to be hostile to a peaceful society.

"The first order of business, our guests." I sat down and banged the gavel again, enjoying the ringing sound it made in this huge space.

222

Jorame stood to speak, Julka next to him at their table. Even though she was seated, the sense of togetherness couldn't have been stronger if they'd been holding hands. He smiled at her, then regarded the rest of the large room. "Ladies and gentlemen, we are here to listen to what these men and women on the stage wish for their lives and their futures. We are willing to have them live among us in conclaves of the old ways, with some modifications. First, no woman can be forced against her will to stay or beaten or killed for not complying. And anyone who wants to leave that life will be allowed to do so. Other than that, those of you who wish to continue in the old ways will be permitted to do so with a pledge that you will not try to force anyone else to live that way if they choose not too."

"A pledge?" Gene stood up, his chains clinking as he took a step forward on the stage. "Are you serious?" His lips twisted. "Why would any of us not take your pledge and then break it anytime we felt like it? What could you do about it?" He gave a short snort of laughter. "You are more naive than I thought!"

"Not really!" Jorame said. "Pendyse, show them."

I unwrapped the Heart of Telling and set it in plain sight on my table.

"So you have some stone plate," one of the women on stage shouted. "What is that to a man like Gene?" She gave Gene a wide grin and tilted her chin in his direction; I felt them take stock of each other. "He will do as he pleases, pledge or no. What does a piece of stone have to do with any of us, anyway?"

"Well," Jorame took a deep breath and began the story of the Heart of Telling, where it came from, how I was given it and what it could do. "So, the pledge you make will be before this 'stone plate,' as you called it, and the truth and honesty of your pledge will be known to us. For those who try to lie to the Heart of Telling will be given a different option than living among us."

Jorame sat down.

Marc Carroll from Califeia stood next. "If any of you wish to speak for yourselves, now is the time. The floor is open to you on the stage," he said, and sat back down.

Gene, still standing, said, "What difference would anything we have to say make in this whole farce? You people have already made up your mind for us, haven't you?"

223

"I want to talk." A diminutive gray mouse of a woman spoke up. "I want to take the pledge. I would like to live without fear of being beaten if I say the wrong thing or do something stupid that a man doesn't like." She stood, even though she seemed afraid, and said, "I'll take the pledge."

I took the Heart of Telling up the steps and onto the stage and stood in front of her holding the disk in my hands so I could also see it. "Will you promise to do no harm to peaceful people if we let you go?"

"Oh, yes!" She was nearly in tears. "I do. I promise. I never wanted to do anyone harm, ever. Never." She sniffed, trembling.

We both watched as the Heart of Telling began to stir. River colors swirled with gold became an image of a simple Women's House, with the fellowship of women doing household chores. "I grew up there," the woman said. "That was the happiest time of my life … before … the men."

"You may go. This is your first and only Telling." I motioned for the guard with the key to unlock her chains. "This woman is no threat to us," I said to the people. They knocked their stones on the table in agreement.

"This woman," I motioned one of our prearranged guides over, "will take you to where you can live until you decide what you wish to do with your life next." The guide lead the small woman from the stage and out of the building.

"You have got to be kidding!" Robert said. "Any one of us can place in our heads images of a happy little scene from our childhood, if that's all it takes." His attitude of braggadocio belied the fear I sensed beneath those words. "All of us men have had Tellings before. Even I could fool the Voice about what appeared in the Tree."

A rumble of assent rose from the chained men on stage. The women were silent, as they had no such experience to speak of.

"I will promise!" A young man stood up. "I am only here because my father made me join with him and the Natural Order. I loved my mother. But he took her back after she gave birth to a girl. He took them both back to the Women's Palace. I never knew what happened to either one of them. I was six when they went away. It left a hole in my heart that is still there. An ache that will never be healed." By the time this young man was finished, there were tears in his eyes and mine. I stood before him and let the Heart of Telling look into him, even as I was also seeing the wound that lay at the core of him. I realized that Robert, who was next to this man, was stone still, eyes wide open, as the image made for the young man showed the young man embracing a woman and saying, "Mother?" Then a thirteen- or fourteen-year-old girl joined them, and they were all crying and hugging.

"This man is no threat to us," I said, and the guard unlocked him. "I think you will see them both again," I told him. A guide came and led him away.

"I'll pledge." Robert stood, holding his head high. "I will do no harm to any of you."

I knew this was not true even as the surface of the Heart of Telling swirled blood red and angry. What we saw in there was murder, lies and deceit. Robert was covered from head to toe in someone else's blood, a mad gleam in his eyes.

He shook his head, "No! That is **not** me! I did not do that!"

"But you will," I said sadly. "It's in your heart, your mind." I turned to the people, "We cannot let this man live among us. He is dangerous and has murder in his heart."

Robert fell back onto his chair and began to howl and weep. He was being such a distraction that he had to be removed back to the temporary cells just so we could proceed.

The woman who had been eyeing Gene stood up. "I always wondered what was so great about a Telling anyway. Let the damn thing show me."

We looked; she was no weak or cowering woman. She was strong, but violence laced her life. She was crafty and deceitful, sneaky, and untrustworthy. Wherever she went, bad things followed. Instead of this unnerving her, she lifted her head and her eyes shone with pride.

"This woman is not to be trusted," I said. "She doesn't feel what others feel. She has no compassion. She will always find a way to do what she wants no matter who that might hurt."

One after another stood and spoke about their life. Some were let go to find a new life, some were held to form communities that would follow more of the old ways. Some were held as the most antisocial among them. We had a special place in mind for them.

We were only a quarter of the way through the lot of them when we took a break for lunch.

It took four days to hear everyone. It may not have been perfect, the way we did these Tellings, but we knew who we could allow to live with us and who we could not. Even among the ones who wanted the old ways, most of them didn't want trouble; they just wanted their old lives back. So that was what they would have, as long as they didn't try to force anyone into the old ways. People would be free to choose. It was the only way we could see peace happening.

Those men and women who were not released, we kept in cells until our council business was finished.

The people of Resort proposed that it become Nueden's capital. We discussed this for several days and then accepted their offer. We began the planning for the new Capital Building, its design and location, and also a factory to make our own transporters and smaller airships. Hadria, Nueden and the Blue Moon were agreeing to exchange knowledge and skills to bring about a better quality of life for all our people. A strong alliance between the three known peoples of this world was being forged.

It felt like the one step behind hope was finally becoming hope itself. There was excitement and possibility in the air, and laughter as people drew close and ideas flowed. I could see family developing in new ways. And I was a part of that. Sometimes I felt so proud of the people that I could hardly believe where this adventure in my life had started.

Resort was a reward and a delight to me. I kept finding new and unexpected insights, not only about the world at large, but about myself also.

And Zarek ... well, we were closer than ever.

CHAPTER TWENTY-NINE
(Day Thirty-four)

"One hundred and three people will be taken to the Island," Verity said. She looked at me, then Wydra, and she nodded thoughtfully. "It will be interesting to see what they make of their new freedom and a whole island to themselves."

We were gathered at the command center tent, the front of it open to the view of the cliffs and the Trillium Sea. John, Zarek and I had gone on a Stinger to Hadria to discuss with Verity and Ilantha the plans we had only talked about by com link.

"Forty-nine men and women were freed to go wherever they chose to live," I said, "and two small groups will be returned to Dunsmier and Brendle to live lives the old way. They can set up their communities outside their old towns, but they will be monitored for any aggressive behavior or the use of force to make people live the old ways. As long as they remain among us peacefully, they can stay; otherwise we will take them to the island."

"Gene and the other one hundred and one men and women will be put to sleep and taken to the island on the opposite side of the planet, thanks to your knowledge of this world's geography ..." Zarek said to Ilantha, "The new island is twice the size of Hadria's island, with everything they will need to sustain life with hard work and cooperation between them, but so far away they will not be a problem."

"And they will be watched on a regular basis with stealth flyovers." Wydra spoke directly to the First Woman, Ilantha.

"We will go once a year and check on them in person," Zarek nodded, "to see if anyone wants to leave or anyone new wants to be taken there."

"It will be our safety valve," said John. "We will leave enough supplies to get them started."

"Tools for building and planting," I added, "and seeds for crops."

"This unexplored island is heavily forested," Verity said. "We have known about it for a long time. It was our next move if we ever outgrew this island." She sighed. "But we have not grown. We have diminished in size over the last few decades of Rexon's treachery, and Keto plots; now we know why we haven't grown."

"Being poisoned will do that to a society, mind or body." Wydra said, and touched Verity's shoulder to reassure her. "That is no longer happening. And this island is bigger then the livable landmass of the Blue Moon, so you could easily have several cities here to add to your living space now that you have found the reason for your troubles."

"Keto told us that he and Ursa were not the first to try to take over the domes. The long, slow sickness was a poisoning time as well. That is why our birth rates have been so desperately low these past few hundred years," Ilantha said. The sadness in her voice nearly made me weep. *I know what that's like, when you think history, is one way, and it turns out to be just the opposite. Maybe that's what brings me so close to tears for her.*

"And now that you have contact with the exiles your Fish Children saved," Zarek said, "you already have a start on one of those towns—well, at least you have a start on communicating with them, anyway."

"Granted," I said, "there is work to be done to bring the bond of trust completely back to life. Your people seem ready to try." I shook my head, clearing away the sad thoughts. "I would not have thought it could be so, but here you are, building Beach Camp and repairing the damage to Hadria. Your people have named the whole island Hadrianna." I smiled at Verity and Ilantha. "You may even decide to live on the island too, someday."

"No." Ilantha smiled but shook her head, her long silver hair shimmering in the morning light as it cascaded over one shoulder. "Not me. Oh, I will spend time on the island, maybe even build a small dwelling here, but I will never leave my ocean home. It is where my heart blossomed, and I love it to much to forsake it." She gave Verity a searching stare. "Verity might choose the up top, maybe even living in the house her father built ..."

At this, Verity hugged Ilantha close and said, "Wherever you live, I will live. How else will I learn the finer details of leading?"

Ilantha laughed and patted Verity's shoulder, then pulled away to look into her indigo eyes. "I have learned far more about leading from you than the other way around, my dear." She brushed at the moisture in her eyes. "And I will be forever grateful. You have saved Hadria, and our people ... and me." The First Woman turned in my direction. "You and Pendyse. It would have all been lost without the two of you."

We talked on for a while until Wydra and John went to find my little brother Lodar and my hound Ibera, who was babysitting him on the beach. The others drifted away, leaving Zarek and I alone to sit on the cliffs and watch the waves roll.

This is beautiful! Zarek spoke to my mind. *It reminds me of home.*

I smiled. The hush-shush of the waves down below at low tide was a music that I felt filling us both. *This place is also home. We no longer belong to only one place, or one people.*

Yet, I believe we can make all people one. He smiled as he spoke to my thoughts.

He took my hand and brought it to his generous lips and kissed my palm. This exchange was not in words, but images. I closed my eyes and melted into the union love brings to two minds.

"OK. This is awkward."

I opened my eyes and looked up to see Kid facing out to sea.

"I didn't mean to interrupt anything ..." he began.

Zarek and I chuckled at his embarrassment. "It's OK," I said. "Did you need something?"

"Well, Dray and I have been thinking about your offer of an education. We would like to go with LaBo to Moon City Library. You know LaBo and Bee are leaving for home in a couple of days, and we were wondering if we could go with them?"

I leaned around Kid and saw Dray and Bee a few steps away. "Come on up, Dray, this is about you too," I said. "Bee, my sweet girl, how have you been these past few weeks?"

"I'm very well, thank you. Hello, great-uncle Zarek." She came over and kissed him on the cheek. He grinned and kissed her on the forehead.

"So you're going home. That is welcome news," Zarek said, and pulled her down to sit between us. The guys sat down next to me and hung their feet over the cliff edge, making me feel a little queasy at their nonchalant daring.

"And have you decided what you want to study?" I asked.

"Everything!" Kid said emphatically.

"Only everything?" Zarek chuckled.

"Well, how else will we learn enough to become Argonauts?" Dray said with a little huff to his answer and question.

"Argonauts?" Zarek looked puzzled.

"Yes, Uncle, we are all going to be Argonauts!" Willobee said, most seriously. "And the Moon City Library is the best in two worlds for learning the most."

She's got you there, I said. "Well, that sounds fine to me. If that is where you choose to study, that is a great place to start your adventure. The Blue Moon will amaze you."

"We would go with you if we didn't have so much still to do here." Zarek hugged Little Bee and added, "So you are going to be one of those brave explorers too, are you?"

"Oh, yes! I'm going to keep these two out of trouble."

The boys laughed and said, "Who's going to keep who out of trouble, little sister?" And, "You wish!"

"Samra and her mother, Lilith, are coming too. I gave them permission." Bee had a very grown-up expression on her newly seven-year-old face.

"All right then," Zarek said, "I guess that is settled. You all go to Moon City on our return trip to Resort. From Resort, you will go to Well Nine and be beamed directly to the phase port in the Library, our main mode of transport between the two places."

Dray, Kid and Bee began excitedly to tell us all the things they were going to do when they got to these places. They weren't going to wait to be explorers. They'd already claimed the name Argonauts: the three Argonauts.

***

Kid, Dray and Bee had three full days to explore Resort and reported to Zarek and I that it was a fine place for the new capital of New Eden. Kid refused to call our land Nueden, all run together as if it were one word, as we had done for hundreds of years. For him and his, it would be New Eden, "as it was meant to be," he would say. "And that is that!"

We all went to a "Song and Dance Drama" in the Concert Hall, where the council held meetings for the time being, and we thoroughly enjoyed ourselves. But the inevitable came to close the door on the children's time in Resort, for they were leaving in the morning.

Jorame and Julka were taking charge of the safari across the Steel Desert on work cycles. Kid, Dray Merry, the foundling Julka had adopted, Julka, and Jorame had a pallets behind their cycle for Lilith and Samra and LaBo, who had never piloted a cycles in her life and didn't want to start now, and Little Bee wanted to ride with Merry and Julka so that was how they left, a caravan of three cycles heading down the only accessible path out of Resort headed to the Domed Wells. At the bottom of the mountains, they would turn right and head around the base of the mountains to the Steel Desert. I was sure Jorame would show them the Desert Blaze at sunset, as he had shown me on my first trip to the Wells. *Kid will love it*, I thought, smiling to myself.

LaBo would take the boys, Little Bee, Lilith and Samra from Well Nine the rest of the way to Moon City. I would have loved to go with them just to see the looks on their faces at the experience of traveling by phase port.

Jorame, Julka and Merry were going home. I was sending them with letters to Father and my sister, Pandasiea. I talked to Father as often as I could by com, but letters were so much more thought out. I liked to send them on a regular basis, filled with all those things I'd forgotten to say when we were talking by com. And for Panda, I was giving her tangible words that she might store up and look back on as proof that I did, that I do, love her. She was thriving in Well One, and her hounds were full-grown and a huge hit in the Wells.

Mergel and Father were deep into the creation of the new stone road to Re-Maid, which was a good thing, as it would connect Ra'Vell Island to Ravenwood again. It would take a couple of years of hard work designing and forging new steel parts before our West Gate Bridge was repaired and functional again. With transporters to help with the heavy lifting, it would be much easier than the first time it was built and the many times it was repaired over the centuries.

I wanted to be everywhere at once, to see it all happening. The painful loss of life with the destruction of Telling Wood was by no means out of our minds, but the movement forward was exhilarating; everywhere we went, building was going on.

***

(Day Fifty-four)

A crew of workers loaded two transporters with supplies for the exiled. Zarek and I were going with them to see the island we were calling Far Away, which someday would most likely be called Farway, what with the people's penchant for smashing names together. *But no doubt it will be moot*, I thought, *as Gene and the people will most likely give it a name of their own, as they live there.*

On my last visit with Gene, he asked me, "What are you going to do with the people left in the cells now that you have let the others go?"

"We are preparing a place for you and the last one hundred," I said. "We will be taking you there soon. How you govern this new place will be up to you and the people who go with you. But you will not have access to Nueden any longer. The trouble you cause, you will have to live with."

"Sounds intriguing," he said. "When do we leave?"

"Now!" I pulled out my Rectifier and put the man to sleep.

It took some time to move them all to the third transporter. We'd keep them asleep for the duration of the journey, as we didn't want them knowing anything about where this island was in relationship to the rest of the inhabited world. Even if they had enough knowledge to build ships that would stay afloat, it would be unlikely they would be able to cross the vast ocean and find Nueden.

All one hundred and one were safely stowed aboard as we lifted away from Resort. The turquoise of Montana Lake glimmered in the sun as the three large air barges shot away over the mountains and desert, past Hadrianna to the island of Far Away.

232

CHAPTER THIRTY
(Day Fifty-five)

It took us all the rest of the day of departure and all that night to reach Far Away. We set down and gave the exiles another small dose of sleep while we unloaded the tools, supplies and them.

Water was readily available, as there was a clean river emptying into the ocean not far away from a clearing close to the beach where we had landed. We were on a beautiful, crescent-shaped, south-facing beach with white sand that shimmered a light purple in the slant of early morning sun. The land rose in a gentle slope to an open area that looked like a good place for a village, close to fresh water and fishing, both river and ocean.

From the back of the natural clearing, the land rose in layers of plateaus with exotic trees of vivid greens and many colorful flowers among the foliage, and even more exotic varieties of birds using their colorful plumage to compete with the trees. The birdcalls were both beautiful and terrifying at the same time: I was thinking of the kinds of wildlife on the Blue Moon. I wondered if we were dooming this spectacular place, these creatures, or perhaps the people, as the Stella Mara didn't have great knowledge to share of what kinds of animals that lived here.

But the Heart of Telling had shown us this place, and the Stella Mara knew where it was, and they'd given it to us as a bond promise to be allies and friends. The Sabostienies had agreed to build a phase port on Hadrianna that would connect them to the Blue Moon.

Standing on the beach that glittered like diamonds, looking up that slope, I saw that some of the trees close by looked as if they grew large fruit or possibly nuts of some kind. The people might not starve even if they chose not to work at planting for their future.

This was a good place to begin, a very good place. They would have every chance here to build a life for themselves, if they could learn to cooperate with one another and not kill each other before they learned that.

We set up a large communal tent that would shelter them until they could build something more permanent. We put the tools and supplies inside the tent and waited for Gene to wake up. The dose of sleep we'd given him wasn't as much as we'd given the rest of the people. Zarek wanted to talk to him before we left. I figured that no matter what anyone else thought, he would probably become the leader of this band of outcasts. The men already looked to him for that, and so, I thought, he might as well be the first to see the place.

To my surprise, it wasn't Gene who woke up first, but the woman who'd spoken out at the council meeting, the crafty, deceitful, not-to-be trusted woman. She seemed to think Gene was a hero for all ages. Her name was Merrill, I remembered. She sat up and stretched like a cat, looking around, first at the transporters and the crew still unloading last-minute items. Then she saw the landscape and the sea. She stood up with one hand on her hip, the other hand held over her eyes like a visor to block the morning glare. She froze when her searching gaze landed of Zarek and me.

"Where am I?" she asked. She kept looking, and soon a wide grin took possession of her face. "If it weren't for you two being here," her lip curled in a nasty sort of way, "I'd think I'd died and gone to Tomorrow Land."

"What the hell..." Gene rumbled as he stood up and moved stiffly onto the beach. He said nothing else, just looked and looked. Two of the transports lifted off the beach and hovered in the air over the island.

"This is your new home," Zarek said to the two of them. "How you choose to live here will be up to the lot of you. We've left supplies that should see you well into the year. By then, you will have decided where best to set up your village or future city, I would imagine. The Hadrians tell us the climate is fairly mild year round, so you should be all right on that score. You might not like the rain. The rainy season is a few

234

months out, so you might want to get some sturdy buildings up before it comes."

"We call this Far Away," I said, "as it is far away from anywhere else. This will be your island to live on according to the old ways -- or new ways, as you please, but because of distance, it makes war on Nuedeners, the Blue Moon or Hadrianna impossible."

The woman, Merrill, began to laugh. Gene stared at her with cold, calculating eyes, showing no emotion at all, and then he asked. "You are leaving us here?" His sharp eyes kept roaming the land. Suddenly he whooped out a harsh laugh and stooped to toss sand in the air like a child at play, but when he straightened up and looked at us again, he asked, "This isn't a joke? You are giving us this place to live in as we please?"

Zarek nodded, silent. *I hope this isn't a mistake,* he said to me alone.

Me too!

"We will come to check on you in a year," I said.

"And bring new supplies if you need them," Zarek added, "and new people, if they want to come. And pick up ones from here who may have changed their minds about making war. We will test anyone who wants to go back to Nueden once a year."

"Among the supplies, you will find a com link to the new capital, Resort," I said. "You will be able to keep in touch that way if you choose too."

"We will be watching you, but you won't see us," Zarek said, "except for once a year. At the appointed time, we will establish some trade agreement with your island if you so choose."

"Zarek, they're beginning to wake up," I said. "It's time for us to go."

Our crew was on board waiting for us. We climbed aboard and lifted away from the beach.

Men and women were standing up from where we had laid them, appearing groggy and disoriented, looks of fear then of wonder on their faces. Our last view of Gene was of a man taking charge, Merrill right beside him giving orders to the women.

Robert Waldorf, stumbling to his feet, looking lost.

"Are we creating another kind of Remode?" I fretted. "I hope not."

"We mustn't second guess what the Heart of Telling has shown us for these people's future," Zarek said. "If this is what the Great Spirit wants, even for these people, giving them a second chance, or maybe a first chance … we might be surprised."

I sighed. "I know. In a way, I almost envy them." My gaze caressed the coastline of this gem of land in the middle of a dark purple and green sea. "What an adventure it would be to start out new, creating and discovering a new world, really." My thoughts flew to Kid, Dray and Bee, the three self-proclaimed Argonauts, wondering if they would ever come here to explore.

"I hope they will be up to the task," Zarek said.

I looked at Zarek to see if he meant the kids or Gene's group of people and decided it didn't matter which. "May Wonannonda bless them with a good future."

Zarek looked at me and smiled. "I'd say that is entirely up to them."

***

(Day Sixty-nine)

At John and Wydra's home in Resort, I sat at the dining table, writing in my journal.

We stayed five days on Hadrianna, both on the island and in the domes. Zarek and I toured every factory and facility, learning many new things that could be implemented in our communities in Nueden and on the Blue Moon.

The First Woman and Zarek spoke in private several times. He told me they often spoke of the Father and Mother, and the Moon City library. Ilantha had always wanted to see it as a child, and that interest was now revived. She wanted to go there and wander the stacks, and sit and read, luxuriating in the pages of real books as well as the neurocap learning centers.

Verity took us to the house by the falls one night to meet some of her newfound siblings, minus Keto, of course; he was still being held captive, the only one on Hadrianna the Heart of Telling showed we could not trust to let go free. What we saw of him in that disk was a twisted, deformed soul. Was Keto evil or just sick? Thinking of the Voice, Zee, and others I had encountered, including Gene and Robert, and Wallace William Waldorf, Robert's father, I found myself asking that question over and over. What do you do with sick individuals who are a

236

danger to the health and wellbeing of the communities they live in? And if they are just sick, what do you do with sick individuals who will not help themselves get better and are a danger to themselves and those around them?

"The realization that I can't help Keto is a hard reality to take in, that I can't reach him. He doesn't listen to anything I say," Verity had said as we talked about what to do with someone set on destroying the people who loved him.

There was no island for him, at least not on this world, although Zarek thought there might be a small island on the Blue Moon on the other side of the Ice Fangs, their main landmass that could work for keto.

"It is a desolate place. Not nearly as nice as the one we left Gene and his crew on," Zarek had said, "but at least he would be free. Alone, but free to move around in nature."

***

In the last few weeks we'd been back in Resort, the rebuilding of the Zap Line Hub had begun, and all over Nueden, things seemed to be settling into new routines. We were all pleased with the progress.

I turned and stood up at the sound of footsteps behind me to find Zarek there, listening to his com.

"Ha!" Zarek whooped, clicking off his wrist com. "I knew this would come, I just didn't expect it so soon." The wide grin on his face and the happy emotion I felt coming from him makes me grin too.

"What?" I asked. "What secret are you keeping hidden behind that wall of yours? You said ..."

"Ah, ah, ah." He wagged a finger at me. "You wouldn't deny me my surprise, would you?" With a big grin on his face, he said, "It's time to go to the Wells. Well Nine, to be exact."

I hadn't been to that Well yet, but I knew it was their most precious city. Though it was the smallest, I had heard it was exquisite in its simple beauty, the center of the spiral, their tallest and deepest Well.

"Father and Mother had their home in Well Nine when they were in the Wells," Zarek said. "Our main phase port is there. And after we make our visit, we will go to Moon City and see about that island for Keto. And prepare for Ilantha's visit."

"OK. How soon can we leave?" I poked him playfully in the ribs. "If you're not going to tell me until we get there what this big secret is, let's leave right now. Today! You know I hate waiting for good news. What's up?"

He cradled me in his arms, smiling, then he became serious. "I love you, Pendyse Ra'Vell," he said, his voice husky with emotion. "And I always will."

Zarek had said this before, but somehow, this time was different. The sparkle in those large, purple, diamond-shaped cat eyes, the light emanating from inside him, made this time more deeply felt in my mind and every cell of my body. I tucked my face against his neck, planting tiny kisses in the hallow of breast bone, and simply breathed in the essence of his scent, that reassuring smell that makes me know I'm safe and loved.

I sighed and mind whispered, *Mutual.*

There is no better feeling in the world than to love and be loved.

***

(Day Seventy)

"How long does this bonding thing take?" Rifkin asked. "We've been here for hours. I'm getting hungry." He grumbled, and James and Ferris nodded agreement. "We're all *starving*," Rifkin said with emphasis.

Just about everyone I knew was there in Well Nine. A huge party was going on, people mingling, music softening the edges of laughter and conversation, but no one could eat or drink anything until the Bond Couple arrived back among us.

Jorame and Julka had entered the Mundus Cavus Arbor Vitae early that morning and had not yet returned.

"The world cave, the womb of the world," Zarek told me, "where the Crystal Tree of Life grew, an ancient crystal formation in the shape of a tree, a mirror image of root and branch reflecting in the Pool of Happiness, deep underground."

"This is an ancient Nuptia," LaBo said. "We have all but forgotten this form of wedding ceremony. We have less formal ways to marry these days. Jorame and Julka are the first in a chiliad to travel to the Pool of Happiness and make their vows before the World Tree of Life."

238

"Trees!" I said, wondering. "We had one above ground, Telling Tree, that was central to our culture, and are now growing anew. The Stella Mara have the Great Sea Tree, and here I learn that the Sabostienie have one called the World Tree of Life. Caves and Trees. What does it mean, LaBo?"

"I am not certain myself, Pen. But one is wood, one coral and one is crystal," LaBo said. "Maybe there is some yet-undiscovered wisdom to be learned about ourselves from the way these three grow, the way we grow. The beauty they are that makes us catch our breath in awe, and pause in the presence of something more than we can see or understand." She shrugged and turned as some of our friends came up to us, laughing and talking.

"So, how much longer must we wait?" John said as he and Wydra, Verity and Ilantha walked up to our small group standing near the center of the room where the sponsal table was being laid out with food fit for the wedding feast. Smaller tables were spread out around the dance floor, currently filled with friends and people I didn't know.

"I'd say soon. They must be back by now," Zarek said, "most likely changing for the celebration." He craned his neck, looking over the heads of the crowd in the direction of the entrance to the Nuptias Cavus, where Mergel, my father Davood and sister Panda, and little Merry waited for the new husband and wife, Jorame and Julka. Mergel was to announce them when they arrived.

Looking around at so many people who had come from the Blue Moon, Hadrianna and many parts of Nueden to celebrate the bonding of these two dear friends, I was awash in feelings of immense pleasure, not only at their bonding but at the drawing together of all these good people.

Mergel climbed the few steps onto a small podium as Jorame and Julka walked out from under the archway and stopped at the edge of the wide, round room. "We have not had a bonding like this in hundreds of years, may it not be our last." Mergel said, and stomped, as with only one arm, he could not clap, which had been the custom we were told. We all stomped in solidarity with Mergel. "I present to you, fresh from the Crystal Tree of Life and the Pool of Happiness, Jorame and Julka. We bless you. May we be, every day of your life, a gift to you both, as you are a gift to us."

The wedding couple, dressed in simple white, faced the crowd. Mergel stepped down from the podium and had them face each other, and he tied a sparkling sand silk ribbon onto Julka's left wrist and Jorame's right, with a few feet of it dangling between them. It was a glittering connection between them, a symbol of the love that would always link them together, even when not visible to the world.

Then Jorame and Julka led us in dining, dancing and singing. At the end of the evening, the ribbon was tossed from the podium by the happy couple, and the World Spirit caught it up and sent it to the next couple who were to exchange vows before the Pool of Happiness.

Without any wind to give it direction, the ribbon floated up and up, and over the crowd, then came drifting down to rest upon Zarek and I.

CHAPTER THIRTY-ONE

"I will be glad to turn him over to you," Verity said, giving me the power staff that held the prisoner, Keto, in a power lock. "He still refuses to speak to me." She looked away from Keto. I felt sorrow well up in her, an undertow of emotion that nearly overwhelmed me too. I felt Zarek shore me up, and I passed that strength along to Verity, who gave us a wan smile.

"Once he's settled, let me know. I'll come to visit him," she said, and turned to join Ilantha, who was boarding the flagship for home. They were returning to Hadria that morning. We saw them off from just outside Well One.

"You three will be leaving soon too," Father said, patting Ibera's back, as we loaded onto the cycle pallet, Father's air chair on the end next to my purple-furred hound.

"Um, four," Davood said, giving Keto a studied look. We were returning to Father's home, where we planned to share a meal before leaving. Jorame and Julka, along with little Merry and my sister Panda, were at Father's preparing for our departure.

"Well, we have to get Keto to someplace safe," I said, giving Keto an appraising stare myself. "Better sooner than later."

Mergel nodded, his mouth a thin, grim line. "Yes!" He glanced sidewise, making a brief survey of Keto's blank, statue-like countenance. Keto did not respond to any of us. He seemed to be in a fugue state. But I didn't trust him. Why should I? He had tried to kill me, and many others.

"I know that island. It will be a good place for him." Mergel shook his head. "I don't know if you know, Zarek, that there is a good-sized house there already. I've never seen it, but I've heard it is quite palatial."

"Yes. I do know, even though the Father and Mother never spoke of it," Zarek said. "They had it built as a family retreat. They didn't use it much after ... well, then Tia grew old and died, and they only went back there to bury her and visit once a year on the anniversary of her death."

"Who was Tia?" I asked, looking from Mergel to Zarek.

"Their first daughter," Zarek said. "She grew old. They did not."

"I didn't think you knew about the house." Mergel patted Zarek on the shoulder. "Your sister, Skitar, told me about it. She didn't think you knew."

"The Library is full of history, my friend, not all of it easy to talk about, not even with friends. And besides, I only discovered the information the last time I was here, when I was reading through their Journals. After Tia, they decided they would have two children at a time, a few years apart, every seventy-five to a hundred years or so. Skitar and I were the last of five sets over as many centuries."

My father looked away, down the spiral tunnel we were travelling, as if to avoid a too-personal moment, but then he changed his mind and asked, "How is it going with the Purple Tea? Are those of you who are giving it up ... all right?" He turned a concerned face to Zarek. "I mean ... has it been hard?"

Zarek thought for a moment, then answered honestly, "Yes! But it would be harder for me to bond with Pen and then watch her age and die while I continued on. I would rather we grow old together." He paused. "And truthfully, I made the commitment to be the next Father because I believed my people needed me to, not because I wanted to take the place of my father. My sister Skitar didn't want to be Mother, and her husband, Bex, when they married, didn't want that responsibility either, so it fell to me to be the leader of our people. I knew we were to be our parents' last children. Even with the Purple Tea, they were passing the years for childbearing."

"But you still are the Father and leader," my father said. "You just won't have the job as long as they did."

Zarek gave a small huff, pursed his lips, nodded and said, "True. And maybe that's a good thing. Our worlds are changing. The old ways don't apply as they once did. The Father and Mother have always been for the people, the community. Even though each is a unique individual of great worth, hearing their stories in the collective, working for the good of all … that is always what mattered most. I believe that can still be so, just in a different way than we have done it before."

I heard my father's words in my head. *I think he is a good man. He will do well for my daughter, Pen.* I knew it was a private thought that had just slipped out. I lowered my head, afraid to look him in the eye. I knew he would know I had listened in. My eyes were misting over with gratitude for a loving father still with me.

There was a long quiet spell as we made our way through the traffic of the city of Well One to Father's place.

"Pen, did you know," Mergel said, finally, "that Davood, Panda, the hounds and I are going to Re-Maid in a few days to start the new road from there to Ravenwood?"

New conversation erupted about the excitement of their trip, the road plans, the workforce, and seeing Father's new granddaughter, Susan, and her mother and father, Minnari, and my old friend, Quill.

The afternoon was a good note to end our visit on, and we headed back to Well Nine with Keto in tow to meet with LaBo, Kid, Dray, Bee and Samra and her mother. We would all be on the Blue Moon by morning.

***

At Phase Port Nine, we huddled together with all our baggage, ready to leave for the Blue Moon. Once on the platform, there was a feeling of speed and distortion, and colors flashing past us, and all I could hear was Keto screaming, and then we were there, in the heart of Moon City, next to Library and the science labs.

When we arrived, Keto was still screaming. His eyes were wild and bone-deep panic rode his face. When he stopped screaming, eyes still wide, he hissed in a ragged breath, "I will kill you all."

"Well, it seems his fugue is over," Zarek said dryly.

Ibera growled. Kid stepped up next to her and stared with hot eyes up at Verity's brother. Kid's nostrils flared in anger. "No one threatens my friends!"

Kid stared at Keto and Keto stared back for a few seconds, then Keto bowed his head, emotions seething like an ocean in turmoil, and mumbled something under his breath that sounded like "You'll be the first to go, brat." It was too low for my ears to catch, but my mind heard those words loud and clear.

"Come on, Kid," Zarek said, placing his hand on the boy's shoulder. "He can't hurt any of us. He's lost everything that is familiar to him. Lighten up. We're all OK."

Kid glanced at Dray and Bee, then LaBo, and back to Zarek and me. "I just want him to understand," Kid said, and shot Keto a glare, "that he had better behave."

We took the man to the cells where John and I had been locked up and kept for a while, almost two years before, and left him there.

***

The three Argonauts came with Zarek and me and Ibera to the island and palatial house to check it out and see what we would need to make it livable for Keto. This initial trip would be without him.

"It will be our first adventure," Andraykin announced proudly.

I laughed. "How can you call it your first? You've been on at least three very dangerous adventures already in your young life."

"Those were not exactly by our own choice. So that makes this one our 'official' first," Kid said with a serious, straight face that punctuated his words. Zarek and I didn't dare laugh, as we both felt the gravity of Kid's thoughts.

We all stood at the ship's rail as we approached the island. It was only about a quarter of the size of Hadrianna, but it had a south-facing beach and a stone harbor and dock next to the beach. It was far enough away from the mainland that the Ice Fangs, as tall as they were, were barely visible, and the line of the southern cliffs could not even be distinguished. They called the island Zagora Falls. At the source of the falls began a river that cascaded down past the house, we were told. There was also a hot spring near the top of Zagora Falls.

Zarek nodded and said, "When you're an Argonaut, you won't always have a choice about what adventure catches you up and whisks you out of your nicely made plans."

Kid look up at him. "I know that!" he said, a little offended. "Kid may be my name, but I'm not one. Haven't been one for a long time ."

"What he means, Uncle Zarek, is that at the beginning of the adventure, we get to choose." Willobee smiled at them both. "We all know there will be dangers and that adventures can and will take us to places unexpected, but that's what we want … after we get educated."

"Yeah," Kid and Dray said together. "What she said."

That did make us all laugh as the captain of the ship bumped us gently up against the stone dock.

The three Argonauts jumped out first, and we followed them at a more sedate pace.

Zarek took my hand, and we walked up the steps to the huge rock structure surrounded by trees that had been shaped by the wind. Even when the wind was not blowing, the small trees scattered about the front wall of the courtyard still looked as if it was. Vegetation was sparse, but the entryway was a grand arch leading into an open courtyard, where there was a rock fountain made with great skill and beauty.

"My sister Tia was an artist." Zarek paused to take in the different-colored stonework and the placement of every detail. "This was her masterpiece. Anyway, that is what I read. And we have many of her stone pieces in our art center." Zarek stood in front of the fountain, feeling the peace of the place. "It is still beautiful, but looks like it needs a little repair on the house side of the fountain over there. Before we bring Keto out here, that should already be done."

I listed the repairs needed in my journal as we went along.

Stairs circled up around both sides of the fountain to the main entrance, another arch with a wide door made of some kind of rose-colored wood with golden streaks in it, and the slightly weathered carving of a welcoming young woman, arms outstretched in greeting.

"Is that your sister, Tia?" Kid asked. "It's weird to think you could have a sister who's been ... well, I mean ..."

"You mean a sister who's been dead for hundreds of years before I was born."

"Well, yeah."

Zarek nodded. "For me too."

There were ornamental trees in the courtyard, well protected from the harshest weather. They had been cared for by someone, it looked like. "Did the Father and Mother have someone look after the place here, even if they didn't come back after Tia was gone except once a year for a while?" I asked.

"I don't know," Zarek said. "It looks as if that's possible."

"Come on, Uncle. Let's go inside," Bee urged.

The boys turned the knob pushed the door open.

Beyond was a wide hall lined with gilt-edged mirrors from floor to high ceiling that caught the light from open spaces between them.

245

We could see into the rooms beyond, and there were windows with thick, wavy glass that let in the light from both sides. There were three large, open main doorways off this huge hall. To the left was what must have been a library at one time, the walls lined with shelves. To the right was a large room with a fireplace. It was too large to be called a living space; it was most likely meant for entertaining at one time. The third door, straight in front of us, led into another hallway, but one of a more normal size. We found a kitchen, huge dining room, other, less-formal looking rooms and, at the end of the hall, another hall that crossed it like a T bar. There were twenty chamber suites, all empty except one, which was filled with plain furnishings.

I said aloud, "That may be where someone stays when they come to check on things here. The place will need more furniture. The kitchen will have to be stocked."

"Keto will have to do for himself," Zarek said. "I won't ask any of my people to put themselves in danger to serve him. We will have to make sure everyone knows to stay away from here."

"I agree," I said. "He isn't to be trusted with any one's life. I hope this place can help him heal. But I think being alone is never a good thing. Maybe with no one to manipulate he will look within for once."

"Well, people are not made to be alone. I don't know how that will help him heal, if he can heal at all."

Each suite had its own small living space, bath and bedchamber, and there were fireplaces in all three rooms. "I wouldn't mind living here," I said. "Even though it's empty, every line of the place has fantastic craftsmanship, an artistic grace that is soothing. Maybe it can do him some good."

After we went through the entire stone mansion, checking every room and wardrobe, we returned to the ship to eat lunch. The four children; Kid, Dray, Samra and Bee, wanted to explore the island. Zarek and I hadn't had much time to ourselves for weeks, so we let them go, with rucksacks full of food for their high adventure. The island was relatively small, so it wasn't as if they could really get lost. They just had to be back before nightfall so we could get back to Moon City and get things together for Keto in the next few weeks.

***

We spent three weeks in Moon City getting all the arrangements taken care of for Keto. Kid, Dray, Samra and Bee were going back to their education at Library with LaBo. The boys already had rooms they shared near Library, and Willobee lived with her greatma and greatpa, Skitar and Bex. Samra and her mother had rooms next to the boys.

"Are you ready to go?" Zarek asked after I'd given everyone a second or third hug before stepping up onto the platform of the phase port. We were going to Ra'Vell Island by phase port to spend some time at home. Then we were going to see friends at Re-Maid.

Zarek put his arm around me, and mine went around his waist. We lifted our hands in farewell and saw their faces slide from view as the phase port was activated.

When we came to rest, Zarek said, "You know our lives will be spent traveling, in meetings, doing for others. We won't really have a home of our own."

"But we will have many homes, places where we belong. Many friends, people we love. My mother told me in a letter that my life would not be my own." I smiled up at him, "I'm good with that, as long as we travel together."

He bent to my lips and kissed me. Ibera whined, making us chuckle and break apart. We picked up our bags and headed up to the shrine where James would be waiting for us with our cycles.

"James! Will!" Zarek gave them a quick embrace, and so did I.

"It's good to be back on Ra'Vell," I said. "Can we go to the tree before heading home?"

"Can't wait to see the Nut Snakes?" James said, laughing, happy to see us. "Well, why not?" We loaded up and headed the short way over to the circular grove.

"Oh, with everything going on lately, I forgot the Nut Snakes are in full summer colors," I said.

The new Wonannonda tree sparkled and shimmered in the sunlight, a gentle wind tugging at the branches, making the leaves flutter in song, the branches clacking together in accompaniment. It took my breath away. A gentle awe filled me at how much it had grown just since the last time I'd been here. I took a deep breath, inhaling the sweet fragrance of the flowers of the Wonannonda Tree.

"Trees and caves," I whispered. I felt Zarek smile beside me.

CHAPTER THIRTY-TWO

"Summer Festivals are the best," I said, excited to share one with Zarek.

"I want to hear the new music, *Wonannonda Born*," Zarek touched my cheek in a tender caress. "Will said his daughter Onamie and her husband Paul wrote the music in honor of your nephew, Mark."

"Yes!" I smiled, sadness tingeing my pleasure at the anticipation of Onamie's gift to all of us in memory of Mark.

Zarek shook me gently. "Hey, it will be good."

I nodded. "I know."

He took my hand and walked me away from the kennels where we'd been visiting Hungry, Ripper and Shadow, who were all ready to give birth again.

"If Rifkin doesn't stop breeding them, everyone on the island will have a guard dog." I laughed. "We could soon have more hounds than people running around here."

"Why don't we take Ibera, make a picnic lunch and check out the progress on the west and east towers and the work being done on the east bridge when we come back?" Zarek suggested.

We went to the castle kitchen, and Chet made us a huge picnic lunch. We loaded up both cycles, Zarek's black one and my first cycle, which the Oaths had given me. Ibera would ride on a short platform behind my cycle. The lunch and overnight supplies were behind Zarek's cycle on another platform. We decided to spend the night beside the west falls. The three-day Summer Festival would start in two days; that would give us plenty of time to look around the south end of Ra'Vell Island.

Are you ready to go? Zarek put his helmet on and straddled the black cycle.

I matched his action and answered, *Lead the way.*

I sensed Ibera flop down on the bed I'd made for her and promptly fall asleep.

We took the road down the west side of the island, past the farmlands, next to the west fork of Rush River. The last time I'd been on this road, Jorame was teaching me how to drive a cycle. I smiled, thinking of him and Julka ... married. I felt very happy for them.

I know. Me too. Zarek spoke gently into my thoughts. *I was afraid for a time that the two of you were going to be that couple who would break my heart forever.*

I admit I was slow on the uptake, but then, I'm young ... not as much experience as you two old men, I teased. There was a time not too long ago when I would never have dared say that to Zarek, as the age difference was part of what had kept him away from me, even though to look at us, you would only think there might be a year or two of difference. It was only because I had come to feel sure that our love was strong enough to take some good-natured kidding now and then that I said anything at all.

I heard him laughing into the helmet com. *We will be the next to visit the Mundus Cavus Arbor Vitae.* This mind touch was as sweet as a caress and a kiss.

The World Cave where the Crystal Tree grows, I sighed. *The Pool of Happiness.*

Yes. Soon. I don't want to wait forever before we are ...

... one in every way, I finished for him. *Me too.*

We ate lunch at a favorite spot of mine overlooking the cliffs and river close to the western falls. It was a sheltered, stony dip in the cliff side, a niche invisible from land but so loud with the rush of water from the cascade that it was an impossible place for conversation—that is, if you couldn't speak mind to mind. After we finished and repacked our basket with the remains of the typical overabundance of provisions Chet always made, we sat with our legs dangling over the edge of the rock face, holding hands, silent, as mist from the falls rose and settled on our skin, making us damp and glistening in the last of the sun's light.

I want to build a small cabin next to the brook where we camped on our way to Resort, I said.

I've been thinking of that too. A small house that could be shielded. It would give us a real place of our own when we need to get away from our responsibilities for some private time alone.

We made plans for the future, talking about what we wanted in a house. We watched the sun set and the moons rise through the mist. A sweet peace settled over us, and we sat a while longer, holding hands over Ibera's back as she lay between us.

Zarek's eyesight being better than mine in the dark, he led me back up to our cycles, and we completed our journey to the southwest tower, which wasn't far away. It loomed large in the dark, a blacker form against the moonslit night sky.

"This watch tower almost tumbled to the ground," I said over my com link.

"Will was telling me about the history of the towers the other day. Looks like it's been completely rebuilt now."

I could still see the outline of some scaffolding on the far side of the tower.

We pulled up and set the cycles to ground. Ibera leapt off and loped over to sniff-greet one of her brothers, the guard tower Nar Hound on duty. He gave her a warning growl. "No funny business, sister, I'm at work here," the growl said. She sat down politely and let him sniff her. Then he howled a greeting to announce that the tower had company.

Roger, the captain of this guard tower, came out, and we all went inside. He introduced us to his thirty guards, and gave us the tour of the four-story tower. By then it was time for dinner, so he led us down to the kitchen and dining hall on the ground floor. All our weapons now were the nonlethal variety, which the guards kept with them at all times, so there was no need for an armory any more. We visited with the men and women stationed there, shared the evening meal and helped them decorate the dining hall for their Summer Festival celebrations.

When all was done and the evening was drawing to a close, we followed Roger up to the unfinished top of the tower for a night view of the stars and the lake by moonlight. The lake held the moons and stars in a deep velvet embrace, and the glory of nature was everywhere we looked.

We spent the night in the guard dorms with the thirty or so other people currently at the tower. The next day, we'd visit the east tower and then head home to the castle and the Summer Festival at Ra'Vell Town before we headed for ReMaid.

In the morning, strangely, even though there were so many people around, I felt as if Zarek and I were alone in the world, just the two of us, and everything had been made for us. Everything took on a sweetness that lit things from within.

Pen, heart of my heart. It's called love.

***

On the morning we were to leave for ReMaid, Zarek got a com that there was some kind of problem on the Blue Moon that required his attention immediately.

"I'll go with you," I said.

"No." He shook his head. "You go on to see your sister Minnari and her new baby. Enjoy some time with your father and little sister Panda. Tell Mergel I'll be along shortly whenever I get this situation smoothed out. The people are used to having a live-in leader, but I'll join you at ReMaid soon, I promise."

So I found myself, and Ibera heading out over the purple plains alone, but not lonely. Zarek was only a thought away if I needed him or if he needed me.

I was amazed at how much the place had grown. It looked bigger than Ra'Vell Town. As I got closer, I realized it *was* bigger than Ra'Vell Town. I could see to the left, some way from the town itself, the Linnaeus Stone Mine. It produced that rare substance needed for the Rectifiers, as well as the black stone they were using for building. All the trees on the lower parts of the mountain where the town had grown up had gone into building as well.

I rode up the switchbacks, through homes and buildings instead of trees, with wide-open vistas of the plains, to the highest part of town, where the old wooden structures had been before they had burned to the ground. There were people about, activity in many directions. I recognized the feel of a happy place. Industry and art were present. I went all the way to the end of the main street and came slowly to a stop among so many cyna-cycles parked along the stone sidewalks that I thought I was back in the Wells. I was wondering where I should go first to try to find my family when I heard a whoop of joy as I was dismounting my cycle, I found my life nearly being squeezed out of me.

"Pendyse!" That's when I knew it was Pepperling, the Mother of ReMaid: when I heard that raspy, warm voice I had come to love.

I turned and hugged her. We both laughed, and she kissed my cheek. "It is about time you came to visit us. In fact, it is past time," she scolded.

She drew back, holding me at arm's length, and looked at me. "You look different. I think you've grown up." She looked around. "Where is this young man of yours? I thought your father said he was coming too."

"He will meet me here later. He had to make a quick trip to Blue Moon. Some dispute that needs settling," I explained.

"I still can't get over it. All these new people and places," Pepperling said, her old eyes round with wonder, "and we here at ReMaid are part of all that." She shook her head. "When this place burned, I never would have thought it could become this." Pepperling raised her hands, indicating the city growing up around her. "And it's all thanks to you, Pen."

"No, this is you and your people ... and I am so impressed."

Pepperling started pointing out the different buildings. "That is our Hearing House," she said, indicating a long, narrow building up against what I knew must be the cave entrance at the end of town, "where we hear the life and times of the people, and if any have problems or complaints." She grinned, eyes asparkle. "And Pen, it's working beautifully."

She pointed to the solar power plant Jorame had helped set up, upslope on the highest point of flat, open land a little above the Hearing House, then to the larger structure in front of us, against the mountain. "This is the school and library, where all our treasures are kept. Children and books! Education!"

"It is so great to see you," I said, "and all that has been done here. So which one of these grand edifices is your domicile?"

"Oh, mine is small, but very nice. I'm only one person, after all. I don't need much." Pepperling smiled sweetly and pointed to the black stone building next to the wooden watchtower that hung on the downslope side of the mountain, overlooking the plains. "Come in and see my little piece of Tomorrow Land."

I followed her into an entryway that reflected her simple but elegant tastes, both in design and furnishing. It was small and sparse, but she had a guest chamber with its own bath. It was directly off the entry, her room across the hall.

"Oh, Pepperling. It's beautiful. I love it."

"I would love to have you stay with me!" she said, leading me into a neat and tidy kitchen and small dining space. Then she opened a door onto a small deck, and I fell in love with the place all over again. We stepped out into the fresh air to a view of the eastern plains. It was a clear day, and I thought I could almost see all the way to the island, even though I knew that was impossible.

"It's beautiful, Pepperling. It's perfect! I am so happy for you."

***

I stayed with Pepperling, and we talked late into the night about all the things going on in Re-Maid. She showed me her new leg and foot, made for her in our plastics factory in Ra'Vell. She was getting around now without using a crutch. She was slower and more careful, but made it around very well.

After breakfast, we walked over to Quill and Minnari's home. I knew Quill would be in school, teaching, and Pandasiea would there, learning, but Father, Mergel and Minnari and baby Susan would be home, Pepperling told me.

Standing at the door of my sister's home, I became a little nervous and was glad that my old friend Quill wouldn't be there.

Pepperling lifted the heavy doorknocker, a rose stone ball on a ring of shiny metal, and banged it against the metal plate on the wooden door a few times.

Soon there was the sound of footsteps approaching, and the door swung open and there was Mergel. We exchanged hugs and greetings. Then Father was there in his air chair, and behind him was Minnari, with babe in arms. An arm shot out from the tight little bundle, a tiny hand making a fist, and Susan announced her existence with an indrawn breath and a sharp little wail, as if to say, "I'm here too."

We all turned to Minnari, and my sister and I embraced with the crying baby snug between us. Susan stopped wailing and looked up at me with the deepest purple eyes I'd ever seen. With one look, this infant captured my heart and I knew it would never be freed from that tiny fist.

"She's beautiful!" I breathed in a whisper, and knew in an instant what Zarek and I would never have as I looked into the smiling

254

face of Minnari gazing down at her child. I had said it didn't matter that we couldn't have a child of our own, but this ... this was so ... beyond words.

We will always have each other. Zarek was there in my thoughts, with an edge of sadness

I know. I smiled. *That's what matters. Life will be good for us. I love you. Are you on your way?*

"Where is Zarek?" Mergel asked.

I'll be there tomorrow.

"He will be here tomorrow," I said. "I am so delighted to meet my little niece," I said to Minnari. "She is perfect."

Minnari led us all back to the kitchen and dining area, where she had been preparing the midday meal, and handed baby Susan to me and went back to her work. The weight and scent of the baby was like an anchor in my soul. I remembered Mark when he was just a toddler, myself little more, how much I loved the fat little hands he would hold out, tiny fingers splayed out as he said, "Up. Up."

I began to cry. I couldn't fathom why. I was happy. I was so happy for my sister and Quill, for Zarek and myself. I found myself whispering, over and over, "You sweet thing. You dear child," and kissing Susan's face, and then a peace I knew well settled on me and I became aware, once again, how precious life is, along with the gifts and blessings that reside in each one born, each child's spirit, if it is allowed to bloom and grow, to discover who they are and what is in them: how very precious. I stood rocking my beautiful purple-eyed niece until Minnari came to put her in her cradle.

Pepperling set a couple of extra places at the table, and she and Mergel helped carry in the food from the kitchen, and we sat down to eat. It felt as if we did this every day, as if we were the closest of sisters, something I had always longed for. I sent Zarek my happy feelings, wanting him to know. Those feelings came back to me, doubled. I smiled.

Throughout the meal, I noticed that Pepperling and Mergel were stealing shy, furtive glances at each other, and I wondered. They both knew what it was like to lose a limb, he his arm, she, her leg from the knee down, so they most likely empathized with each other ... but it seemed as if there were stronger feelings between them than that. My smile broadened.

Life surprises, and life is good.

CHAPTER THIRTY-THREE

It was a good thing I was staying with Pepperling, as it still proved uncomfortable to be in Quill's company, and he excused himself to work in his study on class preparations. He wasn't rude, though, and I counted that as progress.

Father, Panda, our hounds and I had taken a couple of walks through the town. They showed me all the many wonders of ReMaid. I was delighted. Panda and Minnari were happy to be together, and Father was happier than I'd ever seen him. Mergel and Father were gone most of the day, working in the quarry or on the road bed, and with Panda in school, this left Minnari and me free to make up for lost time.

"I can't imagine how hard it must have been for Mother to give us up," Minnari said, gazing down at her nursing baby. "I finally understand why they did what they did, by disguising you as a boy, making you a boy to the eyes of the world, Pen." A big tear slid down her cheek.

"Please, don't cry ..." I began.

"No. I want you to understand. I would do anything to save my child from what happened to Sinnola and me. I no longer blame you for what our parents felt they had to do. I'm just sorry they didn't think of it soon enough for us older girls." She chuckled. "We could have been a family of boys; then Quill wouldn't ..." She stopped in midsentence.

"Do you think he will ever get over it?" I asked with a sigh. "And forgive me?"

"Yes!" Minnari stood up and put the sleeping baby in her cradle, buttoned up the front of her dress, and came back and sat down across from me, taking my hands.

"You, in large part, have made it possible that we will never have to give up our daughter. I know there are people who still want to live according to the old ways, but thankfully, no one here in ReMaid wants that. Quill sees this. And since Susan's birth, he is getting much clearer on the issue of why you had to keep your female identity a secret from everyone, and how it had been drilled into you never to tell anyone."

"Thank you for giving me hope," I said. "I've missed my almost brother."

"It's amazing what having a baby can bring into perspective for a person. And now he is your brother for real. It will happen. He's coming around."

My com buzzed on my wrist, and I pushed the button for audio.

"Pen?" Wydra said, near hysteria in her voice.

"What is it?" I shot to my feet, fear filling me, visions of ruined Telling Wood in my head.

Wydra was weeping uncontrollably. I'd never known her to lose self-control. "We got them," she said, "they're asleep." With big, jagged, shuddering breaths, she said, "but I can't find John." She babbled on; I couldn't make sense of half of her words. Her sentences were all choppy and incoherent, then run together. "Bombs ... we didn't see them coming ... murdered ... the children ... people in the street ..."

"Wydra. Stop!" The feeling I was reading from her was sheer panic, linked to John and Lodar. "Get ahold of yourself. This is not like you." She wailed on, but she began to quiet down some. "What do you mean, you can't find John? What is happening?"

"Or Jorame and Julka or Merry. I'm so afraid. They killed so many people."

"Who? Who killed who?"

"I think it is the Natural Order." I could almost see her chest heaving. "Who else could it be? The guards put them all to sleep; the guards put so many to sleep they're having a hard time sorting them out, and I can't find my family," she sobbed. "People are dead, Pen. Hacked to death. Or bombed. So many."

"When did this happen?"

"Just a little bit ago," Wydra wailed.

"Can you send a ship for me? I'm here in ReMaid."

"Yes, please come!"

"I'll meet you at the entrance of town at the ship fields in a couple of hours. Find some guards and stay with them, just in case some of those men slipped through the sleep net. Gather up as many folks as you can to identify the people you know, separate them from the people you don't know and put the ones you don't know in cells. Pile them in the same cells if there are to many of them to go in single cells. Do what you can to clear the chaos. Can you feel what I'm sending you? Take a deep breath and be strong. Others will follow you."

"Yes." I could feel her settle into a different mind-set. The feelings I gathered were more that calm and resourceful and resolute Wydra I knew. I even sensed her nodding as if she were focusing and aiming her attention on the task at hand.

"I'll be there soon," I said. "Send the ship."

I cut off the com link and found Minnari standing there with an open mouth.

"Now I know why it is you," she said.

"Why what is me?"

"Quill always says that in times of trouble, you take command and just seem to know what to do. Now I understand why it is you the people want in front of them. You are the Mother I hear them call you, you have the voice of authority."

"And some of my children have been very naughty," I said through clenched teeth. "I have to go. I need to talk to Pepperling. I'll be coming back, though, before I leave." I gave her a quick hug. "Don't worry about me."

"But how did you ..." A look of amazed concern washed over her face. I kissed her cheek and hurried out the door.

I ran down the steps and across the street to Pepperling's home, flinging thoughts as I ran. *Zarek. Are you there?*

Yes! I'll meet you in Resort. I just heard two other capitals were attacked at the same time Resort was hit. Somehow the Natural Order has gotten their hands on some communicators, I think. How else could they have coordinated a strike like this?

A ship is coming for me. Wydra can't find John or Jorame's family.

I know. I was there in your thoughts. Your alarm called to me.

Then I'll see you soon.

I wish it were as we planned, in ReMaid and under different circumstances, but I long to hold you. Be safe, my heart.

Ibera ran at my heels. I felt the tension in her matching my own.

258

Pepperling was not home, so I packed up my things and threw them on my cycle's platform pallet. Ibera jumped on, and we rode back to Minnari's home. She answered the door as if she'd been standing there waiting for me the whole time I was gone, Susan clutched tight in her arms. Minnari looked pale and frightened. She had heard the whole exchange, so she had good reason to worry.

"I don't have time to hunt for Pepperling, but I need you to warn her and the people of ReMaid to be on the watch for anything suspicious looking," I said. "Call up your guards. Tell them to be Sleeper ready, with Nar Hounds at heel. The guards should put to sleep *anyone* doing *anything* out of the ordinary first and ask questions later. If you see swords, bows or slingshots, put those people to sleep immediately."

"I can do that!" she said with a bit of a tremble in her voice.

"Zarek told me that two other cities have been attacked at the same time they hit Resort. We don't know how deep this goes, so it's better to be on guard and safe than sorry."

Pen, Zarek said in my mind. *I've commed all the city Fathers and Mothers to warn them of trouble. So far, there's nothing on the horizon, but forewarned is forearmed.*

"Zarek just told me all the capital cities have been warned now too, so as soon as we can get to the bottom of this, we will let you know," I told Minnari.

"But how did he just speak to you?" She looked so puzzled that I had to take pity on her.

"Zarek and I can speak long distance to each other through our thoughts. I wish we would've had more time together." I hugged her so tight that Susan complained about it, being caught in the middle. "There is so much more to say. Zarek and I are going to be married. Not sure when, but hopefully when all this is sorted out. We will come back to finish our visit. I love you. Tell Pepperling and Mergel everything. Father too."

I ran down the steps and turned. "I love you all. Tell them."

I slung myself onto the cycle. "On," I said. It lifted, and we sped away down the gently curving street and down the zigzagging road to the plains. In the distance, I could see the ship coming in. It was a long way off yet, but would arrive sooner than I thought it would take to get here. It was a good thing the ships were that much faster than the cycles.

As the ship approached, I looked back at the small city climbing the mountainside and breathed a prayer for its residents' safety and blessing.

***

I rode my cycle off the small transporter ship onto the ship port-area grounds. I looked around for Wydra; not seeing her anywhere, I rode to the center of town, where I could see damage to some of the buildings. It looked as if the attackers had tried to take down the Concert Center where we had been having our council meetings, but maybe couldn't get close enough to get inside it without being spotted, so had tried to damage it by taking down a couple of buildings next to it. Emergency workers were everywhere, along with dirty and bloody people.

To my relief, the first person I recognized was John, helping a group of men move some rubble away from the side door of the Concert Center.

"John!" I yelled, jumping off the cycle as soon as it set down. I ran over to him and hugged him fiercely.

"Hey, what's this?" He held me at arm's length.

"Have you talked to Wydra yet? Does she know you're not dead?"

He gave me a sad smile and nodded, wiping the sweat off his forehead with the dirty sleeve of his shirt. "We've talked, she's over there at the tent, helping the wounded, Lodar is with her. Zarek will be here soon with more Purple Pearl tea. What we had on hand has saved a good many lives today, people we thought were out of our reach of saving, but we are almost out, and there are still more people who need it."

"What happened?"

"People have been coming into Resort a small group at a time. Grant, one of the city elders, said that was normal; they always have people coming in for Festival and the renowned theater and music here in Resort. We weren't alarmed by small groups of vacationers. We were on watch for anything that looked like an army."

"Oh." I felt sick. "How can you spot an enemy when they look like us?"

"Exactly! They *are* us! That's why we just didn't see them coming."

"I wish I'd been here. Maybe ..."

"I'm glad you were not." He hugged me to him, and I clung to my second father.

"Hey, let go of my man," I heard someone say.

I spun around, and Wydra fell into my arms. "I am so glad you're back," she said. "Things are pretty bad here. We had to put up a tent hospital because the real one is full. We have forty dead, some of them children, and seventy-three close to death. Another fifty people or so with minor wounds have been sent home already," Wydra said.

"The most critical are still with us." John folded his arms over his chest, looking at us, then put an arm around his wife's shoulders, a look of great pain on his face. "Pen, I'm sorry to have to tell you this ... but James's brother, Ferris Steel, died in the attack."

My heart sank. *James has lost another brother* was my first thought, and then I was hit by my own grief at losing another friend.

"Without his warning, though," said John, "many, many more would have died."

"But I thought Ferris was on Hadrianna helping them build ..."

"He was," Wydra said, her lips a grim line. "He came back for some supplies he couldn't find on the island or in Hadria."

"What about Jorame and Julka, and Merry?"

"They were trapped, but safe, in the back of the library building. One of the Natural Order men was trying to place a bomb there and blew himself up. That was the first thing that happened after Ferris sounded the alarm. I think it was a premature start to whatever they had planned and thankfully got their little war off to a bad start," John said, pointing to the still-standing library building, which had a large hole in its side. "That was when Ferris saw about ten men with swords wading into a crowd of people, and he commed me and others and started sleep blasting everyone. We were told that was when someone struck him from behind. Took him down ..." John looked down at the rubble at his feet, "and kept stabbing."

Both my friends shuddered at the same time, almost in unison. John bit his lips and rubbed his eyes. Wydra dashed tears away.

"He had become a very fine friend," John sniffed.

"Ferris saved my life more than once," I said, remembering. "I don't understand why the N.O. would do this. We gave them the freedom to live as they wish. Why kill us when they know we don't want to kill them?"

Wydra shook her head. "Who can understand? All we know is that we think we have all of them separated out from the Resort people. What do you want to do with them?"

"We'll drop them off on Far Away. They can fight each other if that's their inclination," I said, feeling like maybe that would be for the best. But then I remembered my niece, Susan, so precious. *Every life is worthy of love; each of us was once a precious baby, just like her.*

I bowed my head. "Great Creator, Father-Mother, show us how to keep life precious."

Heart of my heart, I'm here.

I turned and watched Zarek walk toward us. I smiled at him, sadness in our touch as our hands met, and then I was in his arms.

"Let's get to work!" he said.

***

It took us days to tend the wounded and send our dead to Tomorrow Land. Eight more died. The Purple Tea saved the lives of all the others with serious wounds, although I knew the wounds on the inside would take longer to heal. The rubble would take weeks to clear away, and the repairs that would have to be made would take months.

The two other cities that were attacked didn't lose as many people as we did, thankfully. They were lucky, as most of the explosives didn't work correctly. Evidently the attackers had damp goods, and no detonator will light damp powder. Numark Kansas and North Harbor Carolina lost a total of twenty-one good souls, murdered by the N.O.

The Head Librarian of the North Harbor Library was the man who sounded the alarm there and was the first one killed. I still grieve his loss, along with the loss of my friend Ferris, two good men the world is poorer without. Everyone who died left a hole in the lives of many other people.

"Are you ready?" Zarek asked as I stepped aboard the transport.

We had just picked up the last of the seventy-three N.O. soldiers who were being taken to Far Away.

"Oh yes! I'm ready," I nodded, looking at the chained men, their sleeping faces slack, immobile, almost serene. Seventy-three men. Murderers. Spoilers all. This was going to create a huge imbalance in the ratio of men to women on Far Away. With this new influx of men, only a quarter of the total population would be women. I could see that might be a real problem for them, everyone on Far Away. But then, in our old order of things, men shared women with ease, so maybe it wouldn't be a problem for them, especially if they didn't care who fathered the children.

"But how likely is that?" Zarek said, touching my forehead with his. He'd been in tune with my thinking.

"I'm glad that the groups that made the covenant with us were not involved with or allies of the N.O.," I said. "At least that is something. In fact, the group that lives closest to Ravenwood felt somewhat outraged at the Natural Order for causing trouble when we've been so reasonable with them."

"I hope they foster that feeling among the other groups, and maybe the N.O. won't have anywhere to draw young men to them from and won't try that sort of thing again." Zarek looked out the window as we left the fast-receding land below, moving out over the vast expanse of the Trillium Sea.

We arrived well after dark, swept the area with the newly installed Sleeper cannon and set down. We offloaded the N.O. men and the batch of supplies Gene had commed us they needed. I hoped he was prepared for these new men. We'd informed him we were leaving them for him to deal with. He had laughed and said "It will be my pleasure. We need more workers."

The ship pulled away from land before anyone woke up. Gene had told Zarek months ago by com that the men had built a community hall first, which would later become the women's first free house once the men started parsing out their own land to build their houses on. So far they were still just staying alive. Gene told us the rainy season was far wetter and windier than any of them had experienced before. But they hunkered down in the new building and weathered the rainy season without trouble other than a few fights because of close quarters.

***

The transport ship pulled into Hadria port, through the two air locks and into one of the bays near the elevator, and shut down. We were still training our own pilots, using the pilots from Hadria to teach our most adaptable people the fine art of commanding ships that move through air and water. The school for the pilots was here at Hadria. We had forty people in training. Captain Saeela was in charge of them. One

263

of her pilots and two of our trainees had taken us to Far Away, along with the N.O.s. We wanted to see how the other thirty-eight were doing.

Zarek, I know this is a business stop, but could we stay a few days longer than planned? I asked. *I need some quiet time. And I'd like to visit Lupa's cave.*

Zarek smiled and took my hand. *Certainly. I'd like to have time to visit with the First and Second Woman at our leisure as well. And I think I would like to see Lupa's cave also.*

But …

Not to worry. By myself … you by yourself. I wouldn't intrude on your time with the Stella Mara Mother.

She is the same Mother to us all, and the same Father Spirit. There is only one Spirit; maybe different images, but the same love, I said as we debarked, and then felt embarrassed as I thought about what I was saying to him. Zarek was at least four times older than me and certainly far more knowledgeable, and understood life in ways I couldn't even imagine yet. How could I keep forgetting that?

"It's not as if I know everything," Zarek said out loud. "You have taught me more than one thing in my life. I suspect there will be more for me to learn from you as time goes on."

That made me smile.

The purple cast to the clear blue-green sea glinted in the sunlight and shadow as the large and small sea life moved through depths and the sea grasses swayed. I saw a mother and child Obaskillian swimming side by side. Zarek stopped at dome edge to watch. I came back to where he stood watching them swim.

"Willobee can mind speak with them," I said, "or, more accurately put, mind picture with them. It's not exactly words, she says. More like images and feelings, and names. I'm not sure what all she uses to communicate with them."

"Yes! We have talked about the Fish Children."

"Bee is an amazing child." I fell silent for a while and just watched the two Obaskillian until they swam out of sight. "Willobee will become something extra special as an adult," I said, "her and those boys, Kid and Dray, and their friend Samra."

"I have a surprise for you," Zarek said, and turned me to face him. "They will be here tomorrow to spend a few weeks here with us. Some of our other friends will be here too, as Reia and Lucus are getting married."

"What?" I punched him lightly on the shoulder. "Why didn't you tell me?"

"I just did." He grinned. "I'm not very good at keeping secrets, especially from you. You can steal your way into all my thoughts, you know. I can only keep you out for short periods of time and with great effort. So no, I'm not very good at keeping secrets."

"Yes you are. How long have you known?"

He laughed. We talked about so many things on the way up to the apartment. I took my old rooms, and Zarek took Reia's suite that had two views of the ocean. The boys would be back in their place and Bee in her rooms. Lucus had helped build a small stone cottage on the island close to the cave we'd come out of to find Bee the time Ursa had tried to drown her. I could hardly wait to see Reia's house.

That night, as I drifted off to sleep watching schools of nesting neon fish drift among the swaying sea grass, I felt completely at peace.

CHAPTER THIRTY-FOUR

LaBo and the children showed up in the morning, along with Samra and her mother, Lily. Samra and her mother took Rifkin and Lucus's rooms. LaBo and the boys took their old rooms. James, Rifkin and other friends of mine were already on Hadrianna in the inn that had recently been completed topside. All of us were spending the afternoon in Ilantha's gathering room for the pre-wedding party.

Lucus and Reia would not be there, as they were observing some ancient Earth custom they had read about in the Library disks I had taken from Library when it burned. They were not to see each other all day. I thought it was an odd custom, but if it meant something to them, it made me happy to oblige them. I wouldn't get to visit with them till after the nuptial promises. I had seen their relationship developing, but it was not one I would ever have thought a possible match to begin with. Two more opposite people in temperament I did not know.

This made me smile. So much was new. In ten years, or twenty, or fifty, would I even recognize holdovers from this time period? Except for a few groups, there seemed to be a sense of freedom to explore our world in new ways. I was seeing and sensing a softening of hearts and opening of minds. Would that develop in good or bad patterns in the long run? How could we know? But I would watch and believe in the good.

We will watch, I heard Zarek say in my mind.

Yes! We.

Everyone was decked out in finery. There was flash and sparkle everywhere, brilliant colors that competed with the neon fish outside the dome wall. It felt good to be back in Ilantha's domain, Hadria. I had actually missed the underwater city. There was a beauty and tranquility there that couldn't be matched anywhere I'd been—that is, when no one was trying to kill us. It was more than stressful then, being under tons of water. I was glad that was over.

At the big double doors of the First Woman's apartment, Ilantha and Verity greeted me. Ilantha embraced me warmly. "It is wonderful to see you again, Pendyse," she said, and kissed both my cheeks. Then Verity and I were hugging as if we'd been long absent from each other. Like Wydra, Verity felt like a sister to me.

"Very wonderful!" she said, smiling hugely. "I can't believe what has come to all our people in this past year ..." *and to me personally. A good friend. A sister,* she finished in mind touch, warming me to the core.

I feel the same. We are chosen sisters, I said back to her.

As the afternoon progressed, Ilantha, Verity, Zarek and I found our selves in Ilantha's private chambers with LaBo and her crew of children, her students, along with Rifkin, James and Lilly.

"We have some very important news we'd like to share with all of you." LaBo's voice held a certain quaver of excitement. My curiosity crested to match the waves of eagerness I felt rolling off her and the children.

"Zarek, you know that Kid and Dray have been doing research in the oldest archives since they learned our language with the neurocaps," LaBo said.

"Yes?" An eyebrow rose along with his tone.

"Well ..." Kid bounced eagerly to his feet and began to pace. "It all started when Dray found a certain book that was ancient, and we began to translate as much of it as we could ... with our limited skill, and we kept seeing mention of a blue planet ..."

"We thought it was referring to the Blue Moon," Dray inserted in a near whisper, sitting on the edge of his seat.

"Yes!" Bee said. "We all thought it was our home it was talking about. The Blue Moon."

"But," Kid took back the telling, "it wasn't. There were things in that book that made me think of some of the books I'd read while I was still in Telling Wood, being held there with Norman."

"They brought the book to my attention," said LaBo.

"And she confirmed what I was beginning to think." Said Kid.

"Well, what were you thinking?" I said in some exasperation. "Please, the suspense is killing me. I can feel it nearly popping off the lot of you."

"Yes, get on with it," Verity and Ilantha said in unison.

"Well, they found proof that the Sabostienie, the Stella Mara *and* the humans all came from the same Earth," LaBo said, her serious demeanor adding emphasis to her statement.

"Not only that!" said Kid, still pacing and gesticulating like a young Librarian. Amused, I thought how Old Earth would have called him a professor. "Not only did we come from the same Earth thousands of years apart in travel, but we discovered that all of us … Are you ready for this?" His eyes were round with anticipation, and he was actually licking his lips.

"Yes!" we all rocketed back at him, laughing in near annoyance.

"Well. It wasn't the first place we came from … "

"Then where?" I shouted. "Tell us already."

"We first came from here," all the children and LaBo said together.

"What?" I said in total shock. We all broke out with questions and exclamations and disbelief.

"What do you mean, we originally came from here?" Zarek held his hands up to quiet all the babbling people. "Tell us what you found."

"Star charts, Uncle Zarek," Bee said in that ultra serious way she had.

"But how do you know they mean we came from here first?" I asked.

"You know how the Sabostienie thought they were the first ones here?" Kid took up the thread of telling again. "Then we humans came. Now we know the Stella Mara and the Obaskillian were part of the Sabostienie that came here about four thousand years ago."

"We had pretty much already come to that conclusion," Ilantha said dryly. "So … carry on."

"This world changes us," Dray said. Samra, sitting next to him, was nodding, "Even you, Pen. Look how purple-black your hair is."

"And your eyes." Bee smiled. "I love your dark purple eyes. And Ibera's purple fur, with her white diamond cap and horn." My hound, lying at my feet, raised her head at the mention of her name, gave an acknowledging chuff and put her head back down again.

"Haven't any of you wondered why the Earth dogs humans brought here with them began to grow a horn?" Kid looked around at each one of us. "This place puts something in us, from the ground, the air, the water, the very sky, maybe. We don't know. But after hundreds and hundreds of years here, we become different, and the animals seem to manifest it first. Maybe the Earth did that to us in reverse when we lived there."

Verity looked stunned. "That's an amazing thought!"

"Yes. I've wondered that before," I said. "Anyway, about the changes I've seen coming."

"But if we came here from your Old Earth," Ilantha began, "after we went there from here, why have we never found ruins of an older civilization on this planet? And it must have been a very advanced civilization to have sent people out to your Old Earth."

"We have!" LaBo beamed. "That book told of a cataclysmic time, an event that made the people flee this world, sending them Earthward, and maybe elsewhere as well."

"Where are such ruins?" Rifkin had a puzzled expression on his face. "How do you know there are such ruins? Maybe you've just come across an old story, a fiction, a fantasy like those of Old Earth."

At this LaBo's crew all smiled, looking around like a Nar Cat that had just eaten a competing family pet.

"Because we went there to see for ourselves," said Kid. "Tell them, LaBo."

"Ground tremblers. The earth shook. Some heaved up, and some ground sank below the seas. Where water had been, earth rose. Cities were suddenly covered with ocean. Off the coast of the Steel Desert, a few hours out, about five fathoms down, is the largest city I've ever seen."

"You mean a domed city?" Ilantha asked.

"No, Ilantha. Not domed, a land city that succumbed to the sea. A ruin. But one of the most beautiful things I've ever seen."

"What do you mean you've seen it?" James asked.

"On our way here, we went to the place we thought might describe the area we've read about and circled around looking for it underwater. It's so huge there's no way to miss it once you're there."

Kid and Dray glowed with the discovery.

"You *are* Argonauts!" I said, in awe of my young friends. "This is a staggering revelation, but in light of the wedding we are celebrating today, I think we should honor Reia and Lucus with our silence about this, at least until tomorrow, after they have had their day. Can we do that?"

There were slow nods of disappointed agreement all around, but now was not the time to share such staggering information.

We had a wedding to attend.

***

The day after the wedding, my head was still in a daze about Kid's news. I had gone to see Ilantha and Verity. The three of us sat in the shell chairs watching the shift of the ocean tides as we drank tea and talked about the discovery, making plans to travel to the city under the sea. We would enlist the help of the Obaskillian and their oxygen balls so we could leave the ships and actually go into the ocean and go among the buildings. We had spent the morning planning the trip. I had not had the opportunity yet of being in the water like that and was looking forward to it. A huge number of us were going. My thoughts drifted until Verity's voice brought me back.

"After that announcement, I could hardly say anything about my brother," Verity said.

"What about Keto?" My brows pinched together in concern.

"Well, he says there's a woman who lives on the island." Verity settled in to tell us about her visit to Fountain Island on the Blue Moon after Ilantha came back from there. Verity herself had just come back to Hadria the day before Reia and Lucus's wedding.

"I'm sure Zarek would know if anyone lived full time on the island," I said. "There have been caretakers from time to time, but no one has lived there in hundreds of years."

"Well, all I can say is what he told me. There is a woman there, and she talks to him."

"Really." Ilantha's disbelieving tone mirrored my own feelings.

"What does this woman talk to him about?" I wanted to know.

"He said she is teaching him how to know himself." Verity's brows formed troubled tents over her intense blue eyes. "He never even tried to attack me or my guards. I didn't even carry my power staff half the time. Of course, my people were always close by, but still ... I expected to see the usual venom coming from him."

"What does this woman look like?" I said. "Zarek should know if someone has sailed to the island and is living there. If she has a sea craft, Keto might escape and cause the Blue Moon trouble."

270

"There was no ship that we could find," Verity said. "He showed me a picture of her."

"A picture?" Ilantha and I said at the same time. We gave a small laugh at how much we were walking the same troubled path in our minds.

"Did he draw you a portrait?" Ilantha asked. "He was always very good with graphite and paper."

"No. It was the carving on the door of the house of a beautiful Sabostienie woman. He said she's always been there."

"That's not possible!" I said, setting my teacup down with a clatter, my back stiff with shock. "That carving is of Zarek's first sister. The one who has been dead near two thousand years now."

We all fell silent. What could this possibly mean?

Had loneliness cracked in half what sanity Keto had left, or was there a lookalike woman with her own motives for being there?

Or ... was she really Zarek's first sister? And if so, was she a flesh and blood woman, or was she the spirit of Zarek's sister?

***

The list of all the people who went to see the ruined city underwater would be too long to name, so suffice it to say, we were around a hundred strong. Hadrian scientists and Blue Moon scholars, councilors and friends were all gathered on the hovering transporter ship. The most reliable Fish Children would take ten in each group down to the city and guard them from any dangerous sea creatures. LaBo and her crew of students were the first group to dive in. Zarek and I and the group we were in would be last to dive. The first time down, they were only letting people stay under for about an hour at a time.

We had taken the ship down, and we had all seen the ruins together. Spiraling steeples of what looked like glass and stone and steel. Inspiring shapes. It was not quite clear how they hung together or what the ones that were broken had once looked like when new. The city was miles and miles of whole and tumbled structures. It looked as if it had been planned as a spiral, as the main street circled from the outside to the center, where what looked like a glass structure was the tallest left standing in the city. The main spiral street was sectioned with many smaller streets that joined one spiral ring to the next one in. It was a fascinating design. Of course, sea life had taken over, and some of the worst broken structures were covered with living organisms building their own communities. Coral colonies. And they were glorious in all their own colorful right, much like what you can see in the coral gardens close to the Sea Tree, all so beautiful and otherworldly.

Zarek dove from the transporter's open door the ten feet to the Trillium Sea. I followed close behind, my oxygen ball firmly clenched in my mouth. It was a very strange feeling, and even though I had a faceplate that fit over my eyes and nose, as my eyes had no nictating eye shield, as Zarek and all the Sabostienie and Stella Mara people have, my first breath was hard to take. My mind kept screaming *No, you're underwater.* But I had to quit holding my breath sometime, so I swallowed down some air and began to believe the oxygen balls really did produce air. I swam a few feet behind Zarek, the remaining eight people in our group behind me. We had decided to go to the glasslike building still intact at the center of the city. The sun above us was now at its zenith, and light flooded down through the ocean, casting shadows among the shafts of light on the floor that was a still-vivid, colorful mosaic of a man and woman who looked remarkably like Zarek and me at first glance. Then my attention was captured by the inside walls and the stone art that had fallen off pedestals. Some pedestals were toppled as well. The size and scope of this place was amazing. Everywhere the eye landed was a new discovery.

I think that chamber has air in it, Zarek thought my way.

What do you mean? It's thousands of years old. It's got to be filled with water.

We swam all the way to the paving stones outside the glasslike entrance and hung onto the metal ribs that held the glass sheets together. I pressed gently on the glass wall and felt a slight give, almost like some plastics. Elastic. I pushed a little harder. It gave a little more.

Careful! Zarek pulled my hand away from the glass wall. *If it breaks and if there is really air in there, we would be sucked in. I don't think that would be a good thing.*

Looking around at the others with us, Zarek signaled for them to keep back.

Then I noticed that the double-boxed entryway looked like an air lock similar to the ones in Hadria. I pointed. *Is that an air lock?*

Zarek and I swam to the area. *Yes. I think it is,* he said. Excitement raced through us both.

Why would they put an air lock on a building they had on land?
My puzzlement went even deeper when Zarek pointed to the mosaic, his face a mask of shock.

That looks like us!

CHAPTER THIRTY-FIVE

You call to Verity to get over here quick. I'll call to LaBo, Zarek thought at me.

Verity! I nearly mind yelled, not knowing how far away she was. I could speak to her and Zarek couldn't. But most of the time I couldn't make contact with LaBo unless she was in the same room, and even then, it was a stretch for both of us.

Yes! What's wrong? Verity answered, a tinge of panic in her mind. *Are you all right?*

Well, we aren't sure exactly, I sent back. *We aren't hurt, just in a state of shock.*

Are you still at the glass building in the center of the city where your group was going?

Yes. You've got to bring your group over here. We found something you're going to want to see. An air lock and a picture.

What?

Just come.

As Verity and I finished, I saw LaBo, Kid, Dray, Bee and Samra swimming like they meant it, like their lives depended on it, the rest of their crew and the Obaskillian protectors fanning out behind.

Verity and her people showed up not long after that, and we gathered around the area that looked like an air lock.

Bee and her Fish Child friend and his father came up between Zarek and me.

Fish Father says not to touch! Bee spoke to Zarek and I at the same time, including LaBo and Verity as an afterthought. Willobee was the real thing when it came to mind touch. *He showed me a picture of an air lock at Hadria. He thinks it could be one. But he wants to check it first. We must move back and let him examine it.*

I was still amazed at her ability to communicate with the Obaskillians, but she said it was a different kind of knowing, and you might have to be a child to understand it. That had made me laugh when she'd first said it, but now, I was beginning to believe that could be true. If there was a building still full of air from maybe ten thousand years ago, with a mosaic of us on the floor, who was to say anything was impossible? In point of fact, a child was the only person I knew of who could communicate with the Fish Children as the Fish Children could communicate with each other.

Fish Father says he will try the air-gate first. You must not yet, Bee said. *He thinks you must be very important to have your images on the floor of very old land city house.*

Everyone moved back, and Fish Father went to the entrance and examined the gate apparatus. After what seemed like a long time, he struggled to lift an exterior handle, and the door began to slide slowly open. Water poured into the space, half the size of one of the ship air locks in Hadria, and Fish Father went inside and closed the door. We could see water being forced outside near the floor, some kind of air pressure working similarly to the Stella Mara air locks. Then Bee's friend opened the inner door and went in.

We could all see the deep lungful of air he took, swelling his chest as he looked over the place. He walked over to the mosaic and gazed down at it for a long time. Then he studied Zarek and me. After a few more glances around the large foyer, the Fish Father motioned for us to come in.

It was a tight squeeze, but we all fit in the exchange chamber. As the air pressure forced out the water, it brought in the ten thousand-year-old air. It was stale, yet it was the sweetest thing I'd ever breathed.

After what seemed like forever, we finally got to move into the foyer, a large, round room with a staircase that wrapped around the glass wall all the way up to the point at the top of the structure, reminding me of the little room in our apartment in Hadria.

We all looked at the likeness of Zarek and me, a sense of wonder and amazement building into a tension that was half fear and half excitement. It was electric, in any case.

Up close, we could all see it was an *exact* likeness of us.

"What does it mean?" Bee looked confused and a little afraid, her brows pinched together under her wet lavender bangs. "I thought this was an ancient building. How come they put your picture on the floor, Uncle Zarek?"

"I don't have a clue, Willobee. This is a mystery to us too."

"Yes!" Kid said. "Mystery. That is what we're here for. Maybe the building will tell us. Let's go in teams and explore?"

"No!" Zarek and I said together, reaching out for the children, alarm racing through us both.

"They are right," LaBo said. "We stick together. The ones who made this place are unknown to us. And we don't know what their motives were for putting your likeness on their floor, or how they knew you would even exist one day and find this place."

"How *could* they know?" Verity said, eyeing Zarek and me worriedly. "How is that even possible?" The floor became wet from our dripping group standing huddled together around the mosaic, and the water trickled out over the two faces on the floor, making them shimmer as if the mosaic was new, laid only yesterday.

Our thirty, plus the nine Obaskillians protectors, went through the first door we came to and found a large records room or library of sorts. It was mind-boggling, and yet so recognizable.

"Don't touch anything. This is a job for the scientists and scholars, people who know how to catalog all these things and see how they work, if they work. Or at least how they once worked," LaBo said. "I am amazed we are actually inside this building at all."

We moved into the room and fanned out, not touching anything. The room was round, like the foyer, and open. All along the walls were niches and shelves lined with things that must be information if we could find out how to understand it. There were stone tables and chairs, delicately carved with fascinating designs on all parts of them, legs, arms and tabletops too, with glasslike overlays. *Not a speck of dust anywhere,* I said to Zarek.

Apparently no decay either, he answered.

We all jumped when we heard a voice speaking what sounded like some form of the Sabostienie-Stella Mara language, and we turned to find a ghostly image of a woman and man. The two of them took turns speaking. LaBo began to interpret.

"Greetings, our Star Sabbath children. You have come home to us at last."

Then Verity took over, catching what LaBo missed.

"Our best and brightest thinkers created this ... uh ... sacred repository ..." The woman and man spoke too fast in unfamiliar accents for Verity to keep up with, and LaBo took over again.

"... to keep for our people, for when the time is right, information you will need as you draw to you your best and brightest to create the world to come."

Then there was a line or two that no one caught, though they struggled to; then Kid, Dray, Bee, Verity and LaBo all joined in the interpretation of the next part.

"And the joy of love must be your foundation for hope to flourish and peace to be made real," they said together, as if it were planned and rehearsed, making it sound like a chant, which echoed in the room, sending shivers down my spine.

"Four Loreia was the name of our world, a good Earth, but nothing stands still and all things change with time," said LaBo.

"And now the time has come again, the time we saw in the Great Spirit Mirror, and you are here, just as we knew you would be." Zarek's words came to a trembling halt.

All eyes were on the see-through couple as they said one last thing. "It is your turn to make Four Loreia into the peaceable people we once were and will be again ... for we have seen it." The one word I caught was redintegrare. "To make whole again," I whispered.

And then they vanished like the drifts of mist in the fields on a warm morning.

We stood there in stunned silence. Time stretched and wobbled like a large soap bubble, then popped.

We broke into a babble of talk and questions and needs, but the Fish Father firmly began to usher us from the room and back toward the air lock.

"Fish Father says we should go now or the ship will worry about us. Our hour is up, past up, and it is time for us to go," Bee said.

We knew he was right, but we didn't want to leave; every last one of us wanted more time here. I wanted to understand what all this meant. What was the Great Spirit Mirror? How did people from so long ago come to us like ghosts? How was this building still standing after a cataclysm like the one that destroyed their world ... our world ... and could that happen again?

We gathered in the exchange room air lock and reinserted our oxygen balls, ready to return to the ship.

Life is never dull when you have so much to learn, I thought to anyone who could hear.

***

(A Month Later)

"This council meeting is called to order," I said, and banged my gavel. We had the witnesses lined up to speak about what had been found under the Trillium Sea and how it might impact our society at large. Our world was already buzzing with the news. The council members were present to hear firsthand from the people who were there, and the next day, they would choose the team who would be the ones to go study what was in that building.

I so wanted to be one of them, but knew I had other things to take care of.

Hundreds of people crowded into the new council building to hear the proceedings. I wondered how we would ever adjust from what had been to what was coming. Could I?

The people settled down, and a hush fell. It was so quiet that Ibera's claws clicking on the stone floor could easily be heard as she stood beside me. The silence held for so long that my horned hound chuffed as she looked at me. A few chuckles released the people from the silence. Someone yelled out, "Even the hound is eager to get on with it." And there were more laughs that spread through the crowd.

I held up my hand. "All right. We will begin."

The stories and questions lasted all day. The midday meal was brought in, and we continued as we ate. No one wanted to stop, even after the sun went down and some people had told their story of what they had seen and heard in the glass-walled spiral building more than once. Everyone seemed hungry for more, even if it was only repeated information from earlier in the day.

The people who were putting themselves up to the scrutiny of the council to be the ones to study the building would be on the next day's agenda. LaBo and her class of adventurers were on the list. Kid wanted this so bad he was hard to speak with because of the naked longing that clung to him and poured from his eyes. I hoped they would be chosen to go. It only seemed right, as none of this would have been possible if it hadn't been for those four children and LaBo. *I guess you can't call them children anymore,* I thought. Kid was thirteen, Andraykin

278

was eleven; Bee, of course, was still a child, only eight; but Samra was eleven too.

My mind drifted back to three years before, when my adventure began, when I turned thirteen and Telling Tree died and was reborn on my island. Three years. In a couple of months, I would be sixteen myself. I no longer looked like a boy, even when I dressed like one, which was most of the time.

As the council session came to a close with everyone eager for the next day's choices to be made, Zarek and I took a walk down by the lake. Ibera played in the water and we sat on a rock as Mother Moon rose.

"I'm going to have to go back to Blue Moon for a couple of months here pretty soon," Zarek finally said with a sigh. "I also know you have to do some traveling to some of Nueden's new schools."

"To say nothing of council meetings," I moaned. "It's going to be a busy time for both of us for awhile."

"Don't worry about your Argonauts." Zarek drew me close. "I know they will be on the list. I feel it, as sure as the sun rises."

***

Zarek and I spent the next three years traveling together and separately to take care of business among the "Peaceable People." We were called on to attend conferences, visit schools, go to meetings on the progress of cataloging the finds under the Trillium Sea, and be kept abreast of the new inventions that came about because of the discoveries there. There were improvements in communications and modes of travel. Then there was the knowledge gathered. They found the Spirit Mirror. It was like a window into the past and future that we didn't understand at all. But maybe, one day, we might. The city had been called Quattuor, meaning four, and the world Loreia. Some people were linking that name, Peaceable People of Loreia, meaning the whole world, even though we all kept local names intact.

And during those three years, James, Rifkin and Hanni spent time traveling with one or the other of us. They also spent a good deal of time helping us build the stone cottage we had dreamed about beside the brook an hour away from Resort. It was about completed, a bright spot in our lives, one Zarek and I would be able to cloak when we didn't want company. But I suspected all our friends and family would be spending a good deal of time there too.

***

At the end of that third year of travel, many of us were back in Resort for another council meeting, and as it drew to a close, Zarek came up holding a bouquet of flowers and handed them to me.

"Will you go with me to the Pool of Happiness, to the World Cave and Crystal Tree?" he asked.

I buried my face in the sweet scent of the flowers, feeling suddenly overwhelmed with the love I felt for Zarek. Looking into his eyes, I said, "Why, Zarek, are you proposing to me?" And the zing of feeling that passed through us both brought us together in a deep kiss, the flowers forgotten and crushed between us. We came to our senses when we realized the council chamber was alive with cheers and clapping.

"It's about time!" I heard Rifkin yell from the far side of the room, and James whistled that shrill two-fingered trademark whistle of his.

I just smiled and waved, then took Zarek by the hand and slipped out the back door of the chamber to get away from the crowd. This was not a moment I wanted to share with anyone but Zarek.

***

Back in Well One, we were staying at Father's place, even though he and the others were still in ReMaid. But they would be coming back soon, along with my sisters and Quill, Mergel and Pepperling, and some other friends from there. Will and Tearveena and all their children from Ra'Vell Island would be here too. For most of them, it would be their first time to the Wells. That thought delighted me. We would have so much fun showing them around.

We set the wedding date for my nineteenth birthday, the first night of the Blue Moon, now less than a month away.

There had been many invitations sent to us to hold receptions in many of the cities around our known world, and we accepted all of them, because we wanted to include as many people as possible in our celebrations.

"It will be the year of the wedding," Zarek laughed, "instead of the wedding of the year."

"To make a tour of the cities will be a good thing anyway, to check on the progress of the schools," I said as we walked down one of the shop-lined, curving streets in Well One.

"I was so amazed to discover, my first time here and on the Blue Moon, that there are no poor or homeless," I said as we strolled along.

"We are aiming for no homeless or hungry in the rest of Nueden by the end of the year," Zarek said dreamily and kissed my hand. "Hadria and Hadrianna have already achieved that. But they have a much smaller territory to cover."

The council members had spent months discussing the meaning of community that first year and decided all would work and contribute what they could in exchange for what they needed and wanted, within reason. No one would receive more than they could use, not even the community Fathers and Mothers. This ruling had only come after many long days of discussion and more than a thousand people from every possible side of life telling their stories of how they lived and why, and how they wanted to live in the future and what they wanted to contribute to society to be a part of the Peaceable People of Loreia. This was what most everyone was calling this new adventure by then. We were living into a more just way of being.

"I hope this is all more than just a beautiful dream," I sighed.

"We will help make it so," Zarek said, "at least, insofar as we can."

Shopping for wedding clothes had become a meander. I needed Verity and Wydra to be with me to really get serious about fancy dresses and shoes. With Zarek along, all that happened was a lot of handholding, strolling, staring into each other's eyes and sighing. We had spent far too much time apart in these past few months, years, and it was just heavenly to be together and have no demands upon our time.

"It is a good thing Wydra and Verity will be here tomorrow," I said, "or I'd have to get married in men's clothes."

I laughed as Zarek kissed my ear and whispered, "Well, you know at the Pool, you take them off anyway."

CHAPTER THIRTY-SIX

Zarek and I stood at the mouth of the tunnel, lit by a soft glow of light like what I remembered on the walls of Lupa's cave in Hadria. It was an otherworldly glow.

He took my hand. *Come, my heart, let's begin our journey.*

We walked for maybe an hour before we came out onto a ledge that led into the largest cavern I had ever seen. Steps were carved into the wall, dropping down to the floor a hundred feet below, just wide enough for two. The Pool of Happiness shimmered with a purple light in the center of the floor at the bottom. The Crystal Tree spread up to the ceiling from a ledge or outcropping of rock at the back of the Pool some distance away, and as we went down the stairs, we saw from the bottom of that outcropping what looked like roots spreading down and into the Pool, forming a bowl like two large hands holding the water. The light sparkled and shifted with each step, springing about the large room and being lost in the shadowy depths of the cavern.

It was breathtaking. We didn't speak. We couldn't.

We walked steadily to the Pool of Happiness, enthralled with the beauty. The Father-Mother Spirit was there to bless our bonding.

At the edge of the Pool, Zarek and I turned to each other and for a long time stared into each other's eyes. Tears began to stream down my face. There was so much I wanted to say to him. But somehow I knew this was not the time or place for words, so I just gave him my emotions, and I was flooded with his. The beauty of our joining, mingling, emotions matched the glory of this place. We slipped out of our robes and into the Pool of Happiness.

We heard, *Be true to each other and to Father - Mother Spirit, and you will always be able to rise above troubles and disappointments. You will have great joy in your lives.*

Time stretched. We didn't know how long we stayed in the Pool. A lingering, easy calm kept us there, dreaming, as we became one.

We finally remembered our wedding guests up in the hall, returned to our robes and took the stairs two at a time in perfect synchronicity, our light laughter echoing in the chamber below as we reached the tunnel back to the wedding hall in half the time it had taken us to go down.

As we reached the changing room, Zarek's friend Mergel was there to help him dress, and Wydra and Verity were there for me. Looking at Zarek, my husband, I thought he fairly shone with a light that radiated from his heart, that pulsing beat that would match my own now and forever, even into Tomorrow Land. They took him to his dressing room, and I was shuffled off to mine. The dual heartbeat remained, reassurance of all the days to come when, no matter how far apart we were in this world, we would always be together.

Once we were dressed, Mergel presented us to our friends and families. We ate, we visited, we danced, and we laughed. Even Quill congratulated me without rancor, a true smile on his face, which I hadn't seen in six years.

I was full of happiness, contentment and peace. Wanting to include our loved ones who were not present with us because they were in Tomorrow Land, and all of us having lost loved ones, we honored them with a toast of sea wine and a sweet silence at end of the evening, then departed quietly for our homes. It was perfect.

***

In the morning, several of our friends gathered with us for the morning meal: John and Wydra, Lodar, Rifkin, James, Hanni, Jorame, Julka and little Merry.

"So where are you going next?" Julka asked. "Are you going to retreat to your cottage by the brook for a while?"

"You certainly deserve to have some time to yourselves before this busy year begins for you," Wydra added.

Zarek and I had set plans in motion the day we left Ra'Vell Island to build the small house at the brook, and it had just recently been completed. We hadn't even been there since it had been finished. A thrill went through me at the thought of spending a month alone with Zarek.

I smiled. "Yes, we are leaving day after tomorrow, we are spending some time with Father and my sisters before we leave."

John put down his fork and glanced at Zarek and me. "You know, don't you, that your father and I finally spoke about … well, you know … about your mother, Allois? I think he is going to be OK about me. We have too many connections to be enemies, he told me. I can tell you, it is a relief to me. Wydra loves him like a father too. So …" He stopped and leaned his head to one side, "I hope that …"

"Yes," I said, "that does make me happy. Thank you, John."

"It's good for family to be together," James said. "Even when they're weird."

Rifkin laughed at that. "Aren't all families a little weird … cousin?"

"We are an unusual family, you might say, ages being what they are." Zarek grinned; then he got more serious. "But the main thing is the genuine regard and love we have for each other. You are all a part of us, and that will only become stronger as we work together to make life richer for everyone. Friendship and family makes a strong fabric that will hold us in good stead."

We all nodded, all kidding aside, appreciating the presence of each one here. I knew this because I felt the emotions that went along with the nods.

"While we are all together," said Jorame, "we have some news. We only confirmed it this morning, but …"

"Wait!" Julka butted in. "Let me tell it."

"What?" Wydra and I said together, laughing at each other. "What news?" I asked, catching Julka's excitement.

"We're going to have a baby," she said.

Zarek stood up in shocked surprise. "But I thought …" He dropped back into his chair.

"As did we all." Jorame beamed. "But maybe things are changing in that regard too."

"I'm going to have a baby sister," Merry said, her hand up to her mouth, whispering loudly to me. Everyone heard it, and smiles went around the table for the sweet child.

"It could be a boy," Lodar said, nodding wisely. "You know it could be."

"No. It's a girl," Merry said stubbornly.

We all laughed. It was a wonderful morning.

284

Maybe that means someday we could have a child of our own too. Zarek watched me as I played with the children. I turned to him. *Someday, as the Spirit sees fit. For now, it is enough that I have you.*

"There they go," Rifkin huffed, lifting his hand in exaggerated exasperation, then letting it fall back to the table, "leaving us out altogether, mind chatting."

"I beg your pardon … it was weightier than chatting," I laughed.

"All right, all right, we'll have none of that." James shoved Rifkin. "You've heard, haven't you, that he has a new lady love?" he asked the gathering. "Don't tell us you don't know."

"What? Again?" John looked at Rifkin in amazement. "A new lady love?"

Teasing and laughter ensued. Rifkin was always in love with someone new.

As the time spent together was ending, Zarek said, "We want to thank you all for the work you have done to help us get the cottage finished before the wedding."

"I love the place!" Wydra smiled. "It's perfect for you."

"I can't wait to see it," Julka said, and touched my hand. "Maybe when you come back after your wedding tour of the country, we can come visit."

"Absolutely," I said, and gave her a hug. "I'm so happy for you and Jorame."

"And me too!" Merry said. "Cuz I'm having a sister."

"No. I think it's a boy. " Lodar said shaking his head. The argument was on and we were all amused as they were both so sure of their of own opinion.

"Well, we will all know for sure when the baby is born," I said, "So there is no reason to fight about it."

Merry, now eight, looked at me with knitted brow, "But I know. I know Lodar is also right, but I just want him to admit that I'm right too."

"What do you mean?" Jorame asked, "Two?"

Then it dawned on us what Merry was saying.

"Twins!" echoed around the table and laughter.

Eventually everyone got up to leave the breakfast café, hugging, chatting and making plans for their next time together.

"I hear you will be meeting with Ilantha, Lupa and Verity this afternoon," John said. "And something about your sister's ghost and Keto."

"Well, we were talking about weird family," Zarek said, shaking his head. "I guess this would qualify."

***

Verity greeted us at the door. Lupa and Ilantha were on the balcony that overlooked the large, round, open space with the clear dome that roofed the city, keeping sand and sea from coming in.

"It is so peaceful here," Ilantha said, squeezing my hand as we came out to the balcony. "I never imagined being here could affect me like this after the sea. But it does."

Lupa stood and gave us both hugs. Zarek and I sat down next to Lupa, and Verity served us tea and then sat down herself.

We chatted about the wonders of the Wells, the wedding party the night before, and Keto and Fountain Island.

"I know you think someone is on Fountain Island with Keto," Zarek said, looking at Verity, "but I assure you, from my first time there three years ago to now, I have seen no sign of anyone else living on the island. I have checked every foot of land and house." He lifted his hands in a helpless gesture. "I don't know what else to tell you. If anyone is there, I've not seen her. He says her name is Nasreen. That was not my sister's name. Maybe he's just ..." I could feel Zarek's embarrassment at what he had been about to say, which was no less than I had thought on a number of occasions.

"This is the most sane I've ever seen him," Verity said. She sipped her tea and set her cup down, leaning forward. "Everyone who has a say in what becomes of him has said he is no longer a danger to himself or others." She shook her head. "I told him he could come home. Do you know what he told me? 'She can't leave the island and I can't, I won't leave her.' Says he would like your permission to spend the rest of his life there."

"Truly, Zarek," Lupa gave him a motherly smile, "can you not see how in some way it might be the spirit of your sister, even if she calls herself Nasreen now? Maybe she loved that place so much she couldn't leave it."

"And after all we have been through and seen," Ilantha added, "whatever this is, it has become the heart of Keto. His saving grace, in a way."

"Maybe someday we will understand what this is," Zarek sighed, "but for now, even though I don't, I'm willing to let him live there. If it gives him peace and makes him happy, we can do that."

"What was your sister's name?" I asked.

"Ahjah. It means heart of light."

***

"Isn't this the most perfect place?" Zarek's arm was around my shoulders, my arm around his waist, as we stood on the covered porch overlooking the brook as it sang over the stones and down the hill in a joyful rush to the river at the bottom of the mountain.

"The first time I met you in the jungle on the Green Path, I had no concept of this life we now share," I said. "I only had a desire for a better life for women, for the poor ... I ..."

"And look what has come of your desires." He grinned, nuzzling my ear.

I slapped him playfully on the stomach. "I'm trying to be serious here."

"So am I," he said, turning me back toward the house. The house was cloaked. I smiled. We sure didn't want company right then. "A whole month to ourselves."

We fished, and we took long walks with Ibera trailing behind us or howling off into the forest. We worked on projects as gifts to each other, even though we were completely unable to keep them a secret to completion, we were so much attuned to each other by then.

We had a great little kitchen that Chet would have loved to cook in, I was sure. We certainly did. Everything we did together was a joy. Work and play.

One morning, Zarek said, "I know the busy life is out there waiting for us, but being here with you has been the best time of my life."

My mind slipped back with a shudder to the time when I thought it would never happen. He took me gently in his arms. *That will never happen again,* he whispered into my thoughts.

I nodded, cuddling under his chin. *I know.*

Early in the month, on one of our walks, we found a fairly large pool at the head of our brook and swam there. We went swimming there almost every day after that.

The time spent together *was* wonderful, but went all too quickly.

The morning of our last day at the cottage, we rose to the sweet sound of White-Winged Whistlers fishing the brook. Dewdrops glistened on the grass, making our world seem rinsed with light, a world gem bright with promise.

ABOUT THE AUTHOR

Linda lives in Bend Oregon with her husband, Duncan, and their magical cat, Panga. Duncan is also a writer. They met in a writer's group thirty-four years ago and married in the fall of that year. A year later they bought Pegasus Books of Bend. Fourteen years ago the couple started a used bookstore, The Bookmark.

From an early age books of all kinds, fiction and non-fiction, fairytales and fantasy, poetry and dictionaries all intrigued her. But it is the character's living at the edge of her dreams that whisper their stories over her shoulders catching her in a web of words. Stories of far away places, different ways of living, strange worlds or our world seen from a different angle, no matter, the character's from those places always whisper, like waves on a beach, **"Write, write, write."**

TRILLIUM TRILOGY

TELLING TREE
ONCE ON A BLUE MOON
UNDER THE TRILLIUM SEA

llmcgeary@gmail.com

Made in the USA
Lexington, KY
16 July 2017